Praise for *The Stories of Edith Wharton*:

"A welcome addition to any library."

—*Library Journal*

"No self-respecting Wharton addict should be without this book." —*Los Angeles Times Book Review*

"Her work is timeless. An excellent choice for inclusion in fiction collections needing representation by this important writer." —ALA *Booklist*

"Edith Wharton honestly explored the human questions that engaged her imagination, writing 'only for that dispassionate and ironic critic who dwells within the breast.' " —*St. Louis Post-Dispatch*

Also available from Carroll & Graf:

The Stories of Edith Wharton—Volume 2
Selected and introduced by Anita Brookner

The Stories of Edith Wharton

Volume I

SELECTED AND INTRODUCED BY
ANITA BROOKNER

Carroll & Graf Publishers, Inc.
New York

Published by arrangement with Simon & Schuster, London.

First Carroll & Graf hardcover edition 1990
First Carroll & Graf paperback edition 1991

Carroll & Graf Publishers, Inc.
260 Fifth Avenue
New York, NY 10001

Library of Congress Cataloging-in-Publication Data

Wharton, Edith, 1862–1937.
　[Short stories]
　The stories of Edith Wharton / selected and introduced by
Anita Brookner.—1st Carroll & Graf ed.
　　p.　　cm.
　ISBN: 0-88184-760-7 : $10.95
　I. Brookner, Anita.　II. Title.
PS3545.H16A6　1990c
813'.52—dc20
　　　　　　　　　　　　　　　　　　　　　　90-1323
　　　　　　　　　　　　　　　　　　　　　　CIP

Manufactured in the United States of America

Contents

Introduction

———◆———

Edith Wharton's autobiography, *A Backward Glance*, is a brilliant exercise in both worldliness and concealment. Both of these qualities are completely authentic: no cover-up is intended. For she was both the great lady she so pleasingly describes and that secret inward-looking creature to whom she only briefly alludes. The writing of fiction – and she was tirelessly prolific, combining her work with an extensive social life – proceeds from the hidden self, a self which exists only on the borders of consciousness. Edith Wharton's outer life was spent in the public gaze. She was *mondaine* in every sense of the word, born into a rigidly stratified society of accepted families, married young to a suitable husband, owner of many beautiful houses, and tirelessly available to a host of friends. She was also a great traveller, a great expatriate, and a great worker: indeed her efforts in the First World War earned her a Légion d'Honneur from the French government. As she tells the story, there would not seem to be either the time or the place for a writer of fiction to emerge and to blossom. Indeed the world in which she grew up saw her literary activity as a sort of aberration or solecism, and only one of her numerous relations ever read her books. Her easy sophistication enables her to dismiss this as she seems to have dismissed every other obstacle in her path.

And yet she was that awkward thing, a born writer. When she was a very small child, before she could read or write, she was subject to compulsive episodes of 'making up'. When one of these came upon her she would seize a book, walk up and down, and chant stories of her own invention, turning the pages at intervals which an adult reader might observe. She was even known to abandon a children's tea party when visited by a sudden desire to 'make up'. Perhaps this is not surprising in a child, but then few children go on to write forty books. The same magic impulse that went into the making up episodes seems to have stayed with her throughout her career, for, as she tells it, she never had to search for a theme or a subject, and even the names of her characters arrived of their own accord, sometimes long in advance of the characters themselves.

Those who seek for a sober explanation for these phenomena would no doubt point to the excellence of her education, the sort of education not enjoyed by anyone today. The young Edith Wharton was allowed to read only the finest works in any language. As she spoke French, German, and Italian from an early age she grew up acquainted with the masterpieces of four languages. At the same time she was introduced to the pleasures of Europe, which was to become her second home, in an age when such pleasures had to be pursued over unmade roads and in occasionally dubious hotels. Although she never went to school, she seems to have had the best and kindest of governesses. And of course agreeable company was assured from the start, the society of old New York reinforcing what her own extensive family habitually provided.

This brilliant education had excellent results. A gracious manner and an inspired way with friends might be qualities one would expect from such an upbringing, but in addition to these qualities Edith Wharton had a characteristic which can only be described as zest. She was zestful in the decoration of her houses, zestful in her long and audacious travels, zestful in the delight and enthusiasm which she felt for her work. She seems not to have known fear or discouragement or everyday depression, but perhaps her innate moral and social code forbade her ever to refer to such moods.

That she was aware of the tensions and restrictions of life lived among others is evident in her writing, particularly in her masterpieces, *The House of Mirth*, *The Custom of the Country*, *The Reef*, and *The Age of Innocence*. These novels have to do with the doomed attempts to challenge the social code, but at the same time they establish the very real validity of the Dionysiac impulse at work in the challenger. Lily Bart and Undine Spragg are far stronger than those among whom they attempt to establish themselves, just as the exquisite Anna Leath is weaker than the coarse beings to whom it is her lot to be superior. Yet if society wins every time it is a society of vaguely disappointed and disappointing people, idle, rigid, without ambition. Although not as nerveless as the heroes of her great friend Henry James, Edith Wharton's men are no match for her women.

The enormous power of sex – a phenomenon to which no overt reference is made – is apparent in everything she wrote, for Edith Wharton, married very young, liberated herself when she was forty. Sex to her was not merely an affair of the body but the untrammelled enjoyment of the will and of destiny. Throwing off a situation which she might see as stagnant or sterile, she would nevertheless be acutely aware of the conventions that existed to frustrate the free soul. Thus many of her novels, and many more of her stories, have to do with a particularly worrying situation: how to preserve the freedom of an affair within the bounds of marriage, or, alternatively, how to safeguard an affair by turning it into a marriage. For it is seen clearly that without some kind of control, some kind of recognition, no illicitly joined couple will enjoy any kind of society, least of all its own.

Edith Wharton was a writer of stories before she was a novelist. She was an early contributor to Scribner's Magazine, and her first collection, called *The Greater Inclination*, appeared in 1899, to be followed by other volumes at regular intervals, her last appearing in 1937. They are notable for the fact that although her material might vary her style varies not at all. It is consistently even, restrained, well-bred, yet at times audaciously acute. The acuteness is disguised by the beautiful tenor of the narrative, yet she has uncomfortable things to say about men and women. She notes their fundamental incompatibility, yet she is so good-natured that only rarely do relations between the sexes become acrimonious. There may be undertones of tension and tragedy but they will be kept within noble boundaries. Nobility is perhaps her most striking characteristic, and although she is always willing to amuse she is at her finest when she is serious. And when she is serious she stands, as she herself said of another author, 'so nearly among the first'.

The stories in the present volume have been taken from several of her collections, ranging from the sprightliness of 'The Pelican' of 1899 to the pitiless social sketch entitled 'The Last Asset' of 1908, from 'Autres Temps', a study of divorce and its legacy, dating from 1916, to the complex little tragedy, 'Her Son', taken from the 1933 collection, *Human Nature*. I have included one or two ghost stories, a genre in which she was extremely interested throughout her life, although she was perhaps too well balanced ever to bring it completely to life. The reader will encounter the true Edith Wharton in stories such as 'The Reckoning' and 'The Letters', or 'Atrophy', stories in which the desires of the heart are accommodated only with difficulty. Her surprising diversity, her unexpected depths, and her consistent good manners make of her a bewitching writer, one to whom both truth and good manners remain not only attractive but, on payment of a small tribute, permanently available.

ANITA BROOKNER

The Pelican

SHE was very pretty when I first knew her, with the sweet straight nose and short upper lip of the cameo-brooch divinity, humanized by a dimple that flowered in her cheek whenever anything was said possessing the outward attributes of humor without its intrinsic quality. For the dear lady was providentially deficient in humor: the least hint of the real thing clouded her lovely eye like the hovering shadow of an algebraic problem.

I don't think nature had meant her to be 'intellectual'; but what can a poor thing do, whose husband has died of drink when her baby is hardly six months old, and who finds her coral necklace and her grandfather's edition of the British Dramatists inadequate to the demands of the creditors?

Her mother, the celebrated Irene Astarte Pratt, had written a poem in blank verse on 'The Fall of Man'; one of her aunts was dean of a girls' college; another had translated Euripides – with such a family, the poor child's fate was sealed in advance. The only way of paying her husband's debts and keeping the baby clothed was to be intellectual; and, after some hesitation as to the form her mental activity was to take, it was unanimously decided that she was to give lectures.

They began by being drawing-room lectures. The first time I saw her she was standing by the piano, against the flippant background of Dresden china and photographs, telling a roomful of women preoccupied with their spring bonnets all she thought she knew about Greek art. The ladies assembled to hear her had given me to understand that she was 'doing it for the baby,' and this fact, together with the shortness of her upper lip and the bewildering co-operation of her dimple, disposed me to listen leniently to her dissertation. Happily, at that time Greek art was still, if I may use the phrase, easily handled: it was as simple as walking down a museum gallery lined with pleasant familiar Venuses and Apollos. All the later complications – the archaic and archaistic conundrums; the influences of Assyria and Asia Minor; the conflicting attributions and the wrangles of the erudite – still slumbered in the bosom of the future 'scientific critic.' Greek art in those days

1

began with Phidias and ended with the Apollo Belvedere; and a child could travel from one to the other without danger of losing his way.

Mrs. Amyot had two fatal gifts: a capacious but inaccurate memory, and an extraordinary fluency of speech. There was nothing she did not remember – wrongly; but her halting facts were swathed in so many layers of rhetoric that their infirmities were imperceptible to her friendly critics. Besides, she had been taught Greek by the aunt who had translated Euripides; and the mere sound of the αἰς and οἰς that she now and then not unskillfully let slip (correcting herself, of course, with a start, and indulgently mistranslating the phrase), struck awe to the hearts of ladies whose only 'accomplishment' was French – if you didn't speak too quickly.

I had then but a momentary glimpse of Mrs. Amyot, but a few months later I came upon her again in the New England university town where the celebrated Irene Astarte Pratt lived on the summit of a local Parnassus, with lesser muses and college professors respectfully grouped on the lower ledges of the sacred declivity. Mrs. Amyot, who, after her husband's death, had returned to the maternal roof (even during her father's lifetime the roof had been distinctively maternal); Mrs. Amyot, thanks to her upper lip, her dimple and her Greek, was already ensconced in a snug hollow of the Parnassian slope.

After the lecture was over it happened that I walked home with Mrs. Amyot. From the incensed glances of two or three learned gentlemen who were hovering on the doorstep when we emerged, I inferred that Mrs. Amyot, at that period, did not often walk home alone; but I doubt whether any of my discomfited rivals, whatever his claims to favor, was ever treated to so ravishing a mixture of shyness and self-abandonment, of sham erudition and real teeth and hair, as it was my privilege to enjoy. Even at the opening of her public career Mrs. Amyot had a tender eye for strangers, as possible links with successive centers of culture to which in due course the torch of Greek art might be handed on.

She began by telling me that she had never been so frightened in her life. She knew, of course, how dreadfully learned I was, and when, just as she was going to begin, her hostess had whispered to her that I was in the room, she had felt ready to sink through the floor. Then (with a flying dimple) she had remembered Emerson's line – wasn't it Emerson's? – that beauty is its own excuse for *seeing* and that had made her feel a little more confident, since she was sure that no one *saw* beauty more vividly than she – as a child she used to sit for hours gazing at an Etruscan vase on the bookcase in the library, while her sisters played with their dolls – and if *seeing* beauty was the only excuse one needed for talking about it, why, she was sure I would make allowances and not be *too* critical and sarcastic, especially if, as she thought probable, I had heard of her having lost her poor husband, and how she had to do it for the baby.

Being abundantly assured of my sympathy on these points, she went on to say that she had always wanted so much to consult me about her lectures. Of course, one subject wasn't enough (this view of the limitations of Greek art as a 'subject' gave me a startling idea of the rate at which a successful lecturer might exhaust the universe); she must find others; she had not ventured on any as yet, but she had thought of Tennyson – didn't I *love* Tennyson? She *worshiped* him so that she was sure she could help others to understand him; or what did I think of a 'course' on Raphael or Michelangelo – or on the heroines of Shakespeare? There were some fine steel engravings of Raphael's Madonnas and of the Sistine ceiling in her mother's library, and she had seen Miss Cushman in several Shakespearian roles, so that on these subjects also she felt qualified to speak with authority.

When we reached her mother's door she begged me to come in and talk the matter over; she wanted me to see the baby – she felt as though I should understand her better if I saw the baby – and the dimple flashed through a tear.

The fear of encountering the author of 'The Fall of Man,' combined with the opportune recollection of a dinner engagement, made me evade this appeal with the promise of returning on the morrow. On the morrow, I left too early to redeem my promise; and for several years afterwards I saw no more of Mrs. Amyot.

My calling at that time took me at irregular intervals from one to another of our larger cities, and as Mrs. Amyot was also peripatetic it was inevitable that sooner or later we should cross each other's path. It was therefore without surprise that, one snowy afternoon in Boston, I learned from the lady with whom I chanced to be lunching that, as soon as the meal was over, I was to be taken to hear Mrs. Amyot lecture.

'On Greek art?' I suggested.

'Oh, you've heard her then? No, this is one of the series called "Homes and Haunts of the Poets." Last week we had Wordsworth and the Lake Poets, today we are to have Goethe and Weimar. She is a wonderful creature – all the women of her family are geniuses. You know, of course, that her mother was Irene Astarte Pratt, who wrote a poem on "The Fall of Man": N. P. Willis called her the female Milton of America. One of Mrs. Amyot's aunts has translated Eurip – '

'And is she as pretty as ever?' I irrelevantly interposed.

My hostess looked shocked. 'She is excessively modest and retiring. She says it is actual suffering for her to speak in public. You know she only does it for the baby.'

Punctually at the hour appointed, we took our seats in a lecture hall full of strenuous females in ulsters. Mrs. Amyot was evidently a favorite with these austere sisters, for every corner was crowded, and as we entered a pale usher with an educated mispronunciation was setting forth to several dejected applicants the impossibility of supplying them with seats.

Our own were happily so near the front that when the curtains at the back of the platform parted, and Mrs. Amyot appeared, I was at once able to establish a comparison between the lady placidly dimpling to the applause of her public and the shrinking drawing-room orator of my earlier recollections.

Mrs. Amyot was as pretty as ever, and there was the same curious discrepancy between the freshness of her aspect and the staleness of her theme, but something was gone of the blushing unsteadiness with which she had fired her first random shots at Greek art. It was not that the shots were less uncertain, but that she now had the air of assuming that, for her purpose, the bull's-eye was everywhere, so that there was no need to be flustered in taking aim. This assurance had so facilitated the flow of her eloquence that she seemed to be performing a trick analogous to that of the conjurer who pulls hundreds of yards of white paper out of his mouth. From a large assortment of stock adjectives she chose, with unerring deftness and rapidity, the one that taste and discrimination would most surely have rejected, fitting out her subject with a whole wardrobe of slop-shop epithets irrelevant in cut and size. To the invaluable knack of not disturbing the association of ideas in her audience, she added the gift of what may be called a confidential manner – so that her fluent generalizations about Goethe and his place in literature (the lecture was, of course, manufactured out of Lewes's book) had the flavor of personal experience, of views sympathetically exchanged with her audience on the best way of knitting children's socks, or of putting up preserves for the winter. It was, I am sure, to this personal accent – the moral equivalent of her dimple – that Mrs. Amyot owed her prodigious, her irrational success. It was her art of transposing secondhand ideas into firsthand emotions that so endeared her to her feminine listeners.

To anyone not in search of 'documents' Mrs. Amyot's success was hardly of a kind to make her more interesting, and my curiosity flagged with the growing conviction that the 'suffering' entailed on her by public speaking was at most a retrospective pang. I was sure that she had reached the point of measuring and enjoying her effects, of deliberately manipulating her public; and there must indeed have been a certain exhilaration in attaining results so considerable by means involving so little conscious effort. Mrs. Amyot's art was simply an extension of coquetry: she flirted with her audience.

In this mood of enlightened skepticism I responded but languidly to my hostess' suggestion that I should go with her that evening to see Mrs. Amyot. The aunt who had translated Euripides was at home on

Saturday evenings, and one met 'thoughtful' people there, my hostess explained: it was one of the intellectual centers of Boston. My mood remained distinctly resentful of any connection between Mrs. Amyot and intellectuality, and I declined to go; but the next day I met Mrs. Amyot in the street.

She stopped me reproachfully. She had heard I was in Boston; why had I not come last night? She had been told that I was at her lecture, and it had frightened her – yes, really, almost as much as years ago in Hillbridge. She never *could* get over that stupid shyness, and the whole business was as distasteful to her as ever; but what could she do? There was the baby – he was a big boy now, and boys were *so* expensive! But did I really think she had improved the least little bit? And why wouldn't I come home with her now, and see the boy, and tell her frankly what I had thought of the lecture? She had plenty of flattery – people were *so* kind, and everyone knew that she did it for the baby – but what she felt the need of was criticism, severe, discriminating criticism like mine – oh, she knew that I was dreadfully discriminating!

I went home with her and saw the boy. In the early heat of her Tennyson worship Mrs. Amyot had christened him Lancelot, and he looked it. Perhaps, however, it was his black velvet dress and the exasperating length of his yellow curls, together with the fact of his having been taught to recite Browning to visitors, that raised to fever heat the itching of my palms in his Infant Samuel-like presence. I have since had reason to think that he would have preferred to be called Billy, and to hunt cats with the other boys in the block: his curls and his poetry were simply another outlet for Mrs. Amyot's irrepressible coquetry.

But if Lancelot was not genuine, his mother's love for him was. It justified everything – the lectures *were* for the baby, after all. I had not been ten minutes in the room before I was pledged to help Mrs. Amyot carry out her triumphant fraud. If she wanted to lecture on Plato she should – Plato must take his chance like the rest of us! There was no use, of course, in being 'discriminating.' I preserved sufficient reason to avoid that pitfall, but I suggested 'subjects' and made lists of books for her with a fatuity that became more obvious as time attenuated the remembrance of her smile; I even remember thinking that some men might have cut the knot by marrying her, but I handed over Plato as a hostage and escaped by the afternoon train.

The next time I saw her was in New York, when she had become so fashionable that it was part of the whole duty of woman to be seen at her lectures. The lady who suggested that of course I ought to go and hear Mrs. Amyot, was not very clear about anything except that she was perfectly lovely, and had had a horrid husband, and was doing it to support her boy. The subject of the discourse (I think it was on Ruskin) was clearly of minor importance, not only to my friend, but to the throng of well-dressed and absent-minded ladies who rustled in late, dropped their muffs, and pocketbooks, and undisguisedly lost themselves in the study of each other's apparel. They received Mrs. Amyot with warmth, but she evidently represented a social obligation like going to church, rather than any more personal interest; in fact I suspect that every one of the ladies would have remained away, had they been sure that none of the others were coming.

Whether Mrs. Amyot was disheartened by the lack of sympathy between herself and her hearers, or whether the sport of arousing it had become a task, she certainly imparted her platitudes with less convincing warmth than of old. Her voice had the same confidential inflections, but it was like a voice reproduced by a gramophone; the real woman seemed far away. She had grown stouter without losing her dewy freshness, and her smart gown might have been taken to show either the potentialities of a settled income, or a politic concession to the taste of her hearers. As I listened I reproached myself for ever having suspected her of self-deception in saying that she took no pleasure in her work. I was sure now that she did it only for Lancelot, and judging from the size of her audience and the price of the tickets I concluded that Lancelot must be receiving a liberal education.

I was living in New York that winter, and in the rotation of dinners I found myself one evening at Mrs. Amyot's side. The dimple came out at my greeting as punctually as a cuckoo in a Swiss clock, and I detected the same automatic quality in the tone in which she made her usual pretty demand for advice. She was like a musical box charged with popular airs. They succeeded one another with breathless rapidity, but there was a moment after each when the cylinders scraped and whizzed.

Mrs. Amyot, as I found when I called on her, was living in a sunny flat, with a sitting room of flowers and a tea table that had the air of expecting visitors. She owned that she had been ridiculously successful. It was delightful, of course, on Lancelot's account. Lancelot had been sent to the best school in the country, and if things went well and people didn't tire of his silly mother he was to go to Harvard afterwards. During the next two or three years Mrs. Amyot kept her flat in New York, and radiated art and literature upon the suburbs. I saw her now and then, always stouter, better dressed, more successful and more automatic: she had become a lecturing machine.

I went abroad for a year or two and when I came back she had disappeared. I asked several people about her, but life had closed over her. She had been last heard of as lecturing – still lecturing – but no one seemed to know when or where.

It was in Boston that I found her at last, forlornly swaying to the oscillations of an overhead strap in a crowded trolley car. Her face had so changed that I lost myself in a startled reckoning of the time that had elapsed since our parting. She spoke to me shyly, as though aware of my hurried calculation, and conscious that in five years she ought not to have altered so much as to upset my notion of time. Then she seemed to set it down to her dress, for she nervously gathered her cloak over a gown that asked only to be concealed, and shrank into a seat behind the line of prehensile bipeds blocking the aisle of the car.

It was perhaps because she so obviously avoided me that I felt for the first time that I might be of use to her; and when she left the car I made no excuse for following her.

She said nothing of needing advice and did not ask me to walk home with her, concealing, as we talked, her transparent preoccupations under the guise of a sudden interest in all I had been doing since she had last seen me. Of what concerned her, I learned only that Lancelot was well and that for the present, she was not lecturing – she was tired and her doctor has ordered her to rest. On the doorstep of a shabby house she paused and held out her hand. She had been so glad to see me and perhaps if I were in Boston again – the tired dimple, as it were, bowed me out and closed the door on the conclusion of the phrase.

Two or three weeks later, at my club in New York, I found a letter from her. In it she owned that she was troubled, that of late she had been unsuccessful, and that, if I chanced to be coming back to Boston, and could spare her a little of that invaluable advice which – . A few days later the advice was at her disposal. She told me frankly what had happened. Her public had grown tired of her. She had seen it coming on for some time and was shrewd enough in detecting the causes. She had more rivals than formerly – younger women, she admitted, with a smile that could still afford to be generous – and then her audiences had grown more critical and consequently more exacting. Lecturing – as she understood it – used to be simple enough. You chose your topic – Raphael, Shakespeare, Gothic Architecture, or some such big familiar 'subject' – and read up about it for a week or so at the Athenaeum or the Astor Library, and then told your audience what you had read. Now, it appeared, that simple process was no longer adequate. People had tired of familiar 'subjects'; it was the fashion to be interested in things that one hadn't always known about – natural selection, animal magnetism, sociology and comparative folklore; while, in literature, the demand had become equally difficult to meet, since Matthew Arnold had introduced the habit of studying the 'influence' of one author on another. She had tried lecturing on influences, and had done very well as long as the public was satisfied with the tracing of such obvious influences as that of Turner on Ruskin, of Schiller on Goethe, of Shakespeare on English literature; but such investigations had soon lost all charm for her too-sophisticated audiences, who now demanded either that the influence or the influenced should be quite unknown, or that there should be no perceptible connection between the two. The zest of the performance lay in the measure of ingenuity with which the

lecturer established a relation between two people who had probably
never heard of each other, much less read each other's work. A pretty
Miss Williams with red hair had, for instance, been lecturing with great
success on the influence of the Rosicrucians upon the poetry of Keats,
while somebody else had given a 'course' on the influence of St. Thomas
Aquinas upon Professor Huxley.

Mrs. Amyot, warmed by my participation in her distress, went on
to say that the growing demand for evolution was what most troubled
her. Her grandfather had been a pillar of the Presbyterian ministry, and
the idea of her lecturing on Darwin or Herbert Spencer was deeply
shocking to her mother and aunts. In one sense the family had staked
its literary as well as its spiritual hopes on the literal inspiration of
Genesis: what became of 'The Fall of Man' in the light of modern
exegesis?

The upshot of it was that she had ceased to lecture because she could
no longer sell tickets enough to pay for the hire of a lecture hall; and
as for the managers, they wouldn't look at her. She had tried her luck
all through the Eastern States and as far south as Washington; but it
was of no use, and unless she could get hold of some new subjects –
or, better still, of some new audiences – she must simply go out of the
business. That would mean the failure of all she had worked for, since
Lancelot would have to leave Harvard. She paused, and wept some of
the unbecoming tears that spring from real grief. Lancelot, it appeared,
was to be a genius. He had passed his opening examinations brilliantly;
he had 'literary gifts'; he had written beautiful poetry, much of which
his mother had copied out, in reverentially slanting characters, in a
velvet-bound volume which she drew from a locked drawer.

Lancelot's verse struck me as nothing more alarming than growing
pains; but it was not to learn this that she had summoned me. What
she wanted was to be assured that he was worth working for, an
assurance which I managed to convey by the simple stratagem of
remarking that the poems reminded me of Swinburne – and so they
did, as well as of Browning, Tennyson, Rossetti, and all the other poets
who supply young authors with original inspirations.

This point being established, it remained to be decided by what
means his mother was, in the French phrase, to pay herself the luxury
of a poet. It was clear that this indulgence could be bought only with
counterfeit coin, and that the one way of helping Mrs. Amyot was to
become a party to the circulation of such currency. My fetish of intellectual integrity went down like a ninepin before the appeal of a woman
no longer young and distinctly foolish, but full of those dear contradic-
tions and irrelevancies that will always make flesh and blood prevail
against a syllogism. When I took leave of Mrs. Amyot I had promised
her a dozen letters to Western universities and had half pledged myself
to sketch out a lecture on the reconciliation of science and religion.

In the West she achieved a success which for a year or more embitt-
ered my perusal of the morning papers. The fascination that lures the
murderer back to the scene of his crime drew my eye to every paragraph
celebrating Mrs. Amyot's last brilliant lecture on the influence of something upon somebody; and her own letters – she overwhelmed me with
them – spared me no detail of the entertainment given in her honor by
the Palimpsest Club of Omaha or of her reception at the university of
Leadville. The college professors were especially kind: she assured me
that she had never before met with such discriminating sympathy. I
winced at the adjective, which cast a sudden light on the vast machinery
of fraud that I had set in motion. All over my native land, men of
hitherto unblemished integrity were conniving with me in urging their
friends to go and hear Mrs. Amyot lecture on the reconciliation of
science and religion! My only hope was that, somewhere among the
number of my accomplices, Mrs. Amyot might find one who would
marry her in the defense of his convictions.

None, apparently, resorted to such heroic measures; for about two
years later I was startled by the announcement that Mrs. Amyot was
lecturing in Trenton, New Jersey, on modern theosophy in the light
of the Vedas. The following week she was at Newark, discussing
Schopenhauer in the light of recent psychology. The week after that I
was on the deck of an ocean steamer, reconsidering my share in Mrs.
Amyot's triumphs with the impartiality with which one views an
episode that is being left behind at the rate of twenty knots an hour.
After all, I had been helping a mother to educate her son.

The next ten years of my life were spent in Europe, and when I
came home the recollection of Mrs. Amyot had become as inoffensive
as one of those pathetic ghosts who are said to strive in vain to make
themselves visible to the living. I did not even notice the fact that I no
longer heard her spoken of; she had dropped like a dead leaf from the
bough of memory.

A year or two after my return I was condemned to one of the worst
punishments a worker can undergo – an enforced holiday. The doctors
who pronounced the inhuman sentence decreed that it should be worked
out in the South, and for a whole winter I carried my cough, my
thermometer and my idleness from one fashionable orange grove to
another. In the vast and melancholy sea of my disoccupation I clutched
like a drowning man at any human driftwood within reach. I took a
critical and depreciatory interest in the coughs, the thermometers and
the idleness of my fellow sufferers; but to the healthy, the occupied,
the transient I clung with undiscriminating enthusiasm.

In no other way can I explain, as I look back on it, the importance
I attached to the leisurely confidences of a new arrival with a brown
beard who, tilted back at my side on a hotel veranda hung with roses,
imparted to me one afternoon the simple annals of his past. There was

nothing in the tale to kindle the most inflammable imagination, and though the man had a pleasant frank face and a voice differing agreeably from the shrill inflections of our fellow lodgers, it is probable that under different conditions his discursive history of successful business ventures in a Western city would have affected me somewhat in the manner of a lullaby.

Even at the time I was not sure I liked his agreeable voice; it had a self-importance out of keeping with the humdrum nature of his story, as though a breeze engaged in shaking out a tablecloth should have fancied itself inflating a banner. But this criticism may have been a mere mark of my own fastidiousness, for the man seemed a simple fellow, satisfied with his middling fortunes, and already (he was not much past thirty) deep sunk in conjugal content.

He had just started on an anecdote connected with the cutting of his eldest boy's teeth, when a lady I knew, returning from her late drive, paused before us for a moment in the twilight, with the smile which is the feminine equivalent of beads to savages.

'Won't you take a ticket?' she said sweetly.

Of course I would take a ticket – but for what? I ventured to inquire.

'Oh, that's *so* good of you – for the lecture this evening. You needn't go, you know; we're none of us going; most of us have been through it already at Aiken and at Saint Augustine and at Palm Beach. I've given away my tickets to some new people who've just come from the North, and some of us are going to send our maids, just to fill up the room.'

'And may I ask to whom you are going to pay this delicate attention?'

'Oh, I thought you knew – to poor Mrs. Amyot. She's been lecturing all over the South this winter; she's simply *haunted* me ever since I left New York – and we had six weeks of her at Bar Harbor last summer! One has to take tickets, you know, because she's a widow and does it for her son – to pay for his education. She's so plucky and nice about it, and talks about him in such a touching unaffected way, that everybody is sorry for her, and we all simply ruin ourselves in tickets. I do hope that boy's nearly educated!'

'Mrs. Amyot? Mrs. Amyot?' I repeated. 'It she *still* educating her son?'

'Oh, do you know about her? Has she been at it long? There's some comfort in that, for I suppose when the boy's provided for the poor thing will be able to take a rest – and give us one!'

She laughed and held out her hand.

'Here's your ticket. Did you say *tickets* – two? Oh, thanks. Of course you needn't go.'

'But I mean to go. Mrs. Amyot is an old friend of mine.'

'Do you really? That's awfully good of you. Perhaps I'll go too if I can persuade Charlie and the others to come. And I wonder' – in a well-directed aside – 'if your friend – ?'

I telegraphed her under cover of the dusk that my friend was of too recent standing to be drawn into her charitable toils, and she masked her mistake under a rattle of friendly adjurations not to be late, and to be sure to keep a seat for her, as she had quite made up her mind to go even if Charlie and the others wouldn't.

The flutter of her skirts subsided in the distance, and my neighbor, who had half turned away to light a cigar, made no effort to reopen the conversation. At length, fearing he might have overheard the allusion to himself, I ventured to ask if he were going to the lecture that evening.

'Much obliged – I have a ticket,' he said abruptly.

This struck me as in such bad taste that I made no answer; and it was he who spoke next.

'Did I understand you to say that you were an old friend of Mrs. Amyot's?'

'I think I may claim to be, if it is the same Mrs. Amyot I had the pleasure of knowing many years ago. My Mrs. Amyot used to lecture too – '

'To pay for her son's education?'

'I believe so.'

'Well – see you later.'

He got up and walked into the house.

In the hotel drawing room that evening there was but a meager sprinkling of guests, among whom I saw my brown-bearded friend sitting alone on a sofa, with his head against the wall. It could not have been curiosity to see Mrs. Amyot that had impelled him to attend the performance, for it would have been impossible for him, without changing his place, to command the improvised platform at the end of the room. When I looked at him he seemed lost in contemplation of the chandelier.

The lady from whom I had bought my tickets fluttered in late, unattended by Charlie and the others, and assuring me that she would *scream* if we had a lecture on Ibsen – she had heard it three times already that winter. A glance at the program reassured her: it informed us (in the lecturer's own slanting hand) that Mrs. Amyot was to lecture on the Cosmogony.

After a long pause, during which the small audience coughed and moved its chairs and showed signs of regretting that it had come, the door opened, and Mrs. Amyot stepped upon the platform. Ah, poor lady!

Someone said 'Hush!' The coughing and chair shifting subsided, and she began.

It was like looking at one's self early in the morning in a cracked

mirror. I had no idea I had grown so old. As for Lancelot, he must
have a beard. A beard? The word struck me, and without knowing
why I glanced across the room at my bearded friend on the sofa.
Oddly enough he was looking at me, with a half-defiant, half-sullen
expression; and as our glances crossed, and his fell, the conviction came
to me that *he was Lancelot.*

I don't remember a word of the lecture; and yet there was enough
of them to have filled a good-sized dictionary. The stream of Mrs.
Amyot's eloquence had become a flood: one had the despairing sense
that she had sprung a leak, and that until the plumber came there was
nothing to be done about it.

The plumber came at length, in the shape of a clock striking ten;
my companion, with a sigh of relief, drifted away in search of Charlie
and the others; the audience scattered with the precipitation of people
who had discharged a duty; and, without surprise, I found the brown-
bearded stranger at my elbow.

We stood alone in the bare-floored room, under the flaring
chandelier.

'I think you told me this afternoon that you were an old friend of
Mrs. Amyot's?' he began awkwardly.

I assented.

'Will you come in and see her?'

'Now? I shall be very glad to, if – '

'She's ready; she's expecting you,' he interposed.

He offered no further explanation, and I followed him in silence.
He led me down the long corridor, and pushed open the door of a
sitting room.

'Mother,' he said, closing the door after we had entered, 'here's the
gentleman who says he used to know you.'

Mrs. Amyot, who sat in an easy chair stirring a cup of bouillon,
looked up with a start. She had evidently not seen me in the audience,
and her son's description had failed to convey my identity. I saw a
frightened look in her eyes; then, like a frost flower on a windowpane,
the dimple expanded on her wrinkled cheek, and she held out her hand.

'I'm so glad,' she said, 'so glad!'

She turned to her son, who stood watching us. 'You must have
told Lancelot all about me – you've known me so long!'

'I haven't had time to talk to your son – since I knew he was your
son,' I explained.

Her brow cleared. 'Then you haven't had time to say anything very
dreadful?' she said with a laugh.

'It is he who has been saying dreadful things,' I returned, trying to
fall in with her tone.

I saw my mistake. 'What things?' she faltered.

'Making me feel how old I am by telling me about his children.'

'My grandchildren!' she exclaimed with a blush.

'Well, if you choose to put it so.'

She laughed again, vaguely, and was silent. I hesitated a moment and then put out my hand.

'I see you are tired. I shouldn't have ventured to come in at this hour if your son – '

The son stepped between us. 'Yes, I asked him to come,' he said to his mother, in his clear self-assertive voice. 'I haven't told him anything yet; but you've got to – now. That's what I brought him for.'

His mother straightened herself, but I saw her eye waver.

'Lancelot – ' she began.

'Mr. Amyot,' I said, turning to the young men, 'If your mother will let me come back tomorrow, I shall be very glad – '

He struck his hand hard against the table on which he was leaning.

'No, sir! It won't take long, but it's got to be said now.'

He moved nearer to his mother, and I saw his lip twitch under his beard. After all, he was younger and less sure of himself than I had fancied.

'See here, Mother,' he went on, 'there's something here that's got to be cleared up, and as you say this gentleman is an old friend of yours it had better be cleared up in his presence. Maybe he can help explain it – and if he can't, it's got to be explained to *him*.'

Mrs. Amyot's lips moved, but she made no sound. She glanced at me helplessly and sat down. My early inclination to thrash Lancelot was beginning to reassert itself. I took up my hat and moved toward the door.

'Mrs. Amyot is under no obligation to explain anything whatever to me,' I said curtly.

'Well! She's under an obligation to me, then – to explain something in your presence.' He turned to her again. 'Do you know what the people in this hotel are saying? Do you know what he thinks – what they all think? That you're doing this lecturing to support me – to pay for my education! They say you go round telling them so. That's what they buy the tickets for – they do it out of charity. Ask him if it isn't what they say – ask him if they weren't joking about it on the piazza before dinner. The others think I'm a little boy, but he's known you for years, and he must have known how old I was. *He* must have known it wasn't to pay for my education!'

He stood before her with his hands clenched, the veins beating in his temples. She had grown very pale, and her cheeks looked hollow. When she spoke her voice had an odd click in it.

'If – if these ladies and gentlemen have been coming to my lectures out of charity, I see nothing to be ashamed of in that – ' she faltered.

'If they've been coming out of charity to *me*,' he retorted, 'don't you see you've been making me a party to a fraud? Isn't there any shame in that?' His forehead reddened. 'Mother! Can't you see the shame of letting people think I was a deadbeat, who sponged on you for my keep? Let alone making us both the laughingstock of every place you go to!'

'I never did that, Lancelot!'

'Did what?'

'Made you a laughingstock – '

He stepped close to her and caught her wrist.

'Will you look me in the face and swear you never told people you were doing this lecturing business to support me?'

There was a long silence. He dropped her wrists and she lifted a limp handkerchief to her frightened eyes. 'I did do it – to support you – to educate you – ' she sobbed.

'We're not talking about what you did when I was a boy. Everybody who knows me knows I've been a grateful son. Have I ever taken a penny from you since I left college ten years ago?'

'I never said you had! How can you accuse your mother of such wickedness, Lancelot?'

'Have you never told anybody in this hotel – or anywhere else in the last ten years – that you were lecturing to support me? Answer me that!'

'How can you,' she wept, 'before a stranger?'

'Haven't you said such things about *me* to strangers?' he retorted.

'Lancelot!'

'Well – answer me, then. Say you haven't, Mother!' His voice broke unexpectedly and he took her hand with a gentler touch. 'I'll believe anything you tell me,' he said almost humbly.

She mistook his tone and raised her head with a rash clutch at dignity.

'I think you'd better ask this gentleman to excuse you first.'

'No, by God, I won't!' he cried. 'This gentleman says he knows all about you and I mean him to know all about me, too. I don't mean that he or anybody else under this roof shall go on thinking for another twenty-four hours that a cent of their money has ever gone into my pockets since I was old enough to shift for myself. And he shan't leave this room till you've made that clear to him.'

He stepped back as he spoke and put his shoulders against the door.

'My dear young gentleman,' I said politely, 'I shall leave this room exactly when I see fit to do so – and that is now. I have already told you that Mrs. Amyot owes me no explanation of her conduct.'

'But I owe you an explanation of mine – you and everyone who has bought a single one of her lecture tickets. Do you suppose a man who's been through what I went through while that woman was talking to you in the porch before dinner is going to hold his tongue, and not attempt to justify himself? No decent man is going to sit down under that sort of thing. It's enough to ruin his character. If you're my mother's friend, you owe it to me to hear what I've got to say.'

He pulled out his handkerchief and wiped his forehead.

'Good God, Mother!' he burst out suddenly, 'what did you do it for? Haven't you had everything you wanted ever since I was able to pay for it? Haven't I paid you back every cent you spent on me when I was in college? Have I ever gone back on you since I was big enough to work?' He turned to me with a laugh. 'I thought she did it to amuse herself – and because there was such a demand for her lectures. *Such a demand!* That's what she always told me. When we asked her to come out and spend this winter with us in Minneapolis, she wrote back that she couldn't because she had engagements all through the South, and her manager wouldn't let her off. That's the reason why I came all the way on here to see her. We thought she was the most popular lecturer in the United States, my wife and I did! We were awfully proud of it too, I can tell you.' He dropped into a chair, still laughing.

'How can you, Lancelot, how can you!' His mother, forgetful of my presence, was clinging to him with tentative caresses. 'When you didn't need the money any longer I spent it all on the chidlren – you know I did.'

'Yes, on lace christening dresses and life-size rocking horses with real manes! The kind of thing children can't do without.'

'Oh, Lancelot, Lancelot – I loved them so! How can you believe such falsehoods about me?'

'What falsehoods about you?'

'That I ever told anybody such dreadful things?'

He put her back gently, keeping his eyes on hers. 'Did you never tell anybody in this house that you were lecturing to support your son?'

Her hands dropped from his shoulders and she flashed round on me in sudden anger.

'I know what I think of people who call themselves friends and who come between a mother and her son!'

'Oh, Mother, Mother!' he groaned.

I went up to him and laid my hand on his shoulder.

'My dear man,' I said, 'don't you see the uselessness of prolonging this?'

'Yes, I do,' he answered abruptly; and before I could forestall his movement he rose and walked out of the room.

There was a long silence, measured by the lessening reverberations of his footsteps down the wooden floor of the corridor.

When they ceased I approached Mrs. Amyot, who had sunk into her chair. I held out my hand and she took it without a trace of resentment on her ravaged face.

'I sent his wife a sealskin jacket at Christmas!' she said, with the tears running down her cheeks.

The Other Two

***

WAYTHORN, on the drawing-room hearth, waited for his wife to come down to dinner.

It was their first night under his own roof, and he was surprised at his thrill of boyish agitation. He was not so old, to be sure – his glass gave him little more than the five-and-thirty years to which his wife confessed – but he had fancied himself already in the temperate zone; yet here he was listening for her step with a tender sense of all it symbolized, with some old trail of verse about the garlanded nuptial doorposts floating through his enjoyment of the pleasant room and the good dinner just beyond it.

They had been hastily recalled from their honeymoon by the illness of Lily Haskett, the child of Mrs. Waythorn's first marriage. The little girl, at Waythorn's desire, had been transferred to his house on the day of her mother's wedding, and the doctor, on their arrival, broke the news that she was ill with typhoid, but declared that all the symptoms were favorable. Lily could show twelve years of unblemished health, and the case promised to be a light one. The nurse spoke as reassuringly, and after a moment of alarm Mrs. Waythorn had adjusted herself to the situation. She was very fond of Lily – her affection for the child had perhaps been her decisive charm in Waythorn's eyes – but she had the perfectly balanced nerves which her little girl had inherited, and no woman ever wasted less tissue in unproductive worry. Waythorn was therefore quite prepared to see her come in presently, a little late because of a last look at Lily, but as serene and well-appointed as if her good-night kiss had been laid on the brow of health. Her composure was restful to him; it acted as ballast to his somewhat unstable sensibilities. As he pictured her bending over the child's bed he thought how soothing her presence must be in illness: her very step would prognosticate recovery.

His own life had been a gray one, from temperament rather than circumstance, and he had been drawn to her by the unperturbed gaiety which kept her fresh and elastic at an age when most women's activities are growing either slack or febrile. He knew what was said about her;

16

for, popular as she was, there had always been a faint undercurrent of detraction. When she had appeared in New York, nine or ten years earlier, as the pretty Mrs. Haskett whom Gus Varick had unearthed somewhere – was it in Pittsburg or Utica? – society, while promptly accepting her, had reserved the right to cast a doubt on its own indiscrimination. Inquiry, however, established her undoubted connection with a socially reigning family, and explained her recent divorce as the natural result of a runaway match at seventeen; and as nothing was known of Mr. Haskett it was easy to believe the worst of him.

Alice Haskett's remarriage with Gus Varick was a passport to the set whose recognition she coveted, and for a few years the Varicks were the most popular couple in town. Unfortunately the alliance was brief and stormy, and this time the husband had his champions. Still, even Varick's stanchest supporters admitted that he was not meant for matrimony, and Mrs. Varick's grievances were of a nature to bear the inspection of the New York courts. A New York divorce is in itself a diploma of virtue, and in the semiwidowhood of this second separation Mrs. Varick took on an air of sanctity, and was allowed to confide her wrongs to some of the most scrupulous ears in town. But when it was known that she was to marry Waythorn there was a momentary reaction. Her best friends would have preferred to see her remain in the role of the injured wife, which was as becoming to her as crepe to a rosy complexion. True, a decent time had elapsed, and it was not even suggested that Waythorn had supplanted his predecessor. People shook their heads over him, however, and one grudging friend, to whom he affirmed that he took the step with his eyes open, replied oracularly: 'Yes – and with your ears shut.'

Waythorn could afford to smile at these innuendos. In the Wall Street phrase, he had 'discounted' them. He knew that society has not yet adapted itself to the consequences of divorce, and that till the adaptation takes place every woman who uses the freedom the law accords her must be her own social justification. Waythorn had an amused confidence in his wife's ability to justify herself. His expectations were fulfilled, and before the wedding took place Alice Varick's group had rallied openly to her support. She took it all imperturbably; she had a way of surmounting obstacles without seeming to be aware of them, and Waythorn looked back with wonder at the trivialities over which he had worn his nerves thin. He had the sense of having found refuge in a richer, warmer nature than his own, and his satisfaction, at the moment, was humorously summed up in the thought that his wife, when she had done all she could for Lily, would not be ashamed to come down and enjoy a good dinner.

The anticipation of such enjoyment was not, however, the sentiment expressed by Mrs. Waythorn's charming face when she presently joined him. Though she had put on her most engaging tea gown she had

neglected to assume the smile that went with it, and Waythorn thought
he had never seen her look so nearly worried.

'What is it?' he asked. 'Is anything wrong with Lily?'

'No; I've just been in and she's still sleeping.' Mrs. Waythorn hesitated. 'But something tiresome has happened.'

He had taken her two hands, and now perceived that he was
crushing a paper between them.

'This letter?'

'Yes – Mr. Haskett has written – I mean his lawyer has written.'

Waythorn felt himself flush uncomfortably. He dropped his wife's
hands.

'What about?'

'About seeing Lily. You know the courts – '

'Yes, yes,' he interrupted nervously.

Nothing was known about Haskett in New York. He was vaguely
supposed to have remained in the outer darkness from which his wife
had been rescued, and Waythorn was one of the few who were aware
that he had given up his business in Utica and followed her to New
York in order to be near his little girl. In the days of his wooing,
Waythorn had often met Lily on the doorstep, rosy and smiling, on
her way 'to see papa.'

'I am so sorry,' Mrs. Waythorn murmured.

He roused himself. 'What does he want?'

'He wants to see her. You know she goes to him once a week.'

'Well – he doesn't expect her to go to him now, does he?'

'No – he has heard of her illness; but he expects to come here.'

'*Here?*'

Mrs. Waythorn reddened under his gaze. They looked away from
each other.

'I'm afraid he has the right. . . . You'll see. . . .' She made a proffer
of the letter.

Waythorn moved away with a gesture of refusal. He stood staring
about the softly-lighted room, which a moment before had seemed so
full of bridal intimacy.

'I'm so sorry,' she repeated. 'If Lily could have been moved – '

'That's out of the question,' he returned impatiently.

'I suppose so.'

Her lip was beginning to tremble, and he felt himself a brute.

'He must come, of course,' he said. 'When is – his day?'

'I'm afraid – tomorrow.'

'Very well. Send a note in the morning.'

The butler entered to announce dinner.

Waythorn turned to his wife. 'Come – you must be tired. It's
beastly, but try to forget about it,' he said, drawing her hand through
his arm.

'You're so good, dear. I'll try,' she whispered back.

Her face cleared at once, and as she looked at him across the flowers, between the rosy candleshades, he saw her lips waver back into a smile.

'How pretty everything is!' she sighed luxuriously.

He turned to the butler. 'The champagne at once, please. Mrs. Waythorn is tired.'

In a moment or two their eyes met above the sparkling glasses. Her own were quite clear and untroubled: he saw that she had obeyed his injunction and forgotten.

• II •

WAYTHORN, the next morning, went downtown earlier than usual. Haskett was not likely to come till the afternoon, but the instinct of flight drove him forth. He meant to stay away all day – he had thoughts of dining at his club. As his door closed behind him he reflected that before he opened it again it would have admitted another man who had as much right to enter it as himself, and the thought filled him with a physical repugnance.

He caught the elevated at the employees' hour, and found himself crushed between two layers of pendulous humanity. At Eighth Street the man facing him wriggled out, and another took his place. Waythorn glanced up and saw that it was Gus Varick. The men were so close together that it was impossible to ignore the smile of recognition on Varick's handsome overblown face. And after all – why not? They had always been on good terms, and Varick had been divorced before Waythorn's intentions to his wife began. The two exchanged a word on the perennial grievance of the congested trains, and when a seat at their side was miraculously left empty the instinct of self-preservation made Waythorn slip into it after Varick.

The latter drew the stout man's breath of relief. 'Lord – I was beginning to feel like a pressed flower.' He leaned back, looking unconcernedly at Waythorn. 'Sorry to hear that Sellers is knocked out again.'

'Sellers?' echoed Waythorn, starting at his partner's name.

Varick looked surprised. 'You didn't know he was laid up with the gout?'

'No. I've been away – I only got back last night.' Waythorn felt himself reddening in anticipation of the other's smile.

'Ah – yes; to be sure. And Sellers' attack came on two days ago. I'm afraid he's pretty bad. Very awkward for me, as it happens, because he was just putting through a rather important thing for me.'

'Ah?' Waythorn wondered vaguely since when Varick had been dealing in 'important things.' Hitherto he had dabbled only in the shallow pools of speculation, with which Waythorn's office did not usually concern itself.

It occurred to him that Varick might be talking at random, to relieve the strain of their propinquity. That strain was becoming momentarily more apparent to Waythorn, and when, at Cortlandt Street, he caught sight of an acquaintance and had a sudden vision of the picture he and Varick must present to an initiated eye, he jumped up with a muttered excuse.

'I hope you'll find Sellers better,' said Varick civilly, and he stammered back: 'If I can be of any use to you – ' and let the departing crowd sweep him to the platform.

At his office he heard that Sellers was in fact ill with the gout, and would probably not be able to leave the house for some weeks.

'I'm sorry it should have happened so, Mr. Waythorn,' the senior clerk said with affable significance. 'Mr. Sellers was very much upset at the idea of giving you such a lot of extra work just now.'

'Oh, that's no matter,' said Waythorn hastily. He secretly welcomed the pressure of additional business, and was glad to think, when the day's work was over, he would have to call at his partner's on the way home.

He was late for luncheon, and turned in at the nearest restaurant instead of going back to his club. The place was full, and the waiter hurried him to the back of the room to capture the only vacant table. In the cloud of cigar smoke Waythorn did not at once distinguish his neighbors: but presently, looking about him, he saw Varick seated a few feet off. This time, luckily, they were too far apart for conversation, and Varick, who faced another way, had probably not even seen him; but there was an irony in their renewed nearness.

Varick was said to be fond of good living, and as Waythorn sat dispatching his hurried luncheon he looked across half enviously at the other's leisurely degustation of his meal. When Waythorn first saw him he had been helping himself with critical deliberation to a bit of Camembert at the ideal point of liquefaction, and now, the cheese removed, he was just pouring his *café double* from its little two-storied earthen pot. He poured slowly, his ruddy profile bent over the task, and one beringed white hand steadying the lid of the coffeepot; then he stretched his other hand to the decanter of cognac at his elbow, filled a liqueur glass, took a tentative sip, and poured the brandy into his coffe cup.

Waythorn watched him in a kind of fascination. What was he thinking of – only of the flavor of the coffee and the liqueur? Had the morning's meeting left no more trace in his thoughts than on his face? Had his wife so completely passed out of his life that even this odd encounter with her present husband, within a week after her remarriage, was no more than an incident in his day? And as Waythorn mused, another idea struck him: had Haskett ever met Varick as Varick and he had just met? The recollection of Haskett perturbed him, and he rose and left the restaurant, taking a circuitous way out to escape the placid irony of Varick's nod.

It was after seven when Waythorn reached home. He thought the footman who opened the door looked at him oddly.

'How is Miss Lily?' he asked in haste.

'Doing very well, sir. A gentleman – '

'Tell Barlow to put off dinner for half an hour,' Waythorn cut him off, hurrying upstairs.

He went straight to his room and dressed without seeing his wife. When he reached the drawing room she was there, fresh and radiant. Lily's day had been good; the doctor was not coming back that evening.

At dinner Waythorn told her of Sellers' illness and of the resulting complications. She listened sympathetically, adjuring him not to let himself be overworked, and asking vague feminine questions about the routine of the office. Then she gave him the chronicle of Lily's day; quoted the nurse and doctor, and told him who had called to inquire. He had never seen her more serene and unruffled. It struck him, with a curious pang, that she was very happy in being with him, so happy that she found a childish pleasure in rehearsing the trivial incidents of her day.

After dinner they went to the library, and the servant put the coffee and liqueurs on a low table before her and left the room. She looked singularly soft and girlish in her rosy-pale dress, against the dark leather of one of his bachelor armchairs. A day earlier the contrast would have charmed him.

He turned away now, choosing a cigar with affected deliberation.

'Did Haskett come?' he asked, with his back to her.

'Oh, yes – he came.'

'You didn't see him, of course?'

She hesitated a moment. 'I let the nurse see him.'

That was all. There was nothing more to ask. He swung round toward her, applying a match to his cigar. Well, the thing was over for a week, at any rate. He would try not to think of it. She looked up at him, a trifle rosier than usual, with a smile in her eyes.

'Ready for your coffee, dear?'

He leaned against the mantelpiece, watching her as she lifted the coffeepot. The lamplight struck a gleam from her bracelets and tipped her soft hair with brightness. How light and slender she was, and how each gesture flowed into the next! She seemed a creature all compact of harmonies. As the thought of Haskett receded, Waythorn felt himself yielding again to the joy of possessorship. They were his, those white hands with flitting motions, his the light haze of hair, the lips and eyes. . . .

She set down the coffeepot, and reaching for the decanter of cognac, measured off a liqueur glass and poured it into his cup.

Waythorn uttered a sudden exclamation.

'What is the matter?' she said, startled.

'Nothing; only – I don't take cognac in my coffee.'

'Oh, how stupid of me,' she cried.

Their eyes met, and she blushed a sudden agonized red.

· III ·

TEN days later, Mr. Sellers, still housebound, asked Waythorn to call on his way downtown.

The senior partner, with his swaddled foot propped up by the fire, greeted his associate with an air of embarrassment.

'I'm sorry, my dear fellow; I've got to ask you to do an awkward thing for me.'

Waythorn waited, and the other went on, after a pause apparently given to the arrangement of his phrases: 'The fact is, when I was knocked out I had just gone into a rather complicated piece of business for – Gus Varick.'

'Well?' said Waythorn, with an attempt to put him at his ease.

'Well – it's this way: Varick came to me the day before my attack. He had evidently had an inside tip from somebody, and had made about a hundred thousand. He came to me for advice, and I suggested his going in with Vanderlyn.'

'Oh, the deuce!' Waythorn exclaimed. He saw in a flash what had happened. The investment was an alluring one, but required negotiation. He listed quietly while Sellers put the case before him, and, the statement ended, he said: 'You think I ought to see Varick?'

'I'm afraid I can't as yet. The doctor is obdurate. And this thing can't wait. I hate to ask you, but no one else in the office knows the ins and outs of it.'

Waythorn stood silent. He did not care a farthing for the success of Varick's venture, but the honor of the office was to be considered, and he could hardly refuse to oblige his partner.

'Very well,' he said, 'I'll do it.'

That afternoon, apprised by telephone, Varick called at the office. Waythorn, waiting in his private room, wondered what the others thought of it. The newspapers, at the time of Mrs. Waythorn's marriage, had acquainted their readers with every detail of her previous matrimonial ventures, and Waythorn could fancy the clerks smiling behind Varick's back as he was ushered in.

Varick bore himself admirably. He was easy without being undignified, and Waythorn was conscious of cutting a much less impressive figure. Varick had no experience of business, and the talk prolonged itself for nearly an hour while Waythorn set forth with scrupulous precision the details of the proposed transaction.

'I'm awfully obliged to you,' Varick said as he rose. 'The fact is I'm not used to having much money to look after, and I don't want to make an ass of myself – ' He smiled, and Waythorn could not help noticing that there was something pleasant about his smile. 'It feels uncommonly queer to have enough cash to pay one's bills. I'd have sold my soul for it a few years ago!'

Waythorn winced at the allusion. He had heard it rumoured that a lack of funds had been one of the determining causes of the Varick separation, but it did not occur to him that Varick's words were intentional. It seemed more likely that the desire to keep clear of embarrassing topics had fatally drawn him into one. Waythorn did not wish to be outdone in civility.

'We'll do the best we can for you,' he said. 'I think this is a good thing you're in.'

'Oh, I'm sure it's immense. It's awfully good of you – ' Varick broke off, embarrassed. 'I suppose the thing's settled now.– but if – '

'If anything happens before Sellers is about, I'll see you again,' said Waythorn quietly. He was glad, in the end, to appear the more self-possessed of the two.

The course of Lily's illness ran smooth, and as the days passed Waythorn grew used to the idea of Haskett's weekly visit. The first time the day came round, he stayed out late, and questioned his wife as to the visit on his return. She replied at once that Haskett had merely seen the nurse downstairs, as the doctor did not wish anyone in the child's sickroom till after the crisis.

The following week Waythorn was again conscious of the recurrence of the day, but had forgotten it by the time he came home to dinner. The crisis of the disease came a few days later, with a rapid decline of fever, and the little girl was pronounced out of danger. In the rejoicing which ensued the thought of Haskett passed out of Waythorn's mind, and one afternoon, letting himself into the house with a latchkey, he went straight to his library without noticing a shabby hat and umbrella in the hall.

In the library he found a small effaced-looking man with a thinnish gray beard sitting on the edge of a chair. The stranger might have been a piano tuner, or one of those mysteriously efficient persons who are summoned in emergencies to adjust some detail of the domestic machinery. He blinked at Waythorn through a pair of gold-rimmed spectacles and said mildly: 'Mr. Waythorn, I presume? I am Lily's father.'

Waythorn flushed. 'Oh – ' he stammered uncomfortably. He broke off, disliking to appear rude. Inwardly he was trying to adjust the actual Haskett to the image of him projected by his wife's reminiscences. Waythorn had been allowed to infer that Alice's first husband was a brute.

'I am sorry to intrude,' said Haskett, with his over-the-counter politeness.

'Don't mention it,' returned Waythorn, collecting himself. 'I suppose the nurse has been told?'

'I presume so. I can wait,' said Haskett. He had a resigned way of speaking, as though life had worn down his natural powers of resistance.

Waythorn stood on the threshold, nervously pulling off his gloves.

'I'm sorry you've been detained. I will send for the nurse,' he said, and as he opened the door he added with an effort: 'I'm glad we can give you a good report of Lily.' He winced as the *we* slipped out, but Haskett seemed not to notice it.

'Thank you, Mr. Waythorn. It's been an anxious time for me.'

'Ah, well, that's past. Soon she'll be able to go to you.' Waythorn nodded and passed out.

In his own room he flung himself down with a groan. He hated the womanish sensibility which made him suffer so acutely from the grotesque chances of life. He had known when he married that his wife's former husbands were both living, and that amid the multiplied contacts of modern existence there were a thousand chances to one that he would run against one or the other, yet he found himself as much disturbed by his brief encounter with Haskett as though the law had not obligingly removed all difficulties in the way of their meeting.

Waythorn sprang up and began to pace the room nervously. He had not suffered half as much from his two meetings with Varick. It was Haskett's presence in his own house that made the situation so intolerable. He stood still, hearing steps in the passage.

'This way, please,' he heard the nurse say. Haskett was being taken upstairs, then: not a corner of the house but was open to him. Waythorn dropped into another chair, staring vaguely ahead of him. On his dressing table stood a photograph of Alice, taken when he had first known her. She was Alice Varick then – how fine and exquisite he had thought her! Those were Varick's pearls about her neck. At Waythorn's instance they had been returned before her marriage. Had Haskett ever given her any trinkets – and what had become of them, Waythorn wondered? He realized suddenly that he knew very little of Haskett's past or present situation; but from the man's appearance and manner of speech he could reconstruct with curious precision the surroundings of Alice's first marriage. And it startled him to think that she had, in the background of her life, a phase of existence so different from anything with which he had connected her. Varick, whatever his faults, was a gentleman, in the conventional, traditional sense of the term: the sense which at that moment seemed, oddly enough, to have most meaning to Waythorn. He and Varick had the same social habits, spoke the same language, understood the same allusions. But this other man . . . it was grotesquely uppermost in Waythorn's mind that Haskett had worn a made-up tie attached with an elastic. Why should that ridiculous detail symbolize the whole man? Waythorn was exasperated by his own paltriness, but the fact of the tie expanded, forced itself on him, became as it were the key to Alice's past. He could see her, as Mrs. Haskett, sitting in a 'front parlor' furnished in plush, with a pianola, and a copy of *Ben Hur* on the center table. He could see her going to the theater with Haskett – or perhaps even to a 'Church Sociable' – she in the 'picture hat' and Haskett in a black frock coat, a little creased, with the made-up tie on an elastic. On the way home they would stop and look at the illuminated shop windows, lingering over the photographs of New York actresses. On Sunday afternoons Haskett would take her for a walk, pushing Lily ahead of them in a white enameled perambulator, and Waythorn had a vision of the people they would stop and talk to. He could fancy how pretty Alice must have looked, in a dress adroitly constructed from the hints of a New York fashion paper, and how she must have looked down on the other women, chafing at her life, and secretly feeling that she belonged in a bigger place.

For the moment his foremost thought was one of wonder at the way in which she had shed the phase of existence which her marriage with Haskett implied. It was as if her whole aspect, every gesture, every inflection, every allusion, were a studied negation of that period of her life. If she had denied being married to Haskett she could hardly have stood more convicted of duplicity than in this obliteration of the self which had been his wife.

Waythorn started up, checking himself in the analysis of her motives. What right had he to create a fantastic effigy of her and then pass judgment on it? She had spoken vaguely of her first marriage as unhappy, had hinted, with becoming reticence, that Haskett had wrought havoc among her young illusions. . . . It was a pity for Waythorn's peace of mind that Haskett's very inoffensiveness shed a new light on the nature of those illusions. A man would rather think that his wife has been brutalized by her first husband than that the process has been reversed.

• IV •

'MR. WAYTHORN, I don't like that French governess of Lily's.'

Haskett, subdued and apologetic, stood before Waythorn in the library, revolving his shabby hat in his hand.

Waythorn, surprised in his armchair over the evening paper, stared back perplexedly at his visitor.

'You'll excuse my asking to see you,' Haskett continued. 'But this is my last visit, and I thought if I could have a word with you it would be a better way than writing to Mrs. Waythorn's lawyer.'

Waythorn rose uneasily. He did not like the French governess either; but that was irrelevant.

'I am not so sure of that,' he returned stiffly; 'but since you wish it I will give your message to – my wife.' He always hesitated over the possessive pronoun in addressing Haskett.

The latter sighed. 'I don't know as that will help much. She didn't like it when I spoke to her.'

Waythorn turned red. 'When did you see her?' he asked.

'Not since the first day I came to see Lily – right after she was taken sick. I remarked to her then that I didn't like the governess.'

Waythorn made no answer. He remembered distinctly that, after that first visit, he had asked his wife if she had seen Haskett. She had lied to him then, but she had respected his wishes since; and the incident cast a curious light on her character. He was sure she would not have seen Haskett that first day if she had divined that Waythorn would object, and the fact that she did not divine it was almost as disagreeable to the latter as the discovery that she had lied to him.

'I don't like the woman,' Haskett was repeating with mild persistency. 'She ain't straight, Mr. Waythorn – she'll teach the child to be underhand. I've noticed a change in Lily – she's too anxious to please – and she don't always tell the truth. She used to be the straightest child, Mr. Waythorn – ' He broke off, his voice a little thick. 'Not but what I want her to have a stylish education,' he ended.

Waythorn was touched. 'I'm sorry, Mr. Haskett; but frankly, I don't quite see what I can do.'

Haskett hesitated. Then he laid his hat on the table, and advanced to the hearthrug, on which Waythorn was standing. There was nothing aggressive in his manner, but he had the solemnity of a timid man resolved on a decisive measure.

'There's just one thing you can do, Mr. Waythorn,' he said. 'You can remind Mrs. Waythorn that, by the decree of the courts, I am entitled to have a voice in Lily's bringing-up.' He paused, and went on more deprecatingly: 'I'm not the kind to talk about enforcing my rights, Mr. Waythorn. I don't know as I think a man is entitled to rights he hasn't known how to hold on to; but this business of the child is different. I've never let go there – and I never mean to.'

The scene left Waythorn deeply shaken. Shamefacedly, in indirect ways, he had been finding out about Haskett; and all that he had learned was favorable. The little man, in order to be near his daughter, had sold

out his share in a profitable business in Utica, and accepted a modest
clerkship in a New York manufacturing house. He boarded in a shabby
street and had few acquaintances. His passion for Lily filled his life.
Waythorn felt that this exploration of Haskett was like groping about
with a dark lantern in his wife's past; but he saw now that there were
recesses his lantern had not explored. He had never inquired into the
exact circumstances of his wife's first matrimonial rupture. On the
surface all had been fair. It was she who had obtained the divorce, and
the court had given her the child. But Waythorn knew how many
ambiguities such a verdict might cover. The mere fact that Haskett
retained a right over his daughter implied an unsuspected compromise.
Waythorn was an idealist. He always refused to recognize unpleasant
contingencies till he found himself confronted with them, and then he
saw them followed by a spectral train of consequences. His next days
were thus haunted, and he determined to try to lay the ghosts by
conjuring them up in his wife's presence.

When he repeated Haskett's request a flame of anger passed over
her face; but she subdued it instantly and spoke with a slight quiver of
outraged motherhood.

'It is very ungentlemanly of him,' she said.

The word grated on Waythorn. 'That is neither here nor there. It's
a bare question of rights.'

She murmured: 'It's not as if he could ever be a help to Lily – '

Waythorn flushed. This was even less to his taste. 'The question is,'
he repeated, 'what authority has he over her?'

She looked downward, twisting herself a little in her seat. 'I am
willing to see him – I thought you objected,' she faltered.

In a flash he understood that she knew the extent of Haskett's claims.
Perhaps it was not the first time she had resisted them.

'My objecting has nothing to do with it,' he said coldly; 'if Haskett
has a right to be consulted you must consult him.'

She burst into tears, and he saw that she expected him to regard
her as a victim.

Haskett did not abuse his rights. Waythorn had felt miserably sure
that he would not. But the governess was dismissed, and from time to
time the little man demanded an interview with Alice. After the first
outburst she accepted the situation with her usual adaptability. Haskett
had once reminded Waythorn of the piano tuner, and Mrs. Waythorn,
after a month or two, appeared to class him with that domestic familiar.
Waythorn could not but respect the father's tenacity. At first he had
tried to cultivate the suspicion that Haskett might be 'up to' something,
that he had an object in securing a foothold in the house. But in his heart
Waythorn was sure of Haskett's single-mindedness; he even guessed in
the latter a mild contempt for such advantages as his relation with the

Waythorns might offer. Haskett's sincerity of purpose made him in vulnerable, and his successor had to accept him as a lien on the property.

Mr. Sellers was sent to Europe to recover from his gout, and Varick's affairs hung on Waythorn's hands. The negotiations were prolonged and complicated; they necessitated frequent conferences between the two men, and the interests of the firm forbade Waythorn's suggesting that his client should transfer his business to another officer.

Varick appeared well in the transaction. In moments of relaxation his coarse streak appeared, and Waythorn dreaded his geniality; but in the office he was concise and clear-headed, with a flattering deference to Waythorn's judgment. Their business relations being so affably established, it would have been absurd for the two men to ignore each other in society. The first time they met in a drawing-room, Varick took up their intercourse in the same easy key, and his hostess' grateful glance obliged Waythorn to respond to it. After that they ran across each other frequently, and one evening at a ball Waythorn, wandering through the remoter rooms, came upon Varick seated beside his wife. She colored a little, and faltered in what she was saying; but Varick nodded to Waythorn without rising, and the latter strolled on.

In the carriage, on the way home, he broke out nervously: 'I didn't know you spoke to Varick.'

Her voice trembled a little. 'It's the first time – he happened to be standing near me; I didn't know what to do. It's so awkward, meeting everywhere – and he said you had been very kind about some business.'

'That's different,' said Waythorn.

She paused a moment. 'I'll do just as you wish,' she returned pliantly. 'I thought it would be less awkward to speak to him when we meet.'

Her pliancy was beginning to sicken him. Had she really no will of her own – no theory about her relation to these men? She had accepted Haskett – did she mean to accept Varick? It was 'less awkward,' as she had said, and her instinct was to evade difficulties or to circumvent them. With sudden vividness Waythorn saw how the instinct had developed. She was 'as easy as an old shoe' – a shoe that too many feet had worn. Her elasticity was the result of tension in too many different directions. Alice Haskett – Alice Varick – Alice Waythorn – she had been each in turn, and had left hanging to each name a little of her privacy, a little of her personality, a little of the inmost self where the unknown god abides.

'Yes – it's better to speak to Varick,' said Waythorn wearily.

• V •

THE winter wore on, and society took advantage of the Waythorn's acceptance of Varick. Harassed hostesses were grateful to them for bridging over a social difficulty, and Mrs. Waythorn was held up as a miracle of good taste. Some experimental spirits could not resist the diversion of throwing Varick and his former wife together, and there were those who thought he found a zest in the propinquity. But Mrs. Waythorn's conduct remained irreproachable. She neither avoided Varick nor sought him out. Even Waythorn could not but admit that she had discovered the solution of the newest social problem.

He had married her without giving much though to that problem. He had fancied that a woman can shed her past like a man. But now he saw that Alice was bound to hers both by the circumstances which forced her into continued relation with it, and by the traces it had left on her nature. With grim irony Waythorn compared himself to a member of a syndicate. He held so many shares in his wife's personality and his predecessors were his partners in the business. If there had been any element of passion in the transaction he would have felt less deteriorated by it. The fact that Alice took her change of husbands like a change of weather reduced the situation to mediocrity. He could have forgiven her for blunders, for excesses; for resisting Haskett, for yielding to Varick; for anything but her acquiescence and her tact. She reminded him of a juggler tossing knives; but the knives were blunt and she knew they would never cut her.

And then, gradually, habit formed a protecting surface for his sensibilities. If he paid for each day's comfort with the small change of his illusions, he grew daily to value the comfort more and set less store upon the coin. He had drifted into a dulling propinquity with Haskett and Varick and he took refuge in the cheap revenge of satirizing the situation. He even began to reckon up the advantages which accrued from it, to ask himself if it were not better to own a third of a wife who knew how to make a man happy than a whole one who had lacked opportunity to acquire the art. For it *was* an art, and made up, like all others, of concessions, eliminations, and embellishments; of lights judiciously thrown and shadows skillfully softened. His wife knew exactly how to manage the lights, and he knew exactly to what training she owed her skill. He even tried to trace the source of his obligations, to discriminate between the influences which had combined to produce his domestic happiness: he perceived that Haskett's commonness had made Alice worship good breeding, while Varick's liberal construction of the marriage bond had taught her to value the conjugal virtues; so that he was directly indebted to his predecessors for the devotion which made his life easy if not inspiring.

From this phase he passed into that of complete acceptance. He ceased to satirize himself because time dulled the irony of the situation and the joke lost its humor with its sting. Even the sight of Haskett's hat on the hall table had ceased to touch the springs of epigram. The hat was often seen there now, for it had been decided that it was better for Lily's father to visit her than for the little girl to go to his boardinghouse. Waythorn, having acquiesced in this arrangement, had been surprised to find how little difference it made. Haskett was never obtrusive, and the few visitors who met him on the stairs were unaware of his identity. Waythorn did not know how often he saw Alice, but with himself Haskett was seldom in contact.

One afternoon, however, he learned on entering that Lily's father was waiting to see him. In the library he found Haskett occupying a chair in his usual provisional way. Waythorn always felt grateful to him for not leaning back.

'I hope you'll excuse me, Mr. Waythorn,' he said rising. 'I wanted to see Mrs. Waythorn about Lily, and your man asked me to wait here till she came in.'

'Of course,' said Waythorn, remembering that a sudden leak had that morning given over the drawing room to the plumbers.

He opened his cigar case and held it out to his visitor, and Haskett's acceptance seemed to mark a fresh stage in their intercourse. The spring evening was chilly, and Waythorn invited his guest to draw up his chair to the fire. He meant to find an excuse to leave Haskett in a moment; but he was tired and cold, and after all the little man no longer jarred on him.

The two were enclosed in the intimacy of their blended cigar smoke when the door opened and Varick walked into the room. Waythorn rose abruptly. It was the first time that Varick had come to the house, and the surprise of seeing him, combined with the singular inopportuneness of his arrival, gave a new edge to Waythorn's blunted sensibilities. He stared at his visitor without speaking.

Varick seemed too preoccupied to notice his host's embarrassment.

'My dear fellow,' he exclaimed in his most expansive tone, 'I must apologize for tumbling in on you in this way, but I was too late to catch you downtown, and so I thought – '

He stopped short, catching sight of Haskett, and his sanguine color deepened to a flush which spread vividly under his scant blond hair. But in a moment he recovered himself and nodded slightly. Haskett returned the bow in silence, and Waythorn was still groping for speech when the footman came in carrying a tea table.

The intrusion offered a welcome vent to Waythorn's nerves. 'What the deuce are you bringing this here for?' he said sharply.

'I beg your pardon, sir, but the plumbers are still in the drawing room, and Mrs. Waythorn said she would have tea in the library.' The footman's perfectly respectful tone implied a reflection on Waythorn's reasonableness.

'Oh, very well,' said the latter resignedly, and the footman proceeded to open the folding tea table and set out its complicated appointments. While this interminable process continued the three men stood motionless, watching it with a fascinated stare, till Waythorn, to break the silence, said to Varick, 'Won't you have a cigar?'

He held out the case he had just tendered to Haskett, and Varick helped himself with a smile. Waythorn looked about for a match, and finding none, proffered a light from his own cigar. Haskett, in the background, held his ground mildly, examining his cigar tip now and then, and stepping forward at the right moment to knock its ash into the fire.

The footman at last withdrew, and Varick immediately began: 'If I could just say half a word to you about this business – '

'Certainly,' stammered Waythorn; 'in the dining room – '

But as he placed his hand on the door it opened from without, and his wife appeared on the threshold.

She came in fresh and smiling, in her street dress and hat, shedding a fragrance from the boa which she loosened in advancing.

'Shall we have tea in here, dear?' she began; and then she caught sight of Varick. Her smiled deepened, veiling a slight tremor of surprise. 'Why, how do you do?' she said with a distinct note of pleasure.

As she shook hands with Varick she saw Haskett standing behind him. Her smile faded for a moment, but she recalled it quickly, with a scarcely perceptible side glance at Waythorn.

'How do you do, Mr. Haskett?' she said, and shook hands with him a shade less cordially.

The three men stood awkwardly before her, till Varick, always the most self-possessed, dashed into an explanatory phrase.

'We – I had to see Waythorn a moment on business,' he stammered, brick-red from chin to nape.

Haskett stepped forward with his air of mild obstinacy. 'I am sorry to intrude; but you appointed five o'clock – ' he directed his resigned glance to the timepiece on the mantel.

She swept aside their embarrassment with a charming gesture of hospitality.

'I'm so sorry – I'm always late; but the afternoon was so lovely.' She stood drawing off her gloves, propitiatory and graceful, diffusing about her a sense of ease and familiarity in which the situation lost its grotesqueness. 'But before talking business,' she added brightly, 'I'm sure everyone wants a cup of tea.'

She dropped into her low chair by the tea table, and the two visitors, as if drawn by her smile, advanced to receive the cups she held out.

She glanced about for Waythorn, and he took the third cup with a laugh.

The Mission of Jane

———❦———

LETHBURY, SURVEYING his wife across the dinner table, found his transient glance arrested by an indefinable change in her appearance.

'How smart you look! Is that a new gown?' he asked.

Her answering look seemed to deprecate his charging her with the extravagance of wasting a new gown on him, and he now perceived that the change lay deeper than any accident of dress. At the same time, he noticed that she betrayed her consciousness of it by a delicate, almost frightened blush. It was one of the compensations of Mrs. Lethbury's protracted childishness that she still blushed as prettily as at eighteen. Her body had been privileged not to outstrip her mind, and the two, as it seemed to Lethbury, were destined to travel together through an eternity of girlishness.

'I don't know what you mean,' she said.

Since she never did, he always wondered at her bringing this out as a fresh grievance against him; but his wonder was unresentful, and he said good-humoredly: 'You sparkle so that I thought you had on your diamonds.'

She sighed and blushed again.

'It must be,' he continued, 'that you've been to a dressmaker's opening. You're absolutely brimming with illicit enjoyment.'

She stared again, this time at the adjective. His adjectives always embarrassed her; their unintelligibleness savored of impropriety.

'In short,' he summed up, 'you've been doing something that you're thoroughly ashamed of.'

To his surprise she retorted: 'I don't see why I should be ashamed of it!'

Lethbury leaned back with a smile of enjoyment. When there was nothing better going he always liked to listen to her explanations.

'Well – ?' he said.

She was becoming breathless and ejaculatory. 'Of course you'll laugh – you laugh at everything!'

'That rather blunts the point of my derision, doesn't it?' he interjected; but she pushed on without noticing.

'It's so easy to laugh at things.'

'Ah,' murmured Lethbury with relish, 'that's Aunt Sophronia's, isn't it?'

Most of his wife's opinions were heirlooms, and he took a quaint pleasure in tracing their descent. She was proud of their age, and saw no reason for discarding them while they were still serviceable. Some, of course, were so fine that she kept them for state occasions, like her great-grandmother's Crown Derby; but from the lady know as Aunt Sophronia she had inherited a stout set of everyday prejudices that were practically as good as new; whereas her husband's, as she noticed, were always having to be replaced. In the early days she had fancied there might be a certain satisfaction in taxing him with the fact; but she had long since been silenced by the reply: 'My dear, I'm not a rich man, but I never use an opinion twice if I can help it.'

She was reduced, therefore, to dwelling on his moral deficiencies; and one of the most obvious of these was his refusal to take things seriously. On this occasion, however, some ulterior purpose kept her from taking up his taunt.

'I'm not in the least ashamed!' she repeated, with the air of shaking a banner to the wind; but the domestic atmosphere being calm, the banner drooped unheroically.

'That,' said Lethbury judicially, 'encourages me to infer that you ought to be, and that, consequently, you've been giving yourself the unusual pleasure of doing something I shouldn't approve of.'

She met this with an almost solemn directness.

'No,' she said. 'You won't approve of it. I've allowed for that.'

'Ah,' he exclaimed, setting down his liqueur glass. 'You've worked out the whole problem, eh?'

'I believe so.'

'That's uncommonly interesting. And what is it?'

She looked at him quietly. 'A baby.'

If it was seldom given her to surprise him, she had attained the distinction for once.

'A baby?'

'Yes.'

'A – human baby?'

'Of course!' she cried, with the virtuous resentment of the woman who has never allowed dogs in the house.

Lethbury's puzzled stare broke into a fresh smile. 'A baby I shan't approve of? Well, in the abstract I don't think much of them, I admit. Is this an abstract baby?'

Again she frowned at the adjective, but she had reached a pitch of exaltation at which such obstacles could not deter her.

'It's the loveliest baby – ' she murmured.

'Ah, then it's concrete. It exists. In this harsh world it draws its breath in pain – '

'It's the healthiest child I ever saw!' she indignantly corrected.

'You've seen it, then?'

Again the accusing blush suffused her. 'Yes – I've seen it.'

'And to whom does this paragon belong?'

And here indeed she confounded him. 'To me – I hope,' she declared.

He pushed his chair back with an articulate murmur. 'To you – ?'

'To *us*,' she corrected.

'Good Lord!' he said. If there had been the least hint of hallucination in her transparent gaze – but no; it was as clear, as shallow, as easily fathomable as when he had first suffered the sharp surprise of striking bottom in it.

It occurred to him that perhaps she was trying to be funny: he knew that there is nothing more cryptic than the humor of the unhumorous.

'Is it a joke?' he faltered.

'Oh, I hope not. I want it so much to be a reality – '

He paused to smile at the limitations of a world in which jokes were not realities, and continued gently: 'But since it is one already – '

'To us, I mean: to you and me. I want – ' her voice wavered, and her eyes with it. 'I have always wanted so dreadfully . . . it has been such a disappointment . . . not to . . .'

'I see,' said Lethbury slowly.

But he had not seen before. It seemed curious now that he had never thought of her taking it in that way, had never surmised any hidden depths beneath her outspread obviousness. He felt as though he had touched a secret spring in her mind.

There was a moment's silence, moist and tremulous on her part, awkward and slightly irritated on his.

'You've been lonely, I suppose?' he began. It was odd, having suddenly to reckon with the stranger who gazed at him out of her trivial eyes.

'At times,' she said.

'I'm sorry.'

'It was not your fault. A man has so many occupations; and women who are clever – or very handsome – I suppose that's an occupation too. Sometimes I've felt that when dinner was ordered I had nothing to do till the next day.'

'Oh,' he groaned.

'It wasn't your fault,' she insisted. 'I never told you – but when I chose that rosebud paper for the front room upstairs, I always thought – '

'Well – ?'

'It would be such a pretty paper – for a baby – to wake up in. That was years ago, of course; but it was rather an expensive paper . . . and it hasn't faded in the least . . .' she broke off incoherently.

'It hasn't faded?'

'No – and so I thought . . . as we don't use the room for anything . . . now that Aunt Sophronia is dead . . . I thought I might . . . you might . . . oh, Julian, if you could only have seen it just waking up in its crib!'

'Seen what – where? You haven't got a baby upstairs?'

'Oh, no – not *yet*,' she said, with her rare laugh – the girlish bubbling of merriment that had seemed one of her chief graces in the early days. It occurred to him that he had not given her enough things to laugh about lately. But then she needed such very elementary things: she was as difficult to amuse as a savage. He concluded that he was not sufficiently simple.

'Alice,' he said almost solemnly, 'what *do* you mean?'

She hesitated a moment: he saw her gather her courage for a supreme effort. Then she said slowly, gravely, as though she were pronouncing a sacramental phrase:

'I'm so lonely without a little child – and I thought perhaps you'd let me adopt one. . . . It's at the hospital . . . its mother is dead . . . and I could . . . pet it, and dress it, and do things for it . . . and it's such a good baby . . . you can ask any of the nurses . . . it would never, *never* bother you by crying. . . .'

• II •

LETHBURY accompanied his wife to the hospital in a mood of chastened wonder. It did not occur to him to oppose her wish. He knew, of course, that he would have to bear the brunt of the situation: the jokes at the club, the inquiries, the explanations. He saw himself in the comic role of the adopted father and welcomed it as an expiation. For in his rapid reconstruction of the past he found himself cutting a shabbier figure than he cared to admit. He had always been intolerant of stupid people, and it was his punishment to be convicted of stupidity. As his mind traversed the years between his marriage and this unexpected assumption of paternity, he saw, in the light of an overheated imagination, many signs of unwonted crassness. It was not that he had ceased to think his wife stupid: she *was* stupid, limited, inflexible; but there was a pathos in the struggles of her swaddled mind, in its blind reachings toward the primal emotions. He had always thought she would have been happier with a child; but he had thought it mechanically, because it had so often been thought before, because it was in the nature of things to think it of every woman, because his wife was so eminently one of a species that she fitted into all the generalizations of the sex.

But he had regarded this generalization as merely typical of the triumph of tradition over experience. Maternity was no doubt the supreme function of primitive woman, the one end to which her whole organism tended; but the law of increasing complexity had operated in both sexes, and he had not seriously supposed that, outside the world of Christmas fiction and anecdotic art, such truisms had any special hold on the feminine imagination. Now he saw that the arts in question were kept alive by the vitality of the sentiments they appealed to.

Lethbury was in fact going through a rapid process of readjustment. His marriage had been a failure, but he had preserved toward his wife the exact fidelity of act that is sometimes supposed to excuse any divagation of feeling; so that, for years, the tie between them had consisted mainly in his abstaining from making love to other women. The abstention had not always been easy, for the world is surprisingly well stocked with the kind of woman one ought to have married but did not; and Lethbury had not escaped the solicitation of such alternatives. His immunity had been purchased at the cost of taking refuge in the somewhat rarefied atmosphere of his perceptions; and his world being thus limited, he had given unusual care to its details, compensating himself for the narrowness of his horizon by the minute finish of his foreground. It was a world of fine shadings and the nicest proportions, where impulse seldom set a blundering foot, and the feast of reason was undisturbed by an intemperate flow of soul. To such a banquet his wife naturally remained uninvited. The diet would have disagreed with her, and she would probably have projected to the other guests. But Lethbury, miscalculating her needs, had hitherto supposed that he had made ample provision for them, and was consequently at liberty to enjoy his own fare without any reproach of mendicancy at his gates. Now he beheld her pressing a starved face against the windows of his life, and in his imaginative reaction he invested her with a pathos borrowed from the sense of his own shortcomings.

In the hospital the imaginative process continued with increasing force. He looked at his wife with new eyes. Formerly she had been to him a mere bundle of negations, a labyrinth of dead walls and bolted doors. There was nothing behind the walls, and the doors led no whither: he had sounded and listened often enough to be sure of that. Now he felt like a traveler who, exploring some ancient ruin, comes on an inner cell, intact amid the general dilapidation, and painted with images which reveal the forgotten uses of the building.

His wife stood by a white crib in one of the wards. In the crib lay a child, a year old, the nurse affirmed, but to Lethbury's eye a mere dateless fragment of humanity projected against a background of conjecture. Over this anonymous particle of life Mrs. Lethbury leaned, such ecstasy reflected in her face as strikes up, in Correggio's 'Nightpiece,' from the child's body to the mother's countenance. It was a light that irradiated and dazzled her. She looked up at an inquiry of Lethbury's, but as their glances met he perceived that she no longer saw him, that he had become as invisible to her as she had long been to him. He had to transfer his question to the nurse.

'What is the child's name?' he asked.

'We call her Jane,' said the nurse.

• III •

LETHBURY, at first, had resisted the idea of a legal adoption; but when he found that his wife could not be brought to regard the child as hers till it had been made so by process of law, he promptly withdrew his objection. On one point only he remained inflexible; and that was the changing of the waif's name. Mrs. Lethbury, almost at once, had expressed a wish to rechristen it: she fluctuated between Muriel and Gladys, deferring the moment of decision like a lady wavering between two bonnets. But Lethbury was unyielding. In the general surrender of his prejudices this one alone held out.

'But Jane is so dreadful,' Mrs. Lethbury protested.

'Well, we don't know that *she* won't be dreadful. She may grow up a Jane.'

His wife exclaimed reproachfully. 'The nurse says she's the loveliest – '

'Don't they always say that?' asked Lethbury patiently. He was prepared to be inexhaustibly patient now that he had reached a firm foothold of opposition.

'It's cruel to call her Jane,' Mrs. Lethbury pleaded.

'It's ridiculous to call her Muriel!'

'The nurse is *sure* she must be a lady's child.'

Lethbury winced: he had tried, all along, to keep his mind off the question of antecedents.

'Well, let her prove it,' he said, with a rising sense of exasperation. He wondered how he could ever have allowed himself to be drawn into such a ridiculous business; for the first time he felt the full irony of it. He had visions of coming home in the afternoon to a house smelling of linseed and paregoric, and of being greeted by a chronic howl as he went upstairs to dress for dinner. He had never been a club man, but he saw himself becoming one now.

The worst of his anticipations were unfulfilled. The baby was surprisingly well and surprisingly quiet. Such infantile remedies as she absorbed were not potent enough to be perceived beyond the nursery; and when Lethbury could be induced to enter that sanctuary, there was nothing to jar his nerves in the mild pink presence of his adopted daughter. Jars there were, indeed: they were probably inevitable in the

disturbed routine of the household, but they occurred between Mrs.
Lethbury and the nurses, and Jane contributed to them only a placid
stare which might have served as a rebuke to the combatants.

In the reaction from his first impulse of atonement, Lethbury noted
with sharpened perceptions the effect of the change on his wife's
character. He saw already the error of supposing that it could work
any transformation in her. It simply magnified her existing qualities.
She was like a dried sponge put in water: she expanded, but she did
not change her shape. From the standpoint of scientific observation it
was curious to see how her stored instincts responded to the pseudo-
maternal call. She overflowed with the petty maxims of the occasion.
One felt in her the epitome, the consummation, of centuries of animal
maternity, so that this little woman, who screamed at a mouse and was
nervous about burglars, came to typify the cave mother rending her
prey for her young.

It was less easy to regard philosophically the practical effects of her
borrowed motherhood. Lethbury found with surprise that she was
becoming assertive and definite. She no longer represented the negative
side of his life; she showed, indeed, a tendency to inconvenient affir-
mations. She had gradually expanded her assumption of motherhood till
it included his own share in the relation, and he suddenly found himself
regarded as the father of Jane. This was a contingency he had not
foreseen, and it took all his philosophy to accept it; but there were
moments of compensation. For Mrs. Lethbury was undoubtedly happy
for the first time in years; and the thought that he had tardily contributed
to this end reconciled him to the irony of the means.

At first he was inclined to reproach himself for still viewing the
situation from the outside, for remaining a spectator instead of a partici-
pant. He had been allured, for a moment, by the vision of severed
hands meeting over a cradle, as the whole body of domestic fiction
bears witness to their doing; and the fact that no such conjunction took
place he could explain only on the ground that it was a borrowed
cradle. He did not dislike the little girl. She still remained to him a
hypothetical presence, a query rather than a fact; but her nearness was
not unpleasant, and there were moments when her tentative utterances,
her groping steps, seemed to loosen the dry accretions enveloping his
inner self. But even at such moments – moments which he invited and
caressed – she did not bring him nearer to his wife. He now perceived
that he had made a certain place in his life for Mrs. Lethbury, and that
she no longer fitted into it. It was too late to enlarge the space, and so
she overflowed and encroached. Lethbury struggled against the sense
of submergence. He let down barrier after barrier, yielding privacy
after privacy; but his wife's personality continued to dilate. She was no
longer herself alone: she was herself and Jane. Gradually, a monstrous
fusion of identity, she became herself, himself and Jane; and instead of

trying to adapt her to a spare crevice of his character, he found himself carelessly squeezed into the smallest compartment of the domestic economy.

• IV •

HE continued to tell himself that he was satisfied if his wife was happy; and it was not till the child's tenth year that he felt a doubt of her happiness.

Jane had been a preternaturally good child. During the eight years of her adoption she had caused her foster parents no anxiety beyond those connected with the usual succession of youthful diseases. But her unknown progenitors had given her a robust constitution, and she passed unperturbed through measles, chicken pox and whooping cough. If there was any suffering it was endured vicariously by Mrs. Lethbury, whose temperature rose and fell with the patient's, and who could not hear Jane sneeze without visions of a marble angel weeping over a broken column. But though Jane's prompt recoveries continued to belie such premonitions, though her existence continued to move forward on an even keel of good health and good conduct, Mrs. Lethbury's satisfaction showed no corresponding advance. Lethbury, at first, was disposed to add her disappointment to the long list of feminine inconsistencies with which the sententious observer of life builds up his favorable induction; but circumstances presently led him to take a kindlier view of the case.

Hitherto his wife had regarded him as a negligible factor in Jane's evolution. Beyond providing for his adopted daughter, and effacing himself before her, he was not expected to contribute to her well-being. But as time passed he appeared to his wife in a new light. It was he who was to educate Jane. In matters of the intellect, Mrs. Lethbury was the first to declare her deficiencies – to proclaim them, even, with a certain virtuous superiority. She said she did not pretend to be clever, and there was no denying the truth of the assertion. Now, however, she seemed less ready, not to own her limitations, but to glory in them. Confronted with the problem of Jane's instruction she stood in awe of the child.

'I have always been stupid, you know,' she said to Lethbury with a new humility, 'and I'm afraid I shan't know what is best for Jane. I'm sure she has a wonderfully good mind, and I should reproach myself if I didn't give her every opportunity.' She looked at him helplessly. 'You must tell me what ought to be done.'

Lethbury was not unwilling to oblige her. Somewhere in his mental lumber room there rusted a theory of education such as usually lingers among the impedimenta of the childless. He brought this out, refurbished it, and applied it to Jane. At first he thought his wife had not overrated the quality of the child's mind. Jane seemed extraordinarily intelligent. Her precocious definiteness of mind was encouraging to her inexperienced preceptor. She had no difficulty in fixing her attention, and he felt that every fact he imparted was being etched in metal. He helped his wife to engage the best teachers, and for a while continued to take an ex-official interest in his adopted daughter's studies. But gradually his interest waned. Jane's ideas did not increase with her acquisitions. Her young mind remained a mere receptacle of facts: a kind of cold storage from which anything which had been put there could be taken out at a moment's notice, intact but congealed. She developed, moreover, an inordinate pride in the capacity of her mental storehouse, and a tendency to pelt her public with its contents. She was overheard to jeer at her nurse for not knowing when the Saxon Heptarchy had fallen, and she alternately dazzled and depressed Mrs. Lethbury by the wealth of her chronological allusions. She showed no interest in the significance of of the facts she amassed: she simply collected dates as another child might have collected stamps or marbles. To her foster mother she seemed a prodigy of wisdom; but Lethbury saw, with a secret movement of sympathy, how the aptitudes in which Mrs. Lethbury gloried were slowly estranging her from her child.

'She is getting too clever for me,' his wife said to him, after one of Jane's historical flights, 'but I am so glad that she will be a companion to you.'

Lethbury groaned in spirit. He did not look forward to Jane's companionship. She was still a good little girl: but there was something automatic and formal in her goodness, as though it were a kind of moral calisthenics which she went through for the sake of showing her agility. An early consciousness of virtue had moreover constituted her the natural guardian and adviser of her elders. Before she was fifteen she had set about reforming the household. She took Mrs Lethbury in hand first; then she extended her efforts to the servants, with consequences more disastrous to the domestic harmony; and lastly she applied herself to Lethbury. She proved to him by statistics that he smoked too much, and that it was injurious to the optic nerve to read in bed. She took him to task for not going to church more regularly, and pointed out to him the evils of desultory reading. She suggested that a regular course of study encourages mental concentration, and hinted that inconsecutiveness of thought is a sign of approaching age.

To her adopted mother her suggestions were equally pertinent. She instructed Mrs. Lethbury in an improved way of making beef stock, and called her attention to the unhygienic qualities of carpets. She poured out distracting facts about bacilli and vegetable mold, and demonstrated that curtains and picture frames are a hotbed of animal organisms. She learned by heart the nutritive ingredients of the principal articles of diet, and revolutionized the cuisine by an attempt to establish a scientific average between starch and phosphates. Four cooks left during this experiment, and Lethbury fell into the habit of dining at the club.

Once or twice, at the outset, he had tried to check Jane's ardor; but his efforts resulted only in hurting his wife's feelings. Jane remained impervious, and Mrs. Lethbury resented any attempt to protect her from her daughter. Lethbury saw that she was consoled for the sense of her own inferiority by the thought of what Jane's intellectual companionship must be to him; and he tried to keep up the illusion by enduring with what grace he might the blighting edification of Jane's discourse.

• V •

As Jane grew up he sometimes avenged himself by wondering if his wife was still sorry that they had not called her Muriel. Jane was not ugly; she developed, indeed, a kind of categorical prettiness which might have been a projection of her mind. She had a creditable collection of features, but one had to take an inventory of them to find out that she was goodlooking. The fusing grace had been omitted.

Mrs. Lethbury took a pride in her daughter's first steps in the world. She expected Jane to take by her complexion those whom she did not capture by her learning. But Jane's rosy freshness did not work any perceptible ravages. Whether the young men guessed the axioms on her lips and detected the encyclopedia in her eye, or whether they simply found no intrinsic interest in these features, certain it is, that, in spite of her mother's heroic efforts, and of incessant calls on Lethbury's purse, Jane, at the end of her first season, had dropped hopelessly out of the running. A few duller girls found her interesting, and one or two young men came to the house with the object of meeting other young women; but she was rapidly becoming one of the social supernumeraries who are asked out only because they are on people's lists.

The blow was bitter to Mrs. Lethbury; but she consoled herself with the idea that Jane had failed because she was too clever. Jane probably shared this conviction; at all events she betrayed no consciousness of failure. She had developed a pronounced taste for society, and went out, unweariedly and obstinately, winter after winter, while Mrs. Lethbury toiled in her wake, showering attentions on oblivious hostesses. To Lethbury there was something at once tragic and exasperating in the sight of their two figures, the one conciliatory, the other dogged, both pursuing with unabated zeal the elusive prize of popularity. He even began to feel a personal stake in the pursuit, not as it concerned

Jane but as it affected his wife. He saw that the latter was the victim of Jane's disappointment: that Jane was not above the crude satisfaction of 'taking it out' of her mother. Experience checked the impulse to come to his wife's defence; and when his resentment was at its height, Jane disarmed him by giving up the struggle.

Nothing was said to mark her capitulation; but Lethbury noticed that the visiting ceased and that the dressmaker's bills diminished. At the same time Mrs. Lethbury made it known that Jane had taken up charities, and before long Jane's conversation confirmed this announcement. At first Lethbury congratulated himself on the change; but Jane's domesticity soon began to weigh on him. During the day she was sometimes absent on errands of mercy; but in the evening she was always there. At first she and Mrs. Lethbury sat in the drawing room together, and Lethbury smoked in the library; but presently Jane formed the habit of joining him there, and he began to suspect that he was included among the objects of her philanthropy.

Mrs. Lethbury confirmed the suspicion. 'Jane has grown very serious-minded lately,' she said. 'She imagines that she used to neglect you and she is trying to make up for it. Don't discourage her,' she added innocently.

Such a plea delivered Lethbury helpless to his daughter's ministrations; and he found himself measuring the hours he spent with her by the amount of relief they must be affording her mother. There were even moments when he read a furtive gratitude in Mrs. Lethbury's eye.

But Lethbury was no hero, and he had nearly reached the limit of vicarious endurance when something wonderful happened. They never quite knew afterward how it had come about, or who first percevied it; but Mrs. Lethbury one day gave tremulous voice to their discovery.

'Of course,' she said, 'he comes here because of Elise.' The young lady in question, a friend of Jane's, was possessed of attractions which had already been found to explain the presence of masculine visitors.

Lethbury risked a denial. 'I don't think he does,' he declared.

'But Elise is thought very pretty,' Mrs. Lethbury insisted.

'I can't help that,' said Lethbury doggedly.

He saw a faint light in his wife's eyes; but she remarked carelessly: 'Mr. Budd would be a very good match for Elise.'

Lethbury could hardly repress a chuckle: he was so exquisitely aware that she was trying to propitiate the gods.

For a few weeks neither said a word; then Mrs. Lethbury once more reverted to the subject.

'It is a month since Elise went abroad,' she said.

'Is it?'

'And Mr Budd seems to come here just as often – '

'Ah,' said Lethbury with heroic indifference, and his wife hastily changed the subject.

Mr. Winstanley Budd was a young man who suffered from an excess of manner. Politeness gushed from him in the driest season. He was always performing feats of drawing-room chivalry, and the approach of the most unobtrusive female threw him into attitudes which endangered the furniture. His features, being of the cherubic order, did not lend themselves to this role; but there were moments when he appeared to dominate them, to force them into compliance with an aquiline ideal. The range of Mr. Budd's social benevolence made its object hard to distinguish. He spread his cloak so indiscriminately that one could not always interpret the gesture, and Jane's impassive manner had the effect of increasing his demonstrations; she threw him into paroxysms of politeness.

At first he filled the house with his amenities; but gradually it became apparent that his most dazzling effects were directed exclusively to Jane. Lethbury and his wife held their breath and looked away from each other. They pretended not to notice the frequence of Mr. Budd's visits, they struggled against an imprudent inclination to leave the young people too much alone. Their conclusions were the result of indirect observation, for neither of them dared to be caught watching Mr. Budd: they behaved like naturalists on the trail of a rare butterfly.

In his efforts not to notice Mr. Budd, Lethbury centered his attention on Jane; and Jane, at this crucial moment, wrung from him a reluctant admiration. While her parents went about dissembling their emotions, she seemed to have none to conceal. She betrayed neither eagerness nor surprise; so complete was her unconcern that there were moments when Lethbury feared it was obtuseness, when he could hardly help whispering to her that now was the moment to lower the net.

Meanwhile the velocity of Mr. Budd's gyrations increased with the ardor of courtship; his politeness became incandescent, and Jane found herself the center of a pyrotechnical display culminating in the 'set piece' of an offer of marriage.

Mrs. Lethbury imparted the news to her husband one evening after their daughter had gone to bed. The announcement was made and received with an air of detachment, as though both feared to be betrayed into unseemly exultation; but Lethbury, as his wife ended, could not repress the inquiry, 'Have they decided on a day?'

Mrs. Lethbury's superior command of her features enabled her to look shocked. 'What can you be thinking of? He only offered himself at five!'

'Of course – of course – ' stammered Lethbury ' – but nowadays people marry after such short engagements – '

'Engagement!' said his wife solemnly. 'There is no engagement.'

Lethbury dropped his cigar. 'What on earth do you mean?'

'Jane is thinking it over.'

'*Thinking it over?*'

'She has asked for a month before deciding.'

Lethbury sank back with a gasp. Was it genius or was it madness? He felt incompetent to decide; and Mrs. Lethbury's next words showed that she shared his difficulty.

'Of course I don't want to hurry Jane – '

'Of course not,' he acquiesced.

'But I pointed out to her that a young man of Mr. Budd's impulsive temperament might – might easily be discouraged – '

'Yes; and what did she say?'

'She said that if she was worth winning she was worth waiting for.'

• VI •

THE period of Mr. Budd's probation could scarcely have cost him as much mental anguish as it caused his would-be parents-in-law.

Mrs. Lethbury, by various ruses, tried to shorten the ordeal, but Jane remained inexorable; and each morning Lethbury came down to breakfast with the certainty of finding a letter of withdrawl from her discouraged suitor.

When at length the decisive day came, and Mrs. Lethbury, at its close, stole into the library with an air of chastened joy, they stood for a moment without speaking; then Mrs. Lethbury paid a fitting tribute to the proprieties by faltering out: 'It will be dreadful to have to give her up – '

Lethbury could not repress a warning gesture, but even as it escaped him he realized that his wife's grief was genuine.

'Of course, of course,' he said, vainly sounding his own emotional shallows for an answering regret. And yet it was his wife who had suffered most from Jane!

He had fancied that these sufferings would be effaced by the milder atmosphere of their last weeks together; but felicity did not soften Jane. Not for a moment did she relax her dominion: she simply widened it to include the new subject. Mr. Budd found himself under orders with the others; and a new fear assailed Lethbury as he saw Jane assume pre-nuptial control of her betrothed. Lethbury had never felt any strong personal interest in Mr. Budd; but as Jane's prospective husband the young man excited his sympathy. To his surprise he found that Mrs. Lethbury shared the feeling.

'I'm afraid he may find Jane a little exacting,' she said, after an evening dedicated to a stormy discussion of the wedding arrangements. 'She really ought to make some concessions. If he *wants* to be married in a black frock coat instead of a dark grey one – ' She paused and looked doubtfully at Lethbury.

'What can I do about it?' he said.

'You might explain to him – tell him that Jane isn't always – '

Lethbury made an impatient gesture. 'What are you afraid of? His finding her out or his not finding her out?'

Mrs. Lethbury flushed. 'You put it so dreadfully!'

Her husband mused for a moment; then he said with an air of cheerful hypocrisy: 'After all, Budd is old enough to take care of himself.'

But the next day Mrs. Lethbury surprised him. Late in the afternoon she entered the library, so breathless and inarticulate that he scented a catastrophe.

'I've done it!' she cried.

'Done what?'

'Told him.' She nodded toward the door. 'He's just gone. Jane is out, and I had a chance to talk to him alone.'

Lethbury pushed a chair forward and she sank into it.

'What did you tell him? That she is *not* always – '

Mrs. Lethbury lifted a tragic eye. 'No; I told him that she always *is* – '

'Always *is* – ?'

'Yes.'

There was a pause. Lethbury made a call on his hoarded philosophy. He saw Jane suddenly reinstated in her evening seat by the library fire; but an answering chord in him thrilled at his wife's heroism.

'Well – what did he say?'

Mrs. Lethbury's agitation deepened. It was clear that the blow had fallen.

'He . . . he said . . . that we . . . had never understood Jane . . . or appreciated her . . .' The final syllables were lost in her handkerchief, and she left him marveling at the mechanism of woman.

After that, Lethbury faced the future with an undaunted eye. They had done their duty – at least his wife had done hers – and they were reaping the usual harvest of ingratitude with a zest seldom accorded to such reaping. There was a marked change in Mr. Budd's manner, and his increasing coldness sent a genial glow through Lethbury's system. It was easy to bear with Jane in the light of Mr. Budd's disapproval.

There was a good deal to be borne in the last days, and the brunt of it fell on Mrs. Lethbury. Jane marked her transition to the married state by a seasonable but incongruous display of nerves. She became sentimental, hysterical and reluctant. She quarreled with her betrothed and threatened to return the ring. Mrs. Lethbury had to intervene, and Lethbury felt the hovering sword of destiny. But the blow was suspended. Mr. Budd's chivalry was proof against all his bride's caprices and his devotion throve on her cruelty. Lethbury feared that he was too faithful, too enduring, and longed to urge him to vary his tactics. Jane presently reappeared with the ring on her finger, and consented to try on the wedding dress; but her uncertainties, her reactions, were prolonged till the final day.

When it dawned, Lethbury was still in an ecstasy of apprehension. Feeling reasonably sure of the principal actors he had centered his fears on incidental possibilities. The clergyman might have a stroke, or the church might burn down, or there might be something wrong with the license. He did all that was humanly possible to avert such contingencies, but there remained that incalculable factor known as the hand of God. Lethbury seemed to feel it groping for him.

At the altar it almost had him by the nape. Mr. Budd was late; and for five immeasurable minutes Lethbury and Jane faced a churchful of conjecture. Then the bridegroom appeared, flushed but chivalrous, and explaining to his father-in-law under cover of the ritual that he had torn his glove and had to go back for another.

'You'll be losing the ring next,' muttered Lethbury; but Mr. Budd produced this article punctually, and a moment or two later was bearing its wearer captive down the aisle.

At the wedding breakfast Lethbury caught his wife's eye fixed on him in mild disapproval, and understood that his hilarity was exceeding the bounds of fitness. He pulled himself together and tried to subdue his tone; but his jubilation bubbled over like a champagne glass perpetually refilled. The deeper his draughts the higher it rose.

It was at the brim when, in the wake of the dispersing guests, Jane came down in her traveling dress and fell on her mother's neck.

'I can't leave you!' she wailed, and Lethbury felt as suddenly sobered as a man under a shower. But if the bride was reluctant her captor was relentless. Never had Mr. Budd been more dominant, more aquiline. Lethbury's last fears were dissipated as the young man snatched Jane from her mother's bosom and bore her off to the brougham.

The brougham rolled away, the last milliner's girl forsook her post by the awning, the red carpet was folded up, and the house door closed. Lethbury stood alone in the hall with his wife. As he turned toward her, he noticed the look of tired heroism in her eyes, the deepened lines of her face. They reflected his own symptoms too accurately not to appeal to him. The nervous tension had been horrible. He went up to her, and an answering impulse made her lay a hand on his arm. He held it there a moment.

'Let us go off and have a jolly little dinner at a restaurant,' he proposed.

There had been a time when such a suggestion would have surprised her to the verge of disapproval; but now she agreed to it at once.

'Oh, that would be so nice,' she murmured with a great sigh of relief and assuagement.

Jane had fulfilled her mission after all: she had drawn them together at last.

The Reckoning

---❦---

'THE MARRIAGE LAW of the new dispensation will be: *Thou shalt not be unfaithful – to thyself.*'

A discreet murmur of approval filled the studio, and through the haze of cigarette smoke Mrs. Clement Westall, as her husband descended from his improvised platform, saw him merged 'in a congratulatory group of ladies. Westall's informal talks on 'The New Ethics' had drawn about him an eager following of the mentally unemployed – those who, as he had once phrased it, liked to have their brain food cut up for them. The talks had begun by accident. Westall's ideas were known to be 'advanced,' but hitherto their advance had not been in the direction of publicity. He had been, in his wife's opinion, almost pusillanimously careful not to let his personal views endanger his professional standing. Of late, however, he had shown a puzzling tendency to dogmatize, to throw down the gauntlet, to flaunt his private code in the face of society; and the relation of the sexes being a topic always sure of an audience, a few admiring friends had persuaded him to give his after-dinner opinions a larger circulation by summing them up in a series of talks at the Van Sideren studio.

The Herbert Van Siderens were a couple who subsisted, socially, on the fact that they had a studio. Van Sideren's pictures were chiefly valuable as accessories to the *mise en scène* which differentiated his wife's 'afternoons' from the blighting functions held in long New York drawing rooms, and permitted her to offer their friends whiskey and soda instead of tea. Mrs. Van Sideren, for her part, was skilled in making the most of the kind of atmosphere which a lay figure and an easel create; and if at times she found the illusion hard to maintain, and lost courage to the extent of almost wishing that Herbert could paint, she promptly overcame such moments of weakness by calling in some fresh talent, some extraneous re-enforcement of the 'artistic' impression. It was in quest of such aid that she had seized on Westall, coaxing him, somewhat to his wife's surprise, into a flattered participation in her fraud. It was vaguely felt, in the Van Sideren circle, that all the audacities were artistic, and that a teacher who pronounced marriage

47

immoral was somehow as distinguished as a painter who depicted purple grass and a green sky. The Van Sideren set were tired of the conventional color scheme in art and conduct.

Julia Westall had long had her own views on the immorality of marriage; she might indeed have claimed her husband as a disciple. In the early days of their union she had secretly resented his disinclination to proclaim himself a follower of the new creed; had been inclined to tax him with moral cowardice, with a failure to live up to the convictions for which their marriage was supposed to stand. That was in the first burst of propagandism, when, womanlike, she wanted to turn her disobedience into a law. Now she felt differently. She could hardly account for the change, yet being a woman who never allowed her impulses to remain unaccounted for, she tried to do so by saying that she did not care to have the articles of her faith misinterpreted by the vulgar. In this connection, she was beginning to think that almost everyone was vulgar; certainly there were few to whom she would have cared to intrust the defence of so esoteric a doctrine. And it was precisely at this point that Westall, discarding his unspoken principles, had chosen to descend from the heights of privacy, and stand hawking his convictions at the street corner!

It was Una Van Sideren who, on this occasion, unconsciously focused upon herself Mrs. Westall's wandering resentment. In the first place, the girl had no business to be there. It was 'horrid' – Mrs. Westfall found herself slipping back into the old feminine vocabulary – simply 'horrid' to think of a young girl's being allowed to listen to such talk. The fact that Una smoked cigarettes and sipped an occasional cocktail did not in the least tarnish a certain radiant innocency which made her appear the victim, rather than the accomplice, of her parents' vulgarities. Julia Westall felt in a hot helpless way that something ought to be done – that someone ought to speak to the girl's mother. And just then Una glided up.

'Oh, Mrs. Westall, how beautiful it was!' Una fixed her with large limpid eyes. 'You believe it all, I suppose?' she asked with seraphic gravity.

'All – what, my dear child?'

The girl shone on her. 'About the higher life – the freer expansion of the individual – the law of fidelity to one's self,' she glibly recited.

Mrs. Westall, to her own wonder, blushed a deep and burning blush.

'My dear Una,' she said, 'you don't in the least understand what it's all about!'

Miss Van Sideren stared, with a slowly answering blush!' 'Don't *you*, then?' she murmured.

Mrs. Westall laughed. 'Not always – or altogether! But I should like some tea, please.'

Una led her to the corner where innocent beverages were dispensed. As Julia received her cup she scrutinized the girl more carefully. It was not such a girlish face, after all – definite lines were forming under the rosy haze of youth. She reflected that Una must be six-and-twenty, and wondered why she had not married. A nice stock of ideas she would have as her dowry! If *they* were to be a part of the modern girl's trousseau – .

Mrs. Westall caught herself up with a start. It was as though someone else had been speaking – a stranger who had borrowed her own voice: she felt herself the dupe of some fantastic mental ventriloquism. Concluding suddenly that the room was stifling and Una's tea too sweet, she set down her cup and looked about for Westall: to meet his eyes had long been her refuge from every uncertainty. She met them now, but only, as she felt, in transit; they included her parenthetically in a larger flight. She followed the flight, and it carried her to a corner to which Una had withdrawn – one of the palmy, nooks to which Mrs. Van Sideren attributed the success of her Saturdays. Westall, a moment later, had overtaken his look, and found a place at the girl's side. She bent forward, speaking eagerly; he leaned back, listening, with the depreciatory smile which acted as a filter to flattery, enabling him to swallow the strongest doses without apparent grossness of appetite. Julia winced at her own definition of the smile.

On the way home, in the deserted winter dusk, Westall surprised his wife by a sudden boyish pressure of her arm. 'Did I open their eyes a bit? Did I tell them what you wanted me to?' he asked gaily.

Almost unconsciously, she let her arm slip from his. 'What *I* wanted – ?'

'Why, haven't you – all this time?' She caught the honest wonder of his tone. 'I somehow fancied you'd rather blamed me for not talking more openly before. You almost made me feel, at times, that I was sacrificing principles to expediency.'

She paused a moment over her reply; then she asked quietly: 'What made you decide not to – any longer?'

She felt again the vibration of a faint surprise. 'Why – the wish to please you!' he answered, almost too simply.

'I wish you would not go on, then,' she said abruptly.

He stopped in his quick walk, and she felt his stare through the darkness.

'Not go on – ?'

'Call a hansom, please. I'm tired,' broke from her with a sudden rush of physical weariness.

Instantly his solicitude enveloped her. The room had been infernally hot – and then that confounded cigarette smoke – he had noticed once or twice that she looked pale – she mustn't come to another Saturday. She felt herself yielding, as she always did, to the warm influence of his concern for her, the feminine in her leaning on the man in him with a conscious intensity of abandonment. He put her in the hansom, and her hand stole into his in the darkness. A tear or two rose, and she let them fall. It was so delicious to cry over imaginary troubles!

That evening, after dinner, he surprised her by reverting to the subject of his talk. He combined a man's dislike of uncomfortable questions with an almost feminine skill in eluding them; and she knew that if he returned to the subject he must have some special reason for doing so.

'You seem not to have cared for what I said this afternoon. Did I put the case badly?'

'No – you put it very well.'

'Then what did you mean by saying that you would rather not have me go on with it?'

She glanced at him nervously, her ignorance of his intention deepening her sense of helplessness.

'I don't think I care to hear such things discussed in public.'

'I don't understand you,' he exclaimed. Again the feeling that his surprise was genuine gave an air of obliquity to her own attitude. She was not sure that she understood herself.

'Won't you explain?' he said with a tingle of impatience.

Her eyes wandered about the familiar drawing room which had been the scene of so many of their evening confidences. The shaded lamps, the quiet-colored walls hung with mezzotints, the pale spring flowers scattered here and there in Venice glasses and bowls of old Sèvres, recalled she hardly knew why, the apartment in which the evenings of her first marriage had been passed – a wilderness of rosewood and upholstery, with a picture of a Roman peasant above the mantelpiece, and a Greek slave in statuary marble between the folding doors of the back drawing room. It was a room with which she had never been able to establish any closer relation than that between a traveler and a railway station; and now, as she looked about at the surroundings which stood for her deepest affinities – the room for which she had left that other room – she was startled by the same sense of strangeness and unfamiliarity. The prints, the flowers, the subdued tones of the old porcelain, seemed to typify a superficial refinement which had no relation to the deeper significances of life.

Suddenly she heard her husband repeating his question.

'I don't know that I can explain,' she faltered.

He drew his armchair forward so that he faced her across the hearth. The light of a reading lamp fell on his finely drawn face, which had a kind of surface sensitiveness akin to the surface refinement of its setting.

'Is it that you no longer believe in our ideas?' he asked.

'In our ideas – ?'

'The ideas I am trying to teach. The ideas you and I are supposed to stand for.' He paused a moment. 'The ideas on which our marriage was founded.'

The blood rushed to her face. He had his reasons, then – she was sure now that he had his reasons! In the ten years of their marriage, how often had either of them stopped to consider the ideas on which it was founded? How often does a man dig about the basement of his house to examine its foundations? The foundation is there, of course – the house rests on it – but one lives abovestairs and not in the cellar. It was she, indeed, who in the beginning had insisted on reviewing the situation now and then, on recapitulating the reasons which justified her course, on proclaiming, for time to time, her adherence to the religion of personal independence; but she had long ceased to feel the want of any such ideal standards, and had accepted her marriage as frankly and naturally as though it had been based on the primitive needs of the heart, and required no special sanction to explain or justify it.

'Of course I still believe in our ideas!' she exclaimed.

'Then I repeat that I don't understand. It was part of your theory that the greatest possible publicity should be given to our view of marriage. Have you changed your mind in that respect?'

She hesitated. 'It depends on circumstances – on the public one is addressing. The set of people that the Van Siderens get about them don't care for the truth or falseness of a doctrine. They are attracted simply by its novelty.'

'And yet it was in just such a set of people that you and I met, and learned the truth from each other.'

'That was different.'

'In what way?'

'I was not a young girl, to begin with. It is perfectly unfitting that young girls should be present at – at such times – should hear such things discussed – '

'I thought you considered it one of the deepest social wrongs that such things never *are* discussed before young girls; but that is beside the point, for I don't remember seeing any young girl in my audience today – '

'Except Una Van Sideren!'

He turned slightly and pushed back the lamp at his elbow.

'Oh, Miss Van Sideren – naturally – '

'Why naturally?'

'The daughter of the house – would you have had her sent out with her governess?'

'If I had a daughter I should not allow such things to go on in my house!'

Westall, stroking his moustache, leaned back with a faint smile. 'I fancy Miss Van Sideren is quite capable of taking care of herself.'

'No girl knows how to take care of herself – till it's too late.'

'And yet you would deliberately deny her the surest means of self-defence?'

'What do you call the surest means of self-defence?'

'Some preliminary knowledge of human nature in its relation to the marriage tie.'

She made an impatient gesture. 'How should you like to marry that kind of girl?'

'Immensely – if she were my kind of girl in other respects.'

She took up the argument at another point.

'You are quite mistaken if you think such talk does not affect young girls. Una was in a state of the most absurd exaltation – ' She broke off, wondering why she had spoken.

Westall reopened a magazine which he had laid aside at the beginning of their discussion. 'What you tell me is immensely flattering to my oratorical talent – but I fear you overrate its effect. I can assure you that Miss Van Sideren doesn't have to have her thinking done for her. She's quite capable of doing it herself.'

'You seem very familiar with her mental processes!' flashed unguardedly from his wife.

He looked up quietly from the pages he was cutting.

'I should like to be,' he answered. 'She interests me.'

• II •

IF there be a distinction in being misunderstood, it was one denied to Julia Westall when she left her first husband. Everyone was ready to excuse and even to defend her. The world she adorned agreed that John Arment was 'impossible,' and hostesses gave a sigh of relief at the thought that it would no longer be necessary to ask him to dine.

There had been no scandal connected with the divorce: neither side had accused the other of the offence euphemistically described as 'statutory'. The Arments had indeed been obliged to transfer their allegiance to a state which recognized desertion as a cause for divorce, and construed the term so liberally that the seeds of desertion were shown to exist in every union. Even Mrs. Arment's second marriage did not make traditional morality stir in its sleep. It was known that she had not met her second husband till after she had parted from the first, and she had, moreover, replaced a rich man by a poor one. Though Clement Westall was acknowledged to be a rising lawyer, it was generally felt that his fortunes would not rise as rapidly as his reputation. The Westalls would probably always have to live quietly and go out to dinner in cabs. Could there be better evidence of Mrs. Arment's complete disinterestedness?

If the reasoning by which her friends justified her course was somewhat cruder and less complex than her own elucidation of the matter, both explanations led to the same conclusion: John Arment was impossible. The only difference was that, to his wife, his impossibility was something deeper than a social disqualification. She had once said, in ironical defence of her marriage, that it had at least preserved her from the necessity of sitting next to him at dinner; but she had not then realized at what cost the immunity was purchased. John Arment was impossible; but the sting of his impossibility lay in the fact that he made it impossible for those about him to be other than himself. By an unconscious process of elimination he had excluded from the world everything of which he did not feel a personal need: had become, as it were, a climate in which only his own requirements survived. This might seem to imply a deliberate selfishness; but there was nothing deliberate about Arment. He was as instinctive as an animal or a child. It was this childish element in his nature which sometimes for a moment unsettled his wife's estimate of him. Was it possible that he was simply undeveloped, that he had delayed, somewhat longer than is usual, the laborious process of growing up? He had the kind of sporadic shrewdness which causes it to be said of a dull man that he is 'no fool'; and it was this quality that his wife found most trying. Even to the naturalist it is annoying to have his deductions disturbed by some unforeseen aberrancy of form or function; and how much more so to the wife whose estimate of herself is inevitably bound up with her judgment of her husband!

Arment's shrewdness did not, indeed, imply any latent intellectual power; it suggested, rather, potentialities of feeling, of suffering, perhaps, in a blind rudimentary way, on which Julia's sensibilities naturally declined to linger. She so fully understood her own reasons for leaving him that she disliked to think they were not as comprehensible to her husband. She was haunted, in her analytic moments, by the look of perplexity, too inarticulate for words, with which he had acquiesced in her explanations.

These moments were rare with her, however. Her marriage had been too concrete a misery to be surveyed philosophically. If she had been unhappy for complex reasons, the unhappiness was as real as though it had been uncomplicated. Soul is more bruisable than flesh, and Julia was wounded in every fiber of her spirit. Her husband's personality seemed to be closing gradually in on her, obscuring the sky and cutting off the air, till she felt herself shut up among the decaying bodies of her starved hopes. A sense of having been decoyed by some world-old conspiracy into this bondage of body and soul filled her with despair. If marriage was the slow lifelong acquittal of a debt contracted in ignorance, then marriage was a crime against human nature. She, for one, would have no share in maintaining the pretense of which she had been a victim: the pretense that a man and a woman, forced into the narrowest of personal relations, must remain there till the end, though they may have outgrown the span of each other's natures as the mature tree outgrows the iron brace about the sapling.

It was in the first heat of her moral indignation that she had met Clement Westall. She had seen at once that he was 'interested,' and had fought off the discovery, dreading any influence that should draw her back into the bondage of conventional relations. To ward off the peril she had, with an almost crude precipitancy, revealed her opinions to him. To her surprise, she found that he shared them. She was attracted by the frankness of a suitor who, while pressing his suit, admitted that he did not believe in marriage. Her worst audacities did not seem to surprise him: he had thought out all that she had felt, and they had reached the same conclusion. People grew at varying rates, and the yoke that was an easy fit for the one might soon become galling to the other. That was what divorce was for: the readjustment of personal relations. As soon as their necessarily transitive nature was recognized they would gain in dignity as well as in harmony. There would be no further need of the ignoble concessions and connivances, the perpetual sacrifice of personal delicacy and moral pride, by means of which imperfect marriages were now held together. Each partner to the contract would be on his mettle, forced to live up to the highest standard of self-development, on pain of losing the other's respect and affection. The low nature could no longer drag the higher down, but must struggle to rise, or remain alone on its inferior level. The only necessary condition to a harmonious marriage was a frank recognition of this truth, and a solemn agreement between the contracting parties to keep faith with themselves, and not to live together for a moment after complete accord had ceased to exist between them. The new adultery was unfaithfulness to self.

It was, as Westall had just reminded her, on this understanding that they had married. The ceremony was an unimportant concession to social prejudice: now that the door of divorce stood open, no marriage need be an imprisonment, and the contract therefore no longer involved any diminution of self-respect. The nature of their attachment placed them so far beyond the reach of such contingencies that it was easy to discuss them with an open mind; and Julia's sense of security made her dwell with a tender insistence on Westall's promise to claim his release when he should cease to love her. The exchange of these vows seemed to make them, in a sense, champions of the new law, pioneers in the forbidden realm of individual freedom: they felt that they had somehow achieved beatitude without martyrdom.

This, as Julia now reviewed the past, she perceived to have been her theoretical attitude toward marriage. It was unconsciously, insidiously, that her ten years of happiness with Westall had developed another conception of the tie; a reversion, rather, to the old instinct of passionate dependency and possessorship that now made her blood revolt at the mere hint of change. Change? Renewal? Was that what they had called it, in their foolish jargon? Destruction, extermination rather – this rending of a myriad fibers interwoven with another's being! Another? But he was not other! He and she were one, one in the mystic sense which alone gave marriage its significance. The new law was not for them, but for the disunited creatures forced into a mockery of union. The gospel she had felt called on to proclaim had no bearing on her own case . . . She sent for the doctor and told him she was sure she needed a nerve tonic.

She took the nerve tonic diligently, but it failed to act as a sedative to her fears. She did not know what she feared; but that made her anxiety the more pervasive. Her husband had not reverted to the subject of his Saturday talks. He was unusually kind and considerate, with a softening of his quick manner, a touch of shyness in his consideration, that sickened her with new fears. She told herself that it was because she looked badly – because he knew about the doctor and the nerve tonic – that he showed this deference to her wishes, this eagerness to screen her from moral drafts; but the explanation simply cleared the way for fresh inferences.

The week passed slowly, vacantly, like a prolonged Sunday. On Saturday the morning post brought a note from Mrs. Van Sideren. Would dear Julia ask Mr. Westall to come half an hour earlier than usual, as there was to be some music after his 'talk'? Westall was just leaving for his office when his wife read the note. She opened the drawing-room door and called him back to deliver the message.

He glanced at the note and tossed it aside. 'What a bore! I shall have to cut my game of racquets. Well, I suppose it can't be helped. Will you write and say it's all right?'

Julia hesitated a moment, her hand stiffening on the chair back against which she leaned.

'You mean to go on with these talks?' she asked.

'I – why not?' he returned; and this time it struck her that his surprise was not quite unfeigned. The perception helped her to find words.

'You said you had started them with the idea of pleasing me – '

'Well?'

'I told you last week that they didn't please me.'

'Last week? – Oh – ' He seemed to make an effort of memory. 'I thought you were nervous then; you sent for the doctor the next day.'

'It was not the doctor I needed; it was your assurance – '

'My assurance?'

Suddenly she felt the floor fail under her. She sank into the chair with a choking throat, her words, her reasons slipping away from her like straws down a whirling flood.

'Clement,' she cried, 'isn't it enough for you to know that I hate it?'

He turned to close the door behind them; then he walked toward her and sat down. 'What is it that you hate?' he asked gently.

She had made a desperate effort to rally her routed argument.

'I can't bear to have you speak as if – as if – our marriage – were like the other kind – the wrong kind. When I heard you there, the other afternoon, before all those inquisitive gossiping people, proclaiming that husbands and wives had a right to leave each other whenever they were tired – or had seen someone else – '

Westall sat motionless, his eyes fixed on a pattern of the carpet.

'You *have* ceased to take this view, then?' he said as she broke off. 'You no longer believe that husbands and wives *are* justified in separating – under such conditions?'

'Under such conditions?' she stammered. 'Yes – I still believe that – but how can we judge for others? What can we know of the circumstances – ?'

He interrupted her. 'I thought it was a fundamental article of our creed that the special circumstances produced by marriage were not to interfere with the full assertion of individual liberty.' He paused a moment. 'I thought that was your reason for leaving Arment.'

She flushed to the forehead. It was not like him to give a personal turn to the argument.

'It was my reason,' she said simply.

'Well, then – why do you refuse to recognize its validity now?'

'I don't – I don't – I only say that one can't judge for others.'

He made an impatient movement. 'This is mere hairsplitting. What you mean is that, the doctrine having served your purpose when you needed it, you now repudiate it.'

'Well,' she exclaimed, flushing again, 'what if I do? What does it matter to us?'

Westall rose from his chair. He was excessively pale, and stood before his wife with something of the formality of a stranger.

'It matters to me,' he said in a low voice, 'because I do *not* repudiate it.'

'Well – ?'

'And because I had intended to invoke it as – '

He paused and drew his breath deeply. She sat silent, almost deafened by her heartbeats.

' –as a complete justification of the course I am about to take.'

Julia remained motionless. 'What course is that?' she asked.

He cleared his throat. 'I mean to claim the fulfilment of your promise.'

For an instant the room wavered and darkened; then she recovered a torturing acuteness of vision. Every detail of her surroundings, pressed upon her: the tick of the clock, the slant of sunlight on the wall, the hardness of the chair arms that she grasped, were a separate wound to each sense.

'My promise – ' she faltered.

'Your part of our mutual agreement to set each other free if one or the other should wish to be released.'

She was silent again. He waited a moment, shifting his position nervously; then he said, with a touch of irritability: 'You acknowledge the agreement?'

The question went through her like a shock. She lifted her head to it proudly. 'I acknowledge the agreement,' she said.

'And – you don't mean to repudiate it?'

A log on the hearth fell forward, and mechanically he advanced and pushed it back.

'No,' she answered slowly, 'I don't mean to repudiate it.'

There was a pause. He remained near the hearth, his elbow resting on the mantelshelf. Close to his hand stood a little cup of jade that he had given her on one of their wedding anniversaries. She wondered vaguely if he noticed it.

'You intend to leave me, then?' she said at length.

His gesture seemed to deprecate the crudeness of the allusion.

'To marry someone else?'

Again his eye and hand protested. She rose and stood before him.

'Why should you be afraid to tell me? Is it Una Van Sideren?'

He was silent.

'I wish you good luck,' she said.

• III •

SHE looked up, finding herself alone. She did not remember when or how he had left the room, or how long afterward she had sat there. The fire still smoldered on the hearth, but the slant of sunlight had left the wall.

Her first conscious thoughts was that she had not broken her word, that she had fulfilled the very letter of their bargain. There had been no crying out, no vain appeal to the past, no attempt at temporizing or evasion. She had marched straight up to the guns.

Now that it was over, she was sickened to find herself alive. She looked about her, trying to recover her hold on reality. Her identity seemed to be slipping from her, as it disappears in a physical swoon. 'This is my room – this is my house,' she heard herself saying. Her room? Her house? She could almost hear the walls laugh back at her.

She stood up, weariness in every bone. The silence of the room frightened her. She remembered, now, having heard the front door close a long time ago: the sound suddenly re-echoed through her brain.

Her husband must have left the house, then – her *husband?* She no longer knew in what terms to think: the simplest phrases had a poisoned edge. She sank back into her chair, overcome by a strange weakness. The clock struck ten – it was only ten o'clock! Suddenly she remembered that she had not ordered dinner . . . or were they dining out that evening? *Dinner – dining out* – the old meaningless phraseology pursued her! She must try to think of herself as she would think of someone else, a someone dissociated from all the familiar routine of the past, whose wants and habits must gradually be learned, as one might spy out the ways of a strange animal. . . .

The clock struck another hour – eleven. She stood up again and walked to the door: she thought she would go upstairs to her room. *Her* room? Again the word derided her. She opened the door, crossed the narrow hall, and walked up the stairs. As she passed, she noticed Westall's sticks and umbrellas: a pair of his gloves lay on the hall table. The same stair carpet mounted between the same walls; the same old French print, and its narrow black frame, faced her on the landing. This visual continuity was intolerable. Within, a gaping chasm; without, the same untroubled and familiar surface. She must get away from it before she could attempt to think. But, once in her room, she sat down on the lounge, a stupor creeping over her. . . .

Gradually her vision cleared. A great deal had happened in the interval – a wild marching and countermarching of emotions, arguments, ideas – a fury of insurgent impulses that fell back spent upon themselves. She had tried, at first, to rally, to organize these chaotic forces. There must be help somewhere, if only she could master the inner tumult. Life could not be broken off short like this, for a whim, a fancy; the law itself would side with her, would defend her. The law? What claim had she upon it? She was the prisoner of her own choice: she had been her own legislator, and she was the predestined victim of the code she had devised. But this was grotesque, intolerable – a mad mistake, for which she could not be held accountable! The law she had despised was still there, might still be invoked . . . invoked, but to what end? Could she ask it to chain Westall to her side? *She* had been allowed to go free when she claimed her freedom – should she show less magnanimity than she had exacted? Magnanimity? The word lashed her with its irony – one does not strike an attitude when one is fighting for life! She would threaten, grovel, cajole . . . she would yield anything to keep her hold on happiness. Ah, but the difficulty lay deeper! The law could not help her – her own apostasy could not help her. She was the victim of the theories she renounced. It was as though some giant machine of her own making had caught her up in its wheels and was grinding her to atoms. . . .

It was afternoon when she found herself out of doors. She walked with an aimless haste, fearing to meet familiar faces. The day was

radiant, metallic: one of those searching American days so calculated
to reveal the shortcomings of our street-cleaning and the excesses of
our architecture. The streets looked bare and hideous; everything stared
and glittered. She called a passing hansom, and gave Mrs. Van Sideren's
address. She did not know what had led up to the act; but she found
herself suddenly resolved to speak, to cry out a warning. It was too
late to save herself – but the girl might still be told. The handsom rattled
up Fifth Avenue; she sat with her eyes fixed, avoiding recognition. At
the Van Siderens' door she sprang out and rang the bell. Action had
cleared her brain, and she felt calm and self-possessed. She knew now
exactly what she meant to say.

The ladies were both out . . . the parlormaid stood waiting for a
card. Julia, with a vague murmur, turned away from the door and
lingered a moment on the sidewalk. Then she remembered that she had
not paid the cab driver. She drew a dollar from her purse and handed
it to him. He touched his hat and drove off, leaving her alone in
the long empty street. She wandered away westward, toward strange
thoroughfares, where she was not likely to meet acquaintances. The
feeling of aimlessness had returned. Once she found herself in the
afternoon torrent of Broadway, swept past tawdry shops and flaming
theatrical posters, with a succession of meaningless faces gliding by in
the opposite direction. . . .

A feeling of faintness reminded her that she had not eaten since
morning. She turned into a side street of shabby houses, with rows of
ash barrels behind bent area railings. In a basement window she saw
the sign 'Ladies' Restaurant': a pie and a dish of doughnuts lay against
the dusty pane like petrified food in an ethnological museum. She
entered and a young woman with a weak mouth and a brazen eye
cleared a table for her near the window. The table was covered with a
red-and-white cotton cloth and adorned with a bunch of celery in a
thick tumbler and a saltcellar full of grayish lumpy salt. Julia ordered
tea, and sat a long time waiting for it. She was glad to be away from
the noise and confusion of the streets. The low-ceilinged room was
empty, and two or three waitresses with thin pert faces lounged in the
background staring at her and whispering together. At last the tea was
brought in a discolored metal teapot. Julia poured a cup and drank it
hastily. It was black and bitter, but it flowed through her veins like an
elixir. She was almost dizzy with exhilaration. Oh, how tired, how
unutterably tired she had been!

She drank a second cup, blacker and bitterer, and now her mind
was once more working clearly. She felt as vigorous, as decisive, as
when she had stood on the Van Siderens' doorstep – but the wish to
return there had subsided. She saw now the futility of such an attempt
– the humiliation to which it might have exposed her. . . . The pity of
it was that she did not know what to do next. The short winter day

was fading, and she realized that she could not remain much longer in the restaurant without attracting notice. She paid for her tea and went out into the street. The lamps were alight, and here and there a basement shop cast an oblong of gaslight across the fissured pavement. In the dusk there was something sinister about the aspect of the street, and she hastened back toward Fifth Avenue. She was not used to being out alone at that hour.

At the corner of Fifth Avenue she paused and stood watching the stream of carriages. At last a policeman caught sight of her and signed to her that he would take her across. She had not meant to cross the street, but she obeyed automatically, and presently found herself on the farther corner. There she paused again for a moment; but she fancied the policemen was watching her, and this sent her hastening down the nearest side street. . . . After that she walked a long time, vaguely. . . . Night had fallen, and now and then, through the windows of a passing carriage, she caught the expanse of an evening waistcoat or the shimmer of an opera cloak. . . .

Suddenly she found herself in a familiar street. She stood still a moment, breathing quickly. She had turned the corner without noticing whither it led; but now, a few yards ahead of her, she saw the house in which she had once lived – her first husband's house. The blinds were drawn, and only a faint translucence marked the windows and the transom above the door. As she stood there she heard a step behind her, and a man walked by in the direction of the house. He walked slowly, with a heavy middle-aged gait, his head sunk a little between the shoulders, the red crease of his neck visible above the fur collar of his overcoat. He crossed the street, went up the steps of the house, drew forth a latchkey, and let himself in. . . .

There was no one else in sight. Julia leaned for a long time against the area rail at the corner, her eyes fixed on the front of the house. The feeling of physical weariness had returned, but the strong tea still throbbed in her veins and lit her brain with an unnatural clearness. Presently she heard another step draw near, and moving quickly away, she too crossed the street and mounted the steps of the house. The impulse which had carried her there prolonged itself in a quick pressure of the electric bell – then she felt suddenly weak and tremulous, and grasped the balustrade for support. The door opened and a young footman with a fresh inexperienced face stood on the threshold. Julia knew in an instant that he would admit her.

'I saw Mr. Arment going in just now,' she said. 'Will you ask him to see me for a moment?'

The footman hesitated. 'I think Mr. Arment has gone up to dress for dinner, madam.'

Julia advanced into the hall. 'I am sure he will see me – I will not detain him long,' she said. She spoke quietly, authoritatively, in the tone which a good servant does not mistake. The footman had his hand on the drawing-room door.

'I will tell him, madam. What name, please?'

Julia trembled: she had not thought of that. 'Merely say a lady', she returned carelessly.

The footman wavered and she fancied herself lost; but at that instant the door opened from within and John Arment stepped into the hall. He drew back sharply as he saw her, his florid face turning sallow with the shock; then the blood poured back to it, swelling the veins on his temples and reddening the lobes of his thick ears.

It was long since Julia had seen him, and she was startled at the change in his appearance. He had thickened, coarsened, settled down into the enclosing flesh. But she noted this insensibly: her one conscious thought was that, now she was face to face with him, she must not let him escape till he had heard her. Every pulse in her body throbbed with the urgency of her message.

She went up to him as he drew back. 'I must speak to you,' she said.

Arment hesitated, red and stammering. Julia glanced at the footman, and her look acted as a warning. The instinctive shrinking from a scene predominated over every other impulse, and Arment said slowly: 'Will you come this way?'

He followed her into the drawing room and closed the door. Julia, as she advanced, was vaguely aware that the room at least was unchanged: time had not mitigated its horrors. The contadina still lurched from the chimney breast, and the Greek slave obstructed the threshold of the inner room. The place was alive with memories; they started out from every fold of the yellow satin curtains and glided between the angles of the rosewood furniture. But while some subordinate agency was carrying these impressions to her brain, her whole conscious effort was centered in the act of dominating Arment's will. The fear that he would refuse to hear her mounted like fever to her brain. She felt her purpose melt before it, words and arguments running into each other in the heat of her longing. For a moment her voice failed her, and she imagined herself thrust out before she could speak; but as she was struggling for a word Arment pushed a chair forward, and said quietly: 'You are not well.'

The sound of his voice steadied her. It was neither kind nor unkind – a voice that suspended judgment, rather, awaiting unforeseen developments. She supported herself against the back of the chair and drew a deep breath.

'Shall I send for something?' he continued, with a cold embarrassed politeness.

Julia raised an entreating hand. 'No – no – thank you. I am quite well.'

He paused midway toward the bell, and turned on her. 'Then may I ask – ?'

'Yes,' she interrupted him. 'I came here because I wanted to see you. There is something I must tell you.'

Arment continued to scrutinize her. 'I am surprised at that,' he said. 'I should have supposed that any communication you may wish to make could have been made through our lawyers.'

'Our lawyers!' She burst into a little laugh. 'I don't think they could help me – this time.'

Arment's face took on a barricaded look. 'If there is any question of help – of course – '

It struck her, whimsically, that she had seen that look when some shabby devil called with a subscription book. Perhaps he thought she wanted him to put his name down for so much in sympathy – or even in money. . . . The thought made her laugh again. She saw his look change slowly to perplexity. All his facial changes were slow, and she remembered, suddenly, how it had once diverted her to shift that lumbering scenery with a word. For the first time it struck her that she had been cruel! 'There *is* a question of help,' she said in a softer key; 'you can help me; but only by listening. . . . I want to tell you something. . . .'

Arment's reistance was not yielding. 'Would it not be easier to – write?' he suggested.

She shook her head. 'There is no time to write . . . and it won't take long.' She raised her head and their eyes met. 'My husband has left me,' she said.

'Westall – ?' he stammered, reddening again.

'Yes. This morning. Just as I left you. Because he was tired of me.'

The words, uttered scarcely above a whisper, seemed to dilate to the limit of the room. Arment looked toward the door; then his embarrassed glance returned returned to Julia.

'I am very sorry,' he said awkwardly.

'Thank you,' she murmured.

'But I don't see – '

'No – but you will – in a moment. Won't you listen to me? Please!' Instinctively she had shifted her position, putting herself between him and the door. 'It happened this morning,' she went on in short breathless phrases. 'I never suspected anything – I thought we were – perfectly happy. . . . Suddenly he told me he was tired of me . . . there is a girl he likes better. . . . He has gone to her. . . .' As he spoke, the lurking anguish rose upon her, possessing her once more to the exclusion of every other emotion. Her eyes ached, her throat swelled with it, and two painful tears ran down her face.

Arment's constraint was increasing visibly. 'This – this is very unfortunate,' he began. 'But I should say the law – '

'The law?' she echoed ironically. 'When he asks for his freedom?'

'You are not obliged to give it.'

'You were not obliged to give me mine – but you did.'

He made a protesting gesture.

'You saw that the law couldn't help you – didn't you?' she went on. 'That is what I see now. The law represents material rights – it can't go beyond. If we don't recognize an inner law . . . the obligation that love creates . . . being loved as well as loving . . . there is nothing to prevent our spreading ruin unhindered . . . is there?' She raised her head plaintively, with the look of a bewildered child. 'That is what I see now . . . what I wanted to tell you. He leaves me because he's tired . . . but *I* was not tired; and I don't understand why he is. That's the dreadful part of it – the not understanding: I hadn't realized what it meant. But I've been thinking of it all day, and things have come back to me – things I hadn't noticed . . . when you and I . . .' She moved closer to him, and fixed her eyes on his with the gaze which tries to reach beyond words. 'I see now that *you* didn't understand – did you?'

Their eyes met in a sudden shock of comprehension: a veil seemed to be lifted between them. Arment's lip trembled.

'No,' he said, 'I didn't understand.'

She gave a little cry, almost of triumph. 'I knew it! I knew it! You wondered – you tried to tell me – but no words came. . . . You saw your life falling in ruins . . . the world slipping from you . . . and you couldn't speak or move!'

She sank down on the chair against which she had been leaning. 'Now I know – now I know,' she repeated.

'I am very sorry for you,' she heard Arment stammer.

She looked up quickly. 'That's not what I came for. I don't want you to be sorry. I came to ask you to forgive me . . . for not understanding that *you* didn't understand. . . . That's all I wanted to say.' She rose with a vague sense that the end had come, and put out a groping hand toward the door.

Arment stood motionless. She turned to him with a faint smile.

'You forgive me?'

'There is nothing to forgive – '

'Then you will shake hands for good-bye?' She felt his hand in hers: it was nerveless, reluctant.

'Good-bye,' she repeated. 'I understand now.'

She opened the door and passed out into the hall. As she did so, Arment took an impulsive step forward; but just then the footman, who was evidently alive to his obligations, advanced from the background to let her out. She heard Arment fall back. The footman threw open the door, and she found herself outside in the darkness.

The Last Asset

'THE DEVIL!' Paul Garnett exclaimed as he reread his note; and the dry old gentleman who was at the moment his only neighbor in the modest restaurant they both frequented, remarked with a smile: 'You don't seem particularly disturbed at meeting him.'

Garnett returned the smile. 'I don't know why I apostrophized him, for he's not in the least present – except inasmuch as he may prove to be at the bottom of anything unexpected.'

The old gentleman who, like Garnett, was an American, and spoke in the thin rarefied voice which seems best fitted to emit sententious truths, twisted his lean neck round to cackle out: 'Ah, it's generally a woman who's at the bottom of the unexpected. Not,' he added, leaning forward with deliberation to select a toothpick, 'that that precludes the devil's being there too.'

Garnett uttered the requisite laugh, and his neighbor, pushing back his plate, called out with a perfectly unbending American intonation: 'Gassong! L'addition, silver play.'

His repast, as usual, had been a simple one, and he left only thirty centimes in the plate on which his account was presented; but the waiter, to whom he was evidently a familiar presence, received the tribute with Latin amenity, and hovered helpfully about the table while the old gentleman cut and lighted his cigar.

'Yes,' the latter proceeded, revolving the cigar meditatively between his thin lips, 'they're generally both in the same hole, like the owl and the prairie dog in the natural history books of my youth. I believe it was all a mistake about the owl and the prairie dog, but it isn't about the unexpected. The fact is, the unexpected *is* the devil – the sooner you find that out, the happier you'll be.' He leaned back, tilting his bald head against the blotched mirror behind him, and rambling on with gentle garrulity while Garnett attacked his omelet.

'Get your life down to routine – eliminate surprises. Arrange things so that, when you get up in the morning, you'll know exactly what's going to happen to you during the day – and the next day and the next. I don't say it's funny – it ain't. But it's better than being hit on the

64

head by a brickbat. That's why I always take my meals at this restaurant.
I know just how much onion they put in things – if I went to the next
place I shouldn't. And I always take the same streets to come here –
I've been doing it for ten years now. I know at which crossing to look
out – I know what I'm going to see in the shop windows. It saves a
lot of wear and tear to know what's coming. For a good many years I
never *did* know, from one minute to another, and now I like to think
that everything's cut and dried, and nothing unexpected can jump out
at me like a tramp from a ditch.'

He paused calmly to knock the ashes from his cigar and Garnett
said with a smile: 'Doesn't such a plan of life cut off nearly all the
possibilities?'

The old gentleman made a contemptuous motion. 'Possibilities of
what? Of being multifariously miserable? There are lots of ways of
being miserable, but there's only one way of being comfortable, and
that is to stop running round after happiness. If you make up your
mind not to be happy there's no reason why you shouldn't have a fairly
good time.'

'That was Schopenhauer's idea, I believe,' the young man said,
pouring his wine with the smile of youthful incredulity.

'I guess he hadn't the monopoly,' responded his friend. 'Lots of
people have found out the secret – the trouble is that so few live up to
it.'

He rose from his seat, pushing the table forward, and standing
passive while the waiter advanced with his shabby overcoat and
umbrella. Then he nodded to Garnett, lifted his hat to the broad-
bosomed lady behind the desk, and passed out into the street.

Garnett looked after him with a musing smile. The two had
exchanged views on life for two years without so much as knowing
each other's names. Garnett was a newspaper correspondent whose
work kept him mainly in London, but on his periodic visits to Paris
he lodged in a dingy hotel of the Latin quarter, the chief merit of which
was its nearness to the cheap and excellent restaurant where the two
Americans had made acquaintance. But Garnett's assiduity in
frequenting the place arose, in the end, less from the excellence of the
food than from the enjoyment of his old friend's conversation. Amid
the flashy sophistications of the Parisian life to which Garnett's trade
introduced him, the American sage's conversation had the crisp and
homely flavor of a native dish – one of the domestic compounds for
which the exiled palate is supposed to yearn. It was a mark of the old
man's impersonality that, in spite of the interest he inspired, Garnett
had never got beyond idly wondering who he might be, where he
lived, and what his occupations were. He was presumably a bachelor
– a man of family ties, however relaxed, though he might have been
as often absent from home, would not have been as regularly present

in the same place – and there was about him a boundless desultoriness which renewed Garnett's conviction that there is no one on earth as idle as an American who is not busy. From certain allusions it was plain that he had lived many years in Paris, yet he had not taken the trouble to adapt his tongue to the local inflections, but spoke French with the accent of one who has formed his notion of the language from a phrase book.

The city itself seemed to have made as little impression on him as its speech. He appeared to have no artistic or intellectual curiosities, to remain untouched by the complex appeal of Paris, while preserving, perhaps the more strikingly from his very detachment, that odd American astuteness which seems the fruit of innocence rather than of experience. His nationality revealed itself again in a mild interest in the political problems of his adopted country, though they appeared to preoccupy him only as illustrating the boundless perversity of mankind. The exhibition of human folly never ceased to divert him, and though his examples of it seemed mainly drawn from the columns of one exiguous daily paper, he found there matter for endless variations on his favorite theme. If this monotony of topic did not weary the younger man, it was because he fancied he could detect under it the tragic note of the fixed idea – of some great moral upheaval which had flung his friend stripped and starving on the desert island of the little restaurant where they met. He hardly knew wherein he read this revelation – whether in the shabbiness of the sage's dress, the impersonal courtesy of his manner, or the shade of apprehension which lurked, indescribably, in his guileless yet suspicious eye. There were moments when Garnett could only define him by saying that he looked like a man who had seen a ghost.

• II •

AN apparition almost as startling had come to Garnett himself in the shape of the mauve note handed to him by his *concierge* as he was leaving the hotel for luncheon.

Not that, on the face of it, a missive announcing Mrs. Sam Newell's arrival at Ritz's, and her need of his presence there that day at five, carried any mark of the portentous. It was not her being at Ritz's that surprised him. The fact that she was chronically hard up, and had once or twice lately been so harshly confronted with the consequences as to accept – indeed solicit – a loan of five pounds from him: this circumstance, as Garnett knew, would never be allowed to affect the general tenor of her existence. If one came to Paris, where could one go but to Ritz's? Did he see her in some grubby hole across the river? Or in a family *pension* near the Place de l'Etoile? There was no affectation in her tendency to gravitate toward what was costliest and most conspicuous. In doing so she obeyed one of the profoundest instincts of her nature, and it was another instinct which taught her to gratify the first at any cost, even to that of dipping into the pocket of an impecunious journalist. It was a part of her strength – and of her charm, too – that she did such things naturally, openly, without any of the grimaces of dissimulation or compunction.

Her recourse to Garnett had of course marked a specially low ebb in her fortunes. Save in moments of exceptional dearth she had richer sources of supply; and he was nearly sure that by running over the 'society column' of the Paris *Herald* he should find an explanation, not perhaps of her presence at Ritz's, but of her means of subsistence there. What perplexed him was not the financial but the social aspect of the case. When Mrs. Newell had left London in July she had told him that, between Cowes and Scotland, she and Hermy were provided for till the middle of October: after that, as she put it, they would have to look about. Why, then, when she had in her hand the opportunity of living for three months at the expense of the British aristocracy, did she rush off to Paris at heaven knew whose expense in the beginning of September? She was not a woman to act incoherently; if she made mistakes they were not of that kind. Garnett felt sure she would never willingly relax her hold on her distinguished friends – was it possible that it was they who had somewhat violently let go of her?

As Garnett reviewed the situation he began to see that his possibility had for some time been latent in it. He had felt that something might happen at any moment – and was not this the something he had obscurely foreseen? Mrs. Newell really moved too fast: her position was as perilous as that of an invading army without a base of supplies. She used up everything too quickly – friends, credit, influence, forbearance. It was so easy for her to acquire all these – what a pity she had never learned to keep them! He himself, for instance – the most insignificant of her acquisitions – was beginning to feel like a squeezed sponge at the mere thought of her; and it was this sense of exhaustion, of the inability to provide more, either materially or morally, which had provoked his exclamation on opening her note. From the first days of their acquaintance her prodigality had amazed him, but he had believed it to be surpassed by the infinity of her resources. If she exhausted old supplies she always had new ones to replace them. When one set of people began to find her impossible, another was always beginning to find her indispensable. Yes – but there were limits – there were only so many sets of people, at least in her classification, and when she came to an end of them, what then? Was this flight to Paris a sign that she had come to an end – was she going to try Paris because London had failed her? The time of year precluded such a conjecture. Mrs. Newell's Paris was nonexistent in September. The town was a desert of gaping trippers – he could as soon think of her seeking social restoration at Margate.

For a moment it occurred to him that she might have come over to renew her wardrobe; but he knew her dates too well to dwell long on this. It was in April and December that she visited the dressmakers: before December, he had heard her explain, one got nothing but 'the American fashions.' Mrs. Newell's scorn of all things American was somewhat illogically coupled with the determination to use her own Americanism to the utmost as a means of social advance. She had found out long ago that, on certain lines, it paid in London to be American, and she had manufactured for herself a personality independent of geographical or social demarcations, and presenting that remarkable blend of plantation dialect, Bowery slang and hyperbolic statement, which expresses the British idea of an unadulterated Americanism. Mrs. Newell, for all her talents, was not by nature either humorous or hyperbolic, and there were times when it would doubtless have been a relief to her to be as stolid as some of the persons whose dullness it was her fate to enliven. It was perhaps the need of relaxing which had drawn her into her odd intimacy with Garnett, with whom she did not have to be either scrupulously English or artificially American, since the impression she made on him was of no more consequence than that which she produced on her footman. Garnett was aware that he owed his success to his insignificance, but the fact affected him only as adding one more element to his knowledge of Mrs. Newell's character. He was as ready to sacrifice his personal vanity in such a cause as he had been, at the outset of their acquaintance, to sacrifice his professional pride to the opportunity of knowing her.

When he had accepted the position of 'London correspondent' (with an occasional side glance at Paris) to the New York *Searchlight*, he had not understood that his work was to include the obligation of 'interviewing': indeed, had the possibility presented itself in advance, he would have met it by packing his valise and returning to the drudgery of his assistant editorship in New York. But when, after three months in Europe, he received a letter from his chief, suggesting that he should enliven the Sunday *Searchlight* by a series of 'Talks with Smart Americans in London' (beginning say, with Mrs. Sam Newell), the change of focus already enabled him to view the proposal without passion. For his life on the edge of the great world caldron of art, politics and pleasure – of that high-spiced brew which is nowhere else so subtly and variously compounded – had bred in him an eagerness to taste of the heady mixture. He knew he should never have the full spoon at his lips, but he recalled the peasant girl in one of Browning's plays, who boasts of having eaten polenta cut with a knife which has carved an ortolan. Might not Mrs. Newell, who had so successfully cut a way into the dense and succulent mass of English society, serve as the knife to season his polenta?

He had expected, as the result of the interview, to which she promptly, almost eagerly, agreed, no more than the glimpse of brightly-lit vistas which a waiting messenger may catch through open doors; but instead he had found himself drawn at once into the inner sanctuary, not of London society, but of Mrs. Newell's relation to it. She had been candidly charmed by the idea of the interview: it struck him that she was conscious of the need of being freshened up. Her appearance was brilliantly fresh, with the inveterate freshness of the toilet table; her paint was as impenetrable as armor. But her personality was a little tarnished: she was in want of social renovation. She had been doing and saying the same things for too long a time. London, Cowes, Hamburg, Scotland, Monte Carlo – that had been the round since Hermy was a baby. Hermy was her daughter, Miss Hermione Newell, who was called in presently to be shown off to the interviewer and add a paragraph to the celebration of her mother's charms.

Miss Newell's appearance was so full of an unassisted freshness that for a moment Garnett made the mistake of fancying that she could fill a paragraph of her own. But he soon found that her vague personality was merely tributary to her parent's; that her youth and grace were, in some mysterious way, her mother's rather than her own. She smiled obediently on Garnett, but could contribute little beyond her smile, and the general sweetness of her presence, to the picture of Mrs. Newell's existence that it was the young man's business to draw. And presently he found that she had left the room without his noticing it.

He learned in time that this unnoticeableness was the most conspicuous thing about her. Burning at best with a mild light, she became invisible in the glare of her mother's personality. It was in fact only as a product of her environment that poor Hermione struck the imagination. With the smartest woman in London as her guide and example she had never developed a taste for dress, and with opportunities for enlightenment from which Garnett's fancy recoiled she remained simple, unsuspicious and tender, with an inclination to good works and afternoon church, a taste for the society of dull girls, and a clinging fidelity to old governesses and retired nursemaids. Mrs. Newell, whose boast it was that she looked facts in the face, frankly owned that she had not been able to make anything of Hermione. 'If she has a role I haven't discovered it,' she confessed to Garnett. 'I've tried everything, but she doesn't fit in anywhere.'

Mrs. Newell spoke as if her daughter were a piece of furniture acquired without due reflection, and for which no suitable place could be found. She got, of course, what she could out of Hermione, who wrote her notes, ran her errands, saw tiresome people for her, and occupied an intermediate office between that of lady's maid and secretary; but such small returns on her investment were not what Mrs. Newell had counted on. What was the use of producing and educating a handsome daughter if she did not, in some more positive way, contribute to her parent's advancement?

•   III   •

'IT's about Hermy,' Mrs. Newell said, rising from the heap of embroidered cushions which formed the background of her afternoon repose. Her sitting room at Ritz's was full of warmth and fragrance. Longstemmed roses filled the vases on the chimney piece, in which a fire sparkled with that effect of luxury which fires produce when the weather is not cold enough to justify them. On the writing table, among notes and cards, and signed photographs of celebrities, Mrs. Newell's gold inkstand, her jeweled pen holder, her heavily monogrammed dispatch box, gave back from their expensive surfaces the glint of the flame, which sought out and magnified the orient of the pearls among the lady's laces and found a mirror in the pink polish of her fingertips. It was just such a scene as a little September fire, lit for show and not for warmth, would delight to dwell on and pick out in all its opulent details; and even Garnett, inured to Mrs. Newell's capacity for extracting manna from the desert, reflected that she must have found new fields to glean.

'It's about Hermy,' she repeated, making room for him at her side, 'I had to see you at once. We came over yesterday from London.'

Garnett, seating himself, continued his leisurely survey of the room. In the blaze of Mrs. Newell's refulgence Hermione, as usual, faded out of sight, and he hardly noticed her mother's allusion.

'I've never seen you more resplendent,' he remarked.

She received the tribute with complacency. 'The rooms are not bad, are they? We came over with the Woolsey Hubbards (you've heard of them, of course? – they're from Detroit), and really they do things very decently. Their motor met us at Boulogne, and the courier always wires ahead to have the rooms filled with flowers. This salon is really a part of their suite, I simply couldn't have afforded it myself.'

She delivered these facts in a high decisive voice, which had a note like the clink of her many bracelets and the rattle of her ringed hands against the enameled cigarette case that she held out to Garnett after helping herself from its contents.

'You are always meeting such charming people,' said the young man with mild irony; and, reverting to her first remark, he bethought himself to add: 'I hope Miss Hermione is not ill?'

'Ill? She was never ill in her life,' exclaimed Mrs. Newell, as though her daughter had been accused of an indelicacy.

'It was only that you said you had come over on her account.'

'So I have. Hermione is to be married.'

Mrs. Newell brought out the words impressively, drawing back to observe their effect on her visitor. It was such that he received them with a long silent stare, which finally passed into a cry of wonder. 'Married? For heaven's sake, to whom?'

Mrs. Newell continued to regard him with a smile so serene and victorious that he saw she took his somewhat unseemly astonishment as a merited tribute to her genius. Presently she extended a glittering hand and took a sheet of notepaper from the blotter.

'You can have that put in tomorrow's *Herald*, she said.

Garnett, receiving the paper, read in Hermione's own finished hand: 'A marriage has been arranged, and will shortly take place, between the Comte Louis du Trayas, son of the Marquis du Trayas de la Baume, and Miss Hermione Newell, daughter of Samuel C. Newell, Esq., of Elmira, N. Y. Comte Louis du Trayas belongs to one of the oldest and most distinguished families in France, and is equally well connected in England, being the nephew of Lord Saint Priscoe and a cousin of the Countess of Morningfield, whom he frequently visits at Adham and Portlow.'

The perusal of this document filled Garnett with such deepening wonder that he could not, for the moment, even do justice to the strangeness of its being written out for publication in the bride's own hand. Hermione a bride! Hermione a future countess! Hermione on the brink of a marriage which would give her not only a great 'situation' in the Parisian world but a footing in some of the best houses in England! Regardless of its unflattering implications, Garnett prolonged his stare of amazement till Mrs. Newell somewhat sharply exclaimed – 'Well, didn't I always tell you she'd marry a Frenchman?'

Garnett, in spite of himself, smiled at this revised version of his hostess's frequent assertion that Hermione was too goody-goody to take in England, but that with her little dowdy air she might very well 'go off' in the Faubourg if only a *dot* could be raked up – and the recollection flashed a new light on the versatility of Mrs. Newell's genius.

'But how did you do it – ?' was on the tip of his tongue; and he had barely time to give the query the more conventional turn of: 'How did it happen?'

'Oh, we were up at Glaish with the Edmund Fitzarthurs. Lady Edmund is a sort of cousin of the Morningfields', who have a shooting lodge near Glaish – a place called Portlow – and young Trayas was there with them. Lady Edmund, who is a dear, drove Hermy over to Portlow, and the thing was done in no time. He simply fell over head and ears in love with her. You know Hermy is really very handsome

in her peculiar way. I don't think you've ever appreciated her,' Mrs.
Newell summed up with a note of reproach.

'I've appreciated her, I assure you; but one somehow didn't think
of her marrying – so soon.'

'Soon? She's three and twenty; but you've no imagination,' said
Mrs. Newell; and Garnett inwardly admitted that he had not enough
to soar to the heights of her invention. For the marriage, of course,
was her invention, a superlative stroke of business in which he was
sure the principal parties had all been passive agents in which everyone,
from the bankrupt and disreputable Fitzarthurs to the rich and immaculate Morningfields, had by some mysterious sleight of hand been made
to fit into Mrs. Newell's designs. But it was not enough for Garnett
to marvel at her work – he wanted to understand it, to take it apart,
to find out how the trick had been done. It was true that Mrs. Newell
had always said Hermy might go off in the Faubourg if she had a *dot*
– but even Mrs. Newell's juggling could hardly conjure up a *dot:* such
feats as she was able to perform in this line were usually made to
serve her own urgent necessities. And besides, who was likely to take
sufficient interest in Hermione to supply her with the means of
marrying a French nobleman? The flowers ordered in advance by the
Woolsey Hubbards' courier made Garnett wonder if that accomplished
functionary had also wired over to have Miss Newell's settlements
drawn up. But of all the comments hovering on his lips the only one
he could decently formulate was the remark that he supposed Mrs.
Newell and her daughter had come over to see the young man's family
and make the final arrangements.

'Oh, they're made – everything's settled,' said Mrs. Newell, looking
him squarely in the eye. 'You're wondering, of course, about the *dot* –
Frenchmen never go off their heads to the extent of forgetting *that;* or
at least their parents don't allow them to.'

Garnett murmured a vague assent, and she went on without the
least appearance of resenting his curiosity: 'It all came about so fortunately. Only fancy, just the week they met I got a little legacy from
an aunt in Elmira – a good soul I hadn't seen or heard of for years. I
suppose I ought to have put on mourning for her, by the way, but it
would have eaten up a good bit of the legacy, and I really needed it all
for poor Hermy. Oh, it's not a fortune, you understand – but the
young man is madly in love, and has always had his own way, so
after a lot of correspondence it's been arranged. They saw Hermy this
morning, and they're enchanted.'

'And the marriage takes place very soon?'

'Yes, in a few weeks, here. His mother is an invalid and couldn't
have gone to England. Besides, the French don't travel. And as Hermy
has become a Catholic – '

'Already?'

Mrs. Newell stared. 'It doesn't take long. And it suits Hermy exactly – she can go to church so much oftener. So I thought,' Mrs. Newell concluded with dignity, 'that a wedding at Saint Philippe du Roule would be the most suitable thing at this season.'

'Dear me,' said Garnett, 'I am left breathless – I can't catch up with you. I suppose even the day is fixed, though Miss Hermione doesn't mention it,' and he indicated the official announcement in his hand.

Mrs. Newell laughed. 'Hermy had to write that herself, poor dear, because my scrawl's too hideous – but I dictated it. No, the day's not fixed – that's why I sent for you.' There was a splendid directness about Mrs. Newell. It would never have occurred to her to pretend to Garnett that she had summoned him for the pleasure of his company.

'You've sent for me – to fix the day?' he inquired humorously.

'To remove the last obstacle to its being fixed.'

'I? What kind of an obstacle could I have the least effect on?'

Mrs. Newell met his banter with a look which quelled it. 'I want you to find her father.'

'Her father? Miss Hermione's – ?'

'My husband, of course. I suppose you know he's living.'

Garnett blushed at his own clumsiness. 'I – yes – that is, I really knew nothing – ' he stammered, feeling that each word added to it. If Hermione was unnoticeable, Mr. Newell had always been invisible. The young man had never so much as given him a thought, and it was awkward to come on him so suddenly at a turn of the talk.

'Well, he is – living here in Paris,' said Mrs. Newell, with a note of asperity which seemed to imply that her friend might have taken the trouble to post himself on this point.

'In Paris? But in that case isn't it quite simple – ?'

'To find him? I dare say it won't be difficult, though he's rather mysterious. But the point is that I can't go to him – and that if I write to him he won't answer.'

'Ah,' said Garnett thoughtfully.

'And so you've got to find him for me, and tell him.'

'Tell him what?'

'That he must come to the wedding – that we must show ourselves together at church and afterward in the sacristy.'

She delivered the behest in her sharp imperative key, the tone of the born commander. But for once Garnett ventured to question her orders.

'And supposing he won't come?'

'He must if he cares for his daughter's happiness. She can't be married without him.'

'Can't be married?'

'The French are like that – especially the old families. I was given to understand at once that my husband must appear – if only to establish the fact that we're not divorced.'

'Ah – you're *not*, then?' escaped from Garnett.

'Mercy no! Divorce is stupid. They don't like it in Europe. And in this case it would have been the end of Hermy's marriage. They wouldn't think of letting their son marry the child of divorced parents.'

'How fortunate, then – '

'Yes: but I always think of such things beforehand. And of course I've told them that my husband will be present.'

'You think he will consent?'

'No; not at first; but you must make him. You must tell him how sweet Hermione is – and you must see Louis, and be able to describe their happiness. You must dine here tonight – he's coming. We're all dining with the Hubbards, and they expect you. They've given Hermy some very good diamonds – though I should have preferred a check, as she'll be horribly poor. But I think Kate Hubbard means to do something about the trousseau – Hermy is at Paquin's with her now. You've no idea how delightful all our friends have been. Ah, here is one of them now,' she broke off smiling, as the door opening to admit, without preliminary announcement, a gentleman so glossy and ancient, with such a fixed unnatural freshness of smile and eye, that he gave Garnett the effect of having been embalmed and then enameled. It needed not the exotic-looking ribbon in the visitor's buttonhole, nor Mr. Newell's introduction of him as her friend Baron Schenkelderff, to assure Garnett of his connection with a race as ancient as his appearance.

Baron Schenkelderff greeted his hostess with paternal playfulness, and the young man with an ease which might have been acquired on the Stock Exchange and in the dressing rooms of 'leading ladies.' He spoke a faultless colorless English, from which one felt he might pass with equal mastery to half a dozen other languages. He inquired patronizingly for the excellent Hubbards, asked his hostess if she did not mean to give him a drop of tea and a cigarette, remarked that he need not ask if Hermione was still closeted with the dressmaker, and, on the waiter's coming in answer to his ring, ordered the tea himself, and added a request for *fine champagne*. It was not the first time that Garnett had seen such minor liberties taken in Mrs. Newell's drawing room, but they had hitherto been taken by persons who had at least the superiority of knowing what they were permitting themselves, whereas the young man felt almost sure that Baron Schenkelderff's manner was the most distinguished he could achieve; and this deepened the disgust with which, as the minutes passed, he yielded to the conviction that the Baron was Mrs. Newell's 'aunt'.

• IV •

GARNETT had always foreseen that Mrs. Newell might someday ask him to do something he should greatly dislike. He had never gone so far as to conjecture what it might be, but had simply felt that if he allowed his acquaintance with her to pass from spectatorship to participation he must be prepared to find himself, at any moment, in a queer situation.

The moment had come; and he was relieved to find that he could meet it by refusing her request. He had not always been sure that she would leave him this alternative. She had a way of involving people in her complications without their being aware of it; and Garnett had pictured himself in holes so tight that there might not be room for a wriggle. Happily in this case he could still move freely. Nothing compelled him to act as an intermediary between Mrs. Newell and her husband, and it was preposterous to suppose that, even in a life of such perpetual upheaval as hers, there were no roots which struck deeper than her casual intimacy with himself. She had simply laid hands on him because he happened to be within reach, and he would put himself out of reach by leaving for London on the morrow.

Having thus inwardly asserted his independence, he felt free to let his fancy dwell on the strangeness of the situation. He had always supposed that Mrs. Newell, in her flight through life, must have thrown a good many victims to the wolves, and had assumed that Mr. Newell had been among the number. That he had been dropped overboard at an early stage in the lady's career seemed probable from the fact that neither his wife nor his daughter ever mentioned him. Mrs. Newell was incapable of reticence, and if her husband had still been an active element in her life he would certainly have figured in her conversation. Garnett, if he thought of the matter at all, had concluded that divorce must long since have elminated Mr. Newell; but he now saw how he had underrated his friend's faculty for using up the waste material of life. She had always struck him as the most extravagant of women, yet it turned out that by a miracle of thrift she had for years kept a superfluous husband on the chance that he might someday be useful. The day had come, and Mr. Newell was to be called from his obscurity. Garnett wondered what had become of him in the interval, and in what shape he would respond to the evocation. The fact that his wife feared he might not respond to it at all seemed to show that his exile was voluntary, or had at least come to appear preferable to other alternatives; but if that were the case it was curious he should not have taken legal means to free himself. He could hardly have had his wife's motives for wishing to maintain the vague tie between them; but conjecture lost itself in trying to picture what his point of view was likely to be, and Garnett, on his way to the Hubbards' dinner that evening, could not help regretting that circumstances denied him the opportunity of meeting so enigmatic a person. The young man's knowledge of Mrs. Newell's methods made him feel that her husband might be an interesting study. This, however, did not affect his resolve to keep clear of the business. He entered the Hubbards' dining room with the firm intention of refusing to execute Mrs. Newell's commission, and if he changed his mind in the course of the evening it was not owing to that lady's persuasions.

Garnett's curiosity as to the Hubbards' share in Hermione's marriage was appeased before he had been five minutes at their table.

Mrs. Woolsey Hubbard was an expansive blonde, whose ample but disciplined outline seemed the result of a well-matched struggle between her cook and her corset maker. She talked a great deal of what was appropriate in dress and conduct, and seemed to regard Mrs. Newell as a final arbiter on both points. To do or to wear anything inappropriate would have been extremely mortifying to Mrs. Hubbard, and she was evidently resolved, at the price of eternal vigilance, to prove her familiarity with what she frequently referred to as 'the right thing.' Mr. Hubbard appeared to have no such preoccupations. Garnett, if called on to describe him, would have done so by saying that he was the American who always pays. The young man, in the course of his foreign wanderings, had come across many fellow citizens of Mr. Hubbard's type in the most diverse company and surroundings; and wherever they were to be found, they always had their hands in their pockets. Mr. Hubbard's standard of gentility was the extent of a man's capacity to 'foot the bill'; and as no one but an occasional compatriot cared to dispute the privilege with him he seldom had reason to doubt his social superiority.

Garnett, nevertheless, did not believe that this lavish pair were, as Mrs. Newell would have phrased it, 'putting up' Hermione's *dot*. They would go very far in diamonds but they would hang back from securities. Their readiness to pay was indefinably mingled with a dread of being expected to, and their prodigalities would take flight at the first hint of coercion. Mrs. Newell, who had had a good deal of experience in managing this type of millionaire, could be trusted not to arouse their susceptibilities, and Garnett was therefore certain that the chimerical legacy had been extracted from other pockets. There were none in view but those of Baron Schenkelderff, who, seated at Mrs. Hubbard's right, with a new order in his buttonhole, and a fresh glaze upon his features, enchanted that lady by his careless references to crowned heads and his condescending approval of the champagne. Garnett was more than ever certain that it was the Baron who was paying; and it was this conviction which made him suddenly resolve that, at any cost, Hermione's marriage must take place. He had felt no special interest in the marriage except as one more proof of Mrs. Newell's extraordinary capacity; but now it appealed to him from the girl's own standpoint. For he saw, with a touch of compunction, that in the mephitic air of her surroundings a love story of miraculous freshness had flowered. He had only to intercept the glances which the young couple exchanged to find himself transported to the candid region of romance. It was evident that Hermione adored and was adored; that the lovers believed in each other and in everyone about them, and that even the legacy of the defunct aunt had not been too great a strain on their faith in human nature.

His first glance at the Comte Louis du Trayas showed Garnett that, by some marvel of fitness, Hermione had happened on a kindred nature. If the young man's long mild features and shortsighted glance revealed no special force of character, they showed a benevolence and simplicity as incorruptible as her own, and declared that their possessor, whatever his failings, would never imperil the illusions she had so wondrously preserved. The fact that the girl took her good fortune naturally, and did not regard herself as suddenly snatched from the jaws of death, added poignancy to the situation; for if she missed this way of escape, and was thrown back on her former life, the day of discovery could not be long deferred. It made Garnett shiver to think of her growing old between her mother and Schenkelderff, or such successors of the Baron's as might probably attend on Mrs. Newell's waning fortunes; for it was clear to him that the Baron marked the first stage in his friend's decline. When Garnett took leave that evening he had promised Mrs. Newell that he would try to find her husband.

• V •

IF Mr. Newell read in the papers the announcement of his daughter's marriage it did not cause him to lift the veil of seclusion in which his wife represented him as shrouded.

A round of the American banks in Paris failed to give Garnett his address, and it was only in chance talk with one of the young secretaries of the Embassy that he was put on Mr. Newell's track. The secretary's father, it appeared, had known the Newells some twenty years earlier. He had had business relations with Mr. Newell, who was then a man of property, with factories or something of the kind, the narrator thought, somewhere in western New York. There had been at this period, for Mrs. Newell, a phase of large hospitality and showy carriages in Washington and at Narragansett. Then her husband had had reverses, had lost heavily in Wall Street, and had finally drifted abroad and disappeared from sight. The young man did not know at what point in his financial decline Mr. Newell had parted company with his wife and daughter; 'though you may bet your hat,' he philosophically concluded, 'that the old girl hung on as long as there were any pickings.' He did not himself know Mr. Newell's address, but opined that it might be extracted from a certain official of the Consulate, if Garnett could give a sufficiently good reason for the request; and here in fact Mrs. Newell's emissary learned that her husband was to be found in an obscure street of the Luxembourg quarter.

In order to be near the scene of action, Garnett went to breakfast at his usual haunt, determined to dispatch his business as early in the day as politeness allowed. The headwaiter welcomed him to a table near that of the transatlantic sage, who sat in his customary corner, his head tilted back against the blistered mirror at an angle suggesting that in a freer civilization his feet would have sought the same level. He greeted Garnett affably and the two exchanged their usual generalizations on life till the sage rose to go; whereupon it occurred to Garnett to accompany him. His friend took the offer in good part, merely remarking that he was going to the Luxembourg Gardens, where it was his invariable habit, on good days, to feed the sparrows with the remains of his breakfast roll; and Garnett replied that, as it happened, his own business lay in the same direction.

'Perhaps, by the way,' he added, 'you can tell me how to find the rue Panonceaux, where I must go presently. I thought I knew this quarter fairly well, but I have never heard of it.'

His companion came to a halt on the narrow pavement, to the confusion of the dense and desultory traffic which flows through the old streets of the Latin quarter. He fixed his mild eye on Garnett and gave a twist to the cigar which lingered in the corner of his mouth.

'The rue Panonceaux? It *is* an out-of-the-way hole, but I can tell you how to find it,' he answered.

He made no motion to do so, however, but continued to bend on the young man the full force of his interrogative gaze; then he added: 'Would you mind telling me your object in going there?'

Garnett looked at him with surprise: a question so unblushingly personal was strangely out of keeping with his friend's usual attitude of detachment. Before he could reply, however, the other had continued: 'Do you happen to be in search of Samuel C. Newell?'

'Why, yes, I am,' said Garnett with a start of conjecture.

His companion uttered a sigh. 'I supposed so,' he said resignedly; 'and in that case,' he added, 'we may as well have the matter out in the Luxembourg.'

Garnett had halted before him with deepening astonishment. 'But you don't mean to tell me – ?' he stammered.

The little man made a motion of assent. 'I am Samuel C. Newell,' he said; 'and if you have no objection, I prefer not to break through my habit of feeding the sparrows. We are five minutes late as it is.'

He quickened his pace without awaiting a reply from Garnett, who walked beside him in unsubdued wonder till they reached the

Luxembourg Gardens, where Mr. Newell, making for one of the less frequented alleys, seated himself on a bench and drew the fragment of a roll from his pocket. His coming was evidently expected, for a shower of little dusky bodies at once descended on him, and the gravel fluttered with battling beaks and wings as he distributed his dole.

It was not till the ground was white with crumbs, and the first frenzy of his pensioners appeased, that he turned to Garnett and said: 'I presume, sir, that you come from my wife.'

Garnett colored with embarrassment: the more simply the old man took his mission the more complicated it appeared to himself.

'From your wife – and from Miss Newell,' he said at length. 'You have perhaps heard that your daughter is to be married.'

'Oh, yes – I read the *Herald* pretty faithfully,' said Miss Newell's parent, shaking out another handful of crumbs.

Garnett cleared his throat. 'Then you have no doubt thought it natural that, under the circumstances, they should wish to communicate with you.'

The sage continued to fix his attention on the sparrows. 'My wife,' he remarked, 'might have written to me.'

'Mrs. Newell was afraid she might not hear from you in reply.'

'In reply? Why should she? I suppose she merely wishes to announce the marriage. She knows I have no money left to buy wedding presents,' said Mr. Newell astonishingly.

Garnett felt his color deepen: he had a vague sense of standing as the representative of something guilty and enormous, with which he had rashly identified himself.

'I don't think you understand,' he said. 'Mrs. Newell and your daughter have asked me to see you because they're anxious that you should consent to appear at the wedding.'

Mr. Newell, at this, ceased to give his attention to the birds, and turned a compassionate gaze on Garnett.

'My dear sir – I don't know your name – ' he remarked, 'would you mind telling me how long you've been acquainted with Mrs. Newell?' And without waiting for an answer he added: 'If you wait long enough she will ask you to do some very disagreeable things for her.'

This echo of his own thoughts gave Garnett a twinge of discomfort, but he made shift to answer good-humoredly: 'If you refer to my present errand, I must tell you that I don't find it disagreeable to do anything which may be of service to Miss Hermione.'

Mr. Newell fumbled in his pocket, as though searching unavailingly for another morsel of bread; then he said: 'From her point of view I shall not be the most important person at the ceremony.'

Garnett smiled. 'That is hardly a reason – ' he began; but he was checked by the brevity of tone with which his companion replied: 'I am not aware that I am called upon to give you my reasons.'

'You are certainly not,' the young man rejoined, 'except in so far as you are willing to consider me as the messenger of your wife and daughter.'

'Oh, I accept your credentials,' said the other with his dry smile; 'What I don't recognize is their right to send a message.'

This reduced Garnett to silence, and after a moment's pause, Mr. Newell drew his watch from his pocket.

'I am sorry to cut the conversation short, but my days are mapped out with a certain regularity, and this is the hour for my nap.' He rose as he spoke and held out his hand with a glint of melancholy humor in his small clear eyes.

'You dismiss me, then? I am to take back a refusal?' the young man exclaimed.

'My dear sir, those ladies have got on very well without me for a number of years: I imagine they can put through this wedding without my help.'

'You're mistaken, then; if it were not for that I shouldn't have undertaken this errand.'

Mr. Newell paused as he was turning away. 'Not for what?' he inquired.

'The fact that, as it happens, the wedding can't be put through without your help.'

Mr. Newell's thin lips formed a noiseless whistle. 'They've got to have my consent, have they? Well, is he a good young man?'

'The bridegroom?' Garnett echoed in surprise. 'I hear the best accounts of him – and Miss Newell is very much in love.'

Her parent met this with an odd smile. 'Well, then, I give my consent – it's all I've got left to give,' he added philosophically.

Garnett hesitated. 'But if you consent – if you approve – why do you refuse your daughter's request?'

Mr. Newell looked at him a moment. 'Ask Mrs. Newell!' he said. And as Garnett was again silent, he turned away with a slight gesture of leave-taking.

But in an instant the young man was at his side. 'I will not ask your reasons, sir,' he said, 'but I will give you mine for being here. Miss Newell cannot be married unless you are present at the ceremony. The young man's parents know that she has a father living, and they give their consent only on condition that he appears at her marriage. I believe it is customary in old French families – '

'Old French families be damned!' said Mr. Newell, 'She had better marry an American.' And he made a more decided motion to free himself from Garnett's importunities.

But his resistance only strengthened the young man's. The more unpleasant the latter's task became, the more unwilling he grew to see his efforts end in failure. During the three days which had been consumed in his quest it had become clear to him that the bridgroom's parents, having been surprised to a reluctant consent, were but too ready to withdraw it on the plea of Mr. Newell's nonappearance. Mrs. Newell, on the last edge of tension, had confided to Garnett that the Morningfields were 'being nasty'; and he could picture the whole powerful clan, on both sides of the Channel, arrayed in a common resolve to exclude poor Hermione from their ranks. The very inequality of the contest stirred in his blood, and made him vow that in this case, at least, the sins of the parents should not be visited on the children. In his talk with the young secretary he had obtained certain glimpses of Baron Schenkelderff's past that fortified this resolve. The Baron, at one time a familiar figure in a much-observed London set, had been mixed up in an ugly money-lending business ending in suicide, which had excluded him from the society most accessible to his race. His alliance with Mrs. Newell was doubtless a desperate attempt at rehabilitation, a forlorn hope on both sides, but likely to be an enduring tie because it represented, to both partners, their last chance of escape from social extinction. That Hermione's marriage was a mere stake in their game did not in the least affect Garnett's view of its urgency. If on their part it was a sordid speculation, to her it had the freshness of the first wooing. If it made of her a mere pawn in their hands, it would put her, so Garnett hoped, beyond further risk of such base uses; and to achieve this had become a necessity to him.

The sense that, if he lost sight of Mr. Newell, the latter might not easily be found again, nerved Garnett to hold his ground in spite of the resistance he encountered; and he tried to put the full force of his plea into the tone with which he cried: 'Ah, you don't know your daughter!'

• VI •

MRS. NEWELL, that afternoon, met him on the threshold of her sitting room with a 'Well?' of pent-up anxiety.

In the room itself, Baron Schenkelderff sat with crossed legs and head thrown back, in an attitude which he did not see fit to alter at the young man's approach.

Garnett hesitated; but it was not the summariness of the Baron's greeting which he resented.

'You've found him?' Mrs. Newell exclaimed.

'Yes; but – '

She followed his glance and answered it with a slight shrug. 'I can't take you into my room, because there's a dressmaker there, and she won't go because she's waiting to be paid. Schenkelderff,' she exclaimed, 'you're not wanted; please go and look out of the window.'

The Baron rose, and, lighting a cigarette, laughingly retired to the embrasure. Mrs. Newell flung herself down and signed to Garnett to take a seat by her side.

'Well – you've found him? You've talked with him?'

'Yes; I've talked with him – for an hour.'

She made an impatient movement. 'That's too long! Does he refuse?'

'He doesn't consent.'

'Then you mean – ?'

'He wants time to think it over.'

'Time? There *is* no time – did you tell him so?'

'I told him so; but you must remember that he has plenty. He has taken twenty-four hours.'

Mrs. Newell groaned. 'Oh, that's too much. When he thinks things over he always refuses.'

'Well, he would have refused at once if I had not agreed to the delay.'

She rose nervously from her seat and pressed her hands to her forehead. 'It's too hard, after all I've done! The trousseau is ordered – think how disgraceful! You must have managed him badly; I'll go and see him myself.'

The Baron, at this, turned abruptly from his study of the Place Vendome.

'My dear creature, for heaven's sake don't spoil everything!' he exclaimed.

Mrs. Newell colored furiously. 'What's the meaning of that brilliant speech?'

'I was merely putting myself in the place of a man on whom you have ceased to smile.'

He picked up his hat and stick, nodded knowingly to Garnett, and walked towards the door with an air of creaking jauntiness.

But on the threshold Mrs. Newell waylaid him.

'Don't go – I must speak to you,' she said, following him into the antechamber; and Garnett remembered the dressmaker who was not to be dislodged from her bedroom.

In a moment Mrs. Newell returned, with a small flat packet which she vainly sought to dissemble in an inaccessible pocket.

'He makes everything too odious!' she exclaimed; but whether she referred to her husband or the Baron it was left to Garnett to decide.

She sat silent, nervously twisting her cigarette case between her fingers, while her visitor rehearsed the details of his conversaiton with Mr. Newell. He did not indeed tell her the arguments he had used to shake her husband's resolve, since in his eloquent sketch of Hermione's situation there had perforce entered hints unflattering to her mother;

but he gave the impression that his hearer had in the end been moved, and for that reason had consented to defer his refusal.

'Ah, it's not that – it's to prolong our misery!' Mrs. Newell exclaimed; and after a moment she added drearily: 'He's been waiting for such an opportunity for years.'

It seemed needless for Garnett to protract his visit, and he took leave with the promise to report at once the result of his final talk with Mr. Newell. But as he was passing through the antechamber a side door opened and Hermione stood before him. Her face was flushed and shaken out of its usual repose, and he saw at once that she had been waiting for him.

'Mr. Garnett!' she said in a whisper.

He paused, considering her with surprise: he had never supposed her capable of such emotion as her voice and eyes revealed.

'I want to speak to you; we are quite safe here. Mamma is with the dressmaker,' she explained, closing the door behind her, while Garnett laid aside his hat and stick.

'I am at your service,' he said.

'You have seen my father? Mamma told me that you were to see him today,' the girl went on, standing close to him in order that she might not have to raise her voice.

'Yes; I've seen him,' Garnett replied with increasing wonder. Hermione had never before mentioned her father to him, and it was by a slight stretch of veracity that he had included her name in her mother's plea to Mr. Newell. He had supposed her to be either unconscious of the transaction, or else too much engrossed in her own happiness to give it a thought; and he had forgiven her the last alternative in consideration of the abnormal character of her filial relations. But he now saw that he must readjust his view of her.

'You went to ask him to come to the wedding: I know about it,' Hermione continued. 'Of course it's the custom – people will think it odd if he does not come.' She paused, and then asked: 'Does he consent?'

'No; he has not yet consented.'

'Ah, I thought so when I saw Mamma just now!'

'But he hasn't quite refused – he has promised to think it over.'

'But he hated it – he hated the idea?'

Garnett hesitated. 'It seemed to arouse painful associations.'

'Ah, it would – it would!' she exclaimed.

He was astonished at the passion of her accent; astonished still more at the tone with which she went on, laying her hand on his arm: 'Mr. Garnett, he must not be asked – he has been asked too often to do things that he hated!'

Garnett looked at the girl with a shock of awe. What abysses of knowledge did her purity hide?'

'But, my dear Miss Hermione – ' he began.

'I know what you are going to say,' she interrupted him. 'It is necessary that he should be present at the marriage, or the du Trayas will break it off. They don't want it very much, at any rate,' she added with a strange candor, 'and they'll not be sorry, perhaps – for of course Louis would have to obey them.'

'So I explained to your father,' Garnett assured her.

'Yes – yes; I knew you would put it to him. But that makes no difference. He must not be forced to come unwillingly.'

'But if he sees the point – after all, no one can force him!'

'No; but if it's painful to him – if it reminds him too much. . . . Oh, Mr. Garnett, I was not a child when he left us. . . . I was old enough to see . . . to see how it must hurt him even now to be reminded. Peace was all he asked for, and I want him to be left in peace!'

Garnett paused in deep embarrassment. 'My dear child, there is no need to remind you that your own future – '

She had a gesture that recalled her mother. 'My future must take care of itself; he must not be made to see us!' she said imperatively. And as Garnett remained silent she went on: 'I have always hoped he didn't hate me, but he would hate me now if he were forced to see me.'

'Not if he could see you at this moment!'

She lifted her face with swimming eyes.

'Well, go to him, then; tell him what I've said to you!'

Garnett continued to stand before her, deeply struck. 'It might be the best thing,' he reflected inwardly; but he did not give utterance to the thought. He merely put out his hand, holding Hermione's in a long pressure.

'I will do whatever you wish,' he replied.

'You understand that I'm in earnest?' she urged.

'I'm quite sure of it.'

'Then I want you to repeat to him what I've said – I want him to be left undisturbed. I don't want him ever to hear of us again!'

The next day, at the appointed hour, Garnett resorted to the Luxembourg Gardens, which Mr. Newell had named as a meeting place in preference to his own lodgings. It was clear he did not wish to admit the young man any farther into his privacy than the occasion required, and the extreme shabbiness of his dress hinted that pride might be the cause of his reluctance.

Garnett found him feeding the sparrows, but he desisted at the young man's approach, and said at once: 'You won't thank me for bringing you all this distance.'

'If that means that you're going to send me away with a refusal, I have come to spare you the necessity,' Garnett answered.

Mr. Newell turned on him a glance of undisguised wonder, in which a tinge of disappointment might almost have been detected.

'Ah – they've got no use for me, after all?' he said ironically.

Garnett, in reply, related without comment his conversation with Hermione, and the message with which she had charged him. He remembered her words exactly and repeated them without modification, heedless of what they implied or revealed.

Mr. Newell listened with an immovable face, occasionally casting a crumb to his flock. When Garnett ended he asked: 'Does her mother know of this?'

'Assuredly not!' cried Garnett with a movement of disgust.

'You must pardon me; but Mrs. Newell is a very ingenious woman.' Mr. Newell shook out his remaining crumbs and turned thoughtfully toward Garnett.

'You believe it's quite clear to Hermione that these people will use my refusal as a pretext for backing out of the marriage?'

'Perfectly clear – she told me so herself.'

'Doesn't she consider the young man rather chickenhearted?'

'No; he has already put up a big fight for her, and you know the French look at these things differently. He's only twenty-three, and his marrying against his parents' approval is in itself an act of heroism.'

'Yes; I believe they look at it that way,' Mr. Newell assented. He rose and picked up the half-smoked cigar which he had laid on the bench beside him.

'What do they wear at these French weddings, anyhow? A dress suit, isn't it?' he asked.

The question was such a surprise to Garnett that for the moment he could only stammer out – 'You consent then? I may go and tell her?'

'You may tell my girl – yes.' He gave a vague laugh and added: 'One way or another, my wife always get what she wants.'

• VII •

MR. NEWELL's consent brought with it no accompanying concessions. In the first flush of success Garnett had pictured himself as bringing together the father and daughter, and hovering in an attitude of benediction over a family group in which Mrs. Newell did not very distinctly figure.

But Mr. Newell's conditions were inflexible. He would 'see the thing through' for his daughter's sake; but he stipulated that in the meantime there should be no meetings or further communications of any kind. He agreed to be ready when Garnett called for him, at the appointed hour on the wedding day; but until then he begged to be left alone. To this decision he adhered immovably, and when Garnett conveyed it to Hermione she accepted it with a deep look of understanding. As for Mrs. Newell she was too much engrossed in the nuptial preparations to give her husband another thought. She had gained her point, she had disarmed her foes, and in the first flush of success she had no time to remember by what means her victory had been won. Even Garnett's services received little recognition, unless he found them sufficiently compensated by the new look in Hermione's eyes.

The principal figures in Mrs. Newell's foreground were the Woolsey Hubbards and Baron Schenkelderff. With these she was in hourly consultation, and Mrs. Hubbard went about aureoled with the importance of her close connection with an 'aristocratic marriage,' and dazzled by the Baron's familiarity with the intricacies of the Almanach de Gotha. In his society and Mrs. Newell's, Mrs. Hubbard evidently felt that she had penetrated to the sacred precincts where 'the right thing' flourished in its native soil. As for Hermione, her look of happiness had returned, but with an undertint of melancholy, visible perhaps only to Garnett, but to him always hauntingly present. Outwardly she sank back into her passive self, resigned to serve as the brilliant lay figure on which Mrs. Newell hung the trophies of conquest. Preparations for the wedding were zealously pressed. Mrs. Newell knew the danger of giving people time to think things over, and her fears about her husband being allayed, she began to dread a new attempt at evasion on the part of the bridegroom's family.

'The sooner it's over the sounder I shall sleep!' she declared to Garnett; and all the mitigations of art could not conceal the fact that she was desperately in need of that restorative. There were movements, indeed, when he was sorrier for her than for her husband or her daughter; so black and unfathomable appeared the abyss into which she must slip back if she lost her hold on this last spar of safety.

But she did not lose her hold; his own experience, as well as her husband's declaration, might have told him that she always got what she wanted. How much she had wanted this particular thing was shown by the way in which, on the last day, when all peril was over, she bloomed out in renovated splendor. It gave Garnett a shivering sense of the ugliness of the alternative which had confronted her.

The day came; the showy coupé provided by Mrs. Newell presented itself punctually at Garnett's door, and the young man entered it and drove to the rue Panonceaux. It was a little melancholy back street, with lean old houses sweating rust and damp, and glimpses of pit-like gardens, black and sunless, between walls bristling with iron spikes. On the narrow pavement a blind man pottered along led by a red-eyed poodle: a little farther on a disheveled woman sat grinding coffee on the threshold of a *buvette*. The bridal carriage stopped before one of the doorways, with a clatter of hoofs and harness which drew the neighborhood to its windows, and Garnett started to mount the ill-smelling stairs to the fourth floor, on which he learned from the *concierge* that Mr. Newell lodged. But halfway up he met the latter descending and they turned and went down together.

Hermione's parent wore his usual imperturbable look, and his eye seemed as full as ever of generalizations on human folly; but there was something oddly shrunken and submerged in his appearance, as though he had grown smaller or his clothes larger. And on the last hypothesis Garnett paused – for it became evident to him that Mr. Newell had hired his dress suit.

Seated at the young man's side on the satin cushions, he remained silent while the carriage rolled smoothly and rapidly through the network of streets leading to the Boulevard Saint-Germain; only once he remarked, glancing at the elaborate fittings of the coupé: 'Is this Mrs. Newell's carriage?'

'I believe so – yes,' Garnett assented, with the guilty sense that in defining that lady's possessions it was impossible not to trespass on those of her friends.

Mr. Newell made no further comment, but presently requested his companion to rehearse to him once more the exact duties which were to devolve on him during the coming ceremony. Having mastered these he remained silent, fixing a dry speculative eye on the panorama of the brilliant streets, till the carriage drew up at the entrance of Saint Philippe du Roule.

With the same air of composure he followed his guide through the mob of spectators, and up the crimson velvet steps, at the head of which, but for a word from Garnett, a formidable Suisse, glittering with cocked hat and mace, would have checked the advance of the small crumpled figure so oddly out of keeping with the magnificence of the bridal party. The French fashion prescribing that the family *cortège* shall follow the bride to the altar, the vestibule of the church was thronged with the participators in the coming procession; but if Mr. Newell felt any nervousness at his sudden projection into this unfamiliar group, nothing in his look or manner betrayed it. He stood beside Garnett till a white-favored carriage, dashing up to the church with superlative glitter of highly groomed horseflesh, and silver-plated harness, deposited the snowy apparition of the bride, supported by her mother; then, as Hermione entered the vestibule, he went forward quietly to meet her.

The girl wrapped in the haze of her bridal veil, and a little confused, perhaps, by the anticipation of the meeting, paused a moment, as if in doubt, before the small oddly-clad figure which blocked her path – a horrible moment to Garnett, who felt a pang of misery at this satire on the infallibility of the filial instinct. He longed to make some sign, to break in some way the pause of uncertainty; but before he could move he saw Mrs. Newell give her daughter a sharp push, he saw a blush of compunction flood Hermione's face, and the girl, throwing back her veil, bent her tall head and flung her arms about her father.

Mr. Newell emerged unshaken from the embrace: it seemed to have no effect beyond giving an odder twist to his tie. He stood beside his daughter till the church doors were thrown open; then, at a sign from the verger, he gave her his arm, and the strange couple with the long train of fashion and finery behind them, started on their march to the altar.

Garnett had already slipped into the church and secured a post of vantage which gave him a side view over the assemblage. The building was thronged – Mrs. Newell had attained her ambition and given Hermione a smart wedding. Garnett's eye traveled curiously from one group to another – from the numerous representatives of the bride-groom's family, all stamped with the same air of somewhat dowdy distinction, the air of having had their thinking done for them for so long that they could no longer perform the act individually, and the heterogeneous company of Mrs. Newell's friends, who presented, on the opposite side of the nave, every variety of individual conviction in dress and conduct. Of the two groups that latter was decidedly the more interesting to Garnett, who observed that it comprised not only such recent acquisitions as the Woolsey Hubbards and the Baron, but also sundry more important figures which of late had faded to the verge of Mrs. Newell's horizon. Hermione's marriage had drawn them back, had once more made her mother a social entity, had in short already accomplished the object for which it had been planned and executed.

And as he looked about him Garnett saw that all the other actors in the show faded into insignificance beside the dominant figure of Mrs. Newell, became mere marionettes pulled hither and thither by the hidden wires of her intention. One and all they were there to serve her ends and accomplish her purpose: Schenkelderff and the Hubbards to pay for the show, the bride and bridegroom to seal and symbolize her social rehabilitation, Garnett himself as the humble instrument adjusting the different parts of the complicated machinery, and her husband, finally, as the last stake in her game, the last asset on which she could draw to rebuild her fallen fortunes. At the thought Garnett was filled with a deep disgust for what the scene signified, and for his own share in it. He had been her tool and dupe like the others; if he imagined that he was serving Hermione, it was for her mother's ends that he had worked. What right had he to sentimentalize a marriage founded on such base connivances, and how could he have imagined that in so doing he was acting a disinterested part?

While these thoughts were passing through his mind the ceremony had already begun, and the principal personages in the drama were ranged before him in the row of crimson velvet chairs which fills the foreground of a Catholic marriage. Through the glow of lights and the perfumed haze about the altar, Garnett's eyes rested on the central figures of the group, and gradually the others disappeared from his view and his mind. After all, neither Mrs. Newell's schemes nor his own share in them could ever unsanctify Hermione's marriage. It was one more testimony to life's indefatigable renewals, to nature's secret of drawing fragrance from corruption; and as his eyes turned from the girl's illuminated presence to the resigned and stoical figure sunk in the adjoining chair, it occurred to him that he had perhaps worked better than he knew in placing them, if only for a moment, side by side.

The Letters

———❦———

Up the hill from the station at St. Cloud, Lizzie West climbed in the cold spring sunshine. As she breasted the incline, she noticed the first waves of wisteria over courtyard railings and the highlights of new foliage against the walls of ivy-matted gardens; and she thought again, as she had thought a hundred times before, that she had never seen so beautiful a spring.

She was on her way to Deerings' house in a street near the hilltop, and every step was dear and familiar to her. She went there five times a week to teach little Juliet Deering, the daughter of Mr. Vincent Deering, the distinguished American artist. Juliet had been her pupil for two years, and day after day, during that time, Lizzie West had mounted the hill in all weathers; sometimes with her umbrella bent against the rain, sometimes with her frail cotton parasol unfurled beneath a fiery sun, sometimes with the snow soaking through her boots or a bitter wind piercing her thin jacket, sometimes with the dust whirling about her and bleaching the flowers of the poor little hat that *had* to 'carry her through' till next summer

At first the ascent had seemed tedious enough, as dull as the trudge to her other lessons. Lizzie was not a heaven-sent teacher; she had no born zeal for her calling, and though she dealt kindly and dutifully with her pupils, she did not fly to them on winged feet. But one day something had happened to change the face of life, and since then the climb to the Deering house had seemed like a dream flight up a heavenly stairway.

Her heart beat faster as she remembered it – no longer in a tumult of fright and self-reproach, but softly, happily, as if brooding over a possession that none could take from her.

It was on a day of the previous October that she had stopped, after Juliet's lesson, to ask if she might speak to Juliet's papa. One had always to apply to Mr. Deering if there was anything to be said about the lessons. Mrs. Deering lay on her lounge upstairs, reading relays of dog-eared novels, the choice of which she left to the cook and the nurse, who were always fetching them for her from the *cabinet de lecture*; and

90

it was understood in the house that she was not to be 'bothered' about Juliet. Mr. Deering's interest in his daughter was fitful rather than consecutive; but at least he was approachable, and listened sympathetically, if a little absently, stroking his long fair mustache, while Lizzie stated her difficulty or put in her plea for maps or copybooks.

'Yes, yes – of course – whatever you think right,' he would always assent, sometimes drawing a five-franc piece from his pocket, and laying it carelessly on the table, or oftener saying, with his charming smile: 'Get what you please, and just put it on your account, you know.'

But this time Lizzie had not come to ask for maps or copybooks, or even to hint, in crimson misery – as once, poor soul, she had had to do – that Mr. Deering had overlooked her last little account – had probably not noticed that she had left it, some two months earlier, on a corner of his littered writing table. That hour had been bad enough, though he had done his best to carry it off gallantly and gaily; but this was infinitely worse. For she had come to complain of her pupil; to say that, much as she loved little Juliet, it was useless, unless Mr. Deering could 'do something,' to go on with the lessons.

'It wouldn't be honest – I should be robbing you; I'm not sure that I haven't already,' she half laughed, through mounting tears, as she put her case. Little Juliet would not work, would not obey. Her poor little drifting existence floated aimlessly between the kitchen and the *lingerie*, and all the groping tendrils of her curiosity were fastened about the life of the backstairs.

It was the same kind of curiosity that Mrs. Deering, overheard in her drug-scented room, lavished on her dog-eared novels and on the 'society notes' of the morning paper; but since Juliet's horizon was not yet wide enough to embrace these loftier objects, her interest was centered in the anecdotes that Céleste and Suzanne brought back from the market and the library. That these were not always of an edifying nature the child's artless prattle too often betrayed; but unhappily they occupied her fancy to the complete exclusion of such nourishing items as dates and dynasties, and the sources of the principal European rivers.

At length the crisis became so acute that poor Lizzie felt herself bound to resign her charge or ask Mr. Deering's intervention; and for Juliet's sake she chose the harder alternative. It *was* hard to speak to him not only because one hated to confess one's failure, and hated still more to ascribe it to such vulgar causes, but because one blushed to bring them to the notice of a spirit engaged with higher things. Mr. Deering was very busy at that moment: he had a new picture 'on.' And Lizzie entered the studio with a flutter of one profanely intruding on some sacred rite; she almost heard the rustle of retreating wings as she approached.

And then – and then – how differently it had all turned out! Perhaps

it wouldn't have, if she hadn't been such a goose – she who so seldom
cried, so prided herself on a stoic control of her little twittering cageful
of 'feelings.' But if she had cried, it was because he had looked at her
so kindly, and because she had nevertheless felt him so pained and
shamed by what she said. The pain, of course, lay for both in the
implication behind her words – in the one word she left unspoken. If
little Juliet was as she was, it was because of the mother upstairs – the
mother who had given the child her frivolous impulses, and grudged
her the care that might have corrected them. The case so obviously
revolved in its own vicious circle that when Mr. Deering had
murmured, 'Of course if my wife were not an invalid,' they both
turned with a spring to the flagrant 'bad example' of Céleste and
Suzanne, fastening on that with a mutual insistence that ended in his
crying out: 'All the more, then, how can you leave her to them?'

'But if I do her no good?' Lizzie wailed; and it was then that, when
he took her hand and assured her gently, 'But you do, you do!' – it
was then that, in the traditional phrase, she 'broke down,' and her poor
little protest quivered off into tears.

'You do *me* good, at any rate – you make the house seem less like
a desert,' she heard him say; and the next moment she felt herself drawn
to him, and they kissed each other through her weeping.

They kissed each other – there was the new fact. One does not, if
one is a poor little teacher living in Mme. Clopin's Pension Suisse at
Passy, and if one has pretty brown hair and eyes that reach out trustfully
to other eyes – one does not, under these common but defenceless
conditions, arrive at the age of twenty-five without being now and
then kissed – waylaid once by a noisy student between two doors,
surprised once by one's grey-bearded professor as one bent over the
'theme' he was correcting – but these episodes, if they tarnish the
surface, do not reach the heart: it is not the kiss endured, but the
kiss returned, that lives. And Lizzie West's first kiss was for Vincent
Deering.

As she drew back from it, something new awoke in her – something
deeper than the fright and the shame, and the penitent thought of Mrs.
Deering. A sleeping germ of life thrilled and unfolded, and started out
to seek the sun.

She might have felt differently, perhaps – the shame and penitence
might have prevailed – had she not known him so kind and tender,
and guessed him so baffled, poor and disappointed. She knew the failure
of his married life, and she divined a corresponding failure in his artistic
career. Lizzie, who had made her own faltering snatch at the same
laurels, brought her thwarted proficiency to bear on the question of his
pictures, which she judged to be remarkable, but suspected of having
somehow failed to affirm their merit publicly. She understood that he
had tasted an earlier moment of success: a *mention*, a medal, something

official and tangible; then the tide of publicity had somehow set the other way, and left him stranded in a noble isolation. It was incredible that any one so naturally eminent and exceptional should have been subject to the same vulgar necessities that governed her own life, should have known poverty and obscurity and indifference. But she gathered that this had been the case, and felt that it formed the miraculous link between them. For through what medium less revealing than that of shared misfortune would he ever have perceived so inconspicuous an object as herself? And she recalled now how gently his eyes had rested on her from the first – the grey eyes that might have seemed mocking if they had not seemed so gentle.

She remembered how kindly he had met her the first day, when Mrs. Deering's inevitable headache had prevented her receiving the new teacher. Insensibly he had led Lizzie to talk of herself and his questions had at once revealed his interest in the little stranded compatriot doomed to earn a precarious living so far from her native shore. Sweet as the moment of unburdening had been, she wondered afterward what had determined it: how she, so shy and sequestered, had found herself letting slip her whole poverty-stricken story, even to the avowal of the ineffectual 'artistic' tendencies that had drawn her to Paris, and had then left her there to the dry task of tuition. She wondered at first, but she understood now; she understood everything after he had kissed her. It was simply because he was as kind as he was great.

She thought of this now as she mounted the hill in the spring sunshine, and she thought of all that had happened since. The intervening months, as she looked back at them, were merged in a vast golden haze, through which here and there rose the outline of a shining island. The haze was the general enveloping sense of his love, and the shining islands were the days they had spent together. They had never kissed again under his own roof. Lizzie's professional honor had a keen edge, but she had been spared the necessity of making him feel it. It was of the essence of her fatality that he always 'understood' when his failing to do so might have imperiled his hold on her.

But her Thursdays and Sundays were free, and it soon became a habit to give them to him. She knew, for her peace of mind, only too much about pictures, and galleries and churches had been the one outlet from the greyness of her personal conditions. For poetry, too, and the other imaginative forms of literature, she had always felt more than she had hitherto had occasion to betray; and now all these folded sympathies shot out their tendrils to the light. Mr. Deering knew how to express with unmatched clearness the thoughts that trembled in her mind: to talk with him was to soar up into the azure on the outspread wings of his intelligence, and look down, dizzily yet clearly, on all the wonders and glories of the world. She was a little ashamed, sometimes, to find how few definite impressions brought back so fast when he was near, and his smile made his words seem like a long quiver of light. Afterward, in quieter hours, fragments of their talk emerged in her memory with wondrous precision, every syllable as minutely chiseled as some of the delicate objects in crystal or ivory that he pointed out in the museums they frequented. It was always a puzzle to Lizzie that some of their hours should be so blurred and others so vivid.

She was reliving all these memories with unusual distinctness, because it was a fortnight since she had seen her friend. Mrs. Deering, some six weeks previously, had gone to visit a relative at St. Raphael; and, after she had been a month absent, her husband and the little girl had joined her. Lizzie's adieux to Deering had been made on a rainy afternoon in the damp corridors of the Aquarium at the Trocadéro. She could not receive him at her own *pension*. That a teacher should be visited by the father of a pupil, especially when that father was still, as Madame Clopin said, *si bien*, was against that lady's austere Helvetian code. And from Deering's first tentative hint of another solution Lizzie had recoiled in a wild flurry of all her scruples. He took her 'No, no, *no!*' as he took all her twists and turns of conscience, with eyes half tender and half mocking, and an instant acquiescence which was the finest homage to the 'lady' she felt he divined and honored in her.

So they continued to meet in museums and galleries, or to extend, on fine days, their explorations to the suburbs, where now and then, in the solitude of grove or garden, the kiss renewed itself, fleeting, isolated, or prolonged in a shy pressure of the hand. But on the day of his leave-taking the rain kept them under cover; and as they threaded the subterranean windings of the Aquarium, and Lizzie gazed unseeingly at the grotesque faces glaring at her through walls of glass, she felt like a drowned wretch at the bottom of the sea, with all her sunlit memories rolling over her like the waves of its surface.

'You'll never see him again – never see him again,' the waves boomed in her ears through his last words; and when she had said goodbye to him at the corner, and had scrambled, wet and shivering, into the Passy omnibus, its grinding wheels took up the derisive burden – 'Never see him, never see him again.'

All that was only two weeks ago, and here she was, as happy as a lark, mounting the hill to his door in the fresh spring sunshine! So weak a heart did not deserve such a radiant fate; and Lizzie said to herself that she would never again distrust her star.

• II •

THE cracked bell tinkled sweetly through her heart as she stood listening for Juliet's feet. Juliet, anticipating the laggard Suzanne, almost always opened the door for her governess, not from any eagerness to hasten the hour of her studies, but from the irrepressible desire to see what was going on in the street. But doubtless on this occasion some unusually absorbing incident had detained the child belowstairs; for Lizzie, after vainly waiting for a step, had to give the bell a second twitch. Even a third produced no response, and Lizzie, full of dawning fears, drew back to look up at the house. She saw that the studio shutters stood wide, and then noticed, without surprise, that Mrs. Deering's were still unopened. No doubt Mrs. Deering was resting after the fatigue of the journey. Instinctively Lizzie's eyes turned again to the studio window; and as she looked, she saw Deering approach it. He caught sight of her, and an instant later was at the door. He lookd paler than usual, and she noticed that he wore a black coat.

'I rang and rang – where is Juliet?' she asked.

He looked at her gravely; then, without answering, he led her down the passage to the studio, and closed the door when she had entered.

'My wife is dead – she died suddenly ten days ago. Didn't you see it in the papers?' he said.

Lizzie, with a cry, sank down on the rickety divan propped against the wall. She seldom saw a newspaper, since she could not afford one for her own perusal, and those supplied to the Pension Clopin were usually in the hands of its more privileged lodgers till long after the hour when she set out on her morning round.

'No; I didn't see it,' she stammered.

Deering was silent. He stood twisting an unlit cigarette in his hand, and looking down at her with a gaze that was both constrained and hesitating.

She, too, felt the constraint of the situation, the impossibility of finding words which, after what had passed between them, should seem neither false nor heartless: and at last she exclaimed, standing up: 'Poor little Juliet! Can't I go to her?'

'Juliet is not here. I left her at St. Raphaël with the relations with whom my wife was staying.'

'Oh,' Lizzie murmured, feeling vaguely that this added to the difficulty of the moment. How differently she had pictured their meeting!

'I'm so – so sorry for her!' she faltered.

Deering made no reply, but, turning on his heel, walked the length of the studio and halted before the picture on the easel. It was the landscape he had begun the previous autumn, with the intention of sending it to the Salon that spring. But it was still unfinished – seemed, indeed, hardly more advanced than on the fateful October day when Lizzie, standing before it for the first time, had confessed her inability to deal with Juliet. Perhaps the same thought struck its creator, for he broke into a dry laugh and turned from the easel with a shrug.

Under his protracted silence Lizzie roused herself to the fact that, since her pupil was absent, there was no reason for her remaining any longer; and as Deering approached her she rose and said with an effort: 'I'll go, then. You'll send for me when she comes back?'

Deering still hesitated, tormenting the cigarette between his fingers. 'She's not coming back – not at present.'

Lizzie heard him with a drop of the heart. Was everything to be changed in their lives? Of course; how could she have dreamed it would be otherwise? She could only stupidly repeat: 'Not coming back? Not this spring?'

'Probably not, since our friends are so good as to keep her. The fact is, I've got to go to America. My wife left a little property, a few pennies, that I must go and see to – for the child.'

Lizzie stood before him, a cold knife in her breast. 'I see – I see,' she reiterated, feeling all the while that she strained her eyes into utter blackness.

'It's a nuisance, having to pull up stakes,' he went on, with a fretful glance about the studio.

She lifted her eyes to his face. 'Shall you be gone long?' she took courage to ask.

'There again – I can't tell. It's all so mixed up.' He met her look for an incredibly long strange moment. 'I hate to go!' he murmured abruptly.

Lizzie felt a rush of moisture to her lashes, and the familiar wave of weakness at her heart. She raised her hand to her face with an instinctive gesture, and as she did so he held out his arms.

'Come here, Lizzie!' he said.

And she went – went with a sweet wild throb of liberation, with the sense that at last the house was his, that *she* was his, if he wanted her; that never again would that silent presence in the room above constrain and shame her rapture.

He pushed back her veil and covered her face with kisses. 'Don't cry, you little goose!' he said.

• III •

THAT they must see each other before his departure, in some place less exposed than their usual haunts, was as clear to Lizzie as it appeared to be to Deering. His expressing the wish seemed, indeed, the sweetest testimony to the quality of his feeling, since, in the first weeks of the most perfunctory widowerhood, a man of his stamp is presumed to abstain from light adventures. If, then, he wished so much to be quietly and gravely with her, it could be only for reasons she did not call by name, but of which she felt the sacred tremor in her heart; and it would have seemed to her vain and vulgar to put forward, at such a moment, the conventional objections with which such little exposed existences defend the treasure of their freshness.

In such a mood as this one may descend from the Passy omnibus at the corner of the Pont de la Concorde (she had not let him fetch her in a cab) with a sense of dedication almost solemn, and may advance to meet one's fate, in the shape of a gentleman of melancholy elegance, with an auto taxi at his call, as one has advanced to the altar steps in some girlish bridal vision.

Even the experienced waiter ushering them into an upper room of the quiet restaurant on the Seine could hardly have supposed their quest for privacy to be based on the familiar motive, so soberly did Deering give his orders, while his companion sat small and grave at his side. She did not, indeed, mean to let her distress obscure their hour together: she was already learning that Deering shrank from sadness. He should see that she had courage and gaiety to face their coming separation, and yet give herself meanwhile to this completer nearness; but she waited, as always for him to strike the opening note.

Looking back at it later, she wondered at the sweetness of the hour. Her heart was unversed in happiness, but he had found the tone to lull her fears, and make her trust her fate for any golden wonder. Deepest of all, he gave her the sense of something tacit and established between them, as if his tenderness were a habit of the heart hardly needing the support of outward proof.

Such proof as he offered came, therefore, as a kind of crowning luxury, the flowering of a profoundly rooted sentiment; and here again the instinctive reserves and defences would have seemed to vulgarize what his confidence ennobled. But if all the tender casuistries of her heart were at his service, he took no grave advantage of them. Even when they sat alone after dinner, with the lights of the river trembling through their one low window, and the rumor of Paris enclosing them in a heart of silence, he seemed, as much as herself, under the spell of hallowing influences. She felt it most of all as she yielded to the arm he presently put about her, to the long caress he laid on her lips and eyes: not a word or gesture missed the note of quiet understanding, or cast a doubt, in retrospect, on the pact they sealed with their last look.

That pact, as she reviewed it through a sleepless night, seemed to have consisted mainly, on his part, in pleadings for full and frequent news of her, on hers in the promise that it should be given as often as he wrote to ask it. She did not wish to show too much eagerness, too great a desire to affirm and define her hold on him. Her life had given her a certain acquaintance with the arts of defence: girls in her situation were supposed to know them all, and to use them as occasion called. But Lizzie's very need of them had intensified her disdain. Just because she was so poor, and had always, materially, so to count her change and calculate her margin, she would at least know the joy of emotional prodigality, and give her heart as recklessly as the rich their millions. She was sure now that Deering loved her, and if he had seized the occasion of their farewell to give her some definitely worded sign of his feeling — if, more plainly, he had asked her to marry him — his doing so would have seemed less a proof of his sincerity than of his suspecting in her the need of such a warrant. That he had abstained seemed to show that he trusted her as she trusted him, and that they were one most of all in this complete security of understanding.

She had tried to make him guess all this in the chariness of her promise to write. She would write; of course she would. But he would be busy, preoccupied, on the move: it was for him to let her know when he wished a word, to spare her the embarrassment of ill-timed intrusions.

'Intrusions?' He had smiled the word away. 'You can't well intrude, my darling, on a heart where you're already established to the complete exclusion of other lodgers.' And then, taking her hands, and looking up from them into her happy dizzy eyes: 'You don't know much about being in love, do you, Lizzie?' he laughingly ended.

It seemed easy enough to reject this imputation in a kiss; but she wondered afterward if she had not deserved it. Was she really cold and conventional, and did other women give more richly and recklessly? She found that it was possible to turn about every one of her reserves and delicacies so that they looked like selfish scruples and petty prud-eries, and at this game she came in time to exhaust all the resources of casuistry.

Meanwhile the first days after Deering's departure wore a soft refracted light like the radiance lingering after sunset. *He*, at any rate, was taxable with no reserves, no calculations, and his letters of farewell, from train and steamer, filled her with long murmurs and echoes of his presence. How he loved her, how he loved her — and how he knew how to tell her so!

She was not sure of possessing the same gift. Unused to the expression of personal emotion, she wavered between the impulse to pour out all she felt and the fear lest her extravagance should amuse or even bore him. She never lost the sense that what was to her the central crisis of experience must be a mere episode in a life so predestined as his to romantic incidents. All that she felt and said would be subjected to the test of comparison with what others had already given him: from all quarters of the globe she saw passionate missives winging their way toward Deering, for whom her poor little swallow flight of devotion could certainly not make a summer. But such moments were succeeded by others in which she raised her head and dared affirm no woman had ever loved him just as she had, and that none, therefore, had probably found just such things to say to him. And this conviction strengthened the other less solidly based belief that *he* also, for the same reason, had found new accents to express his tenderness, and that the three letters she wore all day in her shabby blouse, and hid all night beneath her pillow, not only surpassed in beauty, but differed in quality from, all he had ever penned for other eyes.

They gave her, at any rate, during the weeks that she wore them on her heart, sensations more complex and delicate than Deering's actual presence had ever produced. To be with him was always like breasting a bright rough sea that blinded while it buoyed her; but his letters formed a still pool of contemplation, above which she could bend, and see the reflection of the sky, and the myriad movements of the life that flitted and gleamed below the surface. The wealth of this hidden life – that was what most surprised her! She had had no inkling of it, but had kept on along the narrow track of habit, like a traveler climbing a road in a fog, and suddenly finding himself on a sunlit crag between leagues of sky and dizzy depths of valley. And the odd thing was that all the people about her – the whole world of the Passy pension – seemed plodding along the same dull path, preoccupied with the pebbles underfoot, and unaware of the glory beyond the fog!

There were hours of exultation, when she longed to cry out to them what one saw from the summit – and hours of abasement, when she asked herself why *her* feet had been guided there, while others, no doubt as worthy, stumbled and blundered in obscurity. She felt, in particular, an urgent pity for the two or three other girls at Mme. Clopin's – girls older, duller, less alive than she, and by that very token more thrown upon her sympathy. Would they ever know? Had they ever known? Those were the questions that haunted her as she crossed her companions on the stairs, faced them at the dinner table, and listened to their poor pining talk in the dimly lit slippery-seated *salon*. One of the girls was Swiss, another English; a third, Andora Macy, was a young lady from the Southern States who was studying French with the ultimate object of imparting it to the inmates of a girls' school at Macon, Georgia.

Andora Macy was pale, faded, immature. She had a drooping accent, and a manner which fluctuated between arch audacity and fits of panicky hauteur. She yearned to be admired, and feared to be insulted; and yet seemed wistfully conscious that she was destined to miss both these extremes of sensation, or to enjoy them only in the experiences of her more privileged friends.

It was perhaps for this reason that she took a tender interest in Lizzie, who had shrunk from her at first, as the depressing image of her own probable future, but to whom she now suddenly became an object of sentimental pity.

• IV •

MISS MACY'S room was next to Miss West's, and the Southerner's knock often appealed to Lizzie's hospitality when Mme. Clopin's early curfew had driven her boarders from the *salon*. It sounded thus one evening, just as Lizzie, tired from an unusually long day of tuition, was in the act of removing her dress. She was in too indulgent a mood to withhold her 'Come in,' and as Miss Macy crossed the threshold, Lizzie felt that Vincent Deering's first letter – the letter from the train – had slipped from her bosom to the floor.

Miss Macy, as promptly aware, darted forward to recover it. Lizzie stooped also, instinctively jealous of her touch; but the visitor reached the letter first, and as she seized it, Lizzie knew that she had seen whence it fell, and was weaving round the incident a rapid web of romance.

Lizzie blushed with annoyance. 'It's too stupid, having no pockets! If one gets a letter as one is going out in the morning, one has to carry it in one's blouse all day.'

Miss Macy looked at her fondly. 'It's warm from your heart!' she breathed, reluctantly yielding up the missive.

Lizzie laughed, for she knew it was the letter that had warmed her heart. Poor Andora Macy! *She* would never know. Her bleak bosom would never take fire from such a contact. Lizzie looked at her with kind eyes, chafing at the injustice of fate.

The next evening, on her return home, she found her friend hovering in the entrance hall.

'I thought you'd like me to put this in your own hand,' Andora whispered significantly, pressing a letter upon Lizzie. 'I couldn't *bear* to see it lying on the table with the others.'

It was Deering's letter from the steamer. Lizzie blushed to the forehead, but without resenting Andora's divination. She could not have breathed a word of her bliss, but she was not sorry to have it guessed, and pity for Andora's destitution yielded to the pleasure of using it as a mirror for her own abundance.

Deering wrote again on reaching New York, a long fond dissatisfied letter, vague in its indication to his own projects, specific in the expression of his love. Lizzie brooded over every syllable till they formed the undercurrent of all her waking thoughts, and murmured through her midnight dreams; but she would have been happier if they had shed some definite light on the future.

That would come, no doubt, when he had had time to look about and got his bearings. She counted up the days that must elapse before she received his next letter, and stole down early to peep at the papers, and learn when the next American mail was due. At length the happy date arrived, and she hurried distractedly through the day's work, trying to conceal her impatience by the endearments she bestowed upon her pupils. It was easier, in her present mood, to kiss them than to keep them at their grammars.

That evening, on Mme. Clopin's threshold, her heart beat so wildly that she had to lean a moment against the doorpost before entering. But on the hall table, where the letters lay, there was none for her.

She went over them with an impatient hand, her heart dropping down and down, as she had sometimes fallen down on endless stairway in a dream – the very same stairway up which she had seemed to fly when she climbed the long hill to Deering's door. Then it struck her that Andora might have found and secreted her letter, and with a spring she was on the actual stairs, and rattling Miss Macy's door handle.

'You've a letter for me, haven't you?' she panted.

Miss Macy enclosed her in attenuated arms. 'Oh, darling, did you expect another?'

'Do give it to me!' Lizzie pleaded with eager eyes.

'But I haven't any! There hasn't been a sign of a letter for you.'

'I know there is. There *must* be,' Lizzie cried, stamping her foot.

'But, dearest, I've *watched* for you, and there's been nothing.'

Day after day, for the ensuing weeks, the same scene re-enacted itself with endless variations. Lizzie, after the first sharp spasm of disappointment, made no effort to conceal her anxiety from Miss Macy, and the fond Andora was charged to keep a vigilant eye upon the postman's coming and to spy on the *bonne* for possible negligence or perfidy. But these elaborate precautions remained fruitless, and no letter from Deering came.

During the first fortnight of silence, Lizzie exhausted all the ingenuities of explanation. She marveled afterward at the reasons she had found for Deering's silence: there were moments when she almost argued herself into thinking it more natural than his continuing to write. There was only one reason which her intelligence rejected; and that was the possibility that he had forgotten her, that the whole episode had faded from his mind like a breath from a mirror. From that she resolutely averted her thoughts, conscious that if she suffered herself to contemplate it, the motive power of life would fail, and she would no longer understand why she rose in the morning and lay down at night.

If she had had leisure to indulge her anguish she might have been unable to keep such speculations at bay. But she had to be up and working: the *blanchisseuse* had to be paid, and Mme. Clopin's weekly bill, and all the little 'extras' that even her frugal habits had to reckon with. And in the depths of her thought dwelt the dogging fear of illness and incapacity, goading her to work while she could. She hardly remembered the time when she had been without that fear; it was second nature now, and it kept her on her feet when other incentives might have failed. In the blankness of her misery she felt no dread of death; but the horror of being ill and 'dependent' was in her blood.

In the first weeks of silence she wrote again and again to Deering, entreating him for a word, for a mere sign of life. From the first she had shrunk from seeming to assert any claim on his future, yet in her bewilderment she now charged herself with having been too possessive, too exacting in her tone. She told herself that his fastidiousness shrank from any but a 'light touch,' and that hers had not been light enough. She should have kept to the character of the 'little friend,' the artless consciousness in which tormented genius may find an escape from its complexities; and instead, she had dramatized their relation, exaggerated her own part in it, presumed, forsooth, to share the front of the stage with him, instead of being content to serve as scenery or chorus.

But though, to herself, she admitted, and even insisted on, the episodical nature of the experience, on the fact that for Deering it could be no more than in incident, she was still convinced that his sentiment for her, however fugitive, had been genuine.

His had not been the attitude of the unscrupulous male seeking a vulgar 'advantage.' For a moment he had really needed her, and if he was silent now, it was perhaps because he feared that she had mistaken the nature of the need, and built vain hopes on its possible duration.

It was of the essence of Lizzie's devotion that it sought, instinctively, the larger freedom of its object; she could not conceive of love under any form of exaction or compulsion. To make this clear to Deering became an overwhelming need, and in a last short letter she explicitly freed him from whatever sentimental obligation its predecessors might have seemed to impose. In this communication she playfully accused herself of having unwittingly sentimentalized their relation, affecting, in self-defence, a retrospective astuteness, a sense of the impermanence of the tenderer sentiments, that almost put Deering in the position of having mistaken coquetry for surrender. And she ended, gracefully, with a plea for the continuance of the friendly regard which she had 'always understood' to be the basis of their sympathy. The document, when completed, seemed to her worthy of what she conceived to be Deering's conception of a woman of the world – and she found a spectral satisfaction in the thought of making her final appearance before him in this distinguished character. But she was never destined to learn what effect the appearance produced; for the letter, like those it sought to excuse, remained unanswered.

• V •

THE fresh spring sunshine which had so often attended Lizzie West on her dusty climb up the hill of St. Cloud, beamed on her, some two years later in a scene and a situation of altered import.

Its rays, filtered through the horse chestnuts of the Champs Elysées, shone on the graveled circle about Laurent's restaurant; and Miss West, seated at a table within that privileged space, presented to the light a hat much better able to sustain its scrutiny than those which had shaded the brow of Juliet Deering's instructions.

Her dress was in keeping with the hat, and both belonged to a situation rife with such possibilities as the act of a leisurely luncheon at Laurent's in the opening week of the Salon. Her companions, of both sexes, confirmed this impression by an appropriateness of attire and an case of manner implying the largest range of selection between the forms of Parisian idleness; and even Andora Macy, seated opposite, as in the place of co-hostess or companion, reflected, in coy greys and mauves, the festal note of the occasion.

This note reverberated persistently in the ears of a solitary gentleman straining for glimpses of the group from a table wedged in the remotest corner of the garden; but to Miss West herself the occurrence did not rise above the usual. For nearly a year she had been acquiring the habit of such situations, and the act of offering a luncheon at Laurent's to her cousins, the Harvey Mearses of Providence, and their friend Mr. Jackson Benn, produced in her no emotion beyond the languid glow which Mr. Benn's presence was beginning to impart to such scenes.

'It's frightful, the way you've got used to it,' Andora Macy had wailed, in the first days of her friend's transfigured fortunes, when Lizzie West had waked one morning to find herself among the heirs of an ancient miserly cousin whose testamentary dispositions had formed, since her earliest childhood, the subject of pleasantry and conjecture in her own improvident family. Old Hezron Mears had never given any sign of life to the luckless Wests; had perhaps hardly been conscious of including them in the carefully drawn will which, following the old American convention, scrupulously divided his millions among his kin. It was by a mere genealogical accident that Lizzie, falling just within the golden circle, found herself possessed of a pittance sufficient to release her from the prospect of a long grey future in Mme. Clopin's *pension*.

The release had seemed wonderful at first; yet she presently found that it had destroyed her former world without giving her a new one. On the ruins of the old *pension* life bloomed the only flower that had ever sweetened her path; and beyond the sense of present ease, and the removal of anxiety for the future, her reconstructed existence blossomed with no compensating joys. She had hoped great things from the opportunity to rest, to travel, to look about her, above all, in various artful feminine ways, to be 'nice' to the companions of her less privileged state; but such widenings of scope left her, as it were, but the more conscious of the empty margin of personal life beyond them. It was not till she woke to the leisure of her new days that she had the full sense of what was gone from them.

Their very emptiness made her strain to pack them with transient sensations: she was like the possessor of an unfurnished house, with random furniture and bric-a-brac perpetually pouring in 'on approval.' It was in this experimental character that Mr. Jackson Benn had fixed her attention, and the languid effort of her imagination to adjust him to her taste was seconded by the fond complicity of Andora, and by the smiling approval of her cousins. Lizzie did not discourage these attempts: she suffered serenely Andora's allusions to Mr. Benn's infatuation, and Mrs. Mears's boasts of his business standing. All the better if they could drape his narrow square-shouldered frame and round unwinking countenance in the trailing mists of sentiment: Lizzie looked and listened, not unhopeful of the miracle.

'I never saw anything like the way these Frenchmen stare! Doesn't it make you nervous, Lizzie?' Mrs. Mears broke out suddenly, ruffling her feather boa about an outraged bosom. Mrs. Mears was still in that stage of development when her countrywomen taste to the full the peril of being exposed to the gaze of the licentious Gaul.

Lizzie roused herself from the contemplation of Mr. Benn's round baby cheeks and the square blue jaw resting on his perpendicular collar. 'Is someone staring at me?' she asked.

'Don't turn round, whatever you do! There – just over there, between the rhododendrons – the tall blond man alone at that table. Really, Harvey, I think you ought to speak to the headwaiter, or something, though I suppose in one of these places they'd only laugh at you,' Mrs. Mears shudderingly concluded.

Her husband, as if inclining to this probability, continued the undisturbed dissection of his chicken wing, but Mr. Benn, perhaps conscious that his situation demanded a more punctilious attitude, sternly revolved upon the parapet of his high collar in the direction of Mrs. Mears's glance.

'What, that fellow all alone over there? Why, *he's* not French; he's an American,' he then proclaimed with a perceptible relaxing of the muscles.

'Oh!' murmured Mrs. Mears, as perceptibly disappointed, and Mr. Benn continued: 'He came over on the steamer with me. He's some kind of an artist – a fellow named Deering. He was staring at *me*, I guess: wondering whether I was going to remember him. Why, how d' 'e do? How are you? Why, yes, of course; with pleasure – my friends,

Mrs. Harvey Mears – Mr. Mears; my friends, Miss Macy and Miss West.'

'I have the pleasure of knowing Miss West,' said Vincent Deering with a smile.

• VI •

EVEN through his smile Lizzie had seen, in the first moment, how changed he was; and the impression of the change deepened to the point of pain when, a few days later, in reply to his brief note, she granted him a private hour.

That the first sight of his writing – the first answer to her letters – should have come, after three long years, in the shape of this impersonal line, too curt to be called humble, yet revealing a consciousness of the past in the studied avoidance of its language! As she read, her mind flashed back over what she had dreamed his letters would be, over the exquisite answers she had composed above his name. There was nothing exquisite in the lines before her; but dormant nerves began to throb again at the mere touch of the paper he had touched, and she threw the note into the fire before she dared to reply to it.

Now that he was actually before her again, he became, as usual, the one live spot in her consciousness. Once more her tormented self sank back passive and numb, but now with all its power of suffering mysteriously transferred to the presence, so known yet so unknown, at the opposite corner of her hearth. She was still Lizzie West, and he was still Vincent Deering; but the Styx rolled between them, and she saw his face through its fog. It was his face, really, rather than his words, that told her, as she furtively studied it, the tale of failure and discouragement which had so blurred its handsome lines. She kept, afterward, no precise memory of the details of his narrative: the pain it evidently cost him to impart it was so much the sharpest fact in her new vision of him. Confusedly, however, she gathered that on reaching America he had found his wife's small property gravely impaired; and that, while lingering on to secure what remained of it, he had contrived to sell a picture or two, and had even known a moment of success, during which he received orders and set up a studio. Then the tide had ebbed, his work had remained on his hands, and a tedious illness, with its miserable sequel of debt, soon wiped out his advantage. There followed a period of eclipse, during which she inferred that he had tried his hand at diverse means of livelihood, accepting employment from a fashionable house decorator, designing wallpapers, illustrating magazine articles, and acting for a time – she dimly understood – as the social tout of a new hotel desirous of advertising its restaurant. These disjointed facts were strung on a slender thread of personal allusions –

references to friends who had been kind (jealously, she guessed them to be women), and to enemies who had schemed against him. But, true to his tradition of 'correctness,' he carefully avoided the mention of names, and left her imagination to grope dimly through a crowded world in which there seemed little room for her small shy presence.

As she listened, her private grievance vanished beneath the sense of his unhappiness. Nothing he had said explained or excused his conduct to her; but he had suffered, he had been lonely, had been humiliated, and she felt, with a fierce maternal rage, that there was no possible justification for any scheme of things in which such facts were possible. She could not have said why: she simply knew that it hurt too much to see him hurt.

Gradually it came to her that her absence of resentment was due to her having so definitely settled her own future. She was glad she had decided – as she now felt she had – to marry Jackson Benn, if only for the sense of detachment it gave her in dealing with Vincent Deering. Her personal safety insured her the requisite impartiality, and justified her in lingering as long as she chose over the last lines of a chapter to which her own act had fixed the close. Any lingering hesitations as to the finality of this decision were dispelled by the need of making it known to Deering: and when her visitor paused in his reminiscences to say, with a sigh, 'But many things have happened to you too,' the words did not so much evoke the sense of her altered fortunes as the image of the suitor to whom she was about to entrust them.

'Yes, many things; it's three years,' she answered.

Deering sat leaning forward, in his sad exiled elegance, his eyes gently bent on hers; and at his side she saw the form of Mr. Jackson Benn, with shoulders preternaturally squared by the cut of his tight black coat, and a tall shiny collar sustaining his baby cheeks and hard blue chin. Then the vision faded as Deering began to speak.

'Three years,' he repeated musingly. 'I've so often wondered what they'd brought you.'

She lifted her head with a blush, and the terrified wish that he should not – at the cost of all his notions of correctness – lapse into the blunder of becoming 'personal.'

'You've wondered?' she smiled back bravely.

'Do you suppose I haven't?' His look dwelt on her. 'Yes, I dare say that *was* what you thought of me.'

She had her answer pat – 'Why, frankly, you know, I *didn't* think of you at all.' But the mounting tide of her memories swept it indignantly away. If it was his correctness to ignore, it could never be hers to disavow!

'*Was* that what you thought of me?' she heard him repeat in a tone of sad insistence; and at that, with a lift of her head, she resolutely answered: 'How could I know what to think? I had no word from you.'

If she had expected, and perhaps almost hoped, that this answer would create a difficulty for him, the gaze of quiet fortitude with which he met it proved that she had underestimated his resources.

'No, you had no word. I kept my vow,' he said.

'You vow?'

'That you *shouldn't* have a word – not a syllable. Oh, I kept it through everything!'

Lizzie's heart was sounding in her ears the old confused rumor of the sea of life, but through it she desperately tried to distinguish the still small voice of reason.

'What was your vow? Why shouldn't I have had a syllable from you?'

He sat motionless, still holding her with a look so gentle that it almost seemed forgiving.

Then, abruptly, he rose, and crossing the space between them, sat down in a chair at her side. The movement might have implied a forgetfulness of changed conditions, and Lizzie, as if thus viewing it, drew slightly back; but he appeared not to notice her recoil, and his eyes, at last leaving her face, slowly and approvingly made the round of the small bright drawing room. 'This is charming. Yes, things *have* changed for you,' he said.

A moment before, she had prayed that he might be spared the error of a vain return upon the past. It was as if all her retrospective tenderness, dreading to see him at such a disadvantage, rose up to protect him from it. But his evasiveness exasperated her, and suddenly she felt the desire to hold him fast, face to face with his own words.

Before she could repeat her question, however, he had met her with another.

'You *did* think of me, then? Why are you afraid to tell me that you did?'

The unexpectedness of the challenge wrung a cry from her. 'Didn't my letters tell you so enough?'

'Ah – your letters – ' Keeping her gaze on his with unrelenting fixity, she could detect in him no confusion, not the least quiver of a nerve. He only gazed back at her more sadly.

'They went everywhere with me – your letters,' he said.

'Yet you never answered them.' At last the accusation trembled to her lips.

'Yet I never answered them.'

'Did you ever so much as read them, I wonder?'

All the demons of self-torture were up in her now, and she loosed them on him as if to escape from their rage.

Deering hardly seemed to hear her question. He merely shifted his

attitude, leaning a little nearer to her, but without attempting, by the
least gesture, to remind her of the privileges which such nearness had
once implied.

'There were beautiful, wonderful things in them,' he said, smiling.

She felt herself stiffen under his smile. 'You've waited three years
to tell me so!'

He looked at her with grave surprise. 'And do you resent my telling
you, even now?'

His parries were incredible. They left her with a sense of thrusting
at emptiness, and a desperate, almost vindictive desire to drive him
against the wall and pin him there.

'No. Only I wonder you should take the trouble to tell me, when
at the time – '

And now, with a sudden turn, he gave her the final surprise of
meeting her squarely on her own ground.

'When at the time, I didn't? But how *could* I – at the time?'

'Why couldn't you? You've not yet told me.'

He gave her again his look of disarming patience. 'Do I need to?
Hasn't my whole wretched story told you?'

'Told me why you never answered my letters?'

'Yes – since I could only answer them in one way: by protesting
my love and my longing.'

There was a pause, of resigned expectancy on his part, on hers of
a wild, confused reconstruction of her shattered past. 'You mean, then,
that you didn't write because – '

'Because I found, when I reached America, that I was a pauper: that
my wife's money was gone, and that what I could earn – I've so little
gift that way! – was barely enough to keep Juliet clothed and educated.
It was as if an iron door had been locked and barred between us.'

Lizzie felt herself driven back, panting, on the last defences of her
incredulity. 'You might at least have told me – have explained. Do you
think I shouldn't have understood?'

He did not hesitate. 'You would have understood. It wasn't that.'

'What was it then?' she quavered.

'It's wonderful you shouldn't see! Simply that I couldn't write you
that. Anything else – not *that!*'

'And so you preferred to let me suffer?'

There was a shade of reproach in his eyes. 'I suffered too,' he said.

It was his first direct appeal to her compassion, and for a moment
it nearly unsettled the delicate poise of her sympathies, and sent them
trembling in the direction of scorn and irony. But even as the impulse
rose it was stayed by another sensation. Once again, as so often in the
past, she became aware of a fact which, in his absence, she always failed
to reckon with; the fact of the deep irreducible difference between his
image in her mind and his actual self – the mysterious alteration in her

judgment produced by the inflections of his voice, the look of his eyes, the whole complex pressure of his personality. She had phrased it once, self-reproachfully, by saying to herself that she 'never could remember him – ' so completely did the sight of him supersede the counterfeit about which her fancy wove its perpetual wonders. Bright and breathing as that counterfeit was, it became a figment of the mind at the touch of his presence, and on this occasion the immediate result was to cause her to feel his possible unhappiness with an intensity beside which her private injury paled.

'I suffered horribly,' he repeated, 'and all the more that I couldn't make a sign, couldn't cry out my misery. There was only one escape from it all – to hold my tongue, and pray that you might hate me.'

The blood rushed to Lizzie's forehead. 'Hate you – you prayed that I might hate you?'

He rose from his seat, and moving closer, lifted her hand in his. 'Yes, because your letters showed me that if you didn't, you'd be unhappier still.'

Her hand lay motionless, with the warmth of his flowing through it, and her thoughts, too – her poor fluttering stormy thoughts – felt themselves suddenly penetrated by the same soft current of communion.

'And I meant to keep my resolve,' he went on, slowly releasing his clasp. 'I meant to keep it even after the random stream of things swept me back here, in your way; but when I saw you the other day I felt that what had been possible at a distance was impossible now that we were near each other. How could I see you, and let you hate me?'

He had moved away, but not to resume his seat. He merely paused at a little distance, his hand resting on a chair back, in the transient attitude that precedes departure.

Lizzie's heart contracted. He was going, then, and this was his farewell. He was going, and she could find no word to detain him but the senseless stammer: 'I never hated you.'

He considered her with a faint smile. 'It's not necessary, at any rate, that you should do so now. Time and circumstances have made me so harmless – that's exactly why I've dared to venture back. And I wanted to tell you how I rejoice in your good fortune. It's the only obstacle between us that I can't bring myself to wish away.'

Lizzie sat silent, spellbound, as she listened, by the sudden evocation of Mr. Jackson Benn. He stood there again, between herself and Deering, perpendicular and reproachful, but less solid and sharply outlined than before, with a look in his small hard eyes that desperately wailed for re-embodiment.

Deering was continuing his farewell speech. 'You're rich now – you're free. You will marry.' She saw him holding out his hand.

'It's not true that I'm engaged!' she broke out. They were the last words she had meant to utter; they were hardly related to her conscious thoughts; but she felt her whole will gathered up in the irrepressible impulse to repudiate and fling away from her forever the spectral claim of Mr. Jackson Benn.

• VII •

IT was the firm conviction of Andora Macy that every object in the Vincent Deerings' charming little house at Neuilly had been expressly designed for the Deerings' son to play with.

The house was full of pretty things, some not obviously applicable to the purpose; but Miss Macy's casuistry was equal to the baby's appetite, and the baby's mother was no match for them in the art of defending her possessions. There were moments, in fact, when she almost fell in with Andora's summary division of her works of art into articles safe or unsafe for the baby to lick, or resisted it only to the extent of occasionally substituting some less precious, or less perishable, object for the particular fragility on which her son's desire was fixed. And it was with this intention that, on a certain spring morning – which wore the added luster of being the baby's second birthday – she had murmured, with her mouth in his curls, and one hand holding a bit of Chelsea above his clutch: 'Wouldn't he rather have that beautiful shiny thing in Aunt Andora's hand?'

The two friends were together in Lizzie's morning room – the room she had chosen, on acquiring the house, because, when she sat there, she could hear Deering's step as he paced up and down before his easel in the studio she had built for him. His step had been less regularly audible than she had hoped, for, after three years of wedded bliss, he had somehow failed to settle down to the great work which was to result from that state; but even when she did not hear him she knew that he was there, above her head, stretched out on the old divan from St. Cloud, and smoking countless cigarettes while he skimmed the morning papers; and the sense of his nearness had not yet lost its first keen edge of wonder.

Lizzie herself, on the day in question, was engaged in a more arduous task than the study of the morning's news. She had never unlearned the habit of orderly activity, and the trait she least understood in her husband's character was his way of letting the loose ends of life hang as they would. She had been disposed to ascribe this to the chronic incoherence of his first *ménage;* but now she knew that, though he basked under her beneficent rule, he would never feel any impulse to further its work. He liked to see things fall into place about him at a wave of her wand; but his enjoyment of her household magic in no way diminished his smiling irresponsibility, and it was with one of its least amiable consequences that his wife and her friend were now dealing.

Before them stood two travel-worn trunks and a distended portmanteau, which had shed their heterogeneous contents over Lizzie's rosy carpet. They represented the hostages left by her husband on his somewhat precipitate departure from a New York boardinghouse, and redeemed by her on her learning, in a curt letter from his landlady, that the latter was not disposed to regard them as an equivalent for the arrears of Deering's board.

Lizzie had not been shocked by the discovery that her husband had left America in debt. She had too sad an acquaintance with the economic strain to see any humiliation in such accidents; but it offended her sense of order that he should not have liquidated his obligation in the three years since their marriage. He took her remonstrance with his usual good humor, and left her to forward the liberating draft, though her delicacy had provided him with a bank account which assured his personal independence. Lizzie had discharged the duty without repugnance, since she knew that his delegating it to her was the result of his indolence and not of any design on her exchequer. Deering was not dazzled by money; his altered fortunes had tempted him to no excesses: he was simply too lazy to draw the check, as he had been too lazy to remember the debt it canceled.

'No, dear! No!' Lizzie lifted the Chelsea higher. 'Can't you find something for him, Andora, among that rubbish over there? Where's the beaded bag you had in your hand? I don't think it could hurt him to lick that.'

Miss Macy, bag in hand, rose from her knees, and stumbled across the room through the frayed garments and old studio properties. Before the group of mother and son she fell into a rapturous attitude.

'Do look at him reach for it, the tyrant! Isn't he just like the young Napoleon?'

Lizzie laughed and swung her son in air. 'Dangle it before him, Andora. If you let him have it too quickly, he won't care for it. He's just like any man, I think.'

Andora slowly lowered the bag till the heir of the Deerings closed his masterful fist upon it. 'There – my Chelsea's safe!' Lizzie smiled, setting her boy on the floor, and watching him stagger away with his booty.

Andora stood beside her, watching too. 'Do you know where the bag came from, Lizzie?'

Mrs. Deering, bent above a pile of discollared shirts, shook an inattentive head. 'I never saw such wicked washing! There isn't one that's fit to mend. The bag? No: I've not the least idea.'

Andora surveyed her incredulously. 'Doesn't it make you utterly miserable to think that some woman may have made it for him?'

Lizzie, still bowed in scrutiny above the shirts, broke into a laugh. 'Really, Andora, really! Six, seven, nine; no, there isn't even a dozen. There isn't a whole dozen of *anything*. I don't see how men live alone.'

Andora broodingly pursued her theme. 'Do you mean to tell me it doesn't make you jealous to handle these things of his that other women may have given him?'

Lizzie shook her head again, and, straightening herself with a smile, tossed a bundle in her friend's direction. 'No, I don't feel jealous. Here, count these socks for me, like a darling.'

Andora moaned 'Don't you feel *anything at all*?' as the socks landed in her hollow bosom; but Lizzie, intent upon her task, tranquilly continued to unfold and sort. She felt a great deal as she did so, but her feelings were too deep and delicate for the simplifying processes of speech. She only knew that each article she drew from the trunks sent through her the long tremor of Deering's touch. It was part of her wonderful new life that everything belonging to him contained an infinitesimal fraction of himself – a fraction becoming visible in the warmth of her love as certain secret elements become visible in rare intensities of temperature. And in the case of the objects before her, poor shabby witnesses of his days of failure, what they gave out acquired a special poignancy from its contrast to his present cherished state. His shirts were all in round dozens now, and washed as carefully as old lace. As for his socks, she knew the pattern of every pair, and would have liked to see the washerwoman who dared to mislay one, or bring it home with the colors 'run'! And in these homely tokens of his well-being she saw the symbol of what her tenderness had brought him. He was safe in it, encompassed by it, morally and materially, and she defied the embattled powers of malice to reach him through the armor of her love. Such feelings, however, were not communicable, even had one desired to express them: they were no more to be distinguished from the sense of life itself than bees from the lime blossoms in which they murmur.

'Oh, do *look* at him, Lizzie! He's found out how to open the bag!'

Lizzie lifted her head to look a moment at her son, throned on a heap of studio rubbish, with Andora before him on adoring knees. She thought vaguely 'Poor Andora!' and then resumed the discouraged inspection of a buttonless white waistcoat. The next sound she was conscious of was an excited exclamation from her friend.

'Why, Lizzie, do you know what he used the bag for? To keep your letters in!'

Lizzie looked up more quickly. She was aware that Andora's pronoun had changed its object, and was now applied to Deering. And it struck her as odd, and slightly disagreeable, that a letter of hers should be found among the rubbish abandoned in her husband's New York lodgings.

'How funny! Give it to me, please.'

'Give it to Aunt Andora, darling! Here – look inside, and see what else a big, big boy can find there! Yes, here's another! Why, why – '

Lizzie rose with a shade of impatience and crossed the floor to the romping group beside the other trunk.

'What is it? Give me the letters, please.' As she spoke, she suddenly recalled the day when, in Mme. Clopin's *pension*, she had addressed a similar behest to Andora Macy.

Andora lifted to her a *look* of startled conjecture. 'Why, this one's never been opened! Do you suppose that awful woman could have kept it from him?'

Lizzie laughed. Andora's imaginings were really puerile! 'What awful woman? His landlady? Don't be such a goose, Andora. How can it have been kept back from him, when we've found it among his things?'

'Yes; but then why was it never opened?'

Andora held out the letter, and Lizzie took it. The writing was hers; the envelope bore the Passy postmark; and it was unopened. She looked at it with a sharp drop of the heart.

'Why, so are the others – all unopened!' Andora threw out on a rising note; but Lizzie, stooping over, checked her.

'Give them to me, please.'

'Oh, Lizzie, Lizzie – ' Andora, on her knees, held back the packet, her pale face paler with anger and compassion. 'Lizzie, they're the letters I used to post for you – the letters he never answered! *Look!*'

'Give them back to me, please.' Lizzie possessed herself of the letters.

The two women faced each other, Andora still kneeling, Lizzie motionless before her. The blood had rushed to her face, humming in her ears, and forcing itself into the veins of her temples. Then it ebbed, and she felt cold and weak.

'It must have been some plot – some conspiracy,' Andora cried, so fired by the ecstasy of invention that for the moment she seemed lost to all but the aesthetic aspect of the case.

Lizzie averted her eyes with an effort, and they rested on the boy, who sat at her feet placidly sucking the tassels of the bag. His mother stooped and extracted them from his rosy mouth, which a cry of wrath immediately filled. She lifted him in her arms, and for the first time no current of life ran from his body into hers. He felt heavy and clumsy, like some other woman's child; and his screams annoyed her.

'Take him away, please, Andora.'

'Oh, Lizzie, Lizzie!' Andora wailed.

Lizzie held out the child, and Andora, struggling to her feet, received him.

'I know just how you feel,' she gasped, above the baby's head.

Lizzie, in some dark hollow of herself, heard the faint echo of a laugh. Andora always thought she knew how people felt!

'Tell Marthe to take him with her when she fetches Juliet home from school.'

'Yes, yes.' Andora gloated on her. 'If you'd only give way, my darling!'

The baby, howling, dived over Andora's shoulder for the bag.

'Oh, *take* him!' his mother ordered.

Andora, from the door, cried out: 'I'll be back at once. Remember, love, you're not alone!'

But Lizzie insisted, 'Go with them – I wish you to go with them,' in the tone to which Miss Macy had never learned the answer.

The door closed on her reproachful back, and Lizzie stood alone. She looked about the disordered room, which offered a dreary image of the havoc of her life. An hour or two ago, everything about her had been so exquisitely ordered, without and within: her thoughts and her emotions had all been outspread before her like jewels laid away symmetrically in a collector's cabinet. Now they had been tossed down helter-skelter among the rubbish there on the floor, and had themselves turned to rubbish like the rest. Yes, there lay her life at her feet, among all that tarnished trash.

She picked up her letters, ten in all, and examined the flaps of the envelopes. Not one had been opened – not one. As she looked, every word she had written fluttered to life, and every feeling prompting it sent a tremor through her. With vertiginous speed and microscopic distinctness of vision she was reliving that whole period of her life, stripping bare again the ruin over which the drift of three happy years had fallen.

She laughed at Andora's notion of a conspiracy – of the letters having been 'kept back.' She required no extraneous aid in deciphering the mystery: her three years' experience of Deering shed on it all the light she needed. And yet a moment before she had believed herself to be perfectly happy! Now it was the worst part of her pain that it did not really surprise her.

She knew so well how it must have happened. The letters had reached him when he was busy, occupied with something else, and had been put aside to be read at some future time – a time which never came. Perhaps on the steamer, even, he had met 'someone else' – the 'someone' who lurks, veiled and ominous, in the background of every woman's thoughts about her lover. Or perhaps he had been merely forgetful. She knew now that the sensations which he seemed to feel most intensely left no reverberations in his memory – that he did not relive either his pleasures or his pains. She needed no better proof than the lightness of his conduct toward his daughter. He seemed to have taken it for granted that Juliet would remain indefinitely with the friends who had received her after her mother's death, and it was at Lizzie's suggestion that the little girl was brought home and that they had established themselves at Neuilly to be near her school. But Juliet once with them, he became the model of a tender father, and Lizzie wondered that he had not felt the child's absence, since he seemed so affectionately aware of her presence.

Lizzie had noted all this in Juliet's case, but had taken for granted that her own was different; that she formed, for Deering, the exception which every woman secretly supposes herself to form in the experience of the man she loves. She had learned by this time that she could not modify his habits; but she imagined that she had deepened his sensibilities, had furnished him with an 'ideal' – angelic function! And she now saw that the fact of her letters – her unanswered letters – having on his own assurance, 'meant so much' to him, had been the basis on which this beautiful fabric was reared.

There they lay now, the letters, precisely as when they had left her hands. He had not had time to read them; and there had been a moment in her past when that discovery would have been to her the sharpest pang imaginable. She had traveled far beyond that point. She could have forgiven him now for having forgotten her; but she could never forgive him for having deceived her.

She sat down, and looked again about the room. Suddenly she heard his step overhead, and her heart contracted. She was afraid that he was coming down to her. She sprang up and bolted the door; then she dropped into the nearest chair, tremulous and exhausted, as if the act had required an immense effort. A moment later she heard him on the stairs, and her tremor broke into a fit of shaking. 'I loathe you – I loathe you!' she cried.

She listened apprehensively for his touch on the handle of the door. He would come in, humming a tune, to ask some idle question and lay a caress on her hair. But no, the door was bolted; she was safe. She continued to listen, and the step passed on. He had not been coming to her, then. He must have gone downstairs to fetch something – another newspaper, perhaps. He seemed to read little else, and she sometimes wondered when he had found time to store the material that used to serve for their famous 'literary' talks. The wonder shot through her again, barbed with a sneer. At that moment it seemed to her that everything he had ever done and been was a lie.

She heard the house door close, and started up. Was he going out? It was not his habit to leave the house in the morning.

She crossed the room to the window, and saw him walking, with a quick decided step, between the lilacs to the gate. What could have called him forth at that unusual hour? It was odd that he should not have told her. The fact that she thought it odd suddenly showed her how closely their lives were interwoven. She had become a habit to him, and he was fond of his habits. But to her it was as if a stranger had opened the gate and gone out. She wondered what he would feel if he knew that she felt *that*.

'In a hour he will know,' she said to herself, with a kind of fierce exultation; and immediately she began to dramatize the scene. As soon as he came in she meant to call him up to her room and hand him the letters without a word. For a moment she gloated on the picture; then her imagination recoiled. She was humiliated by the thought of humiliating him. She wanted to keep his image intact; she would not see him.

He had lied to her about her letters – had lied to her when he found it to his interest to regain her favor. Yes, there was the point to hold fast. He had sought her out when he learned that she was rich. Perhaps he had come back from America on purpose to marry her; no doubt he had come back on purpose. It was incredible that she had not seen this at the time. She turned sick at the thought of her fatuity and of the grossness of his arts. Well, the event proved that they were all he needed. . . . But why had he gone out at such an hour? She was irritated to find herself still preoccupied by his comings and goings.

Turning from the window, she sat down again. She wondered what she meant to do next. . . . No, she would not show him the letters; she would simply leave them on his table and go away. She would leave the house with her boy and Andora. It was a relief to feel a definite plan forming itself in her mind – something that her uprooted thoughts could fasten on. She would go away, of course; and meanwhile, in order not to see him, she would feign a headache, and remain in her room till after luncheon. Then she and Andora would pack a few things, and fly with the child while he was dawdling about upstairs in the studio. When one's house fell, one fled from the ruins: nothing could be simpler, more inevitable.

Her thoughts were checked by the impossibility of picturing what would happen next. Try as she would, she could not see herself and the child away from Deering. But that, of course, was because of her nervous weakness. She had youth, money, energy: all the trumps were on her side. It was much more difficult to imagine what would become of Deering. He was do dependent on her, and they had been so happy together! It struck her as illogical and even immoral, and yet she knew he had been happy with her. It never happened like that in novels: happiness 'built on a lie' always crumbled, burying the presumptuous architect beneath its ruins. According to the laws of fiction, Deering, having deceived her once, would inevitably have gone on deceiving her. Yet she knew he had not gone on deceiving her. . . .

She tried again to picture her new life. Her friends, of course, would rally about her. But the prospect left her cold; she did not want them to rally. She wanted only one thing – the life she had been living before she had given her baby the embroidered bag to play with. Oh, why had she given him the bag? She had been so happy, they had all been so happy! Every nerve in her clamored for her lost happiness, angrily, irrationally, as the boy had clamored for his bag! It was horrible to know too much; there was always blood in the foundations. Parents 'kept things' from children – protected them from all the dark secrets of pain and evil. And was any life livable unless it were thus protected? Could anyone look in the Medusa's face and live?

But why should she leave the house, since it was hers? Here, with her boy and Andora, she could still make for herself the semblance of a life. It was Deering who would have to go; he would understand that as soon as he saw the letters.

She saw him going – leaving the house as he had left it just now. She saw the gate closing on him for the last time. Now her vision was acute enough: she saw him as distinctly as if he were in the room. Ah, he would not like returning to the old life of privations and expedients! And yet she knew he would not plead with her.

Suddenly a new thought seized her. What if Andora had rushed to him with the tale of the discovery of the letters – with the 'Fly, you are discovered!' of romantic fiction? What if he *had* left her for good? It would not be unlike him, after all. For all his sweetness he was always evasive and inscrutable. He might have said to himself that he would forestall her action, and place himself at once on the defensive. It might be that she *had* seen him out of the gate for the last time.

She looked about the room again, as if the thought had given it a new aspect. Yes, this alone could explain her husband's going out. It was past twelve o'clock, their usual luncheon hour, and he was scrupulously punctual at meals, and gently reproachful if she kept him waiting. Only some unwanted event could have caused him to leave the house at such an hour and with such marks of haste. Well, perhaps it was better that Andora should have spoken. She mistrusted her own courage; she almost hoped the deed had been done for her. Yet her next sensation was one of confused resentment. She said to herself, 'Why has Andora interfered?' She felt baffled and angry, as though her prey had escaped her. If Deering had been in the house she would have gone to him instantly and overwhelmed him with her scorn. But he had gone out, and she did not know where he had gone, and oddly mingled with her anger against him was the latent instinct of vigilance, the solicitude of the woman accustomed to watch over the man she loves. It would be strange never to feel that solicitude again, never to hear him say, with his hand on her hair: 'You foolish child, were you worried? Am I late?'

The sense of his touch was so real that she stiffened herself against it, flinging back her head as if to throw off his hand. The mere thought of his caress was hateful; yet she felt it in all her veins. Yes, she felt it, but with horror and repugnance. It was something she wanted to escape from, and the fact of struggling against it was what made its hold so strong. It was as though her mind were sounding her body to make sure of its allegiance, spying on it for any secret movement of revolt. . . .

To escape from the sensation, she rose and went again to the window. No one was in sight. But presently the gate began to swing back, and her heart gave a leap – she knew not whether up or down. A moment later the gate opened to admit a perambulator, propelled by the nurse and flanked by Juliet and Andora. Lizzie's eyes rested on the familiar group as if she had never seen it before, and she stood motionless, instead of flying down to meet the children.

Suddenly there was a step on the stairs, and she heard Andora's knock. She unbolted the door, and was strained to her friend's emaciated bosom.

'My darling!' Miss Macy cried. 'Remember you have your child – and me!'

Lizzie loosened herself. She looked at Andora with a feeling of estrangement which she could not explain.

'Have you spoken to my husband?' she asked, drawing coldly back.

'Spoken to him? No.' Andora stared at her, surprised.

'Then you haven't met him since he went out?'

'No, my love. Is he out? I haven't met him.'

Lizzie sat down with a confused sense of relief, which welled up to her throat and made speech difficult.

Suddenly light seemed to come to Andora. 'I understand, dearest. You don't feel able to see him yourself. You want me to go to him for you.' She looked eagerly about her, scenting the battle. 'You're right, darling. As soon as he comes in, I'll go to him. The sooner we get it over, the better.'

She followed Lizzie, who had turned restlessly back to the window. As they stood there, the gate moved again, and Deering entered.

'There he is now!' Lizzie felt Andora's excited clutch upon her arm. 'Where are the letters? I will go down at once. You allow me to speak for you? You trust my woman's heart? Oh, believe me, darling,' Miss Macy panted, 'I shall know exactly what to say to him!'

'What to say to him?' Lizzie absently repeated.

As her husband advanced up the path she had a sudden vision of their three years together. Those years were her whole life; everything before them had been colorless and unconscious, like the blind life of the plant before it reaches the surface of the soil. The years had not been exactly what she had dreamed; but if they had taken away certain illusions they had left richer realities in their stead. She understood now that she had gradually adjusted herself to the new image of her husband as he was, as he would always be. He was not the hero of her dreams, but he was the man she loved, and who had loved her. For she saw now, in this last wide flash of pity and initiation, that, as a comely marble may be made out of worthless scraps of mortar, glass, and pebbles, so out of mean mixed substances may be fashioned a love that will bear the stress of life.

More urgently, she felt the pressure of Miss Macy's hand.

'I shall hand him the letters without a word. You may rely, love, on my sense of dignity. I know everything you're feeling at this moment!'

Deering had reached the doorstep. Lizzie watched him in silence till he disappeared under the projecting roof of the porch; then she turned and looked almost compassionately at her friend.

'Oh, poor Andora, you don't know anything – you don't know anything at all!' she said.

Autres Temps . . .

———— ✦ ————

MRS. LIDCOTE, as the huge menacing mass of New York defined itself
far off across the waters, shrank back into her corner of the deck and
sat listening with a kind of unreasoning terror to the steady onward
drive of the screws.

She had set out on the voyage quietly enough – in what she called
her 'reasonable' mood – but the week at sea had given her too much
time to think of things and had left her too long alone with the past.

When she was alone, it was always the past that occupied her. She
couldn't get away from it, and she didn't any longer care to. During
her long years of exile she had made her terms with it, had learned
to accept the fact that it would always be there, huge, obstructing,
encumbering, bigger and more dominant than anything the future could
ever conjure up. And, at any rate, she was sure of it, she understood
it, knew how to reckon with it; she had learned to screen and manage
and protect it as one does an afflicted member of one's family.

There had never been any danger of her being allowed to forget the
past. It looked out at her from the face of every acquaintance, it appeared
suddenly in the eyes of strangers when a word enlightened them: 'Yes,
the Mrs. Lidcote, don't you know?' It had sprung at her the first day
out, when, across the dining room, from the captain's table, she had
seen Mrs. Lorin Boulger's revolving eyeglass pause and the eye behind
it grow as blank as a dropped blind. The next day, of course, the
captain had asked: 'You know your ambassadress, Mrs. Boulger?' and
she had replied that, No, she seldom left Florence, and hadn't been to
Rome for more than a day since the Boulgers had been sent to Italy.
She was so used to these phrases that it cost her no effort to repeat
them. And the captain had promptly changed the subject.

No, she didn't, as a rule, mind the past, because she was used to it
and understood it. It was a great concrete fact in her path that she had
to walk around every time she moved in any direction. But now, in
the light of the unhappy event that had summoned her from Italy, –
the sudden unanticipated news of her daughter's divorce from Horace
Pursh and remarriage with Wilbour Barkley – the past, her own poor

120

miserable past, started up at her with eyes of accusation, became, to her disordered fancy, like the afflicted relative suddenly breaking away from nurses and keepers and publicly parading the horror and misery she had, all the long years, so patiently screened and secluded.

Yes, there it had stood before her through the agitated weeks since the news had come – during her interminable journey from India, where Leila's letter had overtaken her, and the feverish halt in her apartment in Florence, where she had had to stop and gather up her possessions for a fresh start – there it had stood grinning at her with a new balefulness which seemed to say: 'Oh, but you've got to look at me *now*, because I'm not only your own past but Leila's present.'

Certainly it was a master stroke of those arch-ironists of the shears and spindle to duplicate her own story in her daughter's. Mrs. Lidcote had always somewhat grimly fancied that, having so signally failed to be of use to Leila in other ways, she would at least serve her as a warning. She had even abstained from defending herself, from making the best of her case, had stoically refused to plead extenuating circumstances, lest Leila's impulsive sympathy should lead to deductions that might react disastrously on her own life. And now that very thing had happened, and Mrs. Lidcote could hear the whole of New York saying with one voice: 'Yes, Leila's done just what her mother did. With such an example what could you expect?'

Yet if she had been an example, poor woman, she had been an awful one; she had been, she would have supposed, of more use as a deterrent than a hundred blameless mothers as incentives. For how could anyone who had seen anything of her life in the last eighteen years have had the courage to repeat so disastrous an experiment?

Well, logic in such cases didn't count, example didn't count, nothing probably counted but having the same impulses in the blood; and that was the dark inheritance she had bestowed upon her daughter. Leila hadn't consciously copied her; she had simply 'taken after' her, had been a projection of her own long-past rebellion.

Mrs. Lidcote had deplored, when she started, that the 'Utopia' was a slow steamer, and would take eight full days to bring her to her unhappy daughter; but now, as the moment of reunion approached, she would willingly have turned the boat about and fled back to the high seas. It was not only because she felt still so unprepared to face what New York had in store for her, but because she needed more time to dispose of what the 'Utopia' had already given her. The past was bad enough, but the present and future were worse, because they were less comprehensible, and because, as she grew older, surprises and inconsequences troubled her more than the worst certainties.

There was Mrs. Boulger, for instance. In the light, or rather the darkness, of new developments, it might really be that Mrs. Boulger had not meant to cut her, but had simply failed to recognize her.

Mrs. Lidcote had arrived at this hypothesis simply by listening to the conversation of the persons sitting next to her on deck – two lively young women with the latest Paris hats on their heads and the latest New York ideas in them. These ladies, as to whom it would have been impossible for a person with Mrs. Lidcote's old-fashioned categories to determine whether they were married or unmarried, 'nice' or 'horrid,' or any one or other of the definite things which young women, in her youth and her society, were conveniently assumed to be, had revealed a familiarity with the world of New York that, again according to Mrs. Lidcote's traditions, should have implied a recognized place in it. But in the present fluid state of manners what did anything imply except what their hats implied – that no one could tell what was coming next?

They seemed, at any rate, to frequent a group of idle and opulent people who executed the same gestures and revolved on the same pivots as Mrs. Lidcote's daughter and her friends: their Coras, Matties and Mabels seemed at any moment likely to reveal familiar patronymics, and once one of the speakers, summing up a discussion of which Mrs. Lidcote had missed the beginning, had affirmed with headlong confidence: 'Leila? Oh, *Leila's* all right.'

Could it be *her* Leila, the mother had wondered, with a sharp thrill of apprehension? If only they would mention surnames! But their talk leaped elliptically from allusion to allusion, their unfinished sentences dangled over bottomless pits of conjecture, and they gave their bewildered hearer the impression not so much of talking only of their intimates, as of being intimate with everyone alive.

Her old friend Franklin Ide could have told her, perhaps; but here was the last day of the voyage, and she hadn't yet found courage to ask him. Great as had been the joy of discovering his name on the passenger list and seeing his friendly bearded face in the throng against the taffrail at Cherbourg, she had as yet said nothing to him except, when they had met: 'Of course I'm going out to Leila.'

She had said nothing to Franklin Ide because she had always instinctively shrunk from taking him into her confidence. She was sure he felt sorry for her, sorrier perhaps than anyone had ever felt; but he had always paid her the supreme tribute of not showing it. His attitude allowed her to imagine that compassion was not the basis of his feeling for her, and it was part of her joy in his friendship that it was the one relation seemingly unconditioned by her state, the only one in which she could think and feel and behave like any other woman.

Now, however, as the problem of New York loomed nearer, she began to regret that she had not spoken, had not at least questioned him about the hints she had gathered on the way. He did not know the two ladies next to her, he did not even, as it chanced, know Mrs. Lorin Boulger; but he knew New York, and New York was the sphinx whose riddle she must read or perish.

Almost as the thought passed through her mind his stooping shoulders and grizzled head detached themselves against the blaze of light in the west, and he sauntered down the empty deck and dropped into the chair at her side.

'You're expecting the Barkleys to meet you, I suppose?' he asked.

It was the first time she had heard any one pronounce her daughter's new name, and it occurred to her that her friend, who was shy and inarticulate, had been trying to say it all the way over and had at last shot it out at her only because he felt it must be now or never.

'I don't know. I cabled, of course. But I believe she's at – they're at – *his* place somewhere.'

'Oh, Barkley's; yes, near Lenox, isn't it? But she's sure to come to town to meet you.'

He said it so easily and naturally that her own constraint was relieved, and suddenly, before she knew what she meant to do, she had burst out: 'She may dislike the idea of seeing people.'

Ide, whose absent shortsighted gaze had been fixed on the slowly gliding water, turned in his seat to stare at his companion.

'Who? Leila?' he said with an incredulous laugh.

Mrs. Lidcote flushed to her faded hair and grew pale again. 'It took *me* a long time – to get used to it,' she said.

His look grew gently commiserating. 'I think you'll find' – he paused for a word – 'that things are different now – altogether easier.'

'That's what I've been wondering – ever since we started.' She was determined now to speak. She moved nearer, so that their arms touched, and she could drop her voice to a murmur. 'You see, it all came on me in a flash. My going off to India and Siam on that long trip kept me away from letters for weeks at a time; and she didn't want to tell me beforehand – oh, I understand *that*, poor child! You know how good she's always been to me; how she's tried to spare me. And she knew, of course, what a state of horror I'd be in. She knew I'd rush off to her at once and try to stop it. So she never gave me a hint of anything, and she even managed to muzzle Susy Suffern – you know Susy is the one of the family who keeps me informed about things at home. I don't yet see how she prevented Susy's telling me; but she did. And her first letter, the one I got up at Bangkok, simply said the thing was over – the divorce, I mean – and that the very next day she'd – well, I suppose there was no use waiting; and *he* seems to have behaved as well as possible, to have wanted to marry her as much as – '

'Who? Barkley?' he helped her out. 'I should say so! Why what do you suppose – ' He interrupted himself. 'He'll be devoted to her, I assure you.'

'Oh, of course; I'm sure he will. He's written me – really beautifully. But it's a terrible strain on a man's devotion. I'm not sure that Leila realizes – '

Ide sounded again his little reassuring laugh. 'I'm not sure that you realize, *They're* all right.'

It was the very phrase that the young lady in the next seat had applied to the unknown 'Leila,' and its recurrence on Ide's lips flushed Mrs. Lidcote with fresh courage.

'I wish I knew just what you mean. The two young women next to me – the ones with the wonderful hats – have been talking in the same way.'

'What? About Leila?'

'About *a* Leila; I fancied it might be mine. And about society in general. All their friends seem to be divorced; some of them seem to announce their engagements before they get their decree. One of them – *her* name was Mabel – as far as I could make out, her husband found out that she meant to divorce him by noticing that she wore a new engagement ring.'

'Well, you see Leila did everything "regularly," as the French say,' Ide rejoined.

'Yes; but are these people in society? The people my neighbors talk about?'

He shrugged his shoulders. 'It would take an arbitration commission a good many sittings to define the boundaries of society nowadays. But at any rate they're in New York; and I assure you you're *not*; you're farther and farther from it.'

'But I've been back there several times to see Leila.' She hesitated and looked away from him. Then she brought out slowly: 'And I've never noticed – the least change – in – in my own case – '

'Oh,' he sounded deprecatingly, and she trembled with the fear of having gone too far. But the hour was past when such scruples could restrain her. She must know where she was and where Leila was. 'Mrs. Boulger still cuts me,' she brought out with an embarrassed laugh.

'Are you sure? You've probably cut *her;* if not now, at least in the past. And in a cut if you're not first you're nowhere. That's what keeps up so many quarrels.'

The word roused Mrs. Lidcote to a renewed sense of realities. 'But the Purshes,' she said – 'the Purshes are so strong! There are so many of them, and they all back each other up, just as my husband's family did. I know what it means to have a clan against one. They're stronger than any number of separate friends. The Purshes will *never* forgive Leila for leaving Horace. Why, his mother opposed his marrying her because of – of me. She tried to get Leila to promise that she wouldn't see me when they went to Europe on their honeymoon. And now she'll say it was my example.'

Her companion, vaguely stroking his beard, mused a moment upon this; then he asked, with seeming irrelevance, 'What did Leila say when you wrote that you were coming?'

'She said it wasn't the least necessary, but that I'd better come, because it was the only way to convince me that it wasn't.'

'Well, then, that proves she's not afraid of the Purshes.'

She breathed a long sigh of remembrance. 'Oh, just at first, you know – one never is.'

He laid his hand on hers with a gesture of intelligence and pity. 'You'll see, you'll see,' he said.

A shadow lengthened down the deck before them, and a steward stood there, proffering a Marconigram.

'Oh, now I shall know!' she exclaimed.

She tore the message open, and then let it fall on her knees, dropping her hands on it in silence.

Ide's inquiry roused her: 'It's all right?'

'Oh, quite right. Perfectly. She can't come; but she's sending Susy Suffern. She says Susy will explain.' After another silence she added, with a sudden gush of bitterness: 'As if I needed any explanation!'

She felt Ide's hesitating glance upon her. 'She's in the country?'

'Yes. "Prevented last moment. Longing for you, expecting you. Love from both." Don't you *see*, the poor darling, that she couldn't face it?'

'No, I don't.' He waited. 'Do you mean to go to her immediately?'

'It will be too late to catch a train this evening; but I shall take the first tomorrow morning.' She considered a moment. 'Perhaps it's better. I need a talk with Susy first. She's to meet me at the dock, and I'll take her straight back to the hotel with me.'

As she developed this plan, she had the sense that Ide was still thoughtfully, even gravely, considering her. When she ceased, he remained silent a moment; then he said almost ceremoniously: 'If your talk with Miss Suffern doesn't last too late, may I come and see you when it's over? I shall be dining at my club, and I'll call you up at about ten, if I may. I'm off to Chicago on business tomorrow morning, and it would be a satisfaction to know, before I start, that your cousin's been able to reassure you, as I know she will.'

He spoke with a shy deliberateness that, even to Mrs. Lidcote's troubled perceptions, sounded a long-silenced note of feeling. Perhaps the breaking down of the barrier of reticence between them had released unsuspected emotions in both. The tone of his appeal moved her curiously and loosened the tight strain of her fears.

'Oh, yes, come – do come,' she said, rising. The huge threat of New York was imminent now, dwarfing, under long reaches of embattled masonry, the great deck she stood on and all the little specks of life it carried. One of them, drifting nearer, took the shape of her maid, followed by luggage-laden stewards, and signing to her that it was time to go below. As they descended to the main deck, the throng swept her against Mrs. Lorin Boulger's shoulder, and she heard the ambassa-

dress call out to someone, over the vexed sea of hats: 'So sorry! I should
have been delighted, but I've promised to spend Sunday with some
friends at Lenox.'

• II •

SUSY SUFFERN'S explanation did not end till after ten o'clock, and she
had just gone when Franklin Ide, who, complying with an old New
York tradition, had caused himself to be preceded by a long white box
of roses, was shown into Mrs. Lidcote's sitting room.

He came forward with his shy half-humorous smile and, taking her
hand, looked at her for a moment without speaking.

'It's all right,' he then pronounced.

Mrs. Lidcote returned his smile. 'It's extraordinary. Everything's
changed. Even Susy has changed; and you know the extent to which
Susy used to represent the old New York. There's no old New York
left, it seems. She talked in the most amazing way. She snaps her fingers
at the Purshes. She told me – *me*, that every woman had a right to
happiness and that self-expression was the highest duty. She accused
me of misunderstanding Leila; she said my point of view was conventional! She was bursting with pride at having been in the secret, and
wearing a brooch that Wilbur Barkley'd given her!'

Franklin Ide had seated himself in the armchair she had pushed
forward for him under the electric chandelier. He threw back his head
and laughed. 'What did I tell you?'

'Yes; but I can't believe that Susy's not mistaken. Poor dear, she
has the habit of lost causes; and she may feel that, having stuck to me,
she can do no less than stick to Leila.'

'But she didn't – did she – openly defy the world for you? She
didn't snap her fingers at the Lidcotes?'

Mrs. Lidcote shook her head, still smiling. 'No. It was enough to
defy *my* family. It was doubtful at one time if they would tolerate her
seeing me, and she almost had to disinfect herself after each visit. I
believe that at first my sister-in-law wouldn't let the girls come down
when Susy dined with her.'

'Well, isn't your cousin's present attitude the best possible proof
that times have changed?'

'Yes, yes; I know.' She leaned forward from her sofa-corner, fixing
her eyes on his thin kindly face, which gleamed on her indistinctly
through her tears. 'If it's true, it's – it's dazzling. She says Leila's
perfectly happy. It's as if an angel had gone about lifting gravestones,
and the buried people walked again, and the living didn't shrink from
them.'

'That's about it,' he assented.

She drew a deep breath, and sat looking away from him down the long perspective of lamp-fringed streets over which her windows hung.

'I can understand how happy you must be,' he began at length.

She turned to him impetuously. 'Yes, yes; I'm happy. But I'm lonely, too – lonelier than ever. I didn't take up much room in the world before; but now – where is there a corner for me? Oh, since I've begun to confess myself, why shouldn't I go on? Telling you this lifts a gravestone from *me!* You see, before this, Leila needed me. She was unhappy, and I knew it, and though we hardly ever talked of it I felt that, in a way, the thought that I'd been through the same thing, and down to the dregs of it, helped her. And her needing me helped *me.* And when the news of her marriage came my first thought was that now she'd need me more than ever, that she'd have no one but me to turn to. Yes, under all my distress there was a fierce joy in that. It was so new and wonderful to feel again that there was one person who wouldn't be able to get on without me! And now what you and Susy tell me seems to have taken my child from me; and just at first that's all I can feel.'

'Of course it's all you feel.' He looked at her musingly. 'Why didn't Leila come to meet you?'

'That was really my fault. You see, I'd cabled that I was not sure of being able to get off on the 'Utopia,' and apparently my second cable was delayed, and when she received it she'd already asked some people over Sunday – one or two of her old friends, Susy says. I'm so glad they should have wanted to go to her at once; but naturally I'd rather have been alone with her.'

'You still mean to go, then?'

'Oh, I must. Susy wanted to drag me off to Ridgefield with her over Sunday, and Leila sent me word that of course I might go if I wanted to, and that I was not to think of her; but I know how disappointed she would be. Susy said she was afraid I might be upset at her having people to stay, and that, if I minded, she wouldn't urge me to come. But if *they* don't mind, why should I? And of course, if they're willing to go to Leila it must mean – '

'Of course. I'm glad you recognize that,' Franklin Ide exclaimed abruptly. He stood up and went over to her, taking her head with one of his quick gestures. 'There's something I want to say to you,' he began –

The next morning, in the train, through all the other contending thoughts in Mrs. Lidcote's mind there ran the warm undercurrent of what Franklin Ide had wanted to say to her.

He had wanted, she knew, to say it once before, when, nearly eight years earlier, the hazard of meeting at the end of a rainy autumn in a deserted Swiss hotel had thrown them for a fortnight into unwonted

propinquity. They had walked and talked together, borrowed each
other's books and newspapers, spent the long chill evenings over the
fire in the dim lamplight of her little pitch-pine sitting room; and she
had been wonderfully comforted by his presence, and hard frozen places
in her had melted, and she had known that she would be desperately
sorry when he went. And then, just at the end, in his odd indirect way,
he had let her see that it rested with her to have him stay. She could
still relive the sleepless night she had given to that discovery. It was
preposterous, of course, to think of repaying his devotion by accepting
such a sacrifice; but how find reasons to convince him? She could not
bear to let him think her less touched, less inclined to him than she
was: the generosity of his love deserved that she should repay it with
the truth. Yet how let him see what she felt, and yet refuse what he
offered? How confess to him what had been on her lips when he made
the offer: 'I've seen what it did to one man; and there must never, never
be another'? The tacit ignoring of her past had been the element in
which their friendship lived, and she could not suddenly, to him of all
men, begin to talk of herself like a guilty woman in a play. Somehow,
in the end, she had managed it, had averted a direct explanation, had
made him understand that her life was over, that she existed only for
her daughter, and that a more definite word from him would have been
almost a breach of delicacy. She was so used to behaving as if her life
were over! And, at any rate, he had taken her hint, and she had been
able to spare her sensitiveness and his. The next year, when he came
to Florence to see her, they met again in the old friendly way; and that
till now had continued to be the tenor of their intimacy.

And now, suddenly and unexpectedly, he had brought up the question again, directly this time, and in such a form that she could not
evade it: putting the renewal of his plea, after so long an interval, on
the ground that, on her own showing, her chief argument against it no
longer existed.

'You tell me Leila's happy. If she's happy, she doesn't need you-
need you, that is, in the same way as before. You wanted, I know, to
be always in reach, always free and available if she should suddenly call
you to her or take refuge with you. I understood that – I respected it.
I didn't urge my case because I saw it was useless. You couldn't, I
understand well enough, have felt free to take such happiness as life
with me might give you while she was unhappy, and, as you imagined,
with no hope of release. Even then I didn't feel as you did about it; I
understood better the trend of things here. But ten years ago the change
hadn't really come; and I had no way of convincing you that it was
coming. Still, I always fancied that Leila might not think her case was
closed, and so I chose to think that ours wasn't either. Let me go on
thinking so, at any rate, till you've seen her, and confirmed with your
own eyes what Susy Suffern tells you.'

• III •

ALL through what Susy Suffern told and retold her during their four hours' flight to the hills this plea of Ide's kept coming back to Mrs. Lidcote. She did not yet know what she felt as to its bearing on her own fate, but it was something on which her confused thoughts could stay themselves amid the welter of new impressions, and she was inexpressibly glad that he had said what he had, and said it at that particular moment. It helped her to hold fast to her identity in the rush of strange names and new categories that her cousin's talk poured out on her.

With the progress of the journey Miss Suffern's communications grew more and more amazing. She was like a cicerone preparing the mind of an inexperienced traveler for the marvels about to burst on it.

'You won't know Leila. She's had her pearls reset. Sargent's to paint her. Oh, and I was to tell you that she hopes you won't mind being the least bit squeezed over Sunday. The house was built by Wilbour's father, you know, and it's rather old-fashioned – only ten spare bedrooms. Of course that's small for what they mean to do, and she'll show you the new plans they've had made. Their idea is to keep the present house as a wing. She told me to explain – she's so dreadfully sorry not to be able to give you a sitting room just at first. They're thinking of Egypt for next winter, unless, of course, Wilbour gets his appointment. Oh, didn't she write you about that? Why, he wants Rome, you know – the second secretaryship. Or, rather, he wanted England; but Leila insisted that if they went abroad she must be near you. And of course, what she says is law. Oh, they quite hope they'll get it. You see Horace's uncle is in the Cabinet – one of the assistant secretaries – and I believe he has a good deal of pull – '

'Horace's uncle? You mean Wilbour's, I suppose,' Mrs. Lidcote interjected, with a gasp of which a fraction was given to Miss Suffern's flippant use of the language.

'Wilbour's? No, I don't. I mean Horace's. There's no bad feeling between them, I assure you. Since Horace's engagement was announced – you didn't know Horace was engaged? Why, he's marrying one of Bishop Thorbury's girls: the red-haired one who wrote the novel that everyone's talking about. *This Flesh of Mine*. They're to be married in the cathedral. Of course Horace *can*, because it was Leila who – but, as I say, there's not the *least* feeling, and Horace wrote himself to his uncle about Wilbour.'

Mrs. Lidcote's thoughts fled back to what she had said to Ide the day before on the deck of the 'Utopia.' 'I didn't take up much room before, but now where is there a corner for me?' Where indeed in this crowded, topsy-turvy world, with its headlong changes and helter-skelter readjustments, its new tolerances and indifferences and accom-

modations, was there room for a character fashioned by slower sterner
processes and a life broken under their inexorable pressure? And then,
in a flash, she viewed the chaos from a new angle, and order seemed
to move upon the void. If the old processes were changed, her case was
changed with them; she, too, was a part of the general readjustment, a
tiny fragment of the new pattern worked out in bolder freer harmonies.
Since her daughter had no penalty to pay, was not she herself released
by the same stroke? The rich arrears of youth and joy were gone; but
was there not time enough left to accumulate new stores of happiness?
That, of course, was what Franklin Ide had felt and had meant her to
feel. He had seen at once what the change in her daughter's situation
would make in her view of her own. It was almost – wondrously
enough! – as if Leila's folly had been the means of vindicating hers.

Everything else for the moment faded for Mrs. Lidcote in the glow of
her daughter's embrace. It was unnatural, it was almost terrifying, to
find herself standing on a strange threshold, under an unknown roof,
in a big hall of pictures, flowers, firelight, and hurrying servants, and
in this spacious unfamiliar confusion to discover Leila, bareheaded,
laughing, authoritative, with a strange young man jovially echoing her
welcome and transmitting her orders; but once Mrs. Lidcote had her
child on her breast, and her child's 'It's all right, you old darling!' in
her ears, every other feeling was lost in the deep sense of well-being
that only Leila's hug could give.

The sense was still with her, warming her veins and pleasantly
fluttering her heart, as she went up to her room after luncheon. A little
constrained by the presence of visitors, and not altogether sorry to defer
for a few hours the 'long talk' with her daughter for which she somehow
felt herself tremulously unready, she had withdrawn, on the plea of
fatigue, to the bright luxurious bedroom into which Leila had again
and again apologized for having been obliged to squeeze her. The room
was bigger and finer than any in her small apartment in Florence; but
it was not the standard of affluence implied in her daughter's tone about
it that chiefly struck her, nor yet the finish and complexity of its
appointments. It was the look it shared with the rest of the house, and
with the perspective of the gardens beneath its windows, of being
part of an 'establishment' – of something solid, avowed, founded on
sacraments and precedents and principles. There was nothing about the
place, or about Leila and Wilbour, that suggested either passion or peril:
their relation seemed as comfortable as their furniture and as respectable
as their balance at the bank.

This was, in the whole confusing experience, the thing that confused
Mrs. Lidcote most, that gave her at once the deepest feeling of security
for Leila and the strongest sense of apprehension for herself. Yes, there
was something oppressive in the completeness and compactness of

Leila's well-being. Ide had been right: her daughter did not need her. Leila, with her first embrace, had unconsciously attested the fact in the same phrase as Ide himself and as the two young women with the hats. 'It's all right, you old darling!' she had said: and her mother sat alone, trying to fit herself into the new scheme of things which such a certainty betokened.

Her first distinct feeling was one of irrational resentment. If such a change was to come, why had it not come sooner? Here was she, a woman not yet old, who had paid with the best years of her life for the theft of the happiness that her daughter's contemporaries were taking as their due. There was no sense, no sequence, in it. She had had what she wanted, but she had to pay too much for it. She had had to pay the last bitterest price of learning that love has a price: that it is worth so much and no more. She had known the anguish of watching the man she loved discover this first, and of reading the discovery in his eyes. It was a part of her history that she had not trusted herself to think of for a long time past: she always took a big turn about that haunted corner. But now, at the sight of the young man downstairs, so openly and jovially Leila's, she was overwhelmed at the senseless waste of her own adventure, and wrung with the irony of perceiving that the success or failure of the deepest human experiences may hang on a matter of chronology.

Then gradually the thought of Ide returned to her. 'I chose to think that our case wasn't closed,' he had said. She had been deeply touched by that. To everyone else her case had been closed so long! *Finis* was scrawled all over her. But here was one man who had believed and waited, and what if what he believed in and waited for were coming true? If Leila's 'all right' should really foreshadow hers?

As yet, of course, it was impossible to tell. She had fancied, indeed, when she entered the drawing room before luncheon, that a too-sudden hush had fallen on the assembled group of Leila's friends, on the slender vociferous young women and the lounging golf-stockinged young men. They had all received her politely, with the kind of petrified politeness that may be either a tribute to age or a protest at laxity; but to them, of course, she must be an old woman because she was Leila's mother, and in a society so dominated by youth the mere presence of maturity was a constraint.

One of the young girls, however, had presently emerged from the group, and, attaching herself to Mrs. Lidcote, had listened to her with a blue gaze of admiration which gave the older woman a sudden happy consciousness of her long-forgotten social graces. It was agreeable to find herself attracting this young Charlotte Wynn, whose mother had been among her closest friends, and in whom something of the sober-ness and softness of the earlier manners had survived. But the little colloquy, broken up by the announcement of luncheon, could of course result in nothing more definite than this reminiscent emotion.

No, she could not yet tell how her own case was to be fitted into the new order of things; but there were more people – 'older people' Leila had put it – arriving by the afternoon train, and that evening at dinner she would doubtless be able to judge. She began to wonder nervously who the newcomers might be. Probably she would be spared the embarrassment of finding old acquaintances among them; but it was odd that her daughter had mentioned no names.

Leila had proposed that, later in the afternoon, Wilbour should take her mother for a drive: she said she wanted them to have a 'nice, quiet talk.' But Mrs. Lidcote wished her talk with Leila to come first, and had, moreover, at luncheon, caught stray allusions to an impending tennis match in which her son-in-law was engaged. Her fatigue had been a sufficient pretext for declining the drive, and she had begged Leila to think of her as peacefully resting in her room till such time as they could snatch their quiet moment.

'Before tea, then, you duck!' Leila with a last kiss had decided; and presently Mrs. Lidcote, through her open window, had heard the fresh loud voices of her daughter's visitors chiming across the gardens from the tennis court.

• IV •

LEILA had come and gone, and they had had their talk. It had not lasted as long as Mrs. Lidcote wished, for in the middle of it Leila had been summoned to the telephone to receive an important message from town, and had sent word to her mother that she couldn't come back just then, as one of the young ladies had been called away unexpectedly and arrangements had to be made for her departure. But the mother and daughter had had almost an hour together, and Mrs. Lidcote was happy. She had never seen Leila so tender, so solicitous. The only thing that troubled her was the very excess of this solicitude, the exaggerated expression of her daughter's annoyance that their first moments together should have been marred by the presence of strangers.

'Not strangers to me, darling, since they're friends of yours,' her mother had assured her.

'Yes; but I know your feeling, you queer wild mother. I know how you've always hated people.' (*Hated people!* Had Leila forgotten why?) 'And that's why I told Susy that if you preferred to go with her to Ridgefield on Sunday I should perfectly understand, and patiently wait for our good hug. But you didn't really mind them at luncheon, did you, dearest?'

Mrs. Lidcote, at that, had suddenly thrown a startled look at her daughter. 'I don't mind things of that kind any longer,' she had simply answered.

'But that doesn't console me for having exposed you to the bother of it, for having let you come here when I ought to have *ordered* you off to Ridgefield with Susy. If Susy hadn't been stupid she'd have made you go there with her. I hate to think of you up here all alone.'

Again Mrs. Lidcote tried to read something more than a rather obtuse devotion in her daughter's radiant gaze. 'I'm glad to have had a rest this afternoon, dear; and later – '

'Oh, yes, later, when all this fuss is over, we'll more than make up for it, shan't we, you precious darling?' And at this point Leila had been summoned to the telephone, leaving Mrs. Lidcote to her conjectures.

These were still floating before her in cloudy uncertainty when Miss Suffern tapped at the door.

'You've come to take me down to tea? I'd forgotten how late it was', Mrs. Lidcote exclaimed.

Miss Suffern, a plump peering little woman, with prim hair and a conciliatory smile, nervously adjusted the pendent bugles of her elaborate black dress. Miss Suffern was always in mourning, and always commemorating the demise of distant relatives by wearing the discarded wardrobe of their next of kin. 'It isn't *exactly* mourning,' she would say; 'but it's the only stitch of black poor Julia had – and of course George was only my mother's step-cousin.'

As she came forward Mrs. Lidcote found herself humorously wondering whether she were mourning Horace Pursh's divorce in one of his mother's old black satins.

'Oh, *did* you mean to go down for tea?' Susy Suffern peered at her, a little fluttered. 'Leila sent me up to keep you company. She thought it would be cozier for you to stay here. She was afraid you were feeling rather tired.'

'I was; but I've had the whole afternoon to rest in. And this wonderful sofa to help me.'

'Leila told me to tell you that she'd rush up for a minute before dinner, after everybody had arrived; but the train is always dreadfully late. She's in despair at not giving you a sitting room; she wanted to know if I thought you really minded.'

'Of course I don't mind. It's not like Leila to think I should.' Mrs. Lidcote drew aside to make way for the housemaid, who appeared in the doorway bearing a table spread with a bewildering variety of tea cakes.

'Leila saw to it herself,' Miss Suffern murmured as the door closed. 'Her one idea is that you should feel happy here.'

It struck Mrs. Lidcote as one more mark of the subverted state of things that her daughter's solicitude should find expression in the multiplicity of sandwiches and the piping hotness of muffins; but then everything that had happened since her arrival seemed to increase her confusion.

The note of a motor horn down the drive gave another turn to her thoughts. 'Are those the new arrivals already?' she asked.

'Oh, dear, no; they won't be here till after seven.' Miss Suffern craned her head from the window to catch a glimpse of the motor. 'It must be Charlotte leaving.'

'Was it the little Wynn girl who was called away in a hurry? I hope it's not on account of illness.'

'Oh, no; I believe there was some mistake about dates. Her mother telephoned her that she was expected at the Stepleys, at Fishkill, and she had to be rushed over to Albany to catch a train.'

Mrs. Lidcote meditated. 'I'm sorry. She's a charming young thing. I hoped I should have another talk with her this evening after dinner.'

'Yes; it's too bad.' Miss Sufern's gaze grew vague. 'You *do* look tired, you know,' she continued, seating herself at the tea table and preparing to dispense its delicacies. 'You must go straight back to your sofa and let me wait on you. The excitement has told on you more than you think, and you mustn't fight against it any longer. Just stay quietly up here and let yourself go. You'll have Leila to yourself on Monday.'

Mrs. Lidcote received the teacup which her cousin proffered, but showed no other disposition to obey her injunctions. For a moment she stirred her tea in silence; then she asked: 'Is it your idea that I should stay quietly up here till Monday?'

Miss Suffern set down her cup with a gesture so sudden that it endangered an adjacent plate of scones. When she had assured herself of the safety of the scones she looked up with a fluttered laugh. 'Perhaps, dear, by tomorrow you'll be feeling differently. The air here, you know – '

'Yes, I know.' Mrs. Lidcote bent forward to help herself to a scone. 'Who's arriving this evening?' she asked.

Miss Suffern frowned and peered. 'You know my wretched head for names. Leila told me – but there are so many – '

'So many? She didn't tell me she expected a big party.'

'Oh, not big: but rather outside of her little group. And of course, as it's the first time, she's a little excited at having the older set.'

'The older set? Our contemporaries, you mean?'

'Why – yes.' Miss Suffern paused as if to gather herself up for a leap. 'The Ashton Gileses,' she brought out.

'The Aston Gileses? Really? I shall be glad to see Mary Giles again. It must be eighteen years,' said Mrs. Lidcote steadily.

'Yes,' Miss Suffern gasped, precipitately refilling her cup.

'The Ashton Gileses; and who else?'

'Well, the Sam Fresbies. But the most important person, of course, is Mrs. Lorin Boulger.'

'Mrs. Boulger? Leila didn't tell me she was coming.'

'Didn't she? I suppose she forgot everything when she saw you. But the party was got up for Mrs. Boulger. You see, it's very important that she should – well, take a fancy to Leila and Wilbour; his being appointed to Rome virtually depends on it. And you know Leila insists on Rome in order to be near you. So she asked Mary Giles, who's intimate with the Boulgers, if the visit couldn't possibly be arranged; and Mary's cable caught Mrs. Boulger at Cherbourg. She's to be only a fortnight in America; and getting her to come directly here was rather a triumph.'

'Yes; I see it was,' said Mrs. Lidcote.

'You know, she's rather – rather fussy; and Mary was a little doubtful if – '

'If she would, on account of Leila?' Mrs. Lidcote murmured.

'Well, yes. In her official position. But luckily she's a friend of the Barkleys. And finding the Gileses and Fresbies here will make it all right. The times have changed!' Susy Suffern indulgently summed up.

Mrs. Lidcote smiled. 'Yes; a few years ago it would have seemed improbable that I should ever again be dining with Mary Giles and Harriet Fresbie and Mrs. Lorin Boulger.'

Miss Suffern did not at the moment seem disposed to enlarge upon this theme; and after an interval of silence Mrs. Lidcote suddenly resumed: 'Do they know I'm here, by the way?'

The effect of her question was to produce in Miss Suffern an exaggerated access of peering and frowning. She twitched the tea things about, fingered her bugles, and, looking at the clock, exclaimed amazedly: 'Mercy! Is it seven already?'

'Not that it can make any difference, I suppose,' Mrs. Lidcote continued. 'But did Leila tell them I was coming?'

Miss Suffern looked at her with pain. 'Why, you don't suppose, dearest, that Leila would do anything – '

Mrs. Lidcote went on: 'For, of course, it's of the first importance, as you say, that Mrs. Lorin Boulger should be favorably impressed, in order that Wilbour may have the best possible chance of getting Rome.'

'I *told* Leila you'd feel that, dear. You see, it's actually on *your* account – so that they may get a post near you – that Leila invited Mrs. Boulger.'

'Yes, I see that.' Mrs. Lidcote, abruptly rising from her seat, turned her eyes to the clock. 'But, as you say, it's getting late. Oughtn't we to dress for dinner?'

Miss Suffern, at the suggestion, stood up also, an agitated hand among her bugles. 'I do wish I could persuade you to stay up here this evening. I'm sure Leila'd be happier if you would. Really, you're much too tired to come down.'

'What nonsense, Susy!' Mrs. Lidcote spoke with a sudden sharpness, her hand stretched to the bell. 'When do we dine? At half-past eight? Then I must really send you packing. At my age it takes time to dress.'

Miss Suffern, thus projected toward the threshold, lingered there to repeat: 'Leila'll never forgive herself if you make an effort you're not up to.' But Mrs. Lidcote smiled on her without answering, and the icy light-wave propelled her through the door.

• V •

MRS. LIDCOTE, though she had made the gesture of ringing for her maid, had not done so.

When the door closed, she continued to stand motionless in the middle of her soft spacious room. The fire which had been kindled at twilight danced on the brightness of silver and mirrors and sober gilding; and the sofa toward which she had been urged by Miss Suffern heaped up its cushions in inviting proximity to a table laden with new books and papers. She could not recall having ever been more luxuriously housed, or having ever had so strange a sense of being out alone, under the night, in a wind-beaten plain. She sat down by the fire and thought.

A knock on the door made her lift her head, and she saw her daughter on the threshold. The intricate ordering of Leila's fair hair and the flying folds of her dressing gown showed that she had interrupted her dressing to hasten to her mother; but once in the room she paused a moment, smiling uncertainly, as though she had forgotten the object of her haste.

Mrs. Lidcote rose to her feet. 'Time to dress, dearest? Don't scold! I shan't be late.'

'To dress?' Leila stood before her with a puzzled look. 'Why, I thought, dear – I mean, I hoped you'd decided just to stay here quietly and rest.'

Her mother smiled. 'But I've been resting all the afternoon!'

'Yes, but – you know you *do* look tired. And when Susy told me just now that you meant to make the effort – '

'You came to stop me?'

'I came to tell you that you needn't feel in the least obliged – '

'Of course. I understand that.'

There was a pause during which Leila, vaguely averting herself from her mother's scrutiny, drifted toward the dressing table and began to disturb the symmetry of the brushes and bottles laid out on it. 'Do your visitors know that I'm here?' Mrs. Lidcote suddenly went on.

'Do they – of course – why, naturally,' Leila rejoined, absorbed in trying to turn the stopper of a salts bottle.

'Then won't they think it odd if I don't appear?'

'Oh, not in the least, dearest. I assure you they'll *all* understand.' Leila laid down the bottle and turned back to her mother, her face alight with reassurance.

Mrs. Lidcote stood motionless, her head erect, her smiling eyes on her daughter's. 'Will they think it odd if I *do?*'

Leila stopped short, her lips half parted to reply. As she paused, the color stole over her bare neck, swept up to her throat, and burst into flame in her cheeks. Thence it sent its devastating crimson up to her very temples, to the lobes of her ears, to the edges of her eyelids, beating all over her in fiery waves, as if fanned by some imperceptible wind.

Mrs. Lidcote silently watched the conflagration; then she turned away her eyes with a slight laugh. 'I only meant that I was afraid it might upset the arrangement of your dinner table if I didn't come down. If you can assure me that it won't, I believe I'll take you at your word and go back to this irresistible sofa.' She paused, as if waiting for her daughter to speak; then she held out her arms. 'Run off and dress, dearest; and don't have me on your mind.' She clasped Leila close, pressing a long kiss on the last afterglow of her subsiding blush. 'I do feel the least bit overdone, and if it won't inconvenience you to have me drop out of things, I believe I'll basely take to my bed and stay there till your party scatters. And now run off, or you'll be late; and make my excuses to them all.'

• VI •

THE Barkleys' visitors had dispersed, and Mrs. Lidcote, completely restored by her two days' rest, found herself, on the following Monday, alone with her children and Miss Suffern.

There was a note of jubilation in the air, for the party had 'gone off' so extraordinarily well, and so completely, at it appeared, to the satisfaction of Mrs. Lorin Boulger, that Wilbour's early appointment to Rome was almost to be counted on. So certain did this seem that the prospect of a prompt reunion mitigated the distress with which Leila learned of her mother's decision to return almost immediately to Italy. No one understood this decision; it seemed to Leila absolutely unintelligible that Mrs. Lidcote should not stay on with them till their own fate was fixed, and Wilbour echoed her astonishment.

'Why shouldn't you, as Leila says, wait here till we can all pack up and go together?'

Mrs. Lidcote smiled her gratitude with her refusal. 'After all, it's not yet sure that you'll be packing up.'

'Oh, you ought to have seen Wilbour with Mrs. Boulger,' Leila triumphed.

'No, you ought to have seen Leila with her,' Leila's husband exulted.

Miss Suffern enthusiastically appended: 'I *do* think inviting Harriet Fresbie was a stroke of genius!'

'Oh, we'll be with you soon,' Leila laughed. 'So soon that it's really foolish to separate.'

But Mrs. Lidcote held out with the quiet firmness which her daughter knew it was useless to oppose. After her long months in India, it was really imperative, she declared, that she should get back to Florence and see what was happening to her little place there; and she had been so comfortable on the 'Utopia' that she had a fancy to return by the same ship. There was nothing for it, therefore, but to acquiesce in her decision and keep her with them till the afternoon before the day of the 'Utopia's' sailing. This arrangement fitted in with certain projects which, during her two days' seclusion, Mrs. Lidcote had silently matured. It had become to her of the first importance to get away as soon as she could, and the little place in Florence, which held her past in every fold of its curtains and between every page of its books, seemed now to her the one spot where that past would be endurable to look upon.

She was not unhappy during the intervening days. The sight of Leila's well-being, the sense of Leila's tenderness, were, after all, what she had come for; and of these she had had full measure. Leila had never been happier or more tender; and the contemplation of her bliss, and the enjoyment of her affection, were an absorbing occupation for her mother. But they were also a sharp strain on certain overtightened chords, and Mrs. Lidcote, when at last she found herself alone in the New York hotel to which she had returned the night before embarking, had the feeling that she had just escaped with her life from the clutch of a giant hand.

She had refused to let her daughter come to town with her; she had even rejected Susy Suffern's company. She wanted no viaticum but that of her own thoughts; and she let these come to her without shrinking from them as she sat in the same high-hung sitting room in which, just a week before, she and Franklin Ide had had their memorable talk.

She had promised her friend to let him hear from her, but she had not kept her promise. She knew that he had probably come back from Chicago, and that if he learned of her sudden decision to return to Italy it would be impossible for her not to see him before sailing; and as she wished above all things not to see him she had kept silent, intending to send him a letter from the steamer.

There was no reason why she should wait till then to write it. The actual moment was more favorable, and the task, though not agreeable, would at least bridge over an hour of her lonely evening. She went up to the writing table, drew out a sheet of paper and began to write his name. And as she did so, the door opened and he came in.

The words she met him with were the last she could have imagined herself saying when they had parted. 'How in the world did you know that I was here?'

He caught her meaning in a flash. 'You didn't want me to, then?' He stood looking at her. 'I suppose I ought to have taken your silence as meaning that. But I happened to meet Mrs. Wynn, who is stopping here, and she asked me to dine with her and Charlotte, and Charlotte's young man. They told me they'd seen you arriving this afternoon, and I couldn't help coming up.'

There was a pause between them, which Mrs. Lidcote at last surprisingly broke with the exclamation: 'Ah, she *did* recognize me, then!'

'Recognize you?' he stared. 'Why – '

'Oh, I saw she did, though she never moved an eyelid. I saw it by Charlotte's blush. The child has the prettiest blush. I saw that her mother wouldn't let her speak to me.'

Ide put down his hat with an impatient laugh. 'Hasn't Leila cured you of your delusions?'

She looked at him intently. 'Then you don't think Margaret Wynn meant to cut me?'

'I think your ideas are absurd.'

She paused for a perceptible moment without taking this up; then she said, at a tangent: 'I'm sailing tomorrow early. I meant to write to you – there's the letter I'd begun.'

Ide followed her gesture, and then turned his eyes back to her face. 'You didn't mean to see me, then, or even to let me know that you were going till you'd left?'

'I felt it would be easier to explain to you in a letter – '

'What in God's name is there to explain?' She made no reply, and he pressed on: 'It can't be that you're worried about Leila, for Charlotte Wynn told me she'd been there last week, and there was a big party arriving when she left: Fresbies and Gileses, and Mrs. Lorin Boulger – all the board of examiners! If Leila has passed *that*, she's got her degree.'

Mrs. Lidcote had dropped down into a corner of the sofa where she had sat during their talk of the week before. 'I was stupid,' she began abruptly. 'I ought to have gone to Ridgefield with Susy. I didn't see till afterward that I was expected to.'

'You were expected to?'

'Yes. Oh, it wasn't Leila's fault. She suffered – poor darling; she was distracted. But she'd asked her party before she knew I was arriving.'

'Oh, as to that – ' Ide drew a deep breath of relief. 'I can understand that it must have been a disappointment not to have you to herself just at first. But, after all, you were among old friends or their children: the Gileses and Fresbies – and little Charlotte Wynn.' He paused a moment before the last name, and scrutinized her hesitatingly. 'Even if they came at the wrong time, you must have been glad to see them all at Leila's.'

She gave him back his look with a faint smile. 'I didn't see them.'

'You didn't see them?'

'No. That is, excepting little Charlotte Wynn. That child is exquisite. We had a talk before luncheon the day I arrived. But when her mother found out that I was staying in the house she telephoned her to leave immediately, and so I didn't see her again.'

The color rushed to Ide's sallow face. 'I don't know where you get such ideas!'

She pursued, as if she had not heard him: 'Oh, and I saw Mary Giles for a minute too. Susy Suffern brought her up to my room the last evening, after dinner, when all the others were at bridge. She meant it kindly – but it wasn't much use.'

'But what were you doing in your room in the evening after dinner?'

'Why, you see, when I found out my mistake in coming, – how embarrassing it was for Leila, I mean – I simply told her I was very tired, and preferred to stay upstairs till the party was over.'

Ide, with a groan, struck his hand against the arm of his chair. 'I wonder how much of all this you simply imagined!'

'I didn't imagine the fact of Harriet Fresbie's not even asking if she might see me when she knew I was in the house. Nor of Mary Giles's getting Susy, at the eleventh hour, to smuggle her up to my room when the others wouldn't know where she'd gone; nor poor Leila's ghastly fear lest Mrs. Lorin Boulger, for whom the party was given, should guess I was in the house, and prevent her husband's giving Wilbour the second secretaryship because she'd been obliged to spend a night under the same roof with his mother-in-law!'

Ide continued to drum on his chair arm with exasperated fingers. 'You don't *know* that any of the acts you describe are due to the causes you suppose.'

Mrs. Lidcote paused before replying, as if honestly trying to measure the weight of this argument. Then she said in a low tone: 'I know that Leila was in an agony lest I should come down to dinner the first night. And it was for me she was afraid, not for herself. Leila is never afraid for herself.'

'But the conclusions you draw are simply preposterous. There are narrow-minded women everywhere, but the women who were at Leila's knew perfectly well that their going there would give her a sort of social sanction, and if they were willing that she should have it, why on earth should they want to withhold it from you?'

'That's what I told myself a week ago, in this very room, after my first talk with Susy Suffern.' She lifted a misty smile to his anxious eyes. 'That's why I listened to what you said to me the same evening, and why your arguments half-convinced me, and made me think that what had been possible for Leila might not be impossible for me. If the new dispensation had come, why not for me as well as for the others? I can't tell you the flight my imagination took!'

Franklin Ide rose from his seat and crossed the room to a chair near her sofa corner. 'All I cared about was that it seemed – for the moment – to be carrying you toward me,' he said.

'I cared about that, too. That's why I meant to go away without seeing you.' They gave each other grave look for look. 'Because, you see, I was mistaken,' she went on. 'We were both mistaken. You say it's preposterous that the women who didn't object to accepting Leila's hospitality should have objected to meeting me under her roof. And so it is; but I begin to understand why. It's simply that society is much too busy to revise its own judgments. Probably no one in the house with me stopped to consider that my case and Leila's were identical. They only remembered that I'd done something which, at the time I did it, was condemned by society. My case had been passed on and classified: I'm the woman who has been cut for nearly twenty years. The older people have half-forgotten why, and the younger ones have never really known: it's simply become a tradition to cut me. And traditions that have lost their meaning are the hardest of all to destroy.'

Ide sat motionless while she spoke. As she ended, he stood up with a short laugh and walked across the room to the window. Outside, the immense black prospect of New York, strung with its myriad lines of light, stretched away into the smoky edges of the night. He showed it to her with a gesture.

'What do you suppose such words as you've been using – "society," "tradition," and the rest – mean to all the life out there?'

She came and stood by him in the window. 'Less than nothing, of course. But you and I are not out there. We're shut up in a little tight round of habit and association, just as we're shut up in this room. Remember, I thought I'd got out of it once; but what really happened was that the other people went out, and left me in the same little room. The only difference was that I was there alone. Oh, I've made it habitable now, I'm used to it; but I've lost any illusions I may have had as to an angel's opening the door.'

Ide again laughed impatiently. 'Well, if the door won't open, why not let another prisoner in? At least it would be less of a solitude – '

She turned from the dark window back into the vividly lighted room.

'It would be more of a prison. You forget that I know all about that. We're all imprisoned, of course – all of us middling people, who don't carry our freedom in our brains. But we've accommodated ourselves to our different cells, and if we're moved suddenly into the new ones we're likely to find a stone wall where we thought there was thin air, and to knock ourselves senseless against it. I saw a man do that once.'

Ide, leaning with folded arms against the window frame, watched her in silence as she moved restlessly about the room, gathering together some scattered books and tossing a handful of torn letters into the paper basket. When she ceased, he rejoined: 'All you say is based on preconceived theories. Why didn't you put them to the test by coming down to meet your old friends? Don't you see the inference they would naturally draw from your hiding yourself when they arrived? It looked as though you were afraid of them – or as though you hadn't forgiven them. Either way, you put them in the wrong instead of waiting to let them put you in the right. If Leila had buried herself in a desert do you suppose society would have gone to fetch her out? You say you were afraid for Leila and that she was afraid for you. Don't you see what all these complications of feeling mean? Simply that you were too nervous at the moment to let things happen naturally, just as you're too nervous now to judge them rationally.' He paused and turned her eyes to her face. 'Don't try to just yet. Give yourself a little more time. Give *me* a little more time. I've always known it would take time.'

He moved nearer, and she let him have her hand. With the grave kindness of his face so close above her she felt like a child roused out of frightened dreams and finding a light in the room.

'Perhaps you're right – ' she heard herself begin; then something within her clutched her back, and her hand fell away from him.

'I know I'm right: trust me,' he urged. 'We'll talk of this in Florence soon.'

She stood before him, feeling with despair his kindness, his patience and his unreality. Everything he said seemed like a painted gauze let down between herself and the real facts of life; and a sudden desire seized her to tear the gauze into shreds.

She drew back and looked at him with a smile of superficial reassurance. 'You *are* right – about not talking any longer now. I'm nervous and tired, and it would do no good. I brood over things too much. As you say, I must try not to shrink from people'. She turned away and glanced at the clock. 'Why, it's only ten! If I send you off I shall begin to brood again; and if you stay we shall go on talking about the same thing. Why shouldn't we go down and see Margaret Wynn for half an hour?'

She spoke lightly and rapidly, her brilliant eyes on his face. As she watched him, she saw it change, as if her smile had thrown a too vivid light upon it.

'Oh, no – not tonight!' he exclaimed.

'Not tonight? Why, what other night have I, when I'm off at dawn?

Besides, I want to show you at once that I mean to be more sensible –
that I'm not going to be afraid of people any more. And I should really
like another glimpse of little Charlotte.' He stood before her, his hand
in his beard, with the gesture he had in moments of perplexity. 'Come!'
she ordered him gaily, turning to the door.

He followed her and laid his hand on her arm. 'Don't you think –
hadn't you better let me go first and see? They told me they'd had a
tiring day at the dressmaker's. I dare say they have gone to bed.'

'But you said they'd a young man of Charlotte's dining with them.
Surely he wouldn't have left by ten? At any rate, I'll go down with
you and see. It takes so long if one sends a servant first.' She put him
gently aside, and then paused as a new thought struck her. 'Or wait,
my maid's in the next room. I'll tell her to go and ask if Margaret will
receive me. Yes, that's much the best way.'

She turned back and went toward the door that led to her bedroom;
but before she could open it she felt Ide's quick touch again.

'I believe – I remember now – Charlotte's young man was
suggesting that they should all go out – to a music hall or something
of the sort. I'm sure – I'm positively sure that you won't find them.'

Her hand dropped from the door, his dropped from her arm, and
as they drew back and faced each other she saw the blood rise slowly
through his sallow skin, redden his neck and ears, encroach upon the
edges of his beard, and settle in dull patches under his kind troubled
eyes. She had seen the same blush on another face, and the same impulse
of compassion she had then felt made her turn her gaze away again.

A knock on the door broke the silence, and a porter put his head
into the room.

'It's only just to know how many pieces there'll be to go down to
the steamer in the morning.'

With the words she felt that the veil of painted gauze was torn in
tatters, and that she was moving again among the grim edges of reality.

'Oh, dear,' she exclaimed, 'I never *can* remember! Wait a minute; I
shall have to ask my maid.'

She opened her bedroom door and called out: 'Annette!'

The Long Run

———⚜———

The shade of those our days that had no tongue.

IT WAS LAST WINTER, after a twelve years' absence from New York, that I saw again, at one of the Jim Cumnors' dinners, my old friend Halston Merrick.

The Cumnors' house is one of the few where, even after such a lapse of time, one can be sure of finding familiar faces and picking up old threads; where for a moment one can abandon one's self to the illusion that New York humanity is a shade less unstable than its bricks and mortar. And that evening in particular I remember feeling that there could be no pleasanter way of re-entering the confused and careless world to which I was returning than through the quiet softly-lit dining room in which Mrs. Cumnor, with a characteristic sense of my needing to be broken in gradually, had contrived to assemble so many friendly faces.

I was glad to see them all, including the three or four I did not know, or failed to recognize, that had no difficulty in passing as in the tradition and of the group; but I was most of all glad – as I rather wonderingly found – to set eyes again on Halston Merrick.

He and I had been at Harvard together, for one thing, and had shared there curiosities and ardors a little outside the current tendencies: had, on the whole, been more critical than our comrades, and less amenable to the accepted. Then, for the next following years, Merrick had been a vivid and promising figure in young American life. Handsome, careless, and free, he had wandered and tasted and compared. After leaving Harvard he had spent two years at Oxford; then he had accepted a private secretaryship to our Ambassador in England, and had come back from this adventure with a fresh curiosity about public affairs at home, and the conviction that men of his kind should play a larger part in them. This led, first, to his running for a State Senatorship which he failed to get, and ultimately to a few months of intelligent activity in a municipal office. Soon after being deprived of this post by

144

a change of party he had published a small volume of delicate verse, and, a year later, an odd uneven brilliant book on Municipal Government. After that one hardly knew where to look for his next appearance; but chance rather disappointingly solved the problem by killing off his father and placing Halston at the head of the Merrick Iron Foundry at Yonkers.

His friends had gathered that, whenever this regrettable contingency should occur, he meant to dispose of the business and continue his life of free experiment. As often happens in just such cases, however, it was not the moment for a sale, and Merrick had to take over the management of the foundry. Some two years later he had a chance to free himself; but when it came he did not choose to take it. This tame sequel to an inspiriting start was disappointing to some of us, and I was among those disposed to regret Merrick's drop to the level of the prosperous. Then I went away to a big engineering job in China, and from there to Africa, and spent the next twelve years out of sight and sound of New York doings.

During that long interval I heard of no new phase in Merrick's evolution, but this did not surprise me, as I had never expected from him actions resonant enough to cross the globe. All I knew – and this did surprise me – was that he had not married, and that he was still in the iron business. All through those years, however, I never ceased to wish, in certain situations and at certain turns of thought, that Merrick were in reach, that I could tell this or that to Merrick. I had never, in the interval, found any one with just his quickness of perception and just his sureness of response.

After dinner, therefore, we irresistibly drew together. In Mrs. Cumnor's big easy drawing room cigars were allowed, and there was no break in the communion of the sexes; and, this being the case, I ought to have sought a seat beside one of the ladies among whom we were allowed to remain. But, as had generally happened of old when Merrick was in sight, I found myself steering straight for him past all minor ports of call.

There had been no time, before dinner, for more than the barest expression of satisfaction at meeting, and our seats had been at opposite ends of the longish table, so that we got our first real look at each other in the secluded corner to which Mrs. Cumnor's vigilance now directed us.

Merrick was still handsome in his stooping tawny way: handsomer perhaps, with thinnish hair and more lines in his face, than in the young excess of his good looks. He was very glad to see me and conveyed his gladness by the same charming smile; but as soon as we began to talk I felt a change. It was not merely the change that years and experience and altered values bring. There was something more fundamental the matter with Merrick, something dreadful, unforeseen, unaccountable: Merrick had grown conventional and dull.

In the glow of his frank pleasure in seeing me I was ashamed to analyze the nature of the change; but presently our talk began to flag – fancy a talk with Merrick flagging! – and self-deception became impossible as I watched myself handing out platitudes with the gesture of the salesman offering something to a purchaser 'equally good.' The worst of it was that Merrick – Merrick, who had once felt everything! – didn't seem to feel the lack of spontaneity in my remarks, but hung on them with a harrowing faith in the resuscitating power of our past. It was as if he hugged the empty vessel of our friendship without perceiving that the last drop of its essence was dry.

But after all, I am exaggerating. Through my surprise and disappointment I felt a certain sense of well-being in the mere physical presence of my old friend. I liked looking at the way his dark hair waved away from the forehead, at the tautness of his dry brown cheek, the thoughtful backward tilt of his head, the way his brown eyes mused upon the scene through lowered lids. All the past was in his way of looking and sitting, and I wanted to stay near him, and felt that he wanted me to stay; but the devil of it was that neither of us knew what to talk about.

It was this difficulty which caused me, after a while, since I could not follow Merrick's talk, to follow his eyes in their roaming circuit of the room.

At the moment when our glances joined, his had paused on a lady seated at some distance from our corner. Immersed, at first, in the satisfaction of finding myself again with Merrick, I had been only half aware of this lady, as of one of the few persons present whom I did not know, or had failed to remember. There was nothing in her appearance to challenge my attention or to excite my curiosity, and I don't suppose I should have looked at her again if I had not noticed that my friend was doing so.

She was a woman of about forty-seven, with fair faded hair and a young figure. Her gray dress was handsome but ineffective, and her pale and rather serious face wore a small unvarying smile which might have been pinned on with her ornaments. She was one of the women in whom increasing years show rather what they have taken than what they have bestowed, and only on looking closely did one see that what they had taken must have been good of its kind.

Phil Cumnor and another man were talking to her, and the very intensity of the attention she bestowed on them betrayed the straining of rebellious thoughts. She never let her eyes stray or her smile drop; and at the proper moment I saw she was ready with the proper sentiment.

The party, like most of those that Mrs. Cumnor gathered about her, was not composed of exceptional beings. The people of the old vanished New York set were not exceptional: they were mostly cut on the same convenient and unobtrusive pattern; but they were often exceedingly 'nice.' And this obsolete quality marked every look and gesture of the lady I was scrutinizing.

While these reflections were passing through my mind I was aware that Merrick's eyes rested still on her. I took a cross-section of his look and found in it neither surprise nor absorption, but only a certain sober pleasure just about at the emotional level of the rest of the room. If he continued to look at her, his expression seemed to say, it was only because, all things considered, there were fewer reasons for looking at anybody else.

This made me wonder what were the reasons for looking at *her;* and as a first step toward enlightenment I said: 'I'm sure I've seen the lady over there in gray – '

Merrick detached his eyes and turned them on me with a wondering look.

'Seen her? You know her.' He waited. '*Don't* you know her? It's Mrs. Reardon.'

I wondered that he should wonder, for I could not remember, in the Cumnor group or elsewhere, having known anyone of the name he mentioned.

'But perhaps,' he continued, 'you hadn't heard of her marriage? You knew her as Mrs. Trant.'

I gave him back his stare. 'Not Mrs. Philip Trant?'

'Yes; Mrs. Philip Trant.'

'Not Paulina?'

'Yes – Paulina,' he said, with a just perceptible delay before the name.

In my surprise I continued to stare at him. He averted his eyes from mine after a moment, and I saw that they had strayed back to her. 'You find her so changed?' he asked.

Something in his voice acted as a warning signal, and I tried to reduce my astonishment to less unbecoming proportions. 'I don't find that she looks much older.'

'No. Only different?' he suggested, as if there were nothing new to him in my perplexity.

'Yes – awfully different.'

'I suppose we're all awfully different. To you, I mean – coming from so far?'

'I recognized all the rest of you,' I said, hesitating. 'And she used to be the one who stood out most.'

There was a flash, a wave, a stir of something deep down in his eyes. 'Yes,' he said. '*That's* the difference.'

'I see it is. She – she looks worn down. Soft but blurred, like the figures in that tapestry behind her.'

He glanced at her again, as if to test the exactness of my analogy.

'Life wears everybody down,' he said.

'Yes – except those it makes more distinct. They're the rare ones, of course; but she *was* rare.'

He stood up suddenly, looking old and tired. 'I believe I'll be off. I wish you'd come down to my place for Sunday. . . . No, don't shake hands – I want to slide away unawares.'

He had backed away to the threshold and was turning the noiseless doorknob. Even Mrs. Cumnor's doorknobs had tact and didn't tell.

'Of course I'll come,' I promised warmly. In the last ten minutes he had begun to interest me again.

'All right. Good-bye.' Half through the door he paused to add: '*She* remembers you. You ought to speak to her.'

'I'm going to. But tell me a little more.' I thought I saw a shade of constraint on his face, and did not add as I had meant to: 'Tell me – because she interests me – what wore her down?' Instead, I asked: 'How soon after Trant's death did she remarry?'

He seemed to make an effort of memory. 'It was seven years ago, I think.'

'And is Reardon here tonight?'

'Yes; over there, talking to Mrs. Cumnor.'

I looked across the broken groupings and saw a large glossy man with straw-colored hair and red face, whose shirt and shoes and complexion seemed all to have received a coat of the same expensive varnish.

As I looked there was a drop in the talk about us, and I heard Mr. Reardon pronounce in a big booming voice: 'What I say is: what's the good of disturbing things? Thank the Lord, I'm content with what I've got!'

'Is *that* her husband? What's he like?'

'Oh, the best fellow in the world,' said Merrick, going.

• II •

MERRICK had a little place at Riverdale, where he went occasionally to be near the Iron Works, and where he hid his weekends when the world was too much with him.

Here, on the following Saturday afternoon I found him awaiting me in a pleasant setting of books and prints and faded parental furniture.

We dined late, and smoked and talked afterward in his book-walled study till the terrier on the hearthrug stood up and yawned for bed. When we took the hint and moved toward the staircase I felt, not that

I had found the old Merrick again, but that I was on his track, had come across traces of his passage here and there in the thick jungle that had grown up between us. But I had a feeling that when I finally came on the man himself he might be dead. . . .

As we started upstairs he turned back with one of his abrupt shy movements, and walked into the study.

'Wait a bit!' he called to me.

I waited, and he came out in a moment carrying a limp folio.

'It's typewritten. Will you take a look at it? I've been trying to get to work again,' he explained, thrusting the manuscript into my hand.

'What? Poetry, I hope?' I exclaimed.

He shook his head with a gleam of derision. 'No – just general considerations. The fruit of fifty years of inexperience.'

He showed me to my room and said good night.

The following afternoon we took a long walk inland, across the hills, and I said to Merrick what I could of his book. Unluckily there wasn't much to say. The essays were judicious, polished and cultivated; but they lacked the freshness and audacity of his youthful work. I tried to conceal my opinion behind the usual generalizations, but he broke through these feints with a quick thrust to the heart of my meaning.

'It's worn down – blurred? Like the figures in the Cumnors' tapestry?'

I hesitated. 'It's a little too damned resigned,' I said.

'Ah,' he exclaimed, 'so am I. Resigned.' He switched the bare brambles by the roadside. 'A man can't serve two masters.'

'You mean business and literature?'

'No; I mean theory and instinct. The gray tree and the green. You've got to choose which fruit you'll try; and you don't know till afterward which of the two has the dead core.'

'How can anybody be sure that only one of them has?'

'I'm sure,' said Merrick sharply.

We turned back to the subject of his essays, and I was astonished at the detachment with which he criticized and demolished them. Little by little, as we talked, his old perspective, his old standards came back to him; but with the difference that they no longer seemed like functions of his mind but merely like attitudes assumed or dropped at will. He could still, with an effort, put himself at the angle from which he had formerly seen things; but it was with the effort of a man climbing mountains after a sedentary life in the plain.

I tried to cut the talk short, but he kept coming back to it with nervous insistence, forcing me into the last retrenchments of hypocrisy, and anticipating the verdict I held back. I perceived that a great deal – immensely more than I could see a reason for – had hung for him on my opinion of his book.

Then, as suddenly, his insistence dropped and, as if ashamed of having forced himself so long on my attention, he began to talk rapidly and uninterestingly of other things.

We were alone again that evening, and after dinner, wishing to efface the impression of the afternoon, and above all to show that I wanted him to talk about himself, I reverted to his work. 'You must need an outlet of that sort. When a man's once had it in him, as you have – and when other things begin to dwindle – '

He laughed. 'Your theory is that a man ought to be able to return to the Muse as he comes back to his wife after he's ceased to interest other women?'

'No; as he comes back to his wife after the day's work is done.' A new thought came to me as I looked at him. 'You ought to have had one,' I added.

He laughed again. 'A wife, you mean? So that there'd have been someone waiting for me even if the Muse decamped?' He went on after a pause: 'I've a notion that the kind of woman worth coming back to wouldn't be much more patient than the Muse. But as it happens I never tried – because, for fear they'd chuck me, I put them both out of doors together.'

He turned his head and looked past me with a queer expression at the low-paneled door at my back. 'Out of that very door they went – the two of 'em, on a rainy night like this: and one stopped and looked back, to see if I wasn't going to call her – and I didn't – and so they both went.'

• III •

'THE Muse?' (said Merrick, refilling my glass and stooping to pat the terrier as he went back to his chair) 'Well, you've met the Muse in the little volume of sonnets you used to like; and you've met the woman too, and you used to like *her;* though you didn't know her when you saw her the other evening. . . .

'No, I won't ask you how she struck you when you talked to her: I know. She struck you like that stuff I gave you to read last night. She's conformed – I've conformed – the mills´have caught us and ground us: ground us, oh, exceedingly small!

'But you remember what she was, and that's the reason why I'm telling you this now. . . .

'You may recall that after my father's death I tried to sell the Works. I was impatient to free myself from anything that would keep me tied to New York. I don't dislike my trade, and I've made, in the end, a fairly good thing of it; but industrialism was not, at that time, in the line of my tastes, and I know now that it wasn't what I was meant for.

Above all, I wanted to get away, to see new places and rub up against different ideas. I had reached a time of life – the top of the first hill, so to speak – where the distance draws one, and everything in the foreground seems tame and stale. I was sick to death of the particular set of conformities I had grown up among; sick of being a pleasant popular young man with a long line of dinners on my list, and the dead certainty of meeting the same people, or their prototypes, at all of them.

'Well – I failed to sell the Works, and that increased my discontent. I went through moods of cold unsociability, alternating with sudden flushes of curiosity, when I gloated over stray scraps of talk overheard in railway stations and omnibuses, when strange faces that I passed in the street tantalized me with fugitive promises. I wanted to be among things that were unexpected and unknown; and it seemed to me that nobody about me understood in the least what I felt, but that somewhere just out of reach there was someone who *did*, and whom I must find or despair. . . .

'It was just then that, one evening, I saw Mrs. Trant for the first time.

'Yes: I know – you wonder what I mean. I'd known her, of course, as a girl; I'd met her several times after her marriage; and I'd lately been thrown with her, quite intimately and continuously, during a succession of country-house visits. But I had never, as it happened, really *seen* her. . . .

'It was at a dinner at the Cumnors'; and there she was, in front of the very tapestry we saw her against the other evening, with people about her, and her face turned from me, and nothing noticeable or different in her dress or manner; and suddenly she stood out for me against the familiar unimportant background, and for the first time I saw a meaning in the stale phrase of a picture's walking out of its frame. For, after all, most people *are* just that to us: pictures, furniture, the inanimate accessories of our little island area of sensation. And then sometimes one of these graven images moves and throws out live filaments toward us, and the line they make draws us across the world as the moon track seems to draw a boat across the water. . . .

'There she stood; and as this queer sensation came over me I felt that she was looking steadily at me, that her eyes were voluntarily, consciously resting on me with the weight of the very question I was asking.

'I went over and joined her, and she turned and walked with me into the music room. Earlier in the evening someone had been singing, and there were low lights there, and a few couples still sitting in those confidential corners of which Mrs. Cumnor has the art; but we were under no illusion as to the nature of these presences. We knew that they were just painted in, and that the whole of life was in us two, flowing back and forward between us. We talked, of course; we had the attitudes, even the words, of the others: I remember her telling me her plans for the spring and asking me politely about mine! As if there were the least sense in plans, now that this thing had happened!

'When we went back into the drawing room I had said nothing to her that I might not have said to any other woman of the party; but when we shook hands I knew we should meet the next day – and the next. . . .

'That's the way, I take it, that Nature has arranged the beginning of the great enduring loves; and likewise of the little epidermal flurries. And how is a man to know where he is going?

'From the first my feeling for Paulina Trant seemed to me a grave business; but then the Enemy is given to producing that illusion. Many a man – I'm talking of the kind with imagination – has thought he was seeking a soul when all he wanted was a closer view of its tenement. And I tried – honestly tried – to make myself think I was in the latter case. Because, in the first place, I didn't, just then, want a big disturbing influence in my life; and because I didn't want to be a dupe; and because Paulina Trant was not, according to hearsay, the kind of woman for whom it was worth-while to bring up the big batteries. . . .

'But my resistance was only half-hearted. What I really felt – all I really felt – was the flood of joy that comes of heightened emotion. She had given me that, and I wanted her to give it to me again. That's as near as I've ever come to analyzing my state in the beginning.

'I knew her story, as no doubt you know it: the current version, I mean. She had been poor and fond of enjoyment, and she had married that pompous stick Philip Trant because she needed a home, and perhaps also because she wanted a little luxury. Queer how we sneer at women for wanting the thing that gives them half their attraction!

'People shook their heads over the marriage, and divided, prematurely, into Philip's partisans and hers: for no one thought it would work. And they were almost disappointed when, after all, it did. She and her wooden consort seemed to get on well enough. There was a ripple, at one time, over her friendship with young Jim Dalham, who was always with her during a summer at Newport and an autumn in Italy; then the talk died out, and she and Trant were seen together, as before, on terms of apparent good fellowship.

'This was the more surprising because, from the first, Paulina had never made the least attempt to change her tone or subdue her colors. In the gray Trant atmosphere she flashed with prismatic fires. She smoked, she talked subversively, she did as she liked and went where she chose, and danced over the Trant prejudices and the Trant principles as if they'd been a ballroom floor; and all without apparent offence to her solemn husband and his cloud of cousins. I believe her frankness and directness struck them dumb. She moved like a kind of primitive

Una through the virtuous rout, and never got a finger mark on her freshness.

'One of the finest things about her was the fact that she never, for an instant, used her situation as a means of enhancing her attraction. With a husband like Trant it would have been so easy! He was a man who always saw the small sides of big things. He thought most of life compressible into a set of bylaws and the rest unmentionable; and with his stiff frock-coated and tall-hatted mind, instinctively distrustful of intelligences in another dress, with his arbitrary classification of whatever he didn't understand into "the kind of thing I don't approve of," "the kind of thing that isn't done," and – deepest depth of all – "the kind of thing I'd rather not discuss," he lived in bondage to a shadowy moral etiquette of which the complex rites and awful penalties had cast an abiding gloom upon his manner.

'A woman like his wife couldn't have asked a better foil; yet I'm sure she never consciously used his dullness to relieve her brilliancy. She may have felt that the case spoke for itself. But I believe her reserve was rather due to a lively sense of justice, and to the rare habit (you said she was rare) of looking at facts as they are, without any throwing of sentimental limelights. She knew Trant could no more help being Trant than she could help being herself – and there was an end of it. I've never known a woman who "made up" so little mentally. . . .

'Perhaps her very reserve, the fierceness of her implicit rejection of sympathy, exposed her the more to – well, to what happened when we met. She said afterward that it was like having been shut up for months in the hold of a ship, and coming suddenly on deck on a day that was all flying blue and silver. . . .

'I won't try to tell you what she was. It's easier to tell you what her friendship made of me; and I can do that best by adopting her metaphor of the ship. Haven't you, sometimes, at the moment of starting on a journey, some glorious plunge into the unknown, been tripped up by the thought: "If only one hadn't to come back"? Well, with her one had the sense that one would never have to come back; that the magic ship would always carry one farther. And what an air one breathed on it! And, oh, the wind, and the islands, and the sunsets!

'I said just now "her friendship"; and I used the word advisedly. Love is deeper than friendship, but friendship is a good deal wider. The beauty of our relation was that it included both dimensions. Our thoughts met as naturally as our eyes: it was almost as if we loved each other because we liked each other. The quality of a love may be tested by the amount of friendship it contains, and in our case there was no dividing line between loving and liking, no disproportion between them, no barrier against which desire beat in vain or from which thought fell back unsatisfied. Ours was a robust passion that could give an open-eyed account of itself, and not a beautiful madness shrinking away from the proof. . . .

'For the first months friendship sufficed us, or rather gave us so much by the way that we were in no hurry to reach what we knew it was leading to. But we were moving there nevertheless, and one day we found ourselves on the borders. It came about through a sudden decision of Trant's to start on a long tour with his wife. We had never foreseen that: he seemed rooted in his New York habits and convinced that the whole social and financial machinery of the metropolis would cease to function if he did not keep an eye on it through the columns of his morning paper, and pronounce judgment on it in the afternoon at his club. But something new had happened to him: he caught a cold, which was followed by a touch of pleurisy, and instantly he perceived the intense interest and importance which ill-health may add to life. He took the fullest advantage of it. A discerning doctor recommended travel in a warm climate; and suddenly, the morning paper, the afternoon club, Fifth Avenue, Wall Street, all the complex phenomena of the metropolis, faded into insignificance, and the rest of the terrestrial globe, from being a mere geographical hypothesis, useful in enabling one to determine the latitude of New York, acquired reality and magnitude as a factor in the convalescence of Mr. Philip Trant.

'His wife was absorbed in preparations for the journey. To move him was like mobilizing an army, and weeks before the date set for their departure it was almost as if she were already gone.

'This foretaste of separation showed us what we were to each other. Yet I was letting her go – and there was no help for it, no way of preventing it. Resistance was as useless as the vain struggles in a nightmare. She was Trant's and not mine: part of his luggage when he traveled as she was part of his household furniture when he stayed at home. . . .

'The day she told me that their passages were taken – it was on a November afternoon, in her drawing room in town – I turned away from her and, going to the window, stood looking out at the torrent of traffic interminably pouring down Fifth Avenue. I watched the senseless machinery of life revolving in the rain and mud, and tried to picture myself performing my small function in it after she had gone from me.

' "It can't be – it can't be!" I exclaimed.

' "What can't be?"

'I came back into the room and sat down by her. "This – this – " I hadn't any words. "Two weeks!" I said. "What's two weeks?"

'She answered, vaguely, something about their thinking of Spain for the spring – .

' "Two weeks – two weeks!" I repeated. "And the months we've lost – the days that belonged to us!"

' "Yes," she said, "I'm thankful it's settled."

'Our words seemed irrelevant, haphazard. It was as if each were answering a secret voice, and not what the other was saying.

' "Don't you *feel* anything at all?" I remember bursting out at her. As I asked it the tears were streaming down her face. I felt angry with her, and was almost glad to note that her lids were red and that she didn't cry becomingly. I can't express my sensation to you except by saying that she seemed part of life's huge league against me. And suddenly I thought of an afternoon we had spent together in the country, on a ferny hillside, when we had sat under a beech tree, and her hand had lain palm upward in the moss, close to mine, and I had watched a little black and red beetle creeping over it. . . .

'The bell rang, and we heard the voice of a visitor and the click of an umbrella in the umbrella stand.

'She rose to go into the inner drawing room, and I caught her suddenly by the wrist. "You understand," I said, "that we can't go on like this?"

' "I understand," she answered, and moved away to meet her visitor. As I went out I heard her saying in the other room: "Yes, we're really off on the twelfth."

• IV •

'I wrote her a long letter that night, and waited two days for a reply.

'On the third day I had a brief line saying that she was going to spend Sunday with some friends who had a place near Riverdale, and that she would arrange to see me while she was there. That was all.

'It was on a Saturday that I received the note and I came out here the same night. The next morning was rainy, and I was in despair, for I had counted on her asking me to take her for a drive or a long walk. It was hopeless to try to say what I had to say to her in the drawing room of a crowded country house. And only eleven days were left!

'I stayed indoors all the morning, fearing to go out lest she should telephone me. But no sign came, and I grew more and more restless and anxious. She was too free and frank for coquetry, but her silence and evasiveness made me feel that, for some reason, she did not wish to hear what she knew I meant to say. Could it be that she was, after all, more conventional, less genuine, than I had thought? I went again and again over the whole maddening round of conjecture; but the only conclusion I could rest in was that, if she loved me as I loved her, she would be as determined as I was to let no obstacle come between us during the days that were left.

'The luncheon hour came and passed, and there was no word from her. I had ordered my trap to be ready, so that I might drive over as soon as she summoned me; but the hours dragged on, the early twilight came, and I sat here in this very chair, or measured up and down, up and down, the length of this very rug – and still there was no message and no letter.

'It had grown quite dark, and I had ordered away, impatiently, the servant who came in with the lamps: I couldn't *bear* any definite sign that the day was over! And I was standing there on the rug, staring at the door, and noticing a bad crack in its panel, when I heard the sound of wheels on the gravel. A word at last, no doubt – a line to explain. . . . I didn't seem to care much for her reasons, and I stood where I was and continued to stare at the door. And suddenly it opened and she came in.

'The servant followed her with a light, and then went out and closed the door. Her face looked pale in lamplight, but her voice was as clear as a bell.

' "Well," she said, "you see I've come."

'I started toward her with hands outstretched. "You've come – you've come!" I stammered.

'Yes; it was like her to come in that way – without dissimulation or explanation or excuse. It was like her, if she gave at all, to give not furtively or in haste, but openly, deliberately, without stinting the measure or counting the cost. But her quietness and serenity disconcerted me. She did not look like a woman who has yielded impetuously to an uncontrollable impulse. There was something almost solemn in her face.

'The effect of it stole over me as I looked at her, suddenly subduing the huge flush of gratified longing.

' "You're here, here, here!" I kept repeating, like a child singing over a happy word.

' "You said," she continued, in her grave clear voice, "that we couldn't go on as we were – "

' "Ah, it's divine of you!" I held out my arms to her.

'She didn't draw back from them, but her faint smile said, "Wait," and lifting her hands she took the pins from her hat, and laid the hat on the table.

'As I saw her dear head bare in the lamplight, with the thick hair waving away from the parting, I forgot everything but the bliss and wonder of her being here – here, in my house, on my hearth – that fourth rose from the corner of the rug is the exact spot where she was standing. . . .

'I drew her to the fire, and made her sit down in the chair you're in, and knelt down by her, and hid my face on her knees. She put her hand on my head, and I was happy to the depths of my soul.

' "Oh, I forgot – " she exclaimed suddenly. I lifted my head and our eyes met. Hers were smiling.

'She reached out her hand, opened the little bag she had tossed down with her hat, and drew a small object from it. "I left my trunk at the station. Here's the check. Can you send for it?" she asked.

'Her trunk – she wanted me to send for her trunk! Oh, yes – I see your smile, your "lucky man!" Only, you see, I didn't love her in that way. I knew she couldn't come to my house without running a big risk of discovery, and my tenderness for her, my impulse to shield her, was stronger, even then, than vanity or desire. Judged from the point of view of those emotions I fell terribly short of my part. I hadn't any of the proper feelings. Such an act of romantic folly was so unlike her that it almost irritated me, and I found myself desperately wondering how I could get her to reconsider her plan without – well, without seeming to want her to.

'It's not the way a novel hero feels; it's probably not the way a man in real life ought to have felt. But it's the way I felt – and she saw it.

'She put her hands on my shoulders and looked at me with deep, deep eyes. "Then you didn't expect me to stay?" she asked.

'I caught her hands and pressed them to me, stammering out that I hadn't dared to dream. . . .

' "You thought I'd come – just for an hour?"

' "How could I dare think more? I adore you, you know, for what you've done! But it would be known if you – if you stayed on. My servants – everybody about here knows you. I've no right to expose you to the risk." She made no answer, and I went on tenderly: "Give me, if you will, the next few hours: there's a train that will get you to town by midnight. And then we'll arrange something – in town – where it's safer for you – more easily managed. . . . It's beautiful, it's heavenly of you to have come; but I love you too much – I must take care of you and think for you – '

'I don't suppose it ever took me so long to say so few words, and though they were profoundly sincere they sounded unutterably shallow, irrelevant and grotesque. She made no effort to help me out, but sat silent, listening, with her meditative smile. "It's my duty, dearest, as a man," I rambled on. "The more I love you the more I'm bound – "

' "Yes; but you don't understand," she interrupted.

'She rose as she spoke, and I got up also, and we stood and looked at each other.

' "I haven't come for a night; if you want me I've come for always," she said.

'Here again, if I give you an honest account of my feelings I shall write myself down as the poor-spirited creature I suppose I am. There wasn't, I swear, at the moment, a grain of selfishness, of personal reluctance, in my feeling. I worshiped every hair of her head – when we were together I was happy, when I was away from her something was gone from every good thing; but I had always looked on our love for each other, our possible relation to each other, as such situations are looked on in what is called society. I had supposed her, for all her freedom and originality, to be just as tacitly subservient to that view as I was: ready to take what she wanted on the terms on which society concedes such taking, and to pay for it by the usual restrictions, concealments and hypocrisies. In short, I supposed that she would "play the game" – look out for her own safety, and expect me to look out for it. It sounds cheap enough, put that way – but it's the rule we live under, all of us. And the amazement of finding her suddenly outside of it, oblivious of it, unconscious of it, left me, for an awful minute, stammering at her like a graceless dolt. . . . Perhaps it wasn't even a minute; but in it she had gone the whole round of my thoughts.

' "It's raining," she said, very low. "I suppose you can telephone for a trap?"

'There was no irony or resentment in her voice. She walked slowly across the room and paused before the Brangwyn etching over there. "That's a good impression. *Will* you telephone, please?" she repeated.

'I found my voice again, and with it the power of movement. I followed her and dropped at her feet. "You can't go like this!" I cried.

'She looked down on me from heights and heights. "I can't stay like this," she answered.

'I stood up and we faced each other like antagonists. "You don't know," I accused her passionately, "in the least what you're asking me to ask of you!"

' "Yes, I do; *everything*," she breathed.

' "And it's got to be that or nothing?"

' "Oh, on both sides," she reminded me.

' "*Not* on both sides. It's not fair. That's why – "

' "Why you won't?"

' "Why I cannot – may not!"

' "Why you'll take a night and not a life?"

'The taunt, for a woman usually so sure of her aim, fell so short of the mark that its only effect was to increase my conviction of her helplessness. The very intensity of my longing for her made me tremble where she was fearless. I had to protect her first, and think of my own attitude afterward.

'She was too discerning not to see this too. Her face softened, grew inexpressibly appealing, and she dropped again into that chair you're in, leaned forward, and looked up with her grave smile.

' "You think I'm beside myself – raving? (You're not thinking of yourself, I know.) I'm not: I never was saner. Since I've known you I've often thought this might happen. This thing between us isn't an ordinary thing. If it had been we shouldn't, all these months, have drifted. We should have wanted to skip to the last page – and then throw down the book. We shouldn't have felt we could *trust* the future as we did. We were in no hurry because we knew we shouldn't get tired; and when two people feel that about each other they must live together – or part. I don't see what else they can do. A little trip along the coast won't answer. It's the high seas – or else tied up to Lethe wharf. And I'm for the high seas, my dear!"

'Think of sitting here – here, in this room, in this chair – and listening to that, and seeing the light on her hair, and hearing the sound of her voice! I don't suppose there ever was a scene just like it. . . .

'She was astounding – inexhaustible; through all my anguish of resistance I found a kind of fierce joy in following her. It was lucidity at white heat: the last sublimation of passion. She might have been an angel arguing a point in the empyrean if she hadn't been, so completely, a woman pleading for her life. . . .

'Her life: that was the thing at stake! She couldn't do with less of it than she was capable of; and a woman's life is inextricably part of the man's she cares for.

'That was why, she argued, she couldn't accept the usual solution: couldn't enter into the only relation that society tolerates between people situated like ourselves. Yes: she knew all the arguments on *that* side: didn't I suppose she'd been over them and over them? She knew (for hadn't she often said it of others?) what is said of the woman who, by throwing in her lot with her lover's, binds him to a lifelong duty which has the irksomeness without the dignity of marriage. Oh, she could talk on that side with the best of them: only she asked me to consider the other – the side of the man and woman who love each other deeply and completely enough to want their lives enlarged, and not diminished, by their love. What, in such a case – she reasoned – must be the inevitable effect of concealing, denying, disowning, the central fact, the motive power of one's existence? She asked me to picture the course of such a love: first working as a fever in the blood, distorting and deflecting everything, making all other interests insipid, all other duties irksome, and then, as the acknowledged claims of life regained their hold, gradually dying – the poor starved passion! – for want of the wholesome necessary food of common living and doings, yet leaving life impoverished by the loss of all it might have been.

' "I'm not talking, dear – " I see her now, leaning toward me with shining eyes: "I'm not talking of the people who haven't enough to fill their days, and to whom a little mystery, a little maneuvering, gives an illusion of importance that they can't afford to miss; I'm talking of you and me, with all our tastes and curiosities and activities; and I ask you what our love would become if we had to keep it apart from our lives, like a pretty useless animal that we went to peep at and feed with sweetmeats through its cage?"

'I won't, my dear fellow, go into the other side of our strange duel: the arguments I used were those that most men in my situation would have felt bound to use, and that most women in Paulina's accept instinctively, without even formulating them. The exceptionalness, the significance, of the case lay wholly in the fact that she had formulated them all and then rejected them. . . .

'There was one point I didn't, of course, touch on; and that was the popular conviction (which I confess I shared) that when a man and a woman agree to defy the world together the man really sacrifices much more than the woman. I was not even conscious of thinking of this at the time, though it may have lurked somewhere in the shadow of my scruples for her; but she dragged it out into the daylight and held me face to face with it.

' "Remember, I'm not attempting to lay down any general rule," she insisted; "I'm not theorizing about Man and Woman, I'm talking about you and me. How do I know what's best for the woman in the next house? Very likely she'll bolt when it would have been better for her to stay at home. And it's the same with the man: he'll probably do the wrong thing. It's generally the weak heads that commit follies, when it's the strong ones that ought to: and my point is that you and I are both strong enough to behave like fools if we want to. . . .

' "Take you own case first – because, in spite of the sentimentalists, it's the man who stands to lose most. You'll have to give up the Iron Works: which you don't much care about – because it won't be particularly agreeable for us to live in New York: which you don't care much about either. But you won't be sacrificing what is called 'a career.' You made up your mind long ago that your best chance of self-development, and consequently of general usefulness, lay in thinking rather than doing; and, when we first met, you were already planning to sell out your business, and travel and write. Well! Those ambitions are of a kind that won't be harmed by your dropping out of your social setting. On the contrary, such work as you want to do ought to gain by it, because you'll be brought nearer to life-as-it-is, in contrast to life-as-a-visiting-list. . . ."

'She threw back her head with a sudden laugh. "And the joy of not having any more visits to make! I wonder if you've ever thought of *that?* Just at first, I mean; for society's getting so deplorably lax that, little by little, it will edge up to us – you'll see! I don't want to idealize the situation, dearest, and I won't conceal from you that in time we shall be called on. But, oh, the fun we shall have had in the interval! And then, for the first time we shall be able to dictate our own terms, one of which will be that no bores need apply. Think of being cured of all one's chronic bores! We shall feel as jolly as people do after a successful operation."

'I don't know why this nonsense sticks in my mind when some of the graver things we said are less distinct. Perhaps it's because of a certain iridescent quality of feeling that made gaiety seem like sunshine through a shower. . . .

' "You ask me to think of myself?" she went on. "But the beauty of our being together will be that, for the first time, I shall dare to! Now I have to think of all the tedious trifles I can pack the days with, because I'm afraid – I'm afraid – to hear the voice of the real me, down below, in the windowless underground hole where I keep her. . . .

' "Remember again, please, it's not Woman, it's Paulina Trant, I'm talking of. The woman in the next house may have all sorts of reasons – honest reasons – for staying there. There may be some one there who needs her badly: for whom the light would go out if she went. Whereas to Philip I've been simply – well, what New York was before he decided to travel: the most important thing in life till he made up his mind to leave it; and now merely the starting place of several lines of steamers. Oh, I didn't have to love you to know that! I only had to live with *him*. . . . If he lost his eyeglasses he'd think it was the fault of the eyeglasses; he'd really feel that the eyeglasses had been careless. And he'd be convinced that no others would suit him quite as well. But at the optician's he'd probably be told that he needed something a little different, and after that he'd feel that the old eyeglasses had never suited him at all, and that *that* was their fault too. . . ."

'At one moment – but I don't recall when – I remember she stood up with one of her quick movements, and came toward me, holding out her arms. "Oh, my dear, I'm pleading for my life; do you suppose I shall ever want for arguments?" she cried. . . .

'After that, for a bit, nothing much remains with me except a sense of darkness and of conflict. The one spot of daylight in my whirling brain was the conviction that I couldn't – whatever happened – profit by the sudden impulse she had acted on, and allow her to take, in a moment of passion, a decision that was to shape her whole life. I couldn't so much as lift my little finger to keep her with me then, unless I were prepared to accept for her as well as for myself the full consequences of the future she had planned for us. . . .

'Well – there's the point: I wasn't. I felt in her – poor fatuous idiot that I was! – that lack of objective imagination which had always seemed to me to account, at least in part, for many of the so-called heroic qualities in women. When their feelings are involved they simply can't look ahead. Her unfaltering logic notwithstanding, I felt this about Paulina as I listened. She had a specious air of knowing where she was going, but she didn't. She seemed the genius of logic and understanding, but the demon of illusion spoke through her lips. . . .

'I said just now that I hadn't, at the outset, given my own side of the case a thought. It would have been truer to say that I hadn't given it a *separate* thought. But I couldn't think of her without seeing myself as a factor – the chief factor – in her problem, and without recognizing that whatever the experiment made of me, it must fatally, in the end, make of her. If I couldn't carry the thing through she must break down with me: we should have to throw our separate selves into the melting pot of this mad adventure, and be "one" in a terrible indissoluble completeness of which marriage is only an imperfect counterpart. . . .

'There could be no better proof of her extraordinary power over me, and of the way she had managed to clear the air of sentimental illusion, than the fact that I presently found myself putting this before her with a merciless precision of touch.

' "If we love each other enough to do a thing like this, we must love each other enough to see just what it is we're going to do."

'So I invited her to the dissecting table, and I see now the fearless eye with which she approached the cadaver. "For that's what it is, you know," she flashed out at me, at the end of my long demonstration. "It's a dead body, like all the instances and examples and hypothetical cases that ever were! What do you expect to learn from *that*? The first great anatomist was the man who stuck his knife in a heart that was beating; and the only way to find out what doing a thing will be like is to do it!"

'She looked away from me suddenly, as if she were fixing her eyes on some vision on the outer rim of consciousness. "No: there's one other way," she exclaimed; "and that is, *not* to do it! To abstain and refrain; and then see what we become, or what we don't become, in the long run, and to draw our inferences. That's the game that almost everybody about us is playing, I suppose; there's hardly one of the dull people one meets at dinner who hasn't had, just once, the chance of a berth on a ship that was off for the Happy Isles, and hasn't refused it for fear of sticking on a sandbank!

' "I'm doing my best, you know," she continued, "to see the sequel as you see it, as you believe it's your duty to me to see it. I know the instances you're thinking of: the listless couples wearing out their lives in shabby watering places, and hanging on the favour of hotel acquaint- ances; or the proud quarreling wretches shut up alone in a fine house because they're too good for the only society they can get, and trying to cheat their boredom by squabbling with their tradesmen and spying on their servants. No doubt there are such cases; but I don't recognize either of us in those dismal figures. Why, to do it would be to admit that our life, yours and mine, is in the people about us and not in ourselves; that we're parasites and not self-sustaining creatures; and that the lives we're leading now are so brilliant, full and satisfying that what we should have to give up would surpass even the blessedness of being together!"

'At that stage, I confess, the solid ground of my resistance began to give way under me. It was not that my convictions were shaken, but that she had swept me into a world whose laws were difficult, where one could reach out in directions that the slave of gravity hasn't pictured. But at the same time my opposition hardened from reason into instinct. I knew it was her voice, and not her logic, that was unsettling me. I knew that if she'd written out her thesis and sent it to me by post I should have made short work of it; and again the part of me which I called by all the finest names: my chivalry, my unselfishness, my superior masculine experience, cried out with one voice. "You can't let a woman use her graces to her own undoing – you can't, for her own sake, let her eyes convince you when her reasons don't!"

'And then, abruptly, and for the first time, a doubt entered me: a doubt of her perfect moral honesty. I don't know how else to describe my feeling that she wasn't playing fair, that in coming to my house, in throwing herself at my head (I called things by their names), she had perhaps not so much obeyed an irresistible impulse as deeply, deliberately reckoned on the dissolvent effect of her generosity, her rashness and her beauty. . . .

'From the moment that this mean doubt raised its head in me I was once more the creature of all the conventional scruples: I was repeating, before the looking glass of my self-consciousness, all the stereotyped gestures of the "man of honor." . . . Oh, the sorry figure I must have cut! You'll understand my dropping the curtain on it as quickly as I can. . . .

'Yet I remember, as I made my point, being struck by its impressiveness. I was suffering and enjoying my own suffering. I told her that, whatever step we decided to take, I owed it to her to insist on its being taken soberly, deliberately –

'("No: it's 'advisedly,' isn't it? Oh, I was thinking of the Marriage Service," she interposed with a faint laugh.)

' –That if I accepted, there, on the spot, her headlong beautiful gift of herself, I should feel I had taken an unfair advantage of her, an advantage which she would be justified in reproaching me with afterward; that I was not afraid to tell her this because she was intelligent enough to know that my scruples were the surest proof of the quality of my love; that I refused to owe my happiness to an unconsidered impulse; that we must see each other again, in her own house, in less agitating circumstances, when she had had time to reflect on my words, to study her heart and look into the future. . . .

'The factitious exhilaration produced by uttering these beautiful sentiments did not last very long, as you may imagine. It fell, little by little, under her quiet gaze, a gaze in which there was neither contempt nor irony nor wounded pride, but only a tender wistfulness of interrogation; and I think the acutest point in my suffering was reached when she said, as I ended: "Oh; yes, of course I understand."

' "If only you hadn't come to me here!" I blurted out in the torture of my soul.

'She was on the threshold when I said it, and she turned and laid her hand gently on mine. "There was no other way," she said; and at the moment it seemed to me like some hackneyed phrase in a novel that she had used without any sense of its meaning.

'I don't remember what I answered or what more we either of us said. At the end a desperate longing to take her in my arms and keep her with me swept aside everything else, and I went up to her, pleading, stammering, urging I don't know what. . . . But she held me back with a quiet look, and went. I had ordered the carriage, as she asked me to; and my last definite recollection is of watching her drive off in the rain. . . .

'I had her promise that she would see me, two days later, at her house in town, and that we should then have what I called "a decisive talk"; but I don't think that even at the moment I was the dupe of my phrase. I knew, and she knew, that the end had come. . . .

• V •

'IT was about that time (Merrick went on after a long pause) that I definitely decided not to sell the Works, but to stick to my job and conform my life to it.

'I can't describe to you the rage of conformity that possessed me. Poetry, ideas – all the picture-making processed stopped. A kind of dull self-discipline seemed to me the only exercise worthy of a reflecting mind. I *had* to justify my great refusal, and I tried to do it by plunging myself up to the eyes into the very conditions I had been instinctively struggling to get away from. The only possible consolation would have been to find in a life of business routine and social submission such moral compensations as may reward the citizen if they fail the man; but to attain to these I should have had to accept the old delusion that the social and the individual man are two. Now, on the contrary, I found soon enough that I couldn't get one part of my machinery to work effectively while another wanted feeding: and that in rejecting what had seemed to me a negation of action I had made all my action negative.

'The best solution, of course, would have been to fall in love with another woman; but it was long before I could bring myself to wish that this might happen to me. . . . Then, at length, I suddenly and violently desired it; and as such impulses are seldom without some kind of imperfect issue I contrived, a year or two later, to work myself up into the wished-for state. . . . She was a woman in society, and with all the awe of that institution that Paulina lacked. Our relation was consequently one of those unavowed affairs in which triviality is the only alternative to tragedy. Luckily we had, on both sides, risked only as much as prudent people stake in a drawing-room game; and when the match was over I take it that we came out fairly even.

'My gain, at all events, was of an unexpected kind. The adventure had served only to make me understand Paulina's abhorrence of such experiments, and at every turn of the slight intrigue I had felt how exasperating and belittling such a relation was bound to be between two people who, had they been free, would have mated openly. And so from a brief phase of imperfect forgetting I was driven back to a deeper and more understanding remembrance. . . .

'This second incarnation of Paulina was one of the strangest episodes of the whole strange experience. Things she had said during our extraordinary talk, things I had hardly heard at the time, came back to me with singular vividness and a fuller meaning. I hadn't any longer the cold consolation of believing in my own perspicacity: I saw that her insight had been deeper and keener than mine.

'I remember, in particular, starting up in bed one sleepless night as there flashed into my head the meaning of her last words: "There was no other way; the phrase I had half-smiled at at the time, as a parrot-like echo of the novel heroine's stock farewell. I had never, up to that moment, wholly understood why Paulina had come to my house that night. I had never been able to make that particular act – which could hardly, in the light of her subsequent conduct, be dismissed as a blind surge of passion – square with my conception of her character. She was at once the most spontaneous and the steadiest-minded woman I had ever known, and the last to wish to owe any advantage to surprise, to unpreparedness, to any play on the spring of sex. The better I came, retrospectively, to know her, the more sure I was of this, and the less intelligible her act appeared. And then, suddenly, after a night of hungry restless thinking, the flash of enlightenment came. She had come to my house, had brought her trunk with her, had thrown herself at my head with all possible violence and publicity, in order to give me a pretext, a loophole, an honorable excuse, for doing and saying – why, precisely what I had said and done!

'As the idea came to me it was as if some ironic hand had touched an electric button, and all my fatuous phrases had leapt out on me in fire.

'Of course she had known all along just the kind of thing I should say if I didn't at once open my arms to her; and to save my pride, my dignity, my conception of the figure I was cutting in her eyes, she had recklessly and magnificently provided me with the decentest pretext a man could have for doing a pusillanimous thing. . . .

'With that discovery the whole case took a different aspect. It hurt less to think of Paulina – and yet it hurt more. The tinge of bitterness, of doubt, in my thoughts of her had had a tonic quality. It was harder to go on persuading myself that I had done right as, bit by bit, my theories crumbled under the test of time. Yet, after all, as she herself had said, one could judge of results only in the long run. . . .

'The Trants stayed away for two years; and about a year after they got back, you may remember, Trant was killed in a railway accident. You know Fate's way of untying a knot after everybody has given up tugging at it!

'Well – there I was, completely justified: all my weaknesses turned into merits! I had "saved" a weak woman from herself, I had kept her to the path of duty, I had spared her the humiliation of scandal and the misery of self-reproach; and now I had only to put our my hand and take my reward.

'I had avoided Paulina since her return, and she had made no effort to see me. But after Trant's death I wrote her a few lines, to which she sent a friendly answer, and when a decent interval had elapsed, and I asked if I might call on her, she answered at once that she would see me.

'I went to her house with the fixed intention of asking her to marry me – and I left it without having done so. Why? I don't know that I can tell you. Perhaps you would have had to sit there opposite her, knowing what I did and feeling as I did, to understand why. She was kind, she was compassionate – I could see she didn't want to make it hard for me. Perhaps she even wanted to make it easy. But there, between us, was the memory of the gesture I hadn't made, forever parodying the one I was attempting! There wasn't a word I could think of that hadn't an echo in it of words of hers I had been deaf to; there wasn't an appeal I could make that didn't mock the appeal I had rejected. I sat there and talked of her husband's death, of her plans, of my sympathy; and I knew she understood; and knowing that, in a way, made it harder. . . . The doorbell rang and the footman came in to ask if she would receive other visitors. She looked at me a moment and said "Yes," and I got up and shook hands and went away.

'A few days later she sailed for Europe, and the next time we met she had married Reardon. . . .'

• VI •

It was long past midnight, and the terrier's hints became imperious.

Merrick rose from his chair, pushed back a fallen log and put up the fender. He walked across the room and stared a moment at the Brangwyn etching before which Paulina Trant had paused at a memorable turn of their talk. Then he came back and laid his hand on my shoulder.

'She summed it all up, you know, when she said that one way of finding out whether a risk is worth taking is *not* to take it, and then to see what one becomes in the long run, and draw one's inferences. The long run – well, we've run it, she and I. I know what I've become, but that's nothing to the misery of knowing what she's become. She had to have some kind of life, and she married Reardon. Reardon's a very good fellow in his way; but the worst of it is that it's not her way. . . .

'No: the worst of it is that now she and I meet as friends. We dine at the same houses, we talk about the same people, we play bridge together, and I lend her books. And sometimes Reardon slaps me on the back and says: "Come in and dine with us, old man! What you want is to be cheered up!" And I go and dine with them, and he tells me how jolly comfortable she makes him, and what an ass I am not to marry; and she presses on me a second helping of *poulet Maryland*, and I smoke one of Reardon's cigars, and at half-past ten I get into my overcoat, and walk back alone to my rooms. . . .'

After Holbein

ANSON WARLEY had had his moments of being a rather remarkable man; but they were only intermittent; they recurred at ever-lengthening intervals; and between times he was a small poor creature, chattering with cold inside, in spite of his agreeable and even distinguished exterior.

He had always been perfectly aware of these two sides of himself (which, even in the privacy of his own mind, he contemptuously refused to dub a dual personality); and as the rather remarkable man could take fairly good care of himself, most of Warley's attention was devoted to ministering to the poor wretch who took longer and longer turns at bearing his name, and was more and more insistent in accepting the invitations which New York, for over thirty years, had tirelessly poured out on him. It was in the interest of this lonely fidgety unemployed self that Warley, in his younger days, had frequented the gaudiest restaurants and the most glittering Palace Hotels of two hemispheres, subscribed to the most advanced literary and artistic reviews, bought the pictures of the young painters who were being the most vehemently discussed, missed few of the showiest first nights in New York, London or Paris, sought the company of the men and women – especially the women – most conspicuous in fashion, scandal, or any other form of social notoriety, and thus tried to warm the shivering soul within him at all the passing bonfires of success.

The original Anson Warley had begun by staying at home in his little flat, with his books and his thoughts, when the other poor creature went forth; but gradually – he hardly knew when or how – he had slipped into the way of going too, till finally he made the bitter discovery that he and the creature had become one, except on the increasingly rare occasions when, detaching himself from all casual contingencies, he mounted to the lofty watershed which fed the sources of his scorn. The view from there was vast and glorious, the air was icy but exhilarating; but soon he began to find the place too lonely, and too difficult to get to, especially as the lesser Anson not only refused to go up with him but began to sneer, at first ever so faintly, then with increasing insolence, at this affectation of a taste for the heights.

'What's the use of scrambling up there, anyhow? I could understand it if you brought down anything worth-while – a poem or a picture of your own. But just climbing and staring: what does it lead to? Fellows with the creative gift have got to have their occasional Sinaïs; I can see that. But for a mere looker-on like you, isn't that sort of thing rather a pose? You talk awfully well – brilliantly, even (oh, my dear fellow, no false modesty between you and *me*, please!) But who the devil is there to listen to you, up there among the glaciers? And sometimes, when you come down, I notice that you're rather – well, heavy and tongue-tied. Look out, or they'll stop asking us to dine! And sitting at home every evening – brr! Look here, by the way; if you've got nothing better for tonight, come along with me to Chrissy Torrance's – or the Bob Briggses' – or Princess Kate's; anywhere where there's lots of racket and sparkle, places that people go to in Rollses, and that are smart and hot and overcrowded, and you have to pay a lot – in one way or another – to get in.'

Once and again, it is true, Warley still dodged his double and slipped off on a tour to remote uncomfortable places, where there were churches or pictures to be seen, or shut himself up at home for a good bout of reading, or just, in sheer disgust at his companion's platitude, spent an evening with people who were doing or thinking real things. This happened seldomer than of old, however, and more clandestinely; so that at last he used to sneak away to spend two or three days with an archaeologically-minded friend, or an evening with a quiet scholar, as furtively as if he were stealing to a lover's tryst; which, as lovers' trysts were now always kept in the limelight, was after all a fair exchange. But he always felt rather apologetic to the other Warley about these escapades – and, if the truth were known, rather bored and restless before they were over. And in the back of his mind there lurked an increasing dread of missing something hot and noisy and overcrowded when he went off to one of his mountain tops. 'After all, that highbrow business has been awfully overdone – now hasn't it?' the little Warley would insinuate, rummaging for his pearl studs, and consulting his flat evening watch as nervously as if it were a railway timetable. 'If only we haven't missed something really jolly by all this backing and filling. . . .'

'Oh, you poor creature, you! Always afraid of being left out, aren't you? Well – just for once, to humor you, and because I happen to be feeling rather stale myself. But only to think of a sane man's wanting to go to places just because they're hot and smart and overcrowded!' And off they would dash together. . . .

• II •

ALL that was long ago. It was years now since there had been two distinct Anson Warleys. The lesser one had made away with the other, done him softly to death without shedding of blood; and only a few people suspected (and they no longer cared) that the pale white-haired man, with the small slim figure, the ironic smile and the perfect evening clothes, whom New York still indefatigably invited, was nothing less than a murderer.

Anson Warley – Anson Warley! No party was complete without Anson Warley. He no longer went abroad now; too stiff in the joints; and there had been two or three slight attacks of dizziness. . . . Nothing to speak of, nothing to think of, even; but somehow one dug one's self into one's comfortable quarters, and felt less and less like moving out of them, except to motor down to Long Island for weekends, or to Newport for a few visits in summer. A trip to the Hot Springs, to get rid of the stiffness, had not helped much, and the ageing Anson Warley (who really, otherwise, felt as young as ever) had developed a growing dislike for the promiscuities of hotel life and the monotony of hotel food.

Yes; he was growing more fastidious as he grew older. A good sign, he thought. Fastidious not only about food and comfort but about people also. It was still a privilege, a distinction, to have him to dine. His old friends were faithful, and the new people fought for him, and often failed to get him; to do so they had to offer very special inducements in the way of cuisine, conversation or beauty. Young beauty; yes, that would do it. He did like to sit and watch a lovely face, and call laughter into lovely eyes. But no dull dinners for *him*, not even if they fed you off gold. As to that he was as firm as the other Warley, the distant aloof one with whom he had – er, well, parted company, oh, quite amicably, a good many years ago. . . .

On the whole, since that parting, life had been much easier and pleasanter; and by the time the little Warley was sixty-three he found himself looking forward with equanimity to an eternity of New York dinners.

Oh, but only at the right houses – always at the right houses; that was understood! The right people – the right setting – the right wines. . . . He smiled a little over his perennial enjoyment of them; said 'Nonsense, Filmore,' to his devoted tiresome manservant, who was beginning to hint that really, every night, sir, and sometimes a dance afterward, was too much, especially when you kept at it for months on end; and Dr. –

'Oh, damn your doctors!' Warley snapped. He was seldom ill-tempered; he knew it was foolish and upsetting to lose one's self-control. But Filmore began to be a nuisance, nagging him, preaching at him. As if he himself wasn't the best judge. . . .

Besides, he chose his company. He'd stay at home any time rather than risk a boring evening. Damned rot, what Filmore had said about his going out every night. Not like poor old Mrs. Jaspar, for instance . . . he smiled self-approvingly as he evoked her tottering image. 'That's the kind of fool Filmore takes me for,' he chuckled, his good humor restored by an analogy that was so much to his advantage.

Poor old Evelina Jaspar! In his youth, and even in his prime, she had been New York's chief entertainer – 'leading hostess,' the newspapers called her. Her big house in Fifth Avenue had been an entertaining machine. She had lived, breathed, invested and reinvested her millions, to no other end. At first her pretext had been that she had to marry her daughters and amuse her sons; but when sons and daughters had married and left her she had seemed hardly aware of it; she had just gone on entertaining. Hundreds, no thousands of dinners (on gold plate, of course, and with orchids, and all the delicacies that were out of season), had been served in that vast pompous dining room, which one had only to close one's eyes to transform into a railway buffet for millionaires, at a big junction, before the invention of restaurant trains. . . .

Warley closed his eyes, and did so picture it. He lost himself in amused computation of the annual number of guests, of saddles of mutton, of legs of lamb, of terrapin, canvas backs, magnums of champagne and pyramids of hothouse fruit that must have passed through that room in the last forty years.

And even now, he thought – hadn't one of old Evelina's nieces told him the other day, half bantering, half shivering at the avowal, that the poor old lady, who was gently dying of softening of the brain, still imagined herself to be New York's leading hostess, still sent out invitations (which of course were never delivered), still ordered terrapin, champagne and orchids, and still came down every evening to her great shrouded drawing rooms, with her tiara askew on her purple wig, to receive a stream of imaginary guests?

Rubbish, of course – a macabre pleasantry of the extravagant Nelly Pierce, who had always had her joke at Aunt Evelina's expense. . . . But Warley could not help smiling at the thought that those dull monotonous dinners were still going on in their hostess's clouded imagination. Poor old Evelina, he thought! In a way she was right. There was really no reason why that kind of standardized entertaining should ever cease; a performance so undiscriminating, so undifferentiated, that one could almost imagine, in the hostess' tired brain, all the dinners she had ever given merging into one Gargantuan pyramid of food and drink, with the same faces, perpetually the same faces, gathered stolidly about the same gold plate.

Thank heaven, Anson Warley had never conceived of social values in terms of mass and volume. It was years since he had dined at Mrs. Jaspar's. He even felt that he was not above reproach in that respect. Two or three times, in the past, he had accepted her invitations (always sent out weeks ahead), and then chucked her at the eleventh hour for something more amusing. Finally, to avoid such risks, he had made it a rule always to refuse her dinners. He had even – he remembered – been rather funny about it once, when someone had told him that Mrs. Jaspar couldn't understand . . . was a little hurt . . . said it couldn't be true that he always had another engagement the nights she asked him. . . . *'True?* Is the truth what she wants? All right! Then the next time I get a "Mrs. Jaspar requests the pleasure" I'll answer it with a "Mr. Warley declines the boredom." Think she'll understand that, eh?' And the phrase became a catchword in his little set that winter. ' "Mr. Warley declines the boredom" – good, good, *good!'* 'Dear Anson, I do hope you won't decline the boredom of coming to lunch next Sunday to meet the new Hindu Yoghi' – or the new saxophone soloist, or that genius of a mulatto boy who plays Negro spirituals on a toothbrush; and so on and so on. He only hoped poor old Evelina never heard of it. . . .

'Certainly I shall *not* stay at home tonight – why, what's wrong with me?' he snapped, swinging round on Filmore.

The valet's long face grew longer. His way of answering such questions was always to pull out his face; it was his only means of putting any expression into it. He turned away into the bedroom, and Warley sat alone by his library fire. . . . Now what did the man see that was wrong with him, he wondered? He had felt a little confusion that morning, when he was doing his daily sprint around the Park (his exercise was reduced to that!); but it had been only a passing flurry, of which Filmore could of course know nothing. And as soon as it was over his mind had seemed more lucid, his eye keener, than ever; as sometimes (he reflected) the electric light in his library lamps would blaze up too brightly after a break in the current, and he would say to himself, wincing a little at the sudden glare on the page he was reading: 'That means that it'll go out again in a minute.'

Yes; his mind, at that moment, had been quite piercingly clear and perceptive; his eye had passed with a renovating glitter over every detail of the daily scene. He stood still for a minute under the leafless trees of the Mall, and looking about him with the sudden insight of age, understood that he had reached the time of life when Alps and cathedrals became as transient as flowers.

Everything was fleeting, fleeting . . . yes, that was what had given him the vertigo. The doctors, poor fools, called it the stomach, or high blood pressure; but it was only the dizzy plunge of the sands in the hour glass, the everlasting plunge that emptied one of heart and bowels, like the drop of an elevator from the top floor of a skyscraper.

Certainly, after that moment of revelation, he had felt a little more tired than usual for the rest of the day; the light had flagged in his mind as it sometimes did in his lamps. At Chrissy Torrance's, where he had lunched, they had accused him of being silent, his hostess had said that he looked pale; but he had retorted with a joke, and thrown himself into the talk with a feverish loquacity. It was the only thing to do; for he could not tell all these people at the lunch table that very morning he had arrived at the turn in the path from which mountains look as transient as flowers – and that one after another they would all arrive there too.

He leaned his head back and closed his eyes, but not in sleep. He did not feel sleepy, but keyed up and alert. In the next room he heard Filmore reluctantly, protestingly, laying out his evening clothes. . . . He had no fear about the dinner tonight; a quiet intimate little affair at an old friend's house. Just two or three congenial men, and Elfmann, the pianist (who would probably play), and that lovely Elfrida Flight. The fact that people asked him to dine to meet Elfrida Flight seemed to prove pretty conclusively that he was still in the running! He chuckled softly at Filmore's pessimism, and thought: 'Well, after all, I suppose no man seems young to his valet. . . . Time to dress very soon,' he thought; and luxuriously postponed getting up out of his chair. . . .

• III •

'SHE's worse than usual tonight,' said the day nurse, laying down the evening paper as her colleague joined her. 'Absolutely determined to have her jewels out.'

The night nurse, fresh from a long sleep and an afternoon at the movies with a gentleman friend, threw down her fancy bag, tossed off her hat and rumpled up her hair before old Mrs. Jaspar's tall toilet mirror. 'Oh, I'll settle that – don't you worry,' she said brightly.

'Don't you fret her, though, Miss Cress,' said the other, getting wearily out of her chair. 'We're very well off here, take it as a whole, and I don't want her pressure rushed up for nothing.'

Miss Cress, still looking at herself in the glass, smiled reassuringly at Miss Dunn's pale reflection behind her. She and Miss Dunn got on very well together, and knew on which side their bread was buttered. But at the end of the day Miss Dunn was always fagged out and fearing the worst. The patient wasn't as hard to handle as all that. Just let her ring for her old maid, old Lavinia, and say: 'My sapphire velvet tonight, with the diamond stars' – and Lavinia would know exactly how to manage her.

Miss Dunn had put on her hat and coat, and crammed her knitting, and the newspaper, into her bag, which, unlike Miss Cress's, was capacious and shabby; but she still loitered undecided on the threshold. 'I could stay with you till ten as easy as not. . . .' She looked almost reluctantly about the big high-studded dressing room (everything in the house was high-studded), with its rich dusky carpet and curtains, and its monumental dressing table draped with lace and laden with gold-backed brushes and combs, gold-stoppered toilet bottles, and all the charming paraphernalia of beauty at her glass. Old Lavinia even renewed every morning the roses and carnations in the slim crystal vases between the powder boxes and the nail polishers. Since the family had shut down the hothouses at the uninhabited country place on the Hudson, Miss Cress suspected that old Lavinia bought these flowers out of her own pocket.

'Cold out tonight?' queried Miss Dunn from the door.

'Fierce . . . reg'lar blizzard at the corners. Say, shall I lend you my fur scarf?' Miss Cress, pleased with the memory of her afternoon (they'd be engaged soon, she thought), and with the drowsy prospect of an evening in a deep armchair near the warm gleam of the dressing-room fire, was disposed to kindliness toward that poor thin Dunn girl, who supported her mother, and her brother's idiot twins. And she wanted Miss Dunn to notice her new fur.

'My! Isn't it too lovely? No, not for worlds, thank you. . . .' Her hand on the doorknob, Miss Dunn repeated: 'Don't you cross her now,' and was gone.

Lavinia's bell rang furiously, twice; then the door between the dressing room and Mrs. Jaspar's bedroom opened, and Mrs. Jaspar herself emerged.

'Lavinia!' she called, in a high irritated voice; then, seeing the nurse, who had slipped into her print dress and starched cap, she added in a lower tone: 'Oh, Miss Lemoine, good evening.' Her first nurse, it appeared, had been called Miss Lemoine; and she gave the same name to all the others, quite unaware that there had been any changes in the staff.

'I heard talking, and carriages driving up. Have people begun to arrive?' she asked nervously. 'Where is Lavinia? I still have my jewels to put on.'

She stood before the nurse, the same petrifying apparition which always, at this hour, struck Miss Cress to silence. Mrs. Jaspar was tall; she had been broad; and her bones remained impressive though the flesh had withered on them. Lavinia had encased her, as usual, in her low-necked purple velvet dress, nipped in at the waist in the old-fashioned way, expanding in voluminous folds about the hips and flowing in a long train over the darker velvet of the carpet. Mrs. Jaspar's swollen feet could no longer be pushed into the high-heeled satin slippers which went with the dress; but her skirts were so long and spreading that, by taking short steps, she managed (so Lavinia daily assured her) entirely to conceal the broad round tips of her black orthopedic shoes.

'Your jewels, Mrs. Jaspar? Why, you've got them on,' said Miss Cress brightly.

Mrs. Jaspar turned her porphyry-tinted face to Miss Cress, and looked at her with a glassy incredulous gaze. Her eyes, Miss Cress thought, were the worst. . . . She lifted one old hand, veined and knobbed as a raised map, to her elaborate purple-black wig, groped among the puffs and curls and undulations (queer, Miss Cress thought, that it never occurred to her to look into the glass), and after an interval affirmed: 'You must be mistaken, my dear. Don't you think you ought to have your eyes examined?'

The door opened again, and a very old woman, so old as to make Mrs. Jaspar appear almost young, hobbled in with sidelong steps. 'Excuse me, madam. I was downstairs when the bell rang.'

Lavinia had probably always been small and slight; now, beside her towering mistress, she looked a mere feather, a straw. Everything about her had dried, contracted, been volatilized into nothingness, except her watchful gray eyes, in which intelligence and comprehension burned like two fixed stars. 'Do excuse me, madam,' she repeated.

Mrs. Jaspar looked at her despairingly. 'I hear carriages driving up. And Miss Lemoine says I have my jewels on; and I know I haven't.'

'With that lovely necklace!' Miss Cress ejaculated.

Mrs. Jaspar's twisted hand rose again, this time to her denuded shoulders, which were as stark and barren as the rock from which the hand might have been broken. She felt and felt, and tears rose in her eyes. . . .

'Why do you lie to me?' she burst out passionately.

Lavinia softly intervened. 'Miss Lemoine meant how lovely you'll be when you get the necklace on, madam.'

'Diamonds, diamonds,' said Mrs. Jaspar with an awful smile.

'Of course, madam.'

Mrs. Jaspar sat down at the dressing table, and Lavinia, with eager random hands, began to adjust the *point de Venise* about her mistress' shoulders, and to repair the havoc wrought in the purple-black wig by its wearer's gropings for her tiara.

'Now you do look lovely, madam,' she sighed.

Mrs. Jaspar was on her feet again, stiff but incredibly active. ('Like a cat she is,' Miss Cress used to relate.) 'I do hear carriages – or is it an automobile? The Magraws, I know, have one of those new-fangled automobiles. And now I hear the front door opening. Quick, Lavinia! My fan, my gloves, my handkerchief . . . how often have I got to tell you? I used to have a *perfect* maid – '

Lavinia's eyes brimmed. 'That was me, madam,' she said, bending to straighten out the folds of the long purple-velvet train. ('To watch the two of 'em,' Miss Cress used to tell a circle of appreciative friends, 'is a lot better than any circus.')

Mrs. Jaspar paid no attention. She twitched the train out of Lavinia's vacillating hold, swept to the door, and then paused there as if stopped by a jerk of her constricted muscles. 'Oh, but my diamonds – you cruel woman, you! You're letting me down without my diamonds!' Her ruined face puckered up in a grimace like a new-born baby's, and she began to sob despairingly. 'Everybody . . . every . . . body's . . . against me . . .' she wept in her powerless misery.

Lavinia helped herself to her feet and tottered across the floor. It was almost more than she could bear to see her mistress in distress. 'Madam, madam – if you'll just wait till they're got out of the safe,' she entreated.

The woman she saw before her, the woman she was entreating and consoling, was not the old petrified Mrs. Jaspar with porphyry face and wig awry whom Miss Cress stood watching with a smile, but a young proud creature, commanding and splendid in her Paris gown of amber *moiré*, who, years ago, had burst into just such furious sobs because, as she was sweeping down to receive her guests, the doctor had told her that little Grace, with whom she had been playing all the afternoon, had a diphtheritic throat, and no one must be allowed to enter. 'Everybody's against me, everybody . . .' she sobbed in her fury; and the young Lavinia, stricken by such Olympian anger, had stood speechless, longing to comfort her, and secretly indignant with little Grace and the doctor. . . .

'If you'll just wait, madam, while I go down and ask Munson to open the safe. There's no one come yet, I do assure you. . . .'

Munson was the old butler, the only person who knew the combination of the safe in Mrs. Jaspar's bedroom. Lavinia had once known it too, but now she was no longer able to remember it. The worst of it was that she feared lest Munson, who had been spending the day in the Bronx, might not have returned. Munson was growing old too, and he did sometimes forget about these dinner parties of Mrs. Jaspar's, and then the stupid footman, George, had to announce the names; and you couldn't be sure that Mrs. Jaspar wouldn't notice Munson's absence, and be excited and angry. These dinner party nights were killing old Lavinia, and she did so want to keep alive; she wanted to live long enough to wait on Mrs. Jaspar to the last.

She disappeared, and Miss Cress poked up the fire, and persuaded Mrs. Jaspar to sit down in an armchair and 'tell her who was coming.' It always amused Mrs. Jaspar to say over the long list of her guests' names, and generally she remembered them fairly well, for they were always the same – the last people, Lavinia and Munson said, who had dined at the house, on the very night before her stroke. With recovered complacency she began, counting over one after another on her ring-laden fingers: 'The Italian Ambassador, the Bishop, Mr. and Mrs. Torrington Bligh, Mr. and Mrs. Fred Amesworth, Mr. and Mrs. Mitchell Magraw, Mr. and Mrs. Torrington Bligh. . . .' ('You've said them before,' Miss Cress interpolated, getting out her fancy knitting – a necktie for her friend – and beginning to count the stitches.) And Mrs. Jaspar, distressed and bewildered by the interruption, had to repeat over and over: 'Torrington Bligh, Torrington Bligh,' till the connection was re-established, and she went on again swimmingly with 'Mr. and Mrs. Fred Amesworth, Mr. and Mrs. Mitchell Magraw, Miss Laura Ladew, Mr. Harold Ladew, Mr. and Mrs. Benjamin Bronx, Mr. and Mrs. Torrington Bl – no, I mean, Mr. Anson Warley. Yes, Mr. Anson Warley; that's it,' she ended complacently.

Miss Cress smiled and interrupted her counting. 'No, that's *not* it.'

'What do you mean, my dear – not it?'

'Mr. Anson Warley. He's not coming.'

Mrs. Jaspar's jaw fell, and she stared at the nurse's coldly smiling face. 'Not coming?'

'No. He's not coming. He's not on the list.' (That old list! As if Miss Cress didn't know it by heart! Everybody in the house did, except the booby, George, who heard it reeled off every other night by Munson, and who was always stumbling over the names, and having to refer to the written paper.)

'Not on the list?' Mrs. Jaspar gasped.

Miss Cress shook her pretty head.

Signs of uneasiness gathered on Mrs. Jaspar's face and her lip began to tremble. It always amused Miss Cress to give her these little jolts, though she knew Miss Dunn and the doctors didn't approve of her doing so. She knew also that it was against her own interests, and she did try to bear in mind Miss Dunn's oft-repeated admonition about not sending up the patient's blood pressure; but when she was in high spirits, as she was tonight (they would certainly be engaged), it was irresistible to get a rise out of the old lady. And she thought it funny, this new figure unexpectedly appearing among those time-worn guests. ('I wonder what the rest of 'em 'll say to him,' she giggled inwardly.)

'No; he's not on the list.' Mrs. Jaspar, after pondering deeply, announced the fact with an air of recovered composure.

'That's what I told you,' snapped Miss Cress.

'He's not on the list; but he promised me to come. I saw him yesterday,' continued Mrs. Jaspar, mysteriously.

'You *saw* him – where?'

She considered. 'Last night, at the Fred Amesworths' dance.'

'Ah,' said Miss Cress, with a little shiver; for she knew that Mrs. Amesworth was dead, and she was the intimate friend of the trained nurse who was keeping alive, by dint of *piqûres* and high frequency, the inarticulate and inanimate Mr. Amesworth. 'It's funny,' she remarked to Mrs. Jaspar, 'that you'd never invited Mr. Warley before.'

'No, I hadn't; not for a long time. I believe he felt I'd neglected him; for he came up to me last night, and said he was so sorry he hadn't been able to call. It seems he's been ill, poor fellow. Not as young as he was! So of course I invited him. He was very much gratified.'

Mrs. Jaspar smiled at the remembrance of her little triumph; but Miss Cress's attention had wandered, as it always did when the patient became docile and reasonable. She thought: 'Where's old Lavinia? I bet she can't find Munson.' And she got up and crossed the floor to look into Mrs. Jaspar's bedroom, where the safe was.

There an astonishing sight met her. Munson, as she had expected, was nowhere visible; but Lavinia, on her knees before the safe, was in the act of opening it herself, her twitching hand slowly moving about the mysterious dial.

'Why, I thought you'd forgotten the combination!' Miss Cress exclaimed.

Lavinia turned a startled face over her shoulder. 'So I had, Miss. But I've managed to remember it, thank God. I *had* to, you see, because Munson's forgot to come home.'

'Oh,' said the nurse incredulously ('Old fox,' she thought, 'I wonder why she's always pretended she'd forgotten it.') For Miss Cress did not know that the age of miracles is not yet past.

Joyous, trembling, her cheeks wet with grateful tears, the little old woman was on her feet again, clutching to her breast the diamond stars, the necklace of solitaires, the tiara, the earrings. One by one she spread them out on the velvet-lined tray in which they always used to be carried from the safe to the dressing room; then, with rambling fingers, she managed to lock the safe again, and put the keys in the drawer where they belonged, while Miss Cress continued to stare at her in amazement. 'I don't believe the old witch is as shaky as she makes out,' was her reflection as Lavinia passed her, bearing the jewels to the dressing room where Mrs. Jaspar, lost in pleasant memories, was still computing: 'The Italian Ambassador, the Bishop, the Torrington Blighs, the Mitchell Magraws, the Fred Amesworths. . . .'

Mrs. Jaspar was allowed to go down to the drawing room alone on dinner party evenings because it would have mortified her too much to receive her guests with a maid or a nurse at her elbow; but Miss Cress and Lavinia always leaned over the stair rail to watch her descent, and make sure it was accomplished in safety.

'She do look lovely yet, when all her diamonds is on,' Lavinia sighed, her purblind eyes bedewed with memories, as the bedizened wig and purple velvet disappeared at the last bend of the stairs. Miss

Cress, with a shrug, turned back to the fire and picked up her knitting, while Lavinia set about the slow ritual of tidying up her mistress' room. From below they heard the sound of George's stentorian monologue: 'Mr. and Mrs. Torrington Bligh, Mr. and Mrs. Mitchell Magraw . . . Mr. Ladew, Miss Laura Ladew. . . .'

• IV •

ANSON WARLEY, who had always prided himself on his equable temper, was conscious of being on edge that evening. But it was an irritability which did not frighten him (in spite of what those doctors always said about the importance of keeping calm) because he knew it was due merely to the unusual lucidity of his mind. He was in fact feeling uncommonly well, his brain clear and all his perceptions so alert that he could positively hear the thoughts passing through his manservant's mind on the other side of the door, as Filmore grudgingly laid out the evening clothes.

Smiling at the man's obstinacy, he thought: 'I shall have to tell them tonight that Filmore thinks I'm no longer fit to go into society.' It was always pleasant to hear the incredulous laugh with which his younger friends received any allusion to his supposed senility. 'What, *you?* Well, that's a good one!' And he thought it was, himself.

And then, the moment he was in his bedroom, dressing, the sight of Filmore made him lose his temper again. 'No; *not* those studs, confound it. The black onyx ones – haven't I told you a hundred times? Lost them, I suppose? Sent them to the wash again in a soiled shirt? That it?' He laughed nervously, and sitting down before his dressing table began to brush back his hair in short angry strokes.

'Above all,' he shouted out suddenly, 'don't stand there staring at me as if you were watching to see exactly at what minute to telephone for the undertaker!'

'The under – ? Oh, sir!' gasped Filmore.

'The – the – damn it, are you *deaf* too? Who said undertaker? I said *taxi;* can't you hear what I say?'

'You want me to call a taxi, sir?'

'No; I don't. I've already told you so. I'm going to walk.' Warley straightened his tie, rose and held out his arms toward his dress coat.

'It's bitter cold, sir; better let me call a taxi all the same.'

Warley gave a short laugh. 'Out with it, now! What you'd really like to suggest is that I should telephone to say I can't dine out. You'd scramble me some eggs instead, eh?'

'I wish you would stay in, sir. There's eggs in the house.'

'My overcoat,' snapped Warley.

'Or else let me call a taxi; now do, sir.'

Warley slipped his arms into his overcoat, tapped his chest to see if his watch (the thin evening watch) and his notecase were in their proper pockets, turned back to put a dash of lavender on his handkerchief, and walked with stiff quick steps toward the front door of his flat.

Filmore, abashed, preceded him to ring for the lift; and then, as it quivered upward through the long shaft, said again: 'It's a bitter cold night, sir; and you've had a good deal of exercise today.'

Warley leveled a contemptuous glance at him. 'Dare say that's why I'm feeling so fit,' he retorted as he entered the lift.

It *was* bitter cold; the icy air hit him in the chest when he stepped out of the overheated building, and he halted on the doorstep and took a long breath. 'Filmore's missed his vocation; ought to be nurse to a paralytic,' he thought. 'He'd love to have to wheel me about in a chair.'

After the first shock of the biting air he began to find it exhilarating, and walked along at a good pace, dragging one leg ever so little after the other. (The *masseur* had promised him that he'd soon be rid of that stiffness.) Yes – decidedly a fellow like himself ought to have a younger valet; a more cheerful one, anyhow. He felt like a young'un himself this evening; as he turned into Fifth Avenue he rather wished he could meet someone he knew, some man who'd say afterward at his club: 'Warley? Why, I saw him sprinting up Fifth Avenue the other night like a two-year-old; that night it was four or five below. . . .' He needed a good counter-irritant for Filmore's gloom. 'Always have young people about you,' he thought as he walked along; and at the words his mind turned to Elfrida Flight, next to whom he would soon be sitting in a warm pleasantly lit dining room – *where?*

It came as abruptly as that: the gap in his memory. He pulled up at it as if his advance had been checked by a chasm in the pavement at his feet. Where the dickens was he going to dine? And with whom was he going to dine? God! But things didn't happen in that way; a sound strong man didn't suddenly have to stop in the middle of the street and ask himself where he was going to dine. . . .

'Perfect in mind, body and understanding.' The old legal phrase bobbed up inconsequently into his thoughts. Less than two minutes ago he had answered in every particular to that description; what was he now? He put his hand to his forehead, which was bursting; then he lifted his hat and let the cold air blow for a while over his overheated temples. It was queer, how hot he'd got, walking. Fact was, he'd been sprinting along at a damned good pace. In future he must try to remember not to hurry. . . . Hang it – one more thing to remember! . . . Well, but what was all the fuss about? Of course, as people got older their memories were subject to these momentary lapses; he'd noticed if often enough among his contemporaries. And, brisk and alert though he still was, it wouldn't do to imagine himself totally exempt from human ills. . . .

Where was it he was dining? Why, somewhere farther up Fifth
Avenue; he was perfectly sure of that. With that lovely . . . that
lovely. . . . No; better not make any effort for the moment. Just keep
calm, and stroll slowly along. When he came to the right street corner
of course he'd spot it; and then everything would be perfectly clear
again. He walked on, more deliberately, trying to empty his mind of
all thoughts. 'Above all,' he said to himself, 'don't worry.'

He tried to beguile his nervousness by thinking of amusing things.
'Decline the boredom – ' He thought he might get off that joke tonight.
'Mrs. Jaspar requests the pleasure – Mr. Warley declines the boredom.'
Not so bad, really; and he had an idea he'd never told it to the
people . . . what in hell *was* their name?..the people he was on his way
to dine with . . . *Mrs. Jaspar requests the pleasure*. Poor old Mrs. Jaspar;
again it occurred to him that he hadn't always been very civil to her in
old times. When everybody's running after a fellow it's pardonable
now and then to chuck a boring dinner at the last minute; but all the
same, as one grew older one understood better how an unintentional
slight of that sort might cause offense, cause even pain. And he hated
to cause people pain. . . . He thought perhaps he'd better call on Mrs.
Jaspar some afternoon. She'd be surprised! Or ring her up, poor old
girl, and propose himself, just informally, for dinner. One dull evening
wouldn't kill him – and how pleased she'd be! Yes – he thought
decidedly . . . when he got to be her age, he could imagine how much
he'd like it if somebody still in the running should ring him up unexpectedly and say –

He stopped, and looked up, slowly, wonderingly, at the wide
illuminated façade of the house he was approaching. Queer coincidence
– it was the Jaspar house. And all lit up; for a dinner evidently. And
that was queerer yet; almost uncanny; for here he was, in front of the
door, as the clock struck a quarter past eight; and of course – he
remembered it quite clearly now – it was just here, it was with Mrs.
Jaspar, that he was dining . . . Those little lapses of memory never
lasted more than a second or two. How right he'd been not to let
himself worry. He pressed his hand on the doorbell.

'God,' he thought, as the double doors swung open, 'but it's good
to get in out of the cold.'

• V •

In that hushed sonorous house the sound of the doorbell was as loud
to the two women upstairs as if it had been rung in the next room.

Miss Cress raised her head in surprise, and Lavinia dropped Mrs.
Jaspar's other false set (the more comfortable one) with a clatter on the
marble washstand. She stumbled across the dressing room, and hastened

out to the landing. With Munson absent, there was no knowing how George might muddle things. . . .

Miss Cress joined her. 'Who is it?' she whispered excitedly. Below, they heard the sound of a hat and a walking stick being laid down on the big marble-topped table in the hall, and then George's stentorian drone: 'Mr. Anson Warley.'

'It is – it *is!* I can see him – a gentleman in evening clothes,' Miss Cress whispered, hanging over the stair rail.

'Good gracious – mercy me! And Munson not here! Oh, whatever, whatever shall we do?' Lavinia was trembling so violently that she had to clutch the stair rail to prevent herself from falling. Miss Cress thought, with her cold lucidity: 'She's a good deal sicker than the old woman.'

'What shall we do, Miss Cress? That fool of a George – he's showing him in! Who could have thought it?' Miss Cress knew the images that were whirling through Lavinia's brain: the vision of Mrs. Jaspar's having another stroke at the sight of this mysterious intruder, of Mr. Anson Warley's seeing her there, in her impotence and her abasement, of the family's being summoned, and rushing in to exclaim, to question, to be horrified and furious – and all because poor old Munson's memory was going, like his mistress', like Lavinia's, and because he had forgotten that it was one of the *dinner nights*. Oh, misery! . . . The tears were running down Lavinia's cheeks, and Miss Cress knew she was thinking: 'If the daughters send him off – and they will – where's he going to, old and deaf as he is, and all his people dead? Oh, if only he can hold on till she dies, and get his pension. . . .'

Lavinia recovered herself with one of her supreme efforts. 'Miss Cress, we must go down at once, at once! Something dreadful's going to happen. . . .' She began to totter toward the little velvet-lined lift in the corner of the landing.

Miss Cress took pity on her. 'Come along,' she said. 'But nothing dreadful's going to happen. You'll see.'

'Oh, thank you, Miss Cress. But the shock – the awful shock to her – of seeing that strange gentleman walk in.'

'Not a bit of it.' Miss Cress laughed as she stepped into the lift. 'He's not a stranger. She's expecting him.'

'Expecting him? Expecting Mr. Warley?'

'Sure she is. She told me so just now. She says she invited him yesterday.'

'But, Miss Cress, what are you thinking of? Invite him – how? When you know she can't write nor telephone?'

'Well, she says she saw him; she saw him last night at a dance.'

'Oh, God,' murmured Lavinia, covering her eyes with her hands.

'At a dance at the Fred Amesworths' – that's what she said,' Miss

Cress pursued, feeling the same little shiver run down her back as when Mrs. Jaspar had made the statement to her.

'The Amesworths – oh, not the Amesworths?' Lavinia echoed, shivering too. She dropped her hands from her face, and followed Miss Cress out of the lift. Her expression had become less anguished, and the nurse wondered why. In reality, she was thinking, in a sort of dreary beatitude: 'But if she's suddenly got as much worse as this, she'll go before me, after all, my poor lady, and I'll be able to see to it that she's properly laid out and dressed, and nobody but Lavinia's hands'll touch her.'

'You'll see – if she was expecting him, as she says, it won't give her a shock, anyhow. Only, how did *he* know?' Miss Cress whispered, with an acuter renewal of her shiver. She followed Lavinia with muffled steps down the passage to the pantry, and from there the two women stole into the dining room, and placed themselves noiselessly at its farther end, behind the tall Coromandel screen through the cracks of which they could peep into the empty room.

The long table was set, as Mrs. Jaspar always insisted that it should be on these occasions; but old Munson not having returned, the gold plate (which his mistress also insisted on) had not been got out, and all down the table, as Lavinia saw with horror, George had laid the coarse blue-and-white plates from the servants' hall. The electric wall lights were on, and the candles lit in the branching Sèvres candelabra – so much at least had been done. But the flowers in the great central dish of Rose Dubarry porcelain, and in the smaller dishes which accompanied it – the flowers, oh shame, had been forgotten! They were no longer real flowers; the family had long since suppressed that expense; and no wonder, for Mrs. Jaspar always insisted on orchids. But Grace, the youngest daughter, who was the kindest, had hit on the clever device of arranging three beautiful clusters of artificial orchids and maidenhair, which had only to be lifted from their shelf in the pantry and set in the dishes – only, of course, that imbecile footman had forgotten, or had not known where to find them. And, oh, horror, realizing his oversight too late, no doubt, to appeal to Lavinia, he had taken some old news-papers and bunched them up into something that he probably thought resembled a bouquet, and crammed one into each of the priceless Rose Dubarry dishes.

Lavinia clutched at Miss Cress's arm. 'Oh, look – look what he's done; I shall die of the shame of it. . . . Oh, Miss, hadn't we better slip around to the drawing room and try to coax my poor lady upstairs again, afore she ever notices?'

Miss Cress, peering through the crack of the screen, could hardly suppress a giggle. For at that moment the double doors of the dining room were thrown open, and George, shuffling about in a baggy livery inherited from a long-departed predecessor of more commanding build, bawled out in his loud singsong: 'Dinner is served, madam.'

'Oh, it's too late,' moaned Lavinia. Miss Cress signed to her to keep silent, and the two watchers glued their eyes to their respective cracks of the screen.

What they saw, far off down the vista of empty drawing rooms, and after an interval during which (as Lavinia knew) the imaginary guests were supposed to file in and take their seats, was the entrance, at the end of the ghostly cortège, of a very old woman, still tall and towering, on the arm of a man somewhat smaller than herself, with a fixed smile on a darkly pink face, and a slim erect figure clad in perfect evening clothes, who advanced with short measured steps, profiting (Miss Cress noticed) by the support of the arm he was supposed to sustain. 'Well – I never!' was the nurse's inward comment.

The couple continued to advance, with rigid smiles and eyes staring straight ahead. Neither turned to the other, neither spoke. All their attention was concentrated on the immense, the almost unachievable effort of reaching that point, halfway down the long dinner table, opposite the big Dubarry dish, where George was drawing back a gilt armchair for Mrs. Jaspar. At last they reached it, and Mrs. Jaspar seated herself, and waved a stony hand to Mr. Warley. 'On my right.' He gave a little bow, like the bend of a jointed doll, and with infinite precaution let himself down into his chair. Beads of perspiration were standing on his forehead, and Miss Cress saw him draw out his handkerchief and wipe them stealthily away. He then turned his head somewhat stiffly toward his hostess.

'Beautiful flowers,' he said, with great precision and perfect gravity, waving his hand toward the bunched-up newspaper in the bowl of Sèvres.

Mrs. Jaspar received the tribute with complacency. 'So glad . . . orchids . . . from High Lawn . . . every morning,' she simpered.

'Marvelous,' Mr. Warley completed.

'I always say to the Bishop . . . ,' Mrs. Jaspar continued.

'Ha – of course,' Mr. Warley warmly assented.

'Not that I don't think . . .'

'Ha – rather!'

George had reappeared from the pantry with a blue crockery dish of mashed potatoes. This he handed in turn to one after another of the imaginary guests, and finally presented to Mrs. Jaspar and her right-hand neighbor.

They both helped themselves cautiously, and Mrs. Jaspar addressed an arch smile to Mr. Warley. ''Nother month – no more oysters.'

'Ha – no more!'

George, with a bottle of Apollinaris wrapped in a napkin, was saying to each guest in turn: 'Perrier-Jouet, '95.' (He had picked that up, thought Miss Cress, from hearing old Munson repeat it so often.)

'Hang it – well, then just a sip,' murmured Mr. Warley.

'Old times,' bantered Mrs. Jaspar; and the two turned to each other and bowed their heads and touched glasses.

'I often tell Mrs. Amesworth . . . ,' Mrs. Jaspar continued, bending to an imaginary presence across the table.

'Ha – *ha!*' Mr. Warley approved.

George reappeared and slowly encircled the table with a dish of spinach. After the spinach the Apollinaris also went the rounds again, announced successively as Château Lafite, '74, and 'the old Newbold Madeira.' Each time that George approached his glass, Mr. Warley made a feint of lifting a defensive hand, and then smiled and yielded. 'Might as well – hanged for a sheep . . . ,' he remarked gaily; and Mrs. Jaspar giggled.

Finally a dish of Malaga grapes and apples was handed. Mrs. Jaspar, now growing perceptibly languid, and nodding with more and more effort at Mr. Warley's pleasantries, transferred a bunch of grapes to her plate, but nibbled only two or three. 'Tired,' she said suddenly, in a whimper like a child's; and she rose, lifting herself up by the arms of her chair, and leaning over to catch the eye of an invisible lady, presumably Mrs. Amesworth, seated opposite to her. Mr. Warley was on his feet too, supporting himself by resting one hand on the table in a jaunty attitude. Mrs. Jaspar waved to him to be reseated. 'Join us – after cigars,' she smilingly ordained; and with a great and concentrated effort he bowed to her as she passed toward the double doors which George was throwing open. Slowly, majestically, the purple-velvet train disappeared down the long enfilade of illuminated rooms, and the last door closed behind her.

'Well, I do believe she's enjoyed it!' chuckled Miss Cress, taking Lavinia by the arm to help her back to the hall. Lavinia, for weeping, could not answer.

• VI •

ANSON WARLEY found himself in the hall again, getting into his fur-lined overcoat. He remembered suddenly thinking that the rooms had been intensely overheated, and that all the other guests had talked very loud and laughed inordinately. 'Very good talk though, I must say,' he had to acknowledge.

In the hall, as he got his arms into his coat (rather a job, too, after that Perrier-Jouet) he remembered saying to somebody (perhaps it was to the old butler): 'Slipping off early – going on; 'nother engagement,' and thinking to himself the while that when he got out into the fresh

air again he would certainly remember where the other engagement
was. He smiled a little while the servant, who seemed a clumsy fellow,
fumbled with the fastening of the door. 'And Filmore, who thought I
wasn't even well enough to dine out! Damned ass! What would he say
if he knew I was going on?'

The door opened, and with an immense sense of exhilaration Mr.
Warley issued forth from the house and drew in a first deep breath of
night air. He heard the door closed and bolted behind him, and
continued to stand motionless on the step, expanding his chest, and
drinking in the icy draught.

''Spose it's about the last house where they give you Perrier-Jouet,
'95,' he thought; and then: 'Never heard better talk either. . . .'

He smiled again with satisfaction at the memory of the wine and
the wit. Then he took a step forward, to where a moment before the
pavement had been – and where now there was nothing.

Atrophy

———————

NORA FRENWAY settled down furtively in her corner of the Pullman and, as the express plunged out of the Grand Central Station, wondered at herself for being where she was. The porter came along. 'Ticket?' 'Westover.' She had instinctively lowered her voice and glanced about her. But neither the porter nor her nearest neighbors – fortunately none of them known to her – seemed in the least surprised or interested by the statement that she was traveling to Westover.

Yet what an earth-shaking announcement it was! Not that she cared, now; not that anything mattered except the one overwhelming fact which had convulsed her life, hurled her out of her easy velvet-lined rut, and flung her thus naked to the public scrutiny. . . . Cautiously, again, she glanced about her to make doubly sure that there was no one, absolutely no one, in that Pullman whom she knew by sight.

Her life had been so carefully guarded, so inwardly conventional in a world where all the outer conventions were tottering, that no one had ever known she had a lover. No one – of that she was absolutely sure. All the circumstances of the case had made it necessary that she should conceal her real life – her only real life – from everyone about her; from her half-invalid irascible husband, his prying envious sisters, and the terrible monumental old chieftainess, her mother-in-law, before whom all the family quailed and humbugged and fibbed and fawned.

What nonsense to pretend that nowadays, even in big cities, in the world's greatest social centers, the severe old-fashioned standards had given place to tolerance, laxity and ease! You took up the morning paper, and you read of girl bandits, movie star divorces, 'hold-ups' at balls, murder and suicide and elopement, and a general welter of disjointed disconnected impulses and appetites; then you turned your eyes onto your own daily life, and found yourself as cribbed and cabined, as beset by vigilant family eyes, observant friends, all sorts of embodied standards, as any white muslin novel heroine of the sixties!

In a different way, of course. To the casual eye Mrs. Frenway herself might have seemed as free as any of the young married women of her group. Poker playing, smoking, cocktail drinking, dancing, painting,

187

short skirts, bobbed hair and the rest – when had these been denied to
her? If by any outward sign she had differed too markedly from her
kind – lengthened her skirts, refused to play for money, let her hair
grow, or ceased to make up – her husband would have been the first
to notice it, and to say: 'Are you ill? What's the matter? How queer
you look! What's the sense of making yourself conspicuous?' For he
and his kind had adopted all the old inhibitions and sanctions, blindly
transferring them to a new ritual, as the receptive Romans did when
strange gods were brought into their temples. . . .

The train had escaped from the ugly fringes of the city, and the soft
spring landscape was gliding past her: glimpses of green lawns, budding
hedges, pretty irregular roofs, and miles and miles of alluring tarred
roads slipping away into mystery. How often she had dreamed of
dashing off down an unknown road with Christopher!

Not that she was a woman to be awed by the conventions. She
knew she wasn't. She had always taken their measure, smiled at them
– and conformed. On account of poor George Frenway, to begin with.
Her husband, in a sense, was a man to be pitied; his weak health, his
bad temper, his unsatisfied vanity, all made him a rather forlornly
comic figure. But it was chiefly on account of the two children that
she had always resisted the temptation to do anything reckless. The
least self-betrayal would have been the end of everything. Too many
eyes were watching her, and her husband's family was so strong, so
united – when there was anybody for them to hate – and at all times
so influential, that she would have been defeated at every point, and
her husband would have kept the children.

At the mere thought she felt herself on the brink of an abyss. 'The
children are my religion,' she had once said to herself; and she had no
other.

Yet here she was on her way to Westover. . . . Oh, what did it
matter now? That was the worst of it – it was too late for anything
between her and Christopher to matter! She was sure he was dying.
The way in which his cousin, Gladys Brincker, had blurted it out the
day before at Kate Salmer's dance: 'You didn't know – poor Kit?
Thought you and he were such pals! Yes; awfully bad, I'm afraid.
Return of the old trouble! I know there've been two consultations –
they had Knowlton down. They say there's not much hope; and nobody
but that forlorn frightened Jane mounting guard. . . .'

Poor Christopher! His sister Jane Aldis, Nora suspected, forlorn and
frightened as she was, had played in his life a part nearly as dominant
as Frenway and the children in Nora's. Loyally, Christopher always
pretended that she didn't; talked of her indulgently as 'poor Jenny.' But
didn't she, Nora, always think of her husband as 'poor George'? Jane
Aldis, of course, was much less self-assertive, less demanding, than
George Frenway; but perhaps for that very reason she would appeal all

the more to a man's compassion. And somehow, under her unobtrusive air, Nora had – on the rare occasions when they met – imagined that Miss Aldis was watching and drawing her inferences. But then Nora always felt, where Christopher was concerned, as if her breast were a pane of glass through which her trembling palpitating heart could be seen as plainly as holy viscera in a reliquary. Her sober after-thought was that Jane Aldis was just a dowdy self-effacing old maid whose life was filled to the brim by looking after the Westover place for her brother, and seeing that the fires were lit and the rooms full of flowers when he brought down his friends for a weekend.

Ah, how often he had said to Nora: 'If I could have you to myself for a weekend at Westover' – quite as if it were the easiest thing imaginable, as far as his arrangements were concerned! And they had even pretended to discuss how it could be done. But somehow she fancied he said it because he knew that the plan, for her, was about as feasible as a weekend in the moon. And in reality her only visits to Westover had been made in the company of her husband, and that of other friends, two or three times, at the beginning. . . . For after that she wouldn't. It was three years now since she had been there.

Gladys Brincker, in speaking of Christopher's illness, had looked at Nora queerly, as though suspecting something. But no – what nonsense! No one had ever suspected Nora Frenway. Didn't she know what her friends said of her? 'Nora? No more temperament than a lamp post. Always buried in her books. . . . Never very attractive to men, in spite of her looks.' Hadn't she said that of other women, who perhaps, in secret, like herself . . . ?

The train was slowing down as it approached a station. She sat up with a jerk and looked at her wrist watch. It was half-past two, the station was Ockham; the next would be Westover. In less than an hour she would be under his roof, Jane Aldis would be receiving her in that low paneled room full of books, and she would be saying – what would she be saying?

She had gone over their conversation so often that she knew not only her own part in it but Miss Aldis's by heart. The first moments would of course be painful, difficult; but then a great wave of emotion, breaking down the barriers between the two anxious women, would fling them together. She wouldn't have to say much, to explain; Miss Aldis would just take her by the hand and lead her upstairs to the room.

That room! She shut her eyes, and remembered other rooms where she and he had been together in their joy and their strength. . . . No, not that; she must not think of that now. For the man she had met in those other rooms was dying; the man she was going to was some one so different from that other man that it was like a profanation to associate their images. . . . And yet the man she was going to was her own Christopher, the one who had lived in her soul: and how his soul

must be needing hers, now that it hung alone on the dark brink! As if
anything else mattered at such a moment! She neither thought nor cared
what Jane Aldis might say or suspect; she wouldn't have cared if the
Pullman had been full of prying acquaintances, of if George and all
George's family had got in at that last station.

She wouldn't have cared a fig for any of them. Yet at the same
moment she remembered having felt glad that her old governess, whom
she used to go and see twice a year, lived at Ockham – so that if George
did begin to ask questions, she could always say: 'Yes, I went to see
poor old Fräulein; she's absolutely crippled now. I shall have to give
her a Bath chair. Could you get me a catalogue of prices?' There wasn't
a precaution she hadn't thought of – and now she was ready to scatter
them all to the winds. . . .

Westover – *Junction!*

She started up and pushed her way out of the train. All the people
seemed to be obstructing her, putting bags and suitcases in her way.
And the express stopped for only two minutes. Suppose she should be
carried on to Albany?

Westover Junction was a growing place, and she was fairly sure
there would be a taxi at the station. There was one – she just managed
to get to it ahead of a traveling man with a sample case and a new
straw hat. As she opened the door a smell of damp hay and bad tobacco
greeted her. She sprang in and gasped: 'To Oakfield. You know? Mr.
Aldis's place near Westover.'

• II •

IT began exactly as she had expected. A surprised parlormaid – why
surprised? – showed her into the low paneled room that was so full of
his presence, his books, his pipes, his terrier dozing on the shabby rug.
The parlormaid said she would go and see if Miss Aldis could come
down. Nora wanted to ask if she were with her brother – and how he
was. But she found herself unable to speak the words. She was afraid
her voice might tremble. And why should she question the parlormaid,
when in a moment, she hoped, she was to see Miss Aldis?

The woman moved away with a hushed step – the step which
denotes illness in the house. She did not immediately return, and the
interval of waiting in that room, so strange yet so intimately known,
was a new torture to Nora. It was unlike anything she had imagined.
The writing table with his scattered pens and letters was more than she
could bear. His dog looked at her amicably from the hearth, but made
no advances; and though she longed to stroke him, to let her hand rest
where Christopher's had rested, she dared not for fear he should bark
and disturb the peculiar hush of that dumb watchful house. She stood

in the window and looked out at the budding shrubs and the bulbs pushing up through the swollen earth.

'This way, please.'

Her heart gave a plunge. Was the woman actually taking her upstairs to his room? Her eyes filled, she felt herself swept forward on a great wave of passion and anguish. . . . But she was only being led across the hall into a stiff lifeless drawing room – the kind that bachelors get an upholsterer to do for them, and then turn their backs on forever. The chairs and sofas looked at her with an undisguised hostility, and then resumed the moping expression common to furniture in unfrequented rooms. Even the spring sun slanting in through the windows on the pale marquetry of a useless table seemed to bring no heat or light with it.

The rush of emotion subsided, leaving in Nora a sense of emptiness and apprehension. Supposing Jane Aldis should look at her with the cold eyes of this resentful room? She began to wish she had been friendlier and more cordial to Jane Aldis in the past. In her intense desire to conceal from everyone the tie between herself and Christopher she had avoided all show of interest in his family; and perhaps, as she now saw, excited curiosity by her very affectation of indifference.

No doubt it would have been more politic to establish an intimacy with Jane Aldis; and today, how much easier and more natural her position would have been! Instead of groping about – as she was again doing – for an explanation of her visit, she could have said: 'My dear, I came to see if there was anything in the world I could do to help you.'

She heard a hesitating step in the hall – a hushed step like the parlormaid's – and saw Miss Aldis pause near the half-open door. How old she had grown since their last meeting! Her hair, untidily pinned up, was gray and lanky. Her eyelids, always reddish, were swollen and heavy, her face sallow with anxiety and fatigue. It was odd to have feared so defenseless an adversary. Nora, for an instant, had the impression that Miss Aldis had wavered in the hall to catch a glimpse of her, take the measure of the situation. But perhaps she had only stopped to push back a strand of hair as she passed in front of a mirror.

'Mrs. Frenway – how good of you!' She spoke in a cool detached voice, as if her real self were elsewhere and she were simply an automaton wound up to repeat the familiar forms of hospitality. 'Do sit down,' she said.

She pushed forward one of the sulky armchairs, and Nora seated herself stiffly, her handbag clutched on her knee, in the self-conscious attitude of a country caller.

'I came – '

'So good of you,' Miss Aldis repeated. 'I had no idea you were in this part of the world. Not the slightest.'

Was it a lead she was giving? Or did she know everything, and wish to extend to her visitor the decent shelter of a pretext? Or was she really so stupid –

'You're staying with the Brinckers, I suppose. Or the Northrups? I remember the last time you came to lunch here you motored over with Mr. Frenway from Northrups'. That must have been two years ago, wasn't it?' She put the question with an almost sprightly show of interest.

'No – three years,' said Nora, mechanically.

'Was it? As long ago as that? Yes – you're right. That was the year we moved the big fern-leaved beech. I remember Mr. Frenway was interested in tree moving, and I took him out to show him where the tree had come from. He *is* interested in tree moving, isn't he?'

'Oh, yes; very much.'

'We had those wonderful experts down to do it. "Tree doctors," they call themselves. They have special appliances, you know. The tree is growing better than it did before they moved it. But I suppose you've done a great deal of transplanting on Long Island.'

'Yes. My husband does a good deal of transplanting.'

'So you've come over from the Northrups'? I didn't even know they were down at Maybrook yet. I see so few people.'

'No; not from the Northrups'.'

'Oh – the Brinckers'? Hal Brincker was here yesterday, but he didn't tell me you were staying there.'

Nora hesitated. 'No. The fact is, I have an old governess who lives at Ockham. I go to see her sometimes. And so I came on to Westover –' She paused, and Miss Aldis interrogated brightly: 'Yes?' as if prompting her in a lesson she was repeating.

'Because I saw Gladys Brincker the other day, and she told me that your brother was ill.'

'Oh.' Miss Aldis gave the syllable its full weight, and set a full stop after it. Her eyebrows went up, as if in a faint surprise. The silent room seemed to close in on the two speakers, listening. A resuscitated fly buzzed against the sunny windowpane. 'Yes; he's ill,' she conceded at length.

'I'm so sorry; I . . . he has been . . . such a friend of ours . . . so long. . . .'

'Yes; I've often heard him speak of you and Mr. Frenway.' Another full stop sealed this announcement. ('No, she knows nothing,' Nora thought.) 'I remember his telling me that he thought a great deal of Mr. Frenway's advice about moving trees. But then you see our soil is so different from yours. I suppose Mr. Frenway has had your soil analyzed?'

'Yes; I think he has.'

'Christopher's always been a great gardener.'

'I hope he's not – not very ill? Gladys seemed to be afraid – '

'Illness is always something to be afraid of, isn't it?'

'But you're not – I mean, not anxious . . . not seriously?'

'It's so kind of you to ask. The doctors seem to think there's no particular change since yesterday.'

'And yesterday?'

'Well, yesterday they seemed to think there might be.'

'A change, you mean?'

'Well, yes.'

'A change – I hope for the better?'

'They said they weren't sure; they couldn't say.'

The fly's buzzing had become so insistent in the still room that it seemed to be going on inside of Nora's head, and in the confusion of sound she found it more and more difficult to regain a lead in the conversation. And the minutes were slipping by, and upstairs the man she loved was lying. It was absurd and lamentable to make a pretense of keeping up this twaddle. She would cut through it, no matter how.

'I suppose you've had – a consultation?'

'Oh, yes; Dr. Knowlton's been down twice.'

'And what does he – '

'Well; he seems to agree with the others.'

There was another pause, and then Miss Aldis glanced out of the window. 'Why, who's that driving up?' she inquired. 'Oh, it's your taxi, I suppose, coming up the drive.'

'Yes. I got out at the gate.' She dared not add: 'For fear the noise might disturb him.'

'I hope you had no difficulty in finding a taxi at the Junction?'

'Oh, no; I had no difficulty.'

'I think it was so kind of you to come – not even knowing whether you'd find a carriage to bring you out all this way. And I know how busy you are. There's always so much going on in town, isn't there, even at this time of year?'

'Yes; I suppose so. But your brother – '

'Oh, of course my brother won't be up to any sort of gaiety; not for a long time.'

'A long time; no. But you do hope – '

'I think everybody about a sick bed ought to hope, don't you?'

'Yes; but I mean – '

Nora stood up suddenly, her brain whirling. Was it possible that she and that woman had sat thus facing each other for half an hour, piling up this conversational rubbish, while upstairs, out of sight, the truth, the meaning of their two lives hung on the frail thread of one man's intermittent pulse? She could not imagine why she felt so powerless and baffled. What had a woman who was young and handsome and beloved to fear from a dowdy and insignificant old maid? Why, the antagonism that these very graces and superiorities would create in the other's breast, especially if she knew they were all spent in charming the being on whom her life depended. Weak in herself, but powerful from her circumstances, she stood at bay on the ruins of all that Nora had ever loved. 'How she must hate me – and I never thought of it,' mused Nora, who had imagined that she had thought of everything where her relation to her lover was concerned. Well, it was too late now to remedy her omission; but at least she must assert herself, must say something to save the precious minutes that remained and break through the stifling web of platitudes which her enemy's tremulous hand was weaving around her.

'Miss Aldis – I must tell you – I came to see – '

'How he was? So very friendly of you. He would appreciate it, I know. Christopher is so devoted to his friends.'

'But you'll – you'll tell him that I – '

'Of course. That you came on purpose to ask about him. As soon as he's a little bit stronger.'

'But I mean – now?'

'Tell him now that you called to inquire? How good of you to think of that too! Perhaps tomorrow morning, if he's feeling a little bit brighter – '

Nora felt her lips drying as if a hot wind had parched them. They would hardly move. 'But now – now – today.' Her voice sank to a whisper as she added: 'Isn't he conscious?'

'Oh, yes; he's conscious; he's perfectly conscious.' Miss Aldis emphasized this with another of her long pauses. 'He shall certainly be told that you called.' Suddenly she too got up from her seat and moved toward the window. 'I must seem dreadfully inhospitable, not even offering you a cup of tea. But the fact is, perhaps I ought to tell you – if you're thinking of getting back to Ockham this afternoon there's only one train that stops at the Junction after three o'clock.' She pulled out an old-fashioned enameled watch with a wreath of roses about the dial, and turned almost apologetically to Mrs. Frenway. 'You ought to be at the station by four o'clock at the latest; and with one of those old Junction taxis. . . . I'm so sorry; I know I must appear to be driving you away.' A wan smile drew up her pale lips.

Nora knew just how long the drive from Westover Junction had taken, and understood that she was being delicately dismissed. Dismissed from life – from hope – even from the dear anguish of filling her eyes for the last time with the face which was the one face in the world to her! ('But then she does know everything,' she thought.)

'I mustn't make you miss your train, you know.'

'Miss Aldis, is he – has he seen anyone?' Nora hazarded in a painful whisper.

'Seen anyone? Well, there've been all the doctors – five of them!

And then the nurses. Oh, but you mean friends, of course. Naturally.'
She seemed to reflect. 'Hal Brincker, yes; he saw our cousin Hal
yesterday – but not for very long.'

Hal Brincker! Nora knew what Christopher thought of his Brincker
cousins – blighting bores, one and all of them, he always said. And in
the extremity of his illness the one person privileged to see him had
been – Hal Brincker! Nora's eyes filled; she had to turn them away for
a moment from Miss Aldis's timid inexorable face.

'But today?' she finally brought out.

'No. Today he hasn't seen anyone; not yet.' The two women stood
and looked at each other; then Miss Aldis glanced uncertainly about
the room. 'But couldn't I – Yes, I ought at least to have asked you if
you won't have a cup of tea. So stupid of me! There might still be
time. I never take tea myself.' Once more she referred anxiously to her
watch. 'The water is sure to be boiling, because the nurse's tea is just
being taken up. If you'll excuse me a moment I'll go and see.'

'Oh, no; no!' Nora drew in a quick sob. 'How can you? . . . I mean,
I don't want any. . . .'

Miss Aldis looked relieved. 'Then I shall be quite sure that you
won't reach the station too late.' She waited again, and then held out
a long stony hand. 'So kind – I shall never forget your kindness.
Coming all this way, when you might so easily have telephoned from
town. Do please tell Mr. Frenway how I appreciated it. You will
remember to tell him, won't you? He sent me such an interesting
collection of pamphlets about tree moving. I should like him to know
how much I feel his kindness in letting you come.' She paused again,
and pulled in her lips so that they became a narrow thread, a mere line
drawn across her face by a ruler. 'But, no; I won't trouble you; I'll
write to thank him myself.' Her hand ran out to an electric bell on the
nearest table. It shrilled through the silence, and the parlormaid
appeared with a stagelike promptness.

'The taxi, please? Mrs. Frenway's taxi.'

The room became silent again. Nora thought: 'Yes; she knows
everything.' Miss Aldis peeped for the third time at her watch, and
then uttered a slight unmeaning laugh. The bluebottle banged against
the window, and once more it seemed to Nora that its sonorities were
reverberating inside her head. They were deafeningly mingled there
with the explosion of the taxi's reluctant starting-up and its convulsed
halt at the front door. The driver sounded his horn as if to summon
her. 'He's afraid too that you'll be late!' Miss Aldis smiled.

The smooth slippery floor of the hall seemed to Nora to extend
away in front of her for miles. At its far end she saw a little tunnel of
light, a miniature maid, a toy taxi. Somehow she managed to travel
the distance that separated her from them, though her bones ached with
weariness, and at every step she seemed to be lifting a leaden weight.

The taxi was close to her now, its door was open, she was getting in. The same smell of damp hay and bad tobacco greeted her. She saw her hostess standing on the threshold. 'To the Junction, driver – back to the Junction,' she heard Miss Aldis say. The taxi began to roll toward the gate. As it moved away Nora heard Miss Aldis calling: 'I'll be sure to write and thank Mr. Frenway.'

Pomegranate Seed

———⚬———

CHARLOTTE ASHBY paused on her doorstep. Dark had descended on the brilliancy of the March afternoon, and the grinding rasping street life of the city was at its highest. She turned her back on it, standing for a moment in the old-fashioned, marble-flagged vestibule before she inserted her key in the lock. The sash curtains drawn across the panes of the inner door softened the light within to a warm blur through which no details showed. It was the hour when, in the first months of her marriage to Kenneth Ashby, she had most liked to return to that quiet house in a street long since deserted by business and fashion. The contrast between the soulless roar of New York, its devouring blaze of lights, the oppression of its congested traffic, congested houses, lives, minds and this veiled sanctuary she called home, always stirred her profoundly. In the very heart of the hurricane she had found her tiny islet – or thought she had. And now, in the last months, everything was changed, and she always wavered on the doorstep and had to force herself to enter.

While she stood there she called up the scene within: the hall hung with old prints, the ladder-like stairs, and on the left her husband's long shabby library, full of books and pipes and worn armchairs inviting to meditation. How she had loved that room! Then, upstairs, her own drawing room, in which, since the death of Kenneth's first wife, neither furniture nor hangings had been changed, because there had never been money enough, but which Charlotte had made her own by moving furniture about and adding more books, another lamp, a table for the new reviews. Even on the occasion of her only visit to the first Mrs. Ashby – a distant, self-centered woman, whom she had known very slightly – she had looked about her with an innocent envy, feeling it to be exactly the drawing room she would have liked for herself; and now for more than a year it had been hers to deal with as she chose – the room to which she hastened back at dusk on winter days, where she sat reading by the fire, or answering notes at the pleasant roomy desk, or going over her step-children's copybooks, till she heard her husband's step.

197

Sometimes friends dropped in; sometimes – oftener – she was alone; and she liked that best, since it was another way of being with Kenneth, thinking over what he had said when they parted in the morning, imagining what he would say when he sprang up the stairs, found her by herself and caught her to him.

Now, instead of this, she thought of one thing only – the letter she might or might not find on the hall table. Until she had made sure whether or not it was there, her mind had no room for anything else. The letter was always the same – a square gravish envelope with 'Kenneth Ashby, Esquire,' written on it in bold but faint characters. From the first it had struck Charlotte as peculiar that anyone who wrote such a firm hand should trace the letters so lightly; the address was always written as though there were not enough ink in the pen, or the writer's wrist were too weak to bear upon it. Another curious thing was that, in spite of its masculine curves, the writing was so visibly feminine. Some hands are sexless, some masculine, at first glance; the writing on the gray envelope, for all its strength and assurance, was without doubt a woman's. The envelope never bore anything but the recipient's name; no stamp, no address. The letter was presumably delivered by hand – but by whose? No doubt it was slipped into the letter box, whence the parlormaid, when she closed the shutters and lit the lights, probably extracted it. At any rate, it was always in the evening, after dark, that Charlotte saw it lying there. She thought of the letter in the singular, as 'it,' because, though there had been several since her marriage – seven, to be exact – they were so alike in appearance that they had become merged in one another in her mind, become one letter, become 'it.'

The first had come the day after their return from their honeymoon – a journey prolonged to the West Indies, from which they had returned to New York after an absence of more than two months. Re-entering the house with her husband, late on that first evening – they had dined at his mother's – she had seen, alone on the hall table, the gray envelope. Her eye fell on it before Kenneth's, and her first thought was: 'Why, I've seen that writing before'; but where she could not recall. The memory was just definite enough for her to identify the script whenever it looked up at her faintly from the same pale envelope; but on that first day she would have thought no more of the letter if, when her husband's glance lit on it, she had not chanced to be looking at him. It all happened in a flash – his seeing the letter, putting out his hand for it, raising it to his shortsighted eyes to decipher the faint writing, and then abruptly withdrawing the arm he had slipped through Charlotte's, and moving away to the hanging light, his back turned to her. She had waited – waited for a sound, an exclamation; waited for him to open the letter; but he had slipped it into his pocket without a word and followed her into the library. And there they had sat down by the fire and lit their cigarettes, and he had remained silent, his head thrown back broodingly against the armchair, his eyes fixed on the hearth, and presently had passed his hand over his forehead and said: 'Wasn't it unusually hot at my mother's tonight? I've got a splitting head. Mind if I take myself off to bed?'

That was the first time. Since then Charlotte had never been present when he had received the letter. It usually came before he got home from his office, and she had to go upstairs and leave it lying there. But even if she had not seen it, she would have known it had come by the change in his face when he joined her – which, on those evenings, he seldom did before they met for dinner. Evidently, whatever the letter contained, he wanted to be by himself to deal with it; and when he reappeared he looked years older, looked emptied of life and courage, and hardly conscious of her presence. Sometimes he was silent for the rest of the evening; and if he spoke, it was usually to hint some criticism of her household arrangements, suggest some change in the domestic administration, to ask, a little nervously, if she didn't think Joyce's nursery governess was rather young and flighty, or if she herself always saw to it that Peter – whose throat was delicate – was properly wrapped up when he went to school. At such times Charlotte would remember the friendly warnings she had received when she became engaged to Kenneth Ashby: 'Marrying a heartbroken widower! Isn't that rather risky? You know Elsie Ashby absolutely dominated him'; and how she had jokingly replied: 'He may be glad of a little liberty for a change.' And in this respect she had been right. She had needed no one to tell her, during the first months, that her husband was perfectly happy with her. When they came back from their protracted honeymoon the same friends said: 'What have you done to Kenneth? He looks twenty years younger'; and this time she answered with careless joy: 'I suppose I've got him out of his groove.'

But what she noticed after the gray letters began to come was not so much his nervous tentative faultfinding – which always seemed to be uttered against his will – as the look in his eyes when he joined her after receiving one of the letters. The look was not unloving, not even indifferent; it was the look of a man who had been so far away from ordinary events that when he returns to familiar things they seem strange. She minded that more than the faultfinding.

Though she had been sure from the first that the handwriting on the gray envelope was a woman's, it was long before she associated the mysterious letters with any sentimental secret. She was too sure of her husband's love, too confident of filling his life, for such an idea to occur to her. It seemed far more likely that the letters – which certainly did not appear to cause him any sentimental pleasure – were addressed to the busy lawyer than to the private person. Probably they were from some tiresome client – women, he had often told her, were nearly

always tiresome as clients – who did not want her letters opened by
his secretary and therefore had them carried to his house. Yes; but in
that case the unknown female must be unusually troublesome, judging
from the effect her letters produced. Then again, though his professional
discretion was exemplary, it was odd that he had never uttered an
impatient comment, never remarked to Charlotte, in a moment of
expansion, that there was a nuisance of a woman who kept badgering
him about a case that had gone against her. He had made more than
one semiconfidence of the kind – of course without giving names or
details; but concerning this mysterious correspondent his lips were
sealed.

There was another possibility: what is euphemistically called an 'old
entanglement.' Charlotte Ashby was a sophisticated woman. She had
few illusions about the intricacies of the human heart; she knew that
there were often old entanglements. But when she had married Kenneth
Ashby, her friends, instead of hinting at such a possibility, had said:
'You've got your work cut out for you. Marrying a Don Juan is a
sinecure to it. Kenneth's never looked at another woman since he first
saw Elsie Corder. During all the years of their marriage he was more
like an unhappy lover than a comfortably contented husband. He'll
never let you move an armchair or change the place of a lamp; and
whatever you venture to do, he'll mentally compare with what Elsie
would have done in your place.'

Except for an occasional nervous mistrust as to her ability to manage
the children – a mistrust gradually dispelled by her good humor and
the children's obvious fondness for her – none of these forebodings had
come true. The desolate widower, of whom his nearest friends said
that only his absorbing professional interests had kept him from suicide
after his first wife's death, had fallen in love, two years later, with
Charlotte Gorse, and after an impetuous wooing had married her and
carried her off on a tropical honeymoon. And ever since he had been
as tender and lover-like as during those first radiant weeks. Before
asking her to marry him he had spoken to her frankly of his great love
for his first wife and his despair after her sudden death; but even then
he had assumed no stricken attitude, or implied that life offered no
possibility of renewal. He had been perfectly simple and natural, and
had confessed to Charlotte that from the beginning he had hoped the
future held new gifts for him. And when, after their marriage, they
returned to the house where his twelve years with his first wife had
been spent, he had told Charlotte at once that he was sorry he couldn't
afford to do the place over for her, but that he knew every woman had
her own views about furniture and all sorts of household arrangements
a man would never notice, and had begged her to make any changes
she saw fit without bothering to consult him. As a result, she made as
few as possible; but his way of beginning their new life in the old

setting was so frank and unembarrassed that it put her immediately at her ease, and she was almost sorry to find that the portrait of Elsie Ashby, which used to hang over the desk in his library, had been transferred in their absence to the children's nursery. Knowing herself to be the indirect cause of this banishment, she spoke of it to her husband; but he answered: 'Oh, I thought they ought to grow up with her looking down on them.' The answer moved Charlotte, and satisfied her; and as time went by she had to confess that she felt more at home in her house, more at ease and in confidence with her husband, since that long coldly beautiful face on the library wall no longer followed her with guarded eyes. It was as if Kenneth's love had penetrated to the secret she hardly acknowledged to her own heart – her passionate need to feel herself the sovereign even of his past.

With all this stored-up happiness to sustain her, it was curious that she had lately found herself yielding to a nervous apprehension. But there the apprehension was; and on this particular afternoon – perhaps because she was more tired than usual, or because of the trouble of finding a new cook or, for some other ridiculously trivial reason, moral or physical – she found herself unable to react against the feeling. Latchkey in hand, she looked back down the silent street to the whirl and illumination of the great thoroughfare beyond, and up at the sky already aflare with the city's nocturnal life. 'Outside there,' she thought, 'skyscrapers, advertisements, telephones, wireless, airplanes, movies, motors, and all the rest of the twentieth century; and on the other side of the door something I can't explain, can't relate to them. Something as old as the world, as mysterious as life. . . . Nonsense! What am I worrying about. There hasn't been a letter for three months now – not since the day we came back from the country after Christmas. . . . Queer that they always seem to come after our holidays! . . . Why should I imagine there's going to be one tonight!'

No reason why, but that was the worst of it – one of the worst! – that there were days when she would stand there cold and shivering with the premonition of something inexplicable, intolerable, to be faced on the other side of the curtained panes; and when she opened the door and went in, there would be nothing; and on other days when she felt the same premonitory chill, it was justified by the sight of the gray envelope. So that ever since the last had come she had taken to feeling cold and premonitory every evening, because she never opened the door without thinking the letter might be there.

Well, she'd had enough of it: that was certain. She couldn't go on like that. If her husband turned white and had a headache on the days when the letter came, he seemed to recover afterwards; but she couldn't. With her the strain had become chronic, and the reason was not far to seek. Her husband knew from whom the letter came and what was in it; he was prepared beforehand for whatever he had to deal with, and master of the situation, however bad; whereas she was shut out on the dark with her conjectures.

'I can't stand it! I can't stand it another day!' she exclaimed aloud, as she put her key in the lock. She turned the key and went in; and there, on the table, lay the letter.

• II •

SHE was almost glad of the sight. It seemed to justify everything, to put a seal of definiteness on the whole blurred business. A letter for her husband; a letter from a woman – no doubt another vulgar case of 'old entanglement.' What a fool she had been ever to doubt it, to rack her brains for less obvious explanations! She took up the envelope with a steady contemptuous hand, looked closely at the faint letters, held it against the light and just discerned the outline of the folded sheet within. She knew that now she would have no peace till she found out what was written on that sheet.

Her husband had not come in; he seldom got back from his office before half-past six or seven, and it was not yet six. She would have time to take the letter up to the drawing room, hold it over the tea kettle which at that hour always simmered by the fire in expectation of her return, solve the mystery and replace the letter where she had found it. No one would be the wiser, and her gnawing uncertainty would be over. The alternative, of course, was to question her husband; but to do that seemed even more difficult. She weighed the letter between thumb and finger, looked at it again under the light, started up the stairs with the envelope – and came down again and laid it on the table.

'No, I evidently can't,' she said, disappointed.

What should she do, then. She couldn't go up alone to that warm welcoming room, pour out her tea, look over her correspondence, glance at a book or review – not with that letter lying below and the knowledge that in a little while her husband would come in, open it and turn into the library alone, as he always did on the days when the gray envelope came.

Suddenly she decided. She would wait in the library and see for herself; see what happened between him and the letter when they thought themselves unobserved. She wondered the idea had never occurred to her before. By leaving the door ajar, and sitting in the corner behind it, she could watch him unseen. . . . Well, then, she would watch him! She drew a chair into the corner, sat down, her eyes on the crack, and waited.

As far as she could remember, it was the first time she had ever tried to surprise another person's secret, but she was conscious of no compunction. She simply felt as if she were fighting her way through a stifling fog that she must at all cost get out of.

At length she heard Kenneth's latchkey and jumped up. The impulse to rush out and meet him had nearly made her forget why she was there: but she remembered in time and sat down again. From her post she covered the whole range of his movements – saw him enter the hall, draw the key from the door and take off his hat and overcoat. Then he turned to throw his gloves on the hall table, and at that moment he saw the envelope. The light was full on his face, and what Charlotte first noted there was a look of surprise. Evidently he had not expected the letter – had not thought of the possibility of its being there that day. But though he had not expected it, now that he saw it he knew well enough what it contained. He did not open it immediately, but stood motionless, the color slowly ebbing from his face. Apparently he could not make up his mind to touch it; but at length he put out his hand, opened the envelope, and moved with it to the light. In doing so he turned his back on Charlotte, and she saw only his bent head and slightly stooping shoulders. Apparently all the writing was on one page, for he did not turn the sheet but continued to stare at it for so long that he must have reread it a dozen times – or so it seemed to the woman breathlessly watching him. At length she saw him move; he raised the letter still closer to his eyes, as though he had not fully deciphered it. Then he lowered his head, and she saw his lips touch the sheet.

'Kenneth!' she exclaimed, and went on out into the hall.

The letter clutched in his hand, her husband turned and looked at her. 'Where were you?' he said, in a low bewildered voice, like a man waked out of his sleep.

'In the library, waiting for you.' She tried to steady her voice: 'What's the matter! What's in that letter? You look ghastly.'

Her agitation seemed to calm him, and he instantly put the envelope into his pocket with a slight laugh. 'Ghastly? I'm sorry. I've had a hard day in the office – one or two complicated cases. I look dog-tired, I suppose.'

'You didn't look tired when you came in. It was only when you opened that letter – '

He had followed her into the library, and they stood gazing at each other. Charlotte noticed how quickly he had regained his self-control; his profession had trained him to rapid mastery of face and voice. She saw at once that she would be at a disadvantage in any attempt to surprise his secret, but at the same moment she lost all desire to maneuver, to trick him into betraying anything he wanted to conceal. Her wish was still to penetrate the mystery, but only that she might help him to bear the burden it implied. 'Even if it *is* another woman,' she thought.

'Kenneth,' she said, her heart beating excitedly, 'I waited here on purpose to see you come in. I wanted to watch you while you opened that letter.'

His face, which had paled, turned to dark red; then it paled again. 'That letter? Why especially that letter?'

'Because I've noticed that whenever one of those letters comes it seems to have such a strange effect on you.'

A line of anger she had never seen before came out between his eyes, and she said to herself: 'The upper part of his face is too narrow; this is the first time I ever noticed it.'

She heard him continue, in the cool and faintly ironic tone of the prosecuting lawyer making a point: 'Ah, so you're in the habit of watching people open their letters when they don't know you're there?'

'Not in the habit. I never did such a thing before. But I had to find out what she writes to you, at regular intervals, in those gray envelopes.'

He weighed this for a moment; then: 'The intervals have not been regular,' he said.

'Oh, I dare say you've kept a better account of the dates than I have,' she retorted, her magnanimity vanishing at his tone. 'All I know is that every time that woman writes to you – '

'Why do you assume it's a woman?'

'It's a woman's writing. Do you deny it?'

He smiled. 'No, I don't deny it. I asked only because the writing is generally supposed to look more like a man's.'

Charlotte passed this over impatiently. 'And this woman – what does she write to you about?'

Again he seemed to consider a moment. 'About business.'

'Legal business?'

'In a way, yes. Business in general.'

'You look after her affairs for her?'

'Yes.'

'You've looked after them for a long time?'

'Yes. A very long time.'

'Kenneth, dearest, won't you tell me who she is?'

'No, I can't.' He paused, and brought out, as if with a certain hesitation: 'Professional secrecy.'

The blood rushed from Charlotte's heart to her temples. 'Don't say that – don't!'

'Why not?'

'Because I saw you kiss the letter.'

The effect of the words was so disconcerting that she instantly repented having spoken them. Her husband, who had submitted to her cross-questioning with a sort of contemptuous composure, as though he were humoring an unreasonable child, turned on her a face of terror and distress. For a minute he seemed unable to speak; then, collecting himself, with an effort, he stammered out: 'The writing is very faint; you must have seen me holding the letter close to my eyes to try to decipher it.'

'No; I saw you kissing it.' He was silent. 'Didn't I see you kissing it?'

He sank back into indifference. 'Perhaps.'

'Kenneth! You stand there and say that – to me?'

'What possible difference can it make to you? The letter is on business, as I told you. Do you suppose I'd lie about it? The writer is a very old friend whom I haven't seen for a long time.'

'Men don't kiss business letters, even from women who are very old friends, unless they have been their lovers, and still regret them.'

He shrugged his shoulders slightly and turned away, as if he considered the discussion at an end and were faintly disgusted at the turn it had taken.

'Kenneth!' Charlotte moved toward him and caught hold of his arm.

He paused with a look of weariness and laid his hand over hers. 'Won't you believe me?' he asked gently.

'How can I? I've watched these letters come to you – for months now they've been coming. Ever since we came back from the West Indies – one of them greeted me the very day we arrived. And after each one of them I see their mysterious effect on you, I see you disturbed, unhappy, as if someone were trying to estrange you from me.'

'No dear; not that. Never!'

She drew back and looked at him with passionate entreaty. 'Well, then, prove it to me, darling. It's so easy!'

He forced a smile. 'It's not easy to prove anything to a woman who's once taken an idea into her head.'

'You've only got to show me the letter.'

His hand slipped from hers and he drew back and shook his head.

'You won't?'

'I can't.'

'Then the woman who wrote it is your mistress.'

'No, dear. No.'

'Not now, perhaps. I suppose she's trying to get you back, and you're struggling, out of pity for me. My poor Kenneth.'

'I swear to you she never was my mistress.'

Charlotte felt the tears rushing to her eyes. 'Ah, that's worse, then – that's hopeless! The prudent ones are the kind that keep their hold on a man. We all know that.' She lifted her hands and hid her face in them.

Her husband remained silent; he offered neither consolation nor denial, and at length, wiping away her tears, she raised her eyes almost timidly to his.

'Kenneth, think! We've been married such a short time. Imagine what you're making me suffer. You say you can't show me this letter. You refuse even to explain it.'

'I've told you the letter is on business. I will swear to that too.'

'A man will swear to anything to screen a woman. If you want me to believe you, at least tell me her name. If you'll do that, I promise you I won't ask to see the letter.'

There was a long interval of suspense, during which she felt her heart beating against her ribs in quick admonitory knocks, as if warning her of the danger she was incurring.

'I can't,' he said at length.

'Not even her name?'

'No.'

'You can't tell me anything more?'

'No.'

Again a pause; this time they seemed both to have reached the end of their arguments and to be helplessly facing each other across a baffling waste of incomprehension.

Charlotte stood breathing rapidly, her hands against her breast. She felt as if she had run a hard race and missed the goal. She had meant to move her husband and had succeeded only in irritating him; and this error of reckoning seemed to change him into a stranger, a mysterious incomprehensible being whom no argument or entreaty of hers could reach. The curious thing was that she was aware in him of no hostility or even impatience, but only of a remoteness, an inaccessibility, far more difficult to overcome. She felt herself excluded, ignored, blotted out of his life. But after a moment or two, looking at him more calmly, she saw that he was suffering as much as she was. His distant guarded face was drawn with pain; the coming of the gray envelope, though it always cast a shadow, had never marked him as deeply as this discussion with his wife.

Charlotte took heart; perhaps, after all, she had not spent her last shaft. She drew nearer and once more laid her hand on his arm. 'Poor Kenneth! If you knew how sorry I am for you – '

She thought he winced slightly at this expression of sympathy, but he took her hand and pressed it.

'I can think of nothing worse than to be incapable of loving long,' she continued, 'to feel the beauty of a great love and to be too unstable to bear its burden.'

He turned on her a look of wistful reproach. 'Oh, don't say that of me. Unstable!'

She felt herself at last on the right tack, and her voice trembled with excitement as she went on: 'Then what about me and this other woman? Haven't you already forgotten Elsie twice within a year?'

She seldom pronounced his first wife's name; it did not come naturally to her tongue. She flung it out now as if she were flinging some dangerous explosive into the open space between them, and drew back a step, waiting to hear the mine go off.

Her husband did not move; his expression grew sadder, but showed no resentment. 'I have never forgotten Elsie,' he said.

Charlotte could not repress a faint laugh. 'Then, you poor dear, between the three of us – '

'There are not – ' he began; and then broke off and put his hand to his forehead.

'Not what?'

'I'm sorry; I don't believe I know what I'm saying. I've got a blinding headache.' He looked wan and furrowed enough for the statement to be true, but she was exasperated by his evasion.

'Ah, yes; the gray envelope headache!'

She saw the surprise in his eyes. 'I'd forgotten how closely I've been watched,' he said coldly. 'If you'll excuse me, I think I'll go up and try an hour in the dark, to see if I can get rid of this neuralgia.'

She wavered; then she said, with desperate resolution: 'I'm sorry your head aches. But before you go I want to say that sooner or later this question must be settled between us. Someone is trying to separate us, and I don't care what it costs me to find out who it is.' She looked him steadily in the eyes. 'If it costs me your love, I don't care! If I can't have your confidence I don't want anything from you.'

He still looked at her wistfully. 'Give me time.'

'Time for what? It's only a word to say.'

'Time to show you that you haven't lost my love or my confidence.'

'Well, I'm waiting.'

He turned toward the door, and then glanced back hesitatingly. 'Oh, do wait, my love,' he said, and went out of the room.

She heard his tired step on the stairs and the closing of his bedroom door above. Then she dropped into a chair and buried her face in her folded arms. Her first movement was one of compunction, she seemed to herself to have been hard, unhuman, unimaginative. 'Think of telling him that I didn't care if my insistence cost me his love! The lying rubbish!' She started up to follow him and unsay the meaningless words. But she was checked by a reflection. He had had his way, after all; he had eluded all attacks on his secret, and now he was shut up alone in his room, reading that other woman's letter.

• III •

SHE was still reflecting on this when the surprised parlormaid came in and found her. No, Charlotte said, she wasn't going to dress for dinner; Mr. Ashby didn't want to dine. He was very tired and had gone up to his room to rest; later she would have something brought on a tray to the drawing room. She mounted the stairs to her bedroom. Her dinner dress was lying on the bed, and at the sight the quiet routine of her daily life took hold of her and she began to feel as if the strange talk she had just had with her husband must have taken place in another world, between two beings who were not Charlotte Gorse and Kenneth Ashby, but phantoms projected by her fevered imagination. She recalled the year since her marriage – her husband's constant devotion; his persistent, almost too insistent tenderness; the feeling he had given her at times of being too eagerly dependent on her, too searchingly close to her; as if there were not air enough between her soul and his. It seemed preposterous, as she recalled all this, that a few moments ago she should have been accusing him of an intrigue with another woman! But, then, what –

Again she was moved by the impulse to go up to him, beg his pardon and try to laugh away the misunderstanding. But she was restrained by the fear of forcing herself upon his privacy. He was troubled and unhappy, oppressed by some grief or fear; and he had shown her that he wanted to fight out his battle alone. It would be wiser, as well as more generous, to respect his wish. Only, how strange, how unbearable, to be there, in the next room to his, and feel herself at the other end of the world! In her nervous agitation she almost regretted not having had the courage to open the letter and put it back on the hall table before he came in. At least she would have known what his secret was, and the bogy might have been laid. For she was beginning now to think of the mystery as something conscious, malevolent: a secret persecution before which he quailed, yet from which he could not free himself. Once or twice in his evasive eyes she thought she had detected a desire for help, an impulse of confession, instantly restrained and suppressed. It was as if he felt she could have helped him if she had known, and yet had been unable to tell her!

There flashed through her mind the idea of going to his mother. She was very fond of old Mrs. Ashby, a firm-fleshed clear-eyed old lady, with an astringent bluntness of speech which responded to the forthright and simple in Charlotte's own nature. There had been a tacit bond between them ever since the day when Mrs. Ashby Senior, coming to lunch for the first time with her new daughter-in-law, had been received by Charlotte downstairs in the library, and glancing up at the empty wall above her son's desk, had remarked laconically: 'Elsie gone, eh?' adding, at Charlotte's murmured explanation: 'Nonsense. Don't have her back. Two's company.' Charlotte, at this reading of her thoughts, could hardly refrain from exchanging a smile of complicity with her mother-in-law; and it seemed to her now that Mrs. Ashby's almost uncanny directness might pierce to the core of this new mystery. But here again she hesitated, for the idea almost suggested a betrayal. What right had she to call in anyone, even so close a relation, to surprise a secret which her husband was trying to keep from her? 'Perhaps, by and by, he'll talk to his mother of his own accord,' she thought, and then ended: 'But what does it matter? He and I must settle it between us.'

She was still brooding over the problem when there was a knock on the door and her husband came in. He was dressed for dinner and seemed surprised to see her sitting there, with her evening dress lying unheeded on the bed.

'Aren't you coming down?'

'I thought you were not well and had gone to bed,' she faltered.

He forced a smile. 'I'm not particularly well, but we'd better go down.' His face, though still drawn, looked calmer than when he had fled upstairs an hour earlier.

'There it is; he knows what's in the letter and has fought his battle out again, whatever it is,' she reflected, 'while I'm still in darkness.' She rang and gave a hurried order that dinner should be served as soon as possible – just a short meal, whatever could be got ready quickly, as both she and Mr. Ashby were rather tired and not very hungry.

Dinner was announced, and they sat down to it. At first neither seemed able to find a word to say; then Ashby began to make conversation with an assumption of ease that was more oppressive than his silence. 'How tired he is! How terribly overtired!' Charlotte said to herself, pursuing her own thoughts while he rambled on about municipal politics, aviation, an exhibition of modern French painting, the health of an old aunt and the installing of the automatic telephone. 'Good heavens, how tired he is!'

When they dined alone they usually went into the library after dinner, and Charlotte curled herself up on the divan with her knitting while he settled down in his armchair under the lamp and lit a pipe. But this evening, by tacit agreement, they avoided the room in which their strange talk had taken place, and went up to Charlotte's drawing room.

They sat down near the fire, and Charlotte said: 'Your pipe?' after he had put down his hardly tasted coffee.

He shook his head. 'No, not tonight.'

'You must go to bed early; you look terribly tired. I'm sure they overwork you at the office.'

'I suppose we all overwork at times.'

She rose and stood before him with sudden resolution. 'Well, I'm not going to have you use up your strength slaving in that way. It's absurd. I can see you're ill.' She bent over him and laid her hand on his forehead. 'My poor old Kenneth. Prepare to be taken away soon on a long holiday.'

He looked up at her, startled. 'A holiday?'

'Certainly. Didn't you know I was going to carry you off at Easter? We're going to start in a fortnight on a month's voyage to somewhere or other. On any one of the big cruising steamers.' She paused and bent closer, touching his forehead with her lips. 'I'm tired, too, Kenneth.'

He seemed to pay no heed to her last words, but sat, his hands on his knees, his head drawn back a little from her caress, and looked up at her with a stare of apprehension. 'Again? My dear, we can't; I can't possibly go away.'

'I don't know why you say "again," Kenneth; we haven't taken a real holiday this year.'

'At Christmas we spend a week with the children in the country.'

'Yes, but this time I mean away from the children, from servants, from the house. From everything that's familiar and fatiguing. Your mother will love to have Joyce and Peter with her.'

He frowned and slowly shook his head. 'No, dear; I can't leave them with my mother.'

'Why, Kenneth, how absurd! She adores them. You didn't hesitate to leave them with her for over two months when we went to the West Indies.'

He drew a deep breath and stood up uneasily. 'That was different.'

'Different? Why?'

'I mean, at that time I didn't realize – ' He broke off as if to choose his words and then went on: 'My mother adores the children, as you say. But she isn't always very judicious. Grandmothers always spoil children. And sometimes she talks before them without thinking.' He turned to his wife with an almost pitiful gesture of entreaty. 'Don't ask me to, dear.'

Charlotte mused. It was true that the elder Mrs. Ashby had a fearless tongue, but she was the last woman in the world to say or hint anything before her grandchildren at which the most scrupulous parent could take offense. Charlotte looked at her husband in perplexity.

'I don't understand.'

He continued to turn on her the same troubled and entreating gaze. 'Don't try to,' he muttered.

'Not try to?'

'Not now – not yet.' He put up his hands and pressed them against his temples. 'Can't you see that there's no use in insisting? I can't go away, no matter how much I might want to.'

Charlotte still scrutinized him gravely. 'The question is, *do* you want to?'

He returned her gaze for a moment; then his lips began to tremble, and he said, hardly above his breath. 'I want – anything you want.'

'And yet – '

'Don't ask me. I can't leave – I can't!'

'You mean that you can't go away out of reach of those letters!'

Her husband had been standing before her in an uneasy half-hesitating attitude, now he turned abruptly away and walked once or twice up and down the length of the room, his head bent, his eyes fixed on the carpet.

Charlotte felt her resentfulness rising with her fears. 'It's that,' she persisted. 'Why not admit it? You can't live without them.'

He continued his troubled pacing of the room; then he stopped short, dropped into a chair and covered his face with his hands. From the shaking of his shoulders, Charlotte saw that he was weeping. She had never seen a man cry, except her father after her mother's death, when she was a little girl, and she remembered still how the sight had frightened her. She was frightened now; she felt that her husband was being dragged away from her into some mysterious bondage, and that she must use up her last atom of strength in the struggle for his freedom, and for hers.

'Kenneth – Kenneth!' she pleaded, kneeling down beside him. 'Won't you listen to me? Won't you try to see what I'm suffering? I'm not unreasonable, darling, really not. I don't suppose I should ever have noticed the letters if it hadn't been for their effect on you. It's not my way to pry into other people's affairs; and even if the effect had been different – yes, yes, listen to me – if I'd seen that the letters made you happy, that you were watching eagerly for them, counting the days, between their coming, that you wanted them, that they gave you something I haven't known how to give – why, Kenneth, I don't say I shouldn't have suffered from that, too; but it would have been in a different way, and I should have had the courage to hide what I felt, and the hope that someday you'd come to feel about me as you did about the writer of the letters. But what I can't bear is to see how you dread them, how they make you suffer, and yet how you can't live without them and won't go away lest you should miss one during your absence. Or perhaps,' she added, her voice breaking into a cry of accusation – 'perhaps it's because she's actually forbidden you to leave. Kenneth, you must answer me! Is that the reason? Is it because she's forbidden you that you won't go away with me?'

She continued to kneel at his side, and raising her hands, she drew his gently down. She was ashamed of her persistence, ashamed of uncovering that baffled disordered face, yet resolved that no such scruples should arrest her. His eyes were lowered, the muscles of his face quivered; she was making him suffer even more than she suffered herself. Yet this no longer restrained her.

'Kenneth, is it that? She won't let us go away together?'

Still he did not speak or turn his eyes to her; and a sense of defeat swept over her. After all, she thought, the struggle was a losing one. 'You needn't answer. I see I'm right,' she said.

Suddenly, as she rose, he turned and drew her down again. His hands caught hers and pressed them so tightly that she felt her rings cutting into her flesh. There was something frightened, convulsive in his hold; it was the clutch of a man who felt himself slipping over a precipice. He was staring up at her now as if salvation lay in the face she bent above him. 'Of course we'll go away together. We'll go wherever you want,' he said in a low confused voice; and putting his arm about her, he drew her close and pressed his lips on hers.

• IV •

CHARLOTTE had said to herself: 'I shall sleep tonight,' but instead she sat before her fire into the small hours, listening for any sound that came from her husband's room. But he, at any rate, seemed to be resting after the tumult of the evening. Once or twice she stole to the door and in the faint light that came in from the street through his open window she saw him stretched out in heavy sleep – the sleep of weakness and exhaustion. 'He's ill,' she thought – 'he's undoubtedly ill. And it's not overwork; it's this mysterious persecution.'

She drew a breath of relief. She had fought through the weary fight and the victory was hers – at least for the moment. If only they could have started at once – started for anywhere! She knew it would be useless to ask him to leave before the holidays; and meanwhile the secret influence – as to which she was still so completely in the dark – would continue to work against her, and she would have to renew the struggle day after day till they started on their journey. But after that everything would be different. If once she could get her husband away under other skies, and all to herself, she never doubted her power to release him from the evil spell he was under. Lulled to quiet by the thought, she too slept at last.

When she woke, it was long past her usual hour, and she sat up in bed surprised and vexed at having overslept herself. She always liked to be down to share her husband's breakfast by the library fire; but a glance at the clock made it clear that he must have started long since for his office. To make sure, she jumped out of bed and went into his room, but it was empty. No doubt he had looked in on her before leaving, seen that she still slept, and gone downstairs without disturbing her; and their relations were sufficiently lover-like for her to regret having missed their morning hour.

She rang and asked if Mr. Ashby had already gone. Yes, nearly an hour ago, the maid said. He had given orders that Mrs. Ashby should not be waked and that the children should not come to her till she sent for them. . . . Yes, he had gone up to the nursery himself to give the order. All this sounded usual enough, and Charlotte hardly knew why she asked: 'And did Mr. Ashby leave no other message?'

Yes, the maid said, he did; she was so sorry she'd forgotten. He'd told her, just as he was leaving to say to Mrs. Ashby that he was going to see about their passages, and would she please be ready to sail tomorrow?

Charlotte echoed the woman's 'Tomorrow,' and sat staring at her incredulously. 'Tomorrow – you're sure he said to sail tomorrow?'

'Oh, ever so sure, ma'am. I don't know how I could have forgotten to mention it.'

'Well, it doesn't matter. Draw my bath, please.' Charlotte sprang up, dashed through her dressing, and caught herself singing at her image in the glass as she sat brushing her hair. It made her feel young again to have scored such a victory. The other woman vanished to a speck on the horizon, as this one, who ruled the foreground, smiled back at the reflection of her lips and eyes. He loved her, then – he loved her as passionately as ever. He had divined what she had suffered, had understood that their happiness depended on their getting away at once, and finding each other again after yesterday's desperate groping in the fog. The nature of the influence that had come between them did not much matter to Charlotte now; she had faced the phantom and dispelled it. 'Courage – that's the secret! If only people who are in love weren't always so afraid of risking their happiness by looking it in the eyes.' As she brushed back her light abundant hair it waved electrically above her head, like the palms of victory. Ah, well, some women knew how to manage men, and some didn't – and only the fair – she gaily paraphrased – deserve the brave! Certainly she was looking very pretty.

The morning danced along like a cockleshell on a bright sea – such a sea as they would soon be speeding over. She ordered a particularly good dinner, saw the children off to their classes, had her trunks brought down, consulted with the maid about getting out summer clothes – for of course they would be heading for heat and sunshine – and wondered if she oughtn't to take Kenneth's flannel suits out of camphor. 'But how absurd,' she reflected, 'that I don't yet know where we're going!' She looked at the clock, saw that it was close on noon, and decided to call him up at his office. There was a slight delay; then she heard his secretary's voice saying that Mr. Ashby had looked in for a moment early, and left again almost immediately. . . . Oh, very well; Charlotte would ring up later. How soon was he likely to be back? The secretary answered that she couldn't tell; all they knew in the office was that when he left he had said he was in a hurry because he had to go out of town.

Out of town! Charlotte hung up the receiver and sat blankly gazing into new darkness. Why had he gone out of town? And where had he gone? And of all days, why should he have chosen the eve of their suddenly planned departure? She felt a faint shiver of apprehension. Of course he had gone to see that woman – no doubt to get her permission to leave. He was as completely in bondage as that; and Charlotte had been fatuous enough to see the palms of victory on her forehead. She burst into a laugh and, walking across the room, sat down again before her mirror. What a different face she saw! The smile on her pale lips seemed to mock the rosy vision of the other Charlotte. But gradually her color crept back. After all, she had a right to claim the victory, since her husband was doing what she wanted, not what the other woman exacted of him. It was natural enough, in view of his abrupt decision to leave the next day, that he should have arrangements to make, business matters to wind up; it was not even necessary to suppose that his mysterious trip was a visit to the writer of the letters. He might simply have gone to see a client who lived out of town. Of course they would not tell Charlotte at the office; the secretary had hesitated before imparting even such meager information as the fact of Mr. Ashby's absence. Meanwhile she would go on with her joyful preparation, content to learn later in the day to what particular island of the blest she was to be carried.

The hours wore on, or rather were swept forward on a rush of eager preparations. At last the entrance of the maid who came to draw the curtains roused Charlotte from her labors, and she saw to her surprise that the clock marked five. And she did not yet know where they were going the next day! She rang up her husband's office and was told that Mr. Ashby had not been there since the early morning. She asked for his partner, but the partner could add nothing to her information, for he himself, his suburban train having been behind time, had reached the office after Ashby had come and gone. Charlotte stood perplexed; then she decided to telephone to her mother-in-law. Of course Kenneth, on the eve of a month's absence, must have gone to see his mother. The mere fact that the children – in spite of his vague objections – would certainly have to be left with old Mrs. Ashby, made it obvious that he would have all sorts of matters to decide with her. At another time Charlotte might have felt a little hurt at being excluded from their conference, but nothing mattered now that she had won the day, that her husband was still hers and not another woman's. Gaily she called up Mrs. Ashby, heard her friendly voice, and began: 'Well, did Kenneth's news surprise you? What do you think of our elopement?'

Almost instantly, before Mrs. Ashby could answer, Charlotte knew what her reply would be, Mrs. Ashby had not seen her son, she had had no word from him and did not know what her daughter-in-law meant. Charlotte stood silent in the intensity of her surprise. 'But then, where *has* he been?' she thought. Then, recovering herself, she explained their sudden decision to Mrs. Ashby, and in doing so, gradually regained her own self-confidence, her conviction that nothing could ever again come between Kenneth and herself. Mrs. Ashby took the news calmly and approvingly. She too, had thought that Kenneth looked worried and over-tired, and she agreed with her daughter-in-law that in such cases change was the surest remedy. 'I'm always so glad when he gets away. Elsie hated traveling; she was always finding pretexts to prevent his going anywhere. With you, thank goodness, it's different.' Nor was Mrs. Ashby surprised at his not having had time to let her know of his departure. He must have been in a rush from the moment the decision was taken; but no doubt he'd drop in before dinner. Five minutes' talk was really all they needed. 'I hope you'll gradually cure Kenneth of his mania for going over and over a question that could be settled in a dozen words. He never used to be like that, and if he carried the habit into his professional work he'd soon lose all his clients. . . . Yes, do come in for a minute, dear, if you have time; no doubt he'll turn up while you're here.' The tonic ring of Mrs. Ashby's voice echoed on reassuringly in the silent room while Charlotte continued her preparations.

Toward seven the telephone rang, and she darted to it. Now she would know! But it was only from the conscientious secretary, to say that Mr. Ashby hadn't been back, or sent any word, and before the office closed she thought she ought to let Mrs. Ashby know. 'Oh, that's all right. Thanks a lot!' Charlotte called out cheerfully, and hung up the receiver with a trembling hand. But perhaps by this time, she reflected, he was at his mother's. She shut her drawers and cupboards, put on her hat and coat and called up to the nursery that she was going out for a minute to see the children's grandmother.

Mrs. Ashby lived nearby, and during her brief walk through the cold spring dusk Charlotte imagined that every advancing figure was her husband's. But she did not meet him on the way, and when she entered the house she found her mother-in-law alone. Kenneth had neither telephoned nor come. Old Mrs. Ashby sat by her bright fire, her knitting needles flashing steadily through her active old hands, and her mere bodily presence gave reassurance to Charlotte. Yes, it was certainly odd that Kenneth had gone off for the whole day without letting any of them know; but, after all, it was to be expected. A busy lawyer held so many threads in his hands that any sudden change of plan would oblige him to make all sorts of unforeseen arrangements and adjustments. He might have gone to see some client in the suburbs and been detained there; his mother remembered his telling her that he had charge of the legal business of a queer old recluse somewhere in New Jersey, who was immensely rich but too mean to have a telephone. Very likely Kenneth had been stranded there.

But Charlotte felt her nervousness gaining on her. When Mrs. Ashby asked her at what hour they were sailing the next day and she had to say she didn't know – that Kenneth had simply sent her word he was going to take their passages – the uttering of the words again brought home to her the strangeness of the situation. Even Mrs. Ashby conceded that it was odd; but she immediately added that it only showed what a rush he was in.

'But, mother, it's nearly eight o'clock! He must realize that I've got to know when we're starting tomorrow.'

'Oh, the boat probably doesn't sail till evening. Sometimes they have to wait till midnight for the tide. Kenneth's probably counting on that. After all, he has a level head.'

Charlotte stood up. 'It's not that. Something has happened to him.'

Mrs. Ashby took off her spectacles and rolled up her knitting. 'If you begin to let yourself imagine things – '

'Aren't you in the least anxious?'

'I never am till I have to be. I wish you'd ring for dinner, my dear. You'll stay and dine? He's sure to drop in here on his way home.'

Charlotte called up her own house. No, the maid said, Mr. Ashby hadn't come in and hadn't telephoned. She would tell him as soon as he came that Mrs. Ashby was dining at his mother's. Charlotte followed her mother-in-law into the dining room and sat with parched throat before her empty plate, while Mrs. Ashby dealt calmly and efficiently with a short but carefully prepared repast. 'You'd better eat something, child, or you'll be as bad as Kenneth. . . . Yes, a little more asparagus, please, Jane.'

She insisted on Charlotte's drinking a glass of sherry and nibbling a bit of toast; then they returned to the drawing room, where the fire had been made up, and the cushions in Mrs. Ashby's armchair shaken out and smoothed. How safe and familiar it all looked; and out there, somewhere in the uncertainty and mystery of the night, lurked the answer to the two women's conjectures, like an indistinguishable figure prowling on the threshold.

At last Charlotte got up and said: 'I'd better go back. At this hour Kenneth will certainly go straight home.'

Mrs. Ashby smiled indulgently. 'It's not very late, my dear. It doesn't take two sparrows long to dine.'

'It's after nine.' Charlotte bent down to kiss her. 'The fact is, I can't keep still.'

Mrs. Ashby pushed aside her work and rested her two hands on the arms of her chair. 'I'm going with you,' she said, helping herself up.

Charlotte protested that it was too late, that it was not necessary, that she would call up as soon as Kenneth came in, but Mrs. Ashby had already rung for her maid. She was slightly lame, and stood resting on her stick while her wraps were brought. 'If Mr. Kenneth turns up, tell him he'll find me at his own house,' she instructed the maid as the two women got into the taxi which had been summoned. During the short drive Charlotte gave thanks that she was not returning home alone. There was something warm and substantial in the mere fact of

Mrs. Ashby's nearness, something that corresponded with the clearness of her eyes and the texture of her fresh firm complexion. As the taxi drew up she laid her hand encouragingly on Charlotte's. 'You'll see; there'll be a message.'

The door opened at Charlotte's ring and the two entered. Charlotte's heart beat excitedly; the stimulus of her mother-in-law's confidence was beginning to flow through her veins.

'You'll see – you'll see,' Mrs. Ashby repeated.

The maid who opened the door said no, Mr. Ashby had not come in, and there had been no message from him.

'You're sure the telephone's not out of order?' his mother suggested; and the maid said, well it certainly wasn't half an hour ago; but she'd just go and ring up to make sure. She disappeared, and Charlotte turned to take off her hat and cloak. As she did so her eyes lit on the hall table, and there lay a gray envelope, her husband's name faintly traced on it. 'Oh!' she cried out, suddenly aware that for the first time in months she had entered her house without wondering if one of the gray letters would be there.

'What is it, my dear?' Mrs. Ashby asked with a glance of surprise.

Charlotte did not answer. She took up the envelope and stood staring at it as if she could force her gaze to penetrate to what was within. Then an idea occurred to her. She turned and held out the envelope to her mother-in-law.

'Do you know that writing?' she asked.

Mrs. Ashby took the letter. She had to feel with her other hand for her eyeglasses, and when she had adjusted them she lifted the envelope to the light. 'Why!' she exclaimed, and then stopped. Charlotte noticed that the letter shook in her usually firm hand. 'But this is addressed to Kenneth,' Mrs. Ashby said at length, in a low voice. Her tone seemed to imply that she felt her daughter-in-law's question to be slightly indiscreet.

'Yes, but no matter,' Charlotte spoke with sudden decision. 'I want to know – do you know the writing?'

Mrs. Ashby handed back the letter. 'No,' she said distinctly.

The two women had turned into the library. Charlotte switched on the electric light and shut the door. She still held the envelope in her hand.

'I'm going to open it,' she announced.

She caught her mother-in-law's startled glance. 'But, dearest – a letter not addressed to you? My dear, you can't!'

'As if I cared about that – now!' She continued to look intently at Mrs. Ashby. 'This letter may tell me where Kenneth is.'

Mrs. Ashby's glossy bloom was effaced by a quick pallor; her firm cheeks seemed to shrink and wither. 'Why should it? What makes you believe – It can't possibly – '

Charlotte held her eyes steadily on that altered face. 'Ah, then you *do* know the writing?' she flashed back.

'Know the writing? How should I? With all my son's correspondents. . . . What I do know is – ' Mrs. Ashby broke off and looked at her daughter-in-law entreatingly, almost timidly.

Charlotte caught her by the wrist. 'Mother! What do you know? Tell me! You must!'

'That I don't believe any good ever came of a woman's opening her husband's letters behind his back.'

The words sounded to Charlotte's irritated ears as flat as a phrase culled from a book of moral axioms. She laughed impatiently and dropped her mother-in-law's wrist. 'Is that all? No good can come of this letter, opened or unopened. I know that well enough. But whatever ill comes, I mean to find out what's in it.' Her hands had been trembling as they held the envelope, but now they grew firm, and her voice also. She still gazed intently at Mrs. Ashby. 'This is the ninth letter addressed in the same hand that has come for Kenneth since we've been married. Always these same gray envelopes. I've kept count of them because after each one he has been like a man who has had some dreadful shock. It takes him hours to shake off their effect. I've told him so, I've told him I must know from whom they come, because I can see they're killing him. He won't answer my questions; he says he can't tell me anything about the letters, but last night he promised to go away with me to get away from them.'

Mrs. Ashby, with shaking steps, had gone to one of the armchairs and sat down in it, her head drooping forward on her breast. 'Ah,' she murmured.

'So now you understand – '

'Did he tell you it was to get away from them?'

'He said, to get away – to get away. He was sobbing so that he could hardly speak. But I told him I knew that was why.'

'And what did he say?'

'He took me in his arms and said he'd go wherever I wanted.'

'Ah, thank God!' said Mrs. Ashby. There was a silence, during which she continued to sit with bowed head, and eyes averted from her daughter-in-law. At last she looked up and spoke. 'Are you sure there have been as many as nine?'

'Perfectly. This is the ninth. I've kept count.'

'And he has absolutely refused to explain?'

'Absolutely.'

Mrs. Ashby spoke through pale contracted lips. 'When did they begin to come? Do you remember?'

Charlotte laughed again. 'Remember? The first one came the night we got back from our honeymoon.'

'All that time?' Mrs. Ashby lifted her head and spoke with sudden energy. 'Then – yes, open it.'

The words were so unexpected that Charlotte felt the blood in her temples, and her hands began to tremble again. She tried to slip her finger under the flap of the envelope, but it was so tightly stuck that she had to hunt on her husband's writing table for his ivory letter opener. As she pushed about the familiar objects his own hands had so lately touched, they sent through her the icy chill emanating from the little personal effects of someone newly dead. In the deep silence of the room the tearing of the paper as she slit the envelope sounded like a human cry. She drew out the sheet and carried it to the lamp.

'Well?' Mrs. Ashby asked below her breath.

Charlotte did not move or answer. She was bending over the page with wrinkled brows, holding it nearer and nearer to the light. Her sight must be blurred, or else dazzled by the reflection of the lamplight on the smooth surface of the paper, for, strain her eyes as she would, she could discern only a few faint strokes, so faint and faltering as to be nearly undecipherable.

'I can't make it out,' she said.

'What do you mean, dear?'

'The writing's so indistinct. . . . Wait.'

She went back to the table and, sitting down close to Kenneth's reading lamp, slipped the letter under a magnifying glass. All this time she was aware that her mother-in-law was watching her intently.

'Well?' Mrs. Ashby breathed.

'Well, it's no clearer. I can't read it.'

'You mean the paper is an absolute blank?'

'No, not quite. There is writing on it. I can make out something like "mine" – oh, and "come". It might be "come." '

Mrs. Ashby stood up abruptly. Her face was even paler than before. She advanced to the table and, resting her two hands on it, drew a deep breath. 'Let me see,' she said, as if forcing herself to a hateful effort.

Charlotte felt the contagion of her whiteness. 'She knows,' she thought. She pushed the letter across the table. Her mother-in-law lowered her head over it in silence, but without touching it with her pale wrinkled hands.

Charlotte stood watching her as she herself, when she had tried to read the letter, had been watched by Mrs. Ashby. The latter fumbled for her glasses, held them to her eyes, and bent still closer to the outspread page, in order, as it seemed, to avoid touching it. The light of the lamp fell directly on her old face, and Charlotte reflected what depths of the unknown may lurk under the clearest and most candid lineaments. She had never seen her mother-in-law's features express any but simple and sound emotions – cordiality, amusement, a kindly sympathy; now and again a flash of wholesome anger. Now they

seemed to wear a look of fear and hatred, of incredulous dismay and
almost cringing defiance. It was as if the spirits warring within her had
distorted her face to their own likeness. At length she raised her head.
'I can't – I can't,' she said in a voice of childish distress.

'You can't make it out either?'

She shook her head, and Charlotte saw two tears roll down her
cheeks.

'Familiar as the writing is to you?' Charlotte insisted with twitching
lips.

Mrs. Ashby did not take up the challenge. 'I can make out nothing
– nothing.'

'But you do know the writing?'

Mrs. Ashby lifted her head timidly; her anxious eyes stole with a
glance of apprehension around the quiet familiar room. 'How can I tell?
I was startled at first. . . .'

'Startled by the resemblance?'

'Well, I thought – '

'You'd better say it out, mother! You knew at once it was her
writing?'

'Oh, wait, my dear – wait.'

'Wait for what?'

Mrs. Ashby looked up; her eyes, traveling slowly past Charlotte,
were lifted to the blank wall behind her son's writing table.

Charlotte, following the glance, burst into a shrill laugh of accusation. 'I needn't wait any longer! You've answered me now! You're
looking straight at the wall where her picture used to hang.'

Mrs. Ashby lifted her hand with a murmur of warning. 'Sh-h.'

'Oh, you needn't imagine that anything can ever frighten me again!'
Charlotte cried.

Her mother-in-law still leaned against the table. Her lips moved
plaintively. 'But we're going mad – we're both going mad. We both
know such things are impossible.'

Her daughter-in-law looked at her with a pitying stare. 'I've known
for a long time now that everything was possible.'

'Even this?'

'Yes, exactly this.'

'But this letter – after all, there's nothing in this letter – '

'Perhaps there would be to him. How can I tell? I remember his
saying to me once that if you were used to a handwriting the faintest
stroke of it became legible. Now I see what he meant. He *was* used to
it.'

'But the few strokes that I can make out are so pale. No one could
possibly read that letter.'

Charlotte laughed again. 'I suppose everything's pale about a ghost,'
she said stridently.

'Oh, my child – my child – don't say it!'

'Why shouldn't I say it, when even the bare walls cry it out? What difference does it make if her letters are illegible to you and me? If even you can see her face on that blank wall, why shouldn't he read her writing on this blank paper? Don't you see that she's everywhere in this house, and the closer to him because to everyone else she's become invisible?' Charlotte dropped into a chair and covered her face with her hands. A turmoil of sobbing shook her from head to foot. At length a touch on her shoulder made her look up, and she saw her mother-in-law bending over her. Mrs. Ashby's face seemed to have grown still smaller and more wasted, but it had resumed its usual quiet look. Through all her tossing anguish, Charlotte felt the impact of that resolute spirit.

'Tomorrow – tomorrow. You'll see. There'll be some explanation tomorrow.'

Charlotte cut her short. 'An explanation? Who's going to give it, I wonder?'

Mrs. Ashby drew back and straightened herself heroically. 'Kenneth himself will,' she cried out in a strong voice. Charlotte said nothing and the old woman went on: 'But meanwhile we must act; we must notify the police. Now, without a moment's delay. We must do everything – everything.'

Charlotte stood up slowly and stiffly; her joints felt as cramped as an old woman's. 'Exactly as if we thought it could do any good to do anything?'

Resolutely Mrs. Ashby cried: 'Yes!' and Charlotte went up to the telephone and unhooked the receiver.

Her Son

I DID NOT RECOGNIZE Mrs. Stephen Glenn when I first saw her on the deck of the 'Scythian.'

The voyage was more than half over, and we were counting on Cherbourg within forty-eight hours, when she appeared on deck and sat down beside me. She was as handsome as ever, and not a day older-looking than when we had last met – toward the end of the war, in 1917 it must have been, not long before her only son, the aviator, was killed. Yet now, five years later, I was looking at her as if she were a stranger. Why? Not, certainly, because of her white hair. She had had the American woman's frequent luck of acquiring it while the face beneath was still fresh, and a dozen years earlier, when we used to meet at dinners, at the Opera, that silver diadem already crowned her. Now, looking more closely, I saw that the face beneath was still untouched; what then had so altered her? Perhaps it was the faint line of anxiety between her dark strongly-drawn eyebrows; or the setting of the eyes themselves, those somber starlit eyes which seemed to have sunk deeper into their lids, and showed like glimpses of night through the arch of a cavern. But what a gloomy image to apply to eyes as tender as Catherine Glenn's! Yet it was immediately suggested by the look of the lady in deep mourning who had settled herself beside me, and now turned to say: 'So you don't know me, Mr. Norcutt – Catherine Glenn?'

The fact was flagrant. I acknowledged it, and added: 'But why didn't I? I can't imagine. Do you mind my saying that I believe it's because you're even more beautiful now than when I last saw you?'

She replied with perfect simplicity: 'No, I don't mind – because I ought to be; that is, if there's any meaning in anything.'

'Any meaning – ?'

She seemed to hesitate; she had never been a woman who found words easily. 'Any meaning in life. You see, since we've met I've lost everything: my son, my husband.' She bent her head slightly, as though the words she pronounced were holy. Then she added, with the air of striving for more scrupulous accuracy: 'Or, at least, almost everything.'

The 'almost' puzzled me. Mrs. Glenn, as far as I knew, had had no

222

child but the son she had lost in the war; and the old uncle who had brought her up had died years earlier. I wondered if, in thus qualifying her loneliness, she alluded to the consolations of religion.

I murmured that I knew of her double mourning; and she surprised me still further by saying: 'Yes; I saw you at my husband's funeral. I've always wanted to thank you for being there.'

'But of course I was there.'

She continued: 'I noticed all of Stephen's friends who came. I was very grateful to them, and especially to the young ones.' (This was meant for me.) 'You see,' she added, 'a funeral is – is a very great comfort.'

Again I looked surprise.

'My son – my son Philip – ' (why should she think it necessary to mention his name, since he was her only child?) ' – my son Philip's funeral took place just where his airplane fell. A little village in the Somme; his father and I went there immediately after the Armistice. One of our army chaplains read the service. The people from the village were there – they were so kind to us. But there was no one else – no personal friends; at that time only the nearest relations could get passes. Our boy would have wished it. . . . he would have wanted to stay where he fell. But it's not the same as feeling one's friends about one, as I did at my husband's funeral.'

While she spoke she kept her eyes intently, almost embarrassingly, on mine. It had never occurred to me that Mrs. Stephen Glenn was the kind of woman who would attach any particular importance to the list of names at her husband's funeral. She had always seemed aloof and abstracted, shut off from the world behind the high walls of a happy domesticity. But on adding this new indication of character to the fragments of information I had gathered concerning her first appearance in New York, and to the vague impression she used to produce on me when we met, I began to see that lists of names were probably just what she would care about. And then I asked myself what I really knew of her. Very little, I perceived; but no doubt just as much as she wished me to. For, as I sat there, listening to her voice, and catching unguarded glimpses of her crepe-shadowed profile, I began to suspect that what had seemed in her a rather dull simplicity might be the vigilance of a secretive person; or perhaps of a person who had a secret. There is a world of difference between them, for the secretive person is seldom interesting and seldom has a secret; but I felt inclined – though nothing I knew of her justified it – to put her in the other class.

I began to think over the years of our intermittent acquaintance – it had never been more, for I had known the Glenns well. She had appeared in New York when I was a very young man, in the nineties, as a beautiful girl from Kentucky or Alabama – a niece of old Colonel Reamer's. Left an orphan, and penniless, when she was still almost a child, she had been passed about from one reluctant relation to another, and had finally (the legend ran) gone on the stage, and followed a strolling company across the continent. The manager had deserted his troupe in some far-off state, and Colonel Reamer, fatuous, impecunious, and no doubt perplexed as to how to deal with the situation, had yet faced it manfully, and shaking off his bachelor selfishness had taken the girl into his house. Such a past, though it looks dove-colored now, seemed hectic in the nineties, and gave a touch of romance and mystery to the beautiful Catherine Reamer, who appeared so aloof and distinguished, yet had been snatched out of such promiscuities and perils.

Colonel Reamer was a ridiculous old man: everything about him was ridiculous – his 'toupee' (probably the last in existence), his vague military title, his anecdotes about southern chivalry, and duels between other gentlemen with military titles and civilian pursuits, and all the obsolete swagger of a character dropped out of Martin Chuzzlewit. He was the notorious bore of New York; tolerated only because he was old Mrs. So-and-so's second cousin, because he was poor, because he was kindly – and because, out of his poverty, he had managed, with a smile and a gay gesture, to shelter and clothe his starving niece. Old Reamer, I recalled, had always had a passion for lists of names; for seeing his own appear in the society column of the morning papers, for giving you those of the people he had dined with, or been unable to dine with because already bespoken by others even more important. The young people called him 'Old Previous-Engagement,' because he was so anxious to have you know that, if you hadn't met him at some particular party, it was because he had been previously engaged at another.

Perhaps, I thought, it was from her uncle that Mrs. Glenn had learned to attach such importance to names, to lists of names, to the presence of certain people on certain occasions, to a social suitability which could give a consecration even to death. The profile at my side, so marble-pure, so marble-sad, did not suggest such preoccupation, neither did the deep entreating gaze she bent on me; yet many details fitted into the theory.

Her very marriage to Stephen Glenn seemed to confirm it. I thought back, and began to reconstruct Stephen Glenn. He was considerably older than myself, and had been a familiar figure in my earliest New York; a man who was a permanent ornament to society, who looked precisely as he ought, spoke, behaved, received his friends, filled his space on the social stage, exactly as his world expected him to. While he was still a young man, old ladies in perplexity over some social problem (there were many in those draconian days) would consult Stephen Glenn as if he had been one of the Ancients of the community. Yet there was nothing precociously old or dry about him. He was one of the handsomest men of his day; a good shot, a leader of cotillions. He practiced at the bar, and became a member of a reputed legal firm chiefly occupied with the management of old ponderous New York estates. In process of time the old ladies who had consulted him about social questions began to ask his advice about investments; and on this point he was considered equally reliable. Only one cloud shadowed his early life. He had married a distant cousin, an effaced sort of woman who bore him no children, and presently (on that account, it was said) fell into suicidal melancholia; so that for a good many years Stephen Glenn's handsome and once hospitable house must have been a grim place to go home to. But at last she died, and after a decent interval the widower married Miss Reamer. No one was greatly surprised. It had been observed that the handsome Stephen Glenn and the beautiful Catherine Reamer were drawn to each other; and though the old ladies thought he might have done better, some of the more caustic remarked that he could hardly have done differently, after having made Colonel Reamer's niece so 'conspicuous.' The attentions of a married man, especially of one unhappily married, and virtually separated from his wife, were regarded in those days as likely to endanger a young lady's future. Catherine Reamer, however, rose above these hints as she had above the perils of her theatrical venture. One had only to look at her to see that, in that smooth marble surface there was no crack in which detraction could take root.

Stephen Glenn's house was opened again, and the couple began to entertain in a quiet way. It was thought natural that Glenn should want to put a little life into the house which had so long been a sort of tomb; but though the Glenn dinners were as good as the most carefully chosen food and wine could make them, neither of the pair had the gifts which make hospitality a success, and by the time I knew them, the younger set had come to regard dining with them as somewhat of a bore. Stephen Glenn was still handsone, his wife still beautiful, perhaps more beautiful than ever; but the apathy of prosperity seemed to have settled down on them, and they wore their beauty and affability like expensive clothes put on for the occasion. There was something static, unchanging in their appearance, as there was in their affability, their conversation, the menus of their carefully planned dinners, the studied arrangement of the drawing room furniture. They had a little boy, born after a year of marriage, and they were devoted parents, given to lengthy anecdotes about their son's doings and sayings; but one could not imagine their tumbling about with him on the nursery floor. Someone said they must go to bed with their crowns on, like the kings and queens on packs of cards; and gradually, from being thought distinguished and impressive, they came to be regarded as wooden, pompous and slightly absurd. But the old ladies still spoke of Stephen Glenn as a man who had done his family credit, and his wife began to acquire his figurehead attributes, and to be consulted, as he was, about the minuter social problems. And all the while – I thought as I looked back – there seemed to have been no one in their lives with whom they were really intimate. . . .

Then, of a sudden, they again became interesting. It was when their only son was killed, attacked alone in mid-sky by a German air squadron. Young Phil Glenn was the first American aviator to fall; and when the news came people saw that the Mr.-and-Mrs. Glenn they had known was a mere façade, and that behind it were a passionate father and mother, crushed, rebellious, agonizing, but determined to face their loss dauntlessly, though they should die of it.

Stephen Glenn did die of it, barely two years later. The doctors ascribed his death to a specific disease; but everybody who knew him knew better. 'It was the loss of the boy,' they said; and added: 'It's terrible to have only one child.'

Since her husband's funeral I had not seen Mrs. Glenn; I had completely ceased to think of her. And now, on my way to take up a post at the American Consulate in Paris, I found myself sitting beside her and remembering these things. 'Poor creatures – it's as if two marble busts had been knocked off their pedestals and smashed,' I thought, recalling the faces of husband and wife after the boy's death; 'and she's been smashed twice, poor woman. . . . Yet she says it has made her more beautiful. . . .' Again I lost myself in conjecture.

• II •

I WAS told that a lady in deep mourning wanted to see me on urgent business, and I looked out of my private den at the Paris Consulate into the room hung with maps and Presidents, where visitors were sifted out before being passed on to the Vice-consul or the Chief.

The lady was Mrs. Stephen Glenn.

Six or seven months had passed since our meeting on the 'Scythian,' and I had again forgotten her very existence. She was not a person who stuck in one's mind; and once more I wondered why, for in her statuesque weeds she looked nobler, more striking than ever. She glanced at the people awaiting their turn under the maps and the Presidents, and asked in a low tone if she could see me privately.

I was free at the moment, and I led her into my office and banished the typist.

Mrs. Glenn seemed disturbed by the signs of activity about me. 'I'm afraid we shall be interrupted. I wanted to speak to you alone,' she said.

I assured her we were not likely to be disturbed if she could put what she had to say in a few words –

'Ah, but that's just what I can't do. What I have to say can't be put in a few words.' She fixed her splendid nocturnal eyes on me, and I read in them a distress so deep that I dared not suggest postponement.

I said I would do all I could to prevent our being interrupted, and in reply she just sat silent, and looked at me, as if after all she had nothing further to communicate. The telephone clicked, and I rang for my secretary to take the message; then one of the clerks came in with papers for my signature. I said: 'I'd better sign and get it over,' and she sat motionless, her head slightly bent, as if secretly relieved by the delay. The clerk went off, I shut the door again, and when we were alone she lifted her head and spoke. 'Mr. Norcutt,' she asked, 'have you ever had a child?'

I replied with a smile that I was not married. She murmured: 'I'm sorry – excuse me,' and looked down again at her black-gloved hands, which were clasped about a black bag richly embroidered with dull jet. Everything about her was as finished, as costly, as studied, as if she were a young beauty going forth in her joy; yet she looked like a heartbroken woman.

She began again: 'My reason for coming is that I've promised to help a friend, a poor woman who's lost all trace of her son – her only surviving son – and is hunting for him.' She paused, though my expectant silence seemed to encourage her to continue. 'It's a very sad case; I must try to explain. Long ago, as a girl, my friend fell in love with a married man – a man unhappily married.' She moistened her lips, which had become parched and colorless. 'You mustn't judge them too severely. . . . He had great nobility of character – the highest standards – but the situation was too cruel. His wife was insane; at that time there was no legal release in such cases. If you were married to a lunatic only death could free you. It was a most unhappy affair – the poor girl pitied her friend profoundly. Their little boy. . . .' Suddenly she stood up with a proud and noble movement and leaned to me across the desk. 'I am that woman,' she said.

She straightened herself and stood there, trembling, erect, like a swathed figure of woe on an illustrious grave. I thought: 'What this inexpressive woman was meant to express is grief – ' and marveled at the wastefulness of Nature. But suddenly she dropped back into her chair, bowed her face against the desk, and burst into sobs. Her sobs were not violent; they were soft, low, almost rhythmical, with lengthening intervals between, like the last drops of rain after a long downpour; and I said to myself: 'She's cried so much that this must be the very end.'

She opened the jet bag, took out a delicate handkerchief, and dried her eyes. Then she turned to me again. 'It's the first time I've ever spoken of this . . . to any human being except one.'

I laid my hand on hers. 'It was no use – my pretending,' she went on, as if appealing to me for justification.

'Is it ever? And why should you, with an old friend?' I rejoined, attempting to comfort her.

'Ah, but I've had to – for so many years, to be silent has become my second nature.' She paused, and then continued in a softer tone: 'My baby was so beautiful . . . do you know, Mr. Norcutt, I'm sure I should know him anywhere. . . . Just two years and one month older than my second boy, Philip . . . the one you know.' Again she hesitated, and then, in a warmer burst of confidence, and scarcely above a whisper: 'We christened the eldest Stephen. We knew it was dangerous: it might give a clue – but I felt I must give him his father's name, the name I loved best. . . . It was all I could keep of my baby. And Stephen understood; he consented. . . .'

I sat and stared at her. What! This child of hers that she was telling me of was the child of Stephen Glenn? The two had had a child two years before the birth of their lawful son Philip? And consequently nearly a year before their marriage? I listened in a stupor, trying to reconstruct in my mind the image of a new, of another, Stephen Glenn, of the suffering reckless man behind the varnished image familiar to me. Now and then I murmured: 'Yes . . . yes . . .' just to help her to go on.

'Of course it was impossible to keep the baby with me. Think – at my uncle's! My poor uncle . . . he would have died of it. . . .'

'And so you died instead?'

I had found the right word; her eyes filled again, and she stretched her hands to mine. 'Ah, you've understood! Thank you. Yes; I died.' She added: 'Even when Philip was born I didn't come to life again – not wholly. Because there was always Stevie . . . part of me belonged to Stevie forever.'

'But when you and Glenn were able to marry, why – ?'

She hung her head, and the blood rose to her worn temples. 'Ah, why? . . . Listen; you mustn't blame my husband. Try to remember what life was thirty years ago in New York. He had his professional standing to consider. A woman with a shadow on her was damned. . . . I couldn't discredit Stephen. . . . We knew *positively* that our baby was in the best of hands. . . .'

'You never saw him again?'

She shook her head. 'It was part of the agreement – with the persons who took him. They wanted to imagine he was their own. We knew we were fortunate . . . to find such a safe home, so entirely beyond suspicion . . . we had to accept the conditions.' She looked up with a faint flicker of reassurance in her eyes. 'In a way it no longer makes any difference to me – the interval. It seems like yesterday. I know he's been well cared for, and I should recognize him anywhere. No child ever had such eyes. . . .' She fumbled in her bag, drew out a small morocco case, opened it, and showed me the miniature of a baby a few months old. 'I managed, with the greatest difficulty, to get a photograph of him – and this was done from it. Beautiful? Yes. I shall be able to identify him anywhere. . . . It's only twenty-seven years. . . .'

• III •

OUR talk was prolonged, the next day, at the quiet hotel where Mrs. Glenn was staying; but it led – it could lead – to nothing definite.

The unhappy woman could only repeat and amplify the strange confession stammered out at the Consulate. As soon as her child was born it had been entrusted with the utmost secrecy to a rich childless couple, who at once adopted it, and disappeared forever. Disappeared, that is, in the sense that (as I guessed) Stephen Glenn was as determined as they were that the child's parents should never hear of them again. Poor Catherine had been very ill at her baby's birth. Tortured by the need of concealment, of taking up her usual life at her uncle's as quickly as possible, of explaining her brief absence in such a way as to avert suspicion, she had lived in a blur of fear and suffering, and by the time she was herself again the child was gone, and the adoption irrevocable. Thereafter, I gathered, Glenn made it clear that he wished to avoid the subject, and she learned very little about the couple who had taken her child except that they were of good standing, and came from somewhere in Pennsylvania. They had gone to Europe almost immediately, it appeared, and no more was heard of them. Mrs. Glenn understood that Mr. Brown (their name was Brown) was a painter, and that they went first to Italy, then to Spain – unless it was the other way round. Stephen Glenn, it seemed, had heard of them through an old governess of his sister's, a family confidante, who was the sole recipient of poor Catherine's secret. Soon afterwards the governess died, and with her disappeared the last trace of the mysterious couple; for it was not going to be easy to wander about Europe looking for a Mr. and Mrs. Brown who had gone to Italy or Spain with a baby twenty-seven years ago. But that was what Mrs. Glenn meant to do. She had a fair amount of money, she was desperately lonely, she had no aim or interest or occupation or duty – except to find the child she had lost.

What she wanted was some sort of official recommendation to our consuls in Italy and Spain, accompanied by a private letter hinting at the nature of her errand. I took these papers to her and when I did so I tried to point out the difficulties and risks of her quest, and suggested that she ought to be accompanied by someone who could advise her – hadn't she a man of business, or a relation, a cousin, a nephew? No, she said; there was no one; but for that matter she needed no one. If necessary she could apply to the police, or employ private detectives; and any American consul to whom she appealed would know how to advise her. 'In any case,' she added, 'I couldn't be mistaken – I should always recognize him. He was the very image of his father. And if there were any possibility of my being in doubt, I have the miniature, and photographs of his father as a young man.'

She drew out the little morocco case and offered it again for my contemplation. The vague presentment of a child a few months old – and by its help she expected to identify a man of nearly thirty!

Apparently she had no clue beyond the fact that, all those years ago, the adoptive parents were rumored to have sojourned in Europe. She was starting for Italy because she thought she remembered that they were said to have gone there first – in itself a curious argument. Wherever there was an American consul she meant to apply to him. First at Genoa; then Milan; then Florence, Rome and Naples. In one or the other of these cities she would surely discover some one who could remember the passage there of an American couple named Brown with the most beautiful baby boy in the world. Even the long arm of coincidence could not have scattered so widely over southern Europe American couples of the name of Brown, with a matchlessly beautiful baby called Stephen.

Mrs. Glenn set forth in a mood of almost mystical exaltation. She promised that I should hear from her as soon as she had anything definite to communicate: 'which means that you *will* hear – and soon!' she concluded with a happy laugh. But six months passed without my receiving any direct news, though I was kept on her track by a succession of letters addressed to my chief by various consuls who wrote to say that a Mrs. Stehpen Glenn had called with a letter of recommendation, but that unluckily it had been impossible to give her any assistance 'as she had absolutely no data to go upon.' Alas poor lady –

And, then, one day, about eight months after her departure, there was a telegram. 'Found my boy. Unspeakably happy. Long to see you.' It was signed Catherine Glenn, and dated from a mountain cure in Switzerland.

• IV •

THAT summer, when the time came for my vacation, it was raining in Paris even harder than it had rained all the preceding winter, and I decided to make a dash for the sun.

I had read in the papers that the French Riviera was suffering from a six months' drought; and though I didn't half believe it, I took the next train for the south. I got out at Les Calanques, a small bathing place between Marseilles and Toulon, where there was a fairish hotel, and pine woods to walk in, and there, that very day, I saw seated on

the beach the majestic figure of Mrs. Stephen Glenn. The first thing
that struck me was that she had at last discarded her weeds. She wore
a thin white dress, and a wide brimmed hat of russet straw shaded the
fine oval of her face. She saw me at once, and springing up advanced
across the beach with a light step. The sun, striking on her hat brim,
cast a warm shadow on her face; and in that semishade it glowed with
recovered youth. 'Dear Mr. Norcutt! How wonderful! Is it really you?
I've been meaning to write for weeks; but I think happiness has made
me lazy and my days are so full,' she declared with a joyous smile.

I looked at her with increased admiration. At the Consulate, I
remembered, I had said to myself that grief was what Nature had meant
her features to express; but that was only because I had never seen her
happy. No; even when her husband and her son Philip were alive, and
the circle of her well-being seemed unbroken, I had never seen her look
as she looked now. And I understood that, during all those years, the
unsatisfied longing for her eldest child, the shame at her own cowardice
in disowning and deserting him, and perhaps her secret contempt for
her husband for having abetted (or more probably exacted) that desertion, must have been eating into her soul, deeper, far deeper, than
satisfied affections could reach. Now everything in her was satisfied; I
could see it.

'How happy you look!' I exclaimed.

'But of course.' She took it as simply as she had my former remark
on her heightened beauty; and I perceived that what had illumined her
face when we met on the steamer was not sorrow but the dawn of
hope. Even then she had felt certain that she was going to find her boy;
now she had found him and was transfigured. I sat down beside her
on the sands. 'And now tell me how the incredible thing happened.'

She shook her head. 'Not incredible – inevitable. When one has
lived for more than half a life with one object in view it's bound to
become a reality. I *had* to find Stevie; and I found him.' She smiled
with the inward brooding smile of a Madonna – an image of the eternal
mother who, when she speaks of her children in old age, still feels them
at the breast.

Of details as I made out there were few; or perhaps she was too
confused with happiness to give them. She had hunted up and down
Italy for her Mr. and Mrs. Brown, and then suddenly, at Alassio, just
as she was beginning to give up hope, and had decided (in a less
sanguine mood) to start for Spain, the miracle had happened. Falling
into talk, on her last evening, with a lady in the hotel lounge, she had
alluded vaguely – she couldn't say why – to the object of her quest;
and the lady, snatching the miniature from her, and bursting into tears,
had identified the portrait as her adopted child's, and herself as the
long-sought Mrs. Brown. Papers had been produced, dates compared,
all to Mrs. Glenn's complete satisfaction. There could be no doubt that

she had found her Stevie (thank heaven, they had kept the name!); and
the only shadow on her joy was the discovery that he was lying ill,
menaced with tuberculosis, at some Swiss mountain cure. Or rather,
that was part of another sadness; of the unfortunate fact that his adopted
parents had lost nearly all their money just as he was leaving school,
and hadn't been able to do much for him in the way of medical attention
or mountain air – the very things he needed as he was growing up.
Instead, since he had a passion for painting, they had allowed him to
live in Paris, rather miserably, in the Latin Quarter, and work all day
in one of those big schools – Julian's wasn't it? The very worst thing
for a boy whose lungs were slightly affected; and this last year he had
had to give up, and spend several months in a cheap hole in Switzerland.
Mrs. Glenn joined him there at once – ah, that meeting! – and as soon
as she had seen him, and talked with the doctors, she became convinced
that all that was needed to ensure his recovery was comfort, care and
freedom from anxiety. His lungs, the doctors assured her, were all right
again; and he had such a passion for the sea that after a few weeks in
a good hotel at Montana he had persuaded Mrs. Glenn to come with
him to the Mediterranean. But she was firmly resolved on carrying
him back to Switzerland for another winter, no matter how much he
objected; and Mr. and Mrs. Brown agreed that she was absolutely
right –

'Ah; there's still a Mr. Brown?'

'Oh, yes.' She smiled at me absently, her whole mind on Stevie.
'You'll see them both – they're here with us. I invited them for a few
weeks, poor souls. I can't altogether separate them from Stevie – not
yet.' (It was clear that eventually she hoped to.)

No, I assented; I supposed she couldn't; and just then she exclaimed:
'Ah, there's my boy!' and I saw a tall stooping young man approaching
us with the listless step of convalescence. As he came nearer I felt that
I was going to like him a good deal better than I had expected – though
I don't know why I had doubted his likeableness before knowing him.
At any rate, I was taken at once by the look of his dark-lashed eyes,
deep set in a long thin face which I suspected of being too pale under
the carefully acquired sunburn. The eyes were friendly, humorous,
ironical; I liked a little less the rather hard lines of the mouth, until his
smile relaxed them into boyishness. His body, lank and loose-jointed,
was too thin for his suit of light striped flannel, and the untidy dark
hair tumbling over his forehead adhered to his temples as if they were
perpetually damp. Yes, he looked ill, this young Glenn.

I remembered wondering, when Mrs. Glenn told me her story, why
it had not occurred to her that her oldest son had probably joined the
American forces and might have remained on the field with his junior.
Apparently this tragic possibility had never troubled her. She seemed
to have forgotten that there had ever been a war, and that a son of her

own, with thousands of young Americans of his generation, had lost his life in it. And now it looked as though she had been gifted with a kind of prescience. The war did not last long enough for America to be called on to give her weaklings, as Europe had, and it was clear that Stephen Glenn, with his narrow shoulders and hectic cheekbones, could never have been wanted for active service. I suspected him of having been ill for longer than his mother knew.

Mrs. Glenn shone on him as he dropped down beside us. 'This is an old friend, Stephen, a very dear friend of your father's.' She added, extravagantly, that but for me she and her son might never have found each other. I protested: 'How absurd,' and young Glenn, stretching out his long limbs against the sandbank, and crossing his arms behind his head, turned on me a glance of rather weary good humor. 'Better give me a longer trial, my dear, before you thank him.'

Mrs. Glenn laughed contentedly, and continued, her eyes on her son: 'I was telling him that Mr. and Mrs. Brown are with us.'

'Ah, yes – ' said Stephen indifferently. I was inclined to like him a little less for his undisguised indifference. Ought he to have allowed his poor and unlucky foster parents to be so soon superseded by this beautiful and opulent new mother? But, after all, I mused, I had not yet seen the Browns, and though I had begun to suspect, from Catherine's tone as well as from Stephen's, that they both felt the presence of that couple to be vaguely oppressive, I decided that I must wait before drawing any conclusions. And then suddenly Mrs. Glenn said, in a tone of what I can only describe as icy cordiality: 'Ah, here they come now. They must have hurried back on purpose – '

• V •

MR. and Mrs. Brown advanced across the beach. Mrs. Brown led the way; she walked with a light springing step, and if I had been struck by Mrs. Glenn's recovered youthfulness, her co-mother, at a little distance, seemed to me positively girlish. She was smaller and much slighter than Mrs. Glen, and looked so much younger that I had a moment's doubt as to the possibility of her having, twenty-seven years earlier been of legal age to adopt a baby. Certainly she and Mr. Brown must have had exceptional reasons for concluding so early that heaven was not likely to bless their union. I had to admit, when Mrs. Brown came up, that I had overrated her juvenility. Slim, active and girlish she remained; but the freshness of her face was largely due to artifice, and the golden glints in her chestnut hair were a thought too golden. Still, she was a very pretty woman, with the alert cosmopolitan air of one who had acquired her elegance in places where the very best counterfeits are found. It will be seen that my first impression was none too favorable; but for all I knew of Mrs. Brown it might turn out that she had made the best of meager opportunities. She met my name with a conquering smile, said: 'Ah, yes – dear Mr. Norcutt. Mrs. Glenn has told us all we owe you' – and at the 'we' I detected a faint shadow on Mrs. Glenn's brow. Was it only maternal jealousy that provoked it? I suspected an even deeper antagonism. The women were so different, so diametrically opposed to each other in appearance, dress, manner, and the inherited standards, that if they had met as strangers it would have been hard for them to find a common ground of understanding; and the fact of that ground being furnished by Stephen hardly seemed to ease the situation.

'Well, what's the matter with taking some notice of little me?' piped a small dry man dressed in too-smart flannels, and wearing a too-white Panama which he removed with an elaborate flourish.

'Oh, of course! My husband – Mr. Norcutt.' Mrs. Brown laid a jeweled hand on Stephen's recumbent shoulder. 'Steve, you rude boy, you ought to have introduced your dad.' As she pressed his shoulder I noticed that her long oval nails were freshly lacquered with the last new shade of coral, and that the forefinger was darkly yellowed with nicotine. This familiar color scheme struck me at the moment as peculiarly distasteful.

Stephen vouchsafed no answer, and Mr. Brown remarked to me sardonically. 'You know you won't lose your money or your morals in this secluded spot.'

Mrs. Brown flashed a quick glance at him. 'Don't be so silly! It's much better for Steve to be in a quiet place where he can just sleep and eat and bask. His mother and I are going to be firm with him about that – aren't we, dearest?' She transferred her lacquered talons to Mrs. Glenn's shoulder, and the latter, with a just perceptible shrinking, replied gaily: 'As long as we can hold out against him!'

'Oh, this is the very place I was pining for,' said Stephen placidly. ('Gosh – *pining!*' Mr. Brown interpolated.) Stephen tilted his hat forward over his sunburnt nose with the drawn nostrils, crossed his arms under his thin neck, and closed his eyes. Mrs. Brown bent over Mrs. Glenn with one of her quick gestures. 'Darling – before we go in to lunch do let me fluff you out a little: so.' With a flashing hand she loosened the soft white waves under Mrs. Glenn's spreading hat brim. 'There – that's better; isn't it, Mr. Norcutt?'

Mrs. Glenn's face was a curious sight. The smile she had forced gave place to a marble rigidity; the old statuesqueness which had melted to flesh and blood stiffened her features again. 'Thank you . . . I'm afraid I never think. . . .'

'No, you never do; that's the trouble!' Mrs. Brown shot an arch glance at me. 'With her looks, oughtn't she to think? But perhaps it's lucky for the rest of us poor women she didn't – eh, Stevie?'

The color rushed to Mrs. Glenn's face; she was going to retort; to snub the dreadful woman. But the new softness had returned, and she merely lifted a warning finger. 'Oh, don't, please . . . speak to him. Can't you see that he's fallen asleep?'

O great King Solomon, I thought – and bowed my soul before the mystery.

I spent a fortnight at Les Calanques, and every day my perplexity deepened. The most conversible member of the little group was undoubtedly Stephen. Mrs. Glenn was as she had always been; beautiful, benevolent and inarticulate. When she sat on the beach beside the dozing Stephen, in her flowing dress, her large white umbrella tilted to shelter him, she reminded me of a carven angel spreading broad wings above a tomb (I could never look at her without being reminded of statuary); and to converse with a marble angel so engaged can never have been easy. But I was perhaps not wrong in suspecting that her smiling silence concealed a reluctance to talk about the Browns. Like many perfectly unegotistical women Catherine Glenn had no subject of conversation except her own affairs; and these at present so visibly hinged on the Browns that it was easy to see why silence was simpler.

Mrs. Brown, I may as well confess, bored me acutely. She was a perfect specimen of the middle-aged flapper, with layers and layers of hard-headed feminine craft under her romping ways. All this I suffered from chiefly because I knew it was making Mrs. Glenn suffer. But after all it was thanks to Mrs. Brown that she had found her son; Mrs. Brown had brought up Stephen, had made him (one was obliged to suppose) the whimsical dreamy charming creature he was; and again and again, when Mrs. Brown outdid herself in girlish archness or middle-aged craft, Mrs. Glenn's wounded eyes said to mine: 'Look at Stephen, isn't that enough?'

Certainly it was enough, enough even to excuse Mr. Brown's jocular allusions and arid anecdotes, his boredom at Les Calanques, and the too-liberal potations in which he drowned it. Mr. Brown, I may add, was not half as trying as his wife. For the first two or three days I was mildly diverted by his contempt for the quiet watering place in which his women had confined him, and his lordly conception of the life of pleasure, as exemplified by intimacy with the headwaiters of gilt-edged restaurants and the lavishing of large sums on horse racing and cards. 'Damn it, Norcutt, I'm not used to being mewed up in this kind of place. Perhaps it's different with you – all depends on a man's standards, don't it? Now before I lost my money – ' and so on. The odd thing was that, though this loss of fortune played a large part in the conversation of both husband and wife, I never somehow believed in it – I mean in the existence of the fortune. I hinted as much one day to Mrs. Glenn, but she only opened her noble eyes reproachfully, as if

I had implied that it discredited the Browns to dream of a fortune they had never had. 'They tell me Stephen was brought up with every luxury. And besides – their own tastes seem rather expensive, don't they?' she argued gently.

'That's the very reason.'

'The reason – ?'

'The only people I know who are totally without expensive tastes are the overwhelmingly wealthy. You see it when you visit palaces. They sleep on camp beds and live on boiled potatoes.'

Mrs. Glenn smiled. 'Stevie wouldn't have liked that.'

Stephen smiled also when I alluded to these past splendors. 'It must have been before I cut my first teeth. I know Boy's always talking about it; but I've got to take it on faith, just as you have.'

'Boy – ?'

'Didn't you know? He's always called "Boy." Boydon Brown – abbreviated by friends and family to "Boy." The Boy Browns. Suits them, doesn't it?'

It did; but I was sure that it suited him to say so.

'And you've always addressed your adopted father in that informal style?'

'Lord, yes; nobody's formal with Boy except headwaiters. They bow down to him; I don't know why. He's got the manner. I haven't. When I go to a restaurant they always give me the worst table and the stupidest waiter.' He leaned back against the sandbank and blinked contentedly seaward. 'Got a cigarette?'

'You know you oughtn't to smoke,' I protested.

'I know; but I do.' He held out a lean hand with prominent knuckles. 'As long as Kit's not about.' He called the marble angel, his mother, 'Kit'! And yet I was not offended – I let him do it, just as I let him have one of my cigarettes. If 'Boy' had a way with headwaiters his adopted son undoubtedly had one with lesser beings; his smile, his faint hoarse laugh would have made me do his will even if his talk had not conquered me. We sat for hours on the sands, discussing and dreaming; not always undisturbed, for Mrs. Brown had a tiresome way of hovering and 'listening in', as she archly called it – ('I don't want Stevie to depreciate his poor ex-mamma to you.' she explained one day); and whenever Mrs. Brown (who, even at Les Calanques, had contrived to create a social round for herself) was bathing, dancing, playing bridge, or being waved, massaged or manicured, the other mother, assuring herself from an upper window that the coast was clear, would descend in her gentle majesty and turn our sandbank into a throne by sitting on it. But now and then Stephen and I had a half hour to ourselves and then I tried to lead his talk to the past.

He seemed willing enough that I should, but uninterested, and unable to recover many details. 'I never can remember things that don't matter – and so far nothing about me has mattered,' he said with a humorous melancholy. 'I mean, not till I struck mother Kit.'

He had vague recollections of continental travels as a little boy; had afterward been at a private school in Switzerland; had tried to pass himself off as a Canadian volunteer in 1915, and in 1917 to enlist in the American army, but had failed in each case – one had only to look at him to see why. The war over, he had worked for a time at Julian's and then broken down; and after that it had been a hard row to hoe till mother Kit came along. By George, but he'd never forget what she'd done for him – never!

'Well, it's a way mothers have with their sons,' I remarked.

He flushed under his bronze tanning, and said simply: 'Yes – only you see I didn't know.'

His view of the Browns, while not unkindly, was so detached that I suspected him of regarding his own mother with the same objectivity; but when we spoke of her there was a different note in his voice. 'I didn't know' – it was a new experience to him to be really mothered. As a type, however, she clearly puzzled him. He was too sensitive to class her (as the Browns obviously did) as a simple-minded woman to whom nothing had ever happened: but he could not conceive what sort of thing could happen to a woman of her kind. I gathered that she had explained the strange episode of his adoption by telling him that at the time of his birth she had been 'secretly married' – poor Catherine! – to his father, but that 'family circumstances' had made it needful to conceal his existence till the marriage could be announced; by which time he had vanished with his adopted parents. I guessed how it must have puzzled Stephen to adapt his interpretation of this ingenuous tale to what, in the light of Mrs. Glenn's character, he could make out of her past. Of obvious explanations there were plenty; but evidently none fitted into his vision of her. For a moment (I could see) he had suspected a sentimental lie, a tender past, between Mrs. Glenn and myself; but this his quick perceptions soon discarded, and he apparently resigned himself to regarding her as inscrutably proud and incorrigibly perfect. 'I'd like to paint her some day – if ever I'm fit to,' he said; and I wondered whether his scruples applied to his moral or artistic inadequacy.

At the doctor's orders he had dropped his painting altogether since his last breakdown; but it was manifestly the one thing he cared for, and perhaps the only reason he had for wanting to get well. 'When you've dropped to a certain level, it's so damnably easy to keep on till you're altogether down and out. So much easier than dragging up hill again. But I do want to get well enough to paint mother Kit. She's a subject.'

One day it rained, and he was confined to the house. I went up to sit with him, and he got out some of his sketches and studies. Instantly he was transformed from an amiably mocking dilettante into an absorbed and passionate professional. 'This is the only life I've ever had. All the rest – !' He made a grimace that turned his thin face into a death's-head. 'Cinders!'

The studies were brilliant – there was no doubt of that. The question was – the eternal question – what would they turn into when he was well enough to finish them? For the moment the problem did not present itself and I could praise and encourage him in all sincerity. My words brought a glow into his face, but also, as it turned out, sent up his temperature. Mrs. Glenn reproached me mildly; she begged me not to let him get excited about his pictures. I promised not to, and reassured on that point she asked if I didn't think he had talent – real talent? 'Very great talent, yes,' I assured her, and she burst into tears – not of grief or agitation, but of a deep unwelling joy. 'Oh, what have I done to deserve it all – to deserve such happiness? Yet I always knew if I could find him he'd make me happy!' She caught both my hands, and pressed her wet cheek on mine. That was one of her unclouded hours.

There were others not so radiant. I could see that the Browns were straining at the leash. With the seductions of Juan-les-Pins and Antibes in the offing, why, their frequent allusions implied, must they remain marooned at Les Calanques? Of course, for one thing, Mrs. Brown admitted she hadn't the clothes to show herself on a smart *plage*. Though so few were worn they had to come from the big dressmakers; and the latter's charges, everybody knew, were in inverse ration to the amount of material used. 'So that to be really naked is ruinous.' she concluded, laughing; and I saw the narrowing of Catherine's lips. As for Mr. Brown, he added morosely that if a man couldn't take a hand at baccarat, or offer his friends something decent to eat and drink, it was better to vegetate at Les Calanques, and be done with it. Only, when a fellow'd been used to having plenty of money. . . .

I saw at once what had happened. Mrs. Glenn, whose material wants did not extend beyond the best plumbing and expensive clothes (and the latter were made to do for three seasons), did not fully understand the Brown's aspirations. Her fortune, though adequate, was not large, and she had settled on Stephen's adoptive parents an allowance which, converted into francs, made a generous showing. It was obvious, however, that what they hoped was to get more money. There had been debts in the background, perhaps; who knew but the handsome Stephen had had his share of them? One day I suggested discreetly to Mrs. Glenn that if she wished to be alone with her son she might offer the Browns a trip to Juan-les-Pins, or some such center of gaiety. But I pointed out that the precedent might be dangerous, and advised her first to consult Stephen. 'I suspect he's as anxious to have them go as you are,' I said recklessly; and her flush of pleasure rewarded me. 'Oh, you mustn't say that,' she reproved me, laughing, and added that she would think over my advice, I am not sure if she did consult Stephen, but she offered the Browns a holiday, and they accepted it without false pride.

• VI •

AFTER my departure from Les Calanques I had no news of Mrs. Glenn till she returned to Paris in October. Then she begged me to call at the hotel where I had previously seen her, and where she was now staying with Stephen – and the Browns.

She suggested, rather mysteriously, my dining with her on a particular evening, when, as she put it, 'everybody' would be out; and when I arrived she explained that Stephen had gone to the country for the week-end, with some old comrades from Julian's, and that the Browns were dining at a smart nightclub in Montmartre. 'So we'll have a quiet time all by ourselves.' She added that Steve was so much better that he was trying his best to persuade her to spend the winter in Paris, and let him get back to his painting, but in spite of the good news I thought she looked worn and dissatisfied.

I was surprised to find the Browns still with her, and told her so.

'Well, you see, it's difficult,' she returned with a troubled frown. 'They love Stephen so much that they won't give him up; and how can I blame them? What are my rights, compared to theirs?'

Finding this hard to answer, I put another question 'Did you enjoy your quiet time with Stephen while they were in Juan-les-Pins?'

'Oh, they didn't go; at least Mrs. Brown didn't – Chrissy she likes me to call her,' Mrs. Glenn corrected herself hurriedly. 'She couldn't bear to leave Stephen.'

'So she sacrificed Juan-les-Pins, and that handsome check?'

'Not the check; she kept that. Boy went,' Mrs. Glenn added apologetically. Boy and Chrissy – it had come to that! I looked away from my old friend's troubled face before putting my next question. 'And Stephen – ?'

'Well, I can't exactly tell how he feels. But I sometimes think he'd like to be alone with me.' A passing radiance smoothed away her frown. 'He's hinted that, if we decide to stay here, they might be tempted by winter sports, and go to the Engadine later.'

'So that they would have the benefit of the high air instead of Stephen?' She coloured a little, looked down, and then smiled at me. 'What can I do?'

I resolved to sound Stephen on his adopted parents. The present situation would have to be put an end to somehow; but it had puzzling elements. Why had Mrs. Brown refused to go to Juan-les-Pins? Was it, as I had suspected, because there were debts, and more pressing uses for the money? Or was it that she was so much attached to her adopted son as to be jealous of his mother's influence? This was far more to be feared; but it did not seem to fit in with what I knew of Mrs. Brown. The trouble was that what I knew was so little. Mrs. Brown, though in one way so intelligble, was in another as cryptic to me as Catherine Glenn was to Stephen. The surface was transparent enough; but what did the blur beneath conceal? Troubled waters, or just a mud flat? My only hope was to try to get Stephen to tell me.

Stephen had hired a studio – against his doctor's advice, I gathered – and spent most of his hours there, in the company of his old group of painting friends. Mrs. Glenn had been there once or twice, but in spite of his being so sweet and dear to her she had felt herself in the way – as she undoubtedly was. 'I can't keep up with their talk, you know,' she explained. With whose talk could she, poor angel?

I suggested that, for the few weeks of their Paris sojourn, it would be kinder to let Stephen have his fling; and she agreed. Afterward, in the mountains, he could recuperate, youth had such powers of self-healing. But I urged her to insist on his spending another winter in the Engadine; not at one of the big fashionable places –

She interrupted me. 'I'm afraid Boy and Chrissy wouldn't like – '

'Oh, for God's sake; can't you give Boy and Chrissy another check, and send them off to Egypt, or to Monte Carlo?'

She hesitated. 'I could try; but I don't believe she'd go. Not without Stevie.'

'And what does Stevie say?'

'What can he say? She brought him up. She was there – all the years when I'd failed him.'

It was unanswerable, and I felt the uselessness of any advice I could give. The situation could be changed only by some internal readjustment. Still, out of pity for the poor mother, I determined to try a word with Stephen. She gave me the address of his studio, and the next day I went there.

It was in a smart-looking modern building in the Montparnasse quarter; lofty, well-lit and well-warmed. What a contrast to his earlier environment! I climbed to his door, rang the bell and waited. There were sounds of moving about within, but as no one came I rang again; and finally Stephen opened the door. His face lit up pleasantly when he saw me. 'Oh, it's you, my dear fellow!' But I caught a hint of constraint in his voice.

'I'm not in the way? Don't mind throwing me out if I am.'

'I've got a sitter – ' he began, visibly hesitating.

'Oh, in that case – '

'No, no; it's only – the fact is, it's Chrissy. I was trying to do a study of her – '

He led me across the passage and into the studio. It was large and flooded with light. Divans against the walls; big oak tables; shaded lamps, a couple of tall screens. From behind one of them emerged Mrs. Brown, hatless, and slim, in a pale summer-like frock, her chestnut hair becomingly tossed about her eyes. 'Dear Mr. Norcutt. So glad you turned up! I was getting such a stiff neck – Stephen's merciless.'

'May I see the result?' I asked; and 'Oh, no,' she protested in mock terror, 'it's too frightful – it really is. I think he thought he was doing a *nature morte* – lemons and a bottle of beer, or something!'

'It's not fit for inspection,' Stephen agreed.

The room was spacious, and not overcrowded. Glancing about, I could see only one easel with a painting on it. Stephen went up and turned the canvas face inward, with the familiar gesture of the artist who does not wish to challenge attention. But before he did so I had remarked that the painting was neither a portrait of Mrs. Brown nor a still-life. It was a rather brilliant three-quarter sketch of a woman's naked back and hips. A model, no doubt – but why did he wish to conceal it?

'I'm so glad you came.' Mrs. Brown repeated, smiling intensely. I stood still, hoping she was about to go; but she dropped down on one of the divans, tossing back her tumbled curls. 'He works too hard, you know; I wish you'd tell him so. Steve, come here and stretch out,' she commanded, indicating the other end of the divan. 'You ought to take a good nap.'

The hint was so obvious that I said: 'In that case I'd better come another time.'

'No, no; wait till I give you a cocktail. We all need cocktails. Where's the shaker, darling?' Mrs. Brown was on her feet again, alert and gay. She dived behind the screen which had previously concealed her, and reappeared with the necessary appliances. 'Bring up that little table, Mr. Norcutt, please. Oh I know – dear Kit doesn't approve of cocktails; and she's right. But look at him – dead-beat! If he will slave at his painting, what's he to do? I was scolding him about it when you came in.'

The shaker danced in her flashing hands, and in a trice she was holding a glass out to me, and another to Stephen, who had obediently flung himself down on the divan. As he took the glass she bent and laid her lips on his damp hair. 'You bad boy, you!'

I looked at Stephen. 'You ought to get out of this, and start straight off for Switzerland,' I admonished him.

'Oh, hell,' he groaned. 'Can't you get Kit to drop all that?'

Mrs. Brown made an impatient gesture. 'Isn't he too foolish? Of course he ought to go away. He looks like nothing on earth. But his only idea of Switzerland is one of those awful places we used to have to go to because they were cheap, where there's nothing to do in the evening but to sit with clergyman's wives looking at stereopticon views of glaciers. I tell him he'll love St. Moritz. There's a thrill there every minute.'

Stephen closed his eyes and sank his head back in the cushions without speaking. His face was drawn and weary; I was startled at the change in him since we had parted at Les Calanques.

Mrs. Brown, following my glance, met it with warning brows and a finger on her painted lips. It was like a parody of Mrs. Glenn's maternal gesture, and I perceived that it meant. 'Can't you see that he's falling asleep? Do be tactful and slip out without disturbing him.'

What could I do but obey? A moment later the studio door had closed on me, and I was going down the long flights of stairs. The worst of it was that I was not at all sure that Stephen was really asleep.

• VII •

THE next morning I received a telephone call from Stephen asking me to lunch. We met at a quiet restaurant near his studio, and when, after an admirably-chosen meal, we settled down to coffe and cigars, he said carelessly: 'Sorry you got thrown out that way yesterday.'

'Oh, well – I saw you were tired, and I didn't want to interfere with your nap.'

He looked down moodily at his plate. 'Tired – yes, I'm tired. But I didn't want a nap. I merely simulated slumber to try and make Chrissy shut up.'

'Ah – ' I said.

He shot a quick glance at me, almost resentfully, I thought. Then he went on: 'There are times when aimless talk nearly kills me. I wonder,' he broke out suddenly, 'If you can realize what it feels like for a man who's never – I mean for an orphan – suddenly to find himself with two mothers?'

I said I could see it might be arduous.

'Arduous! It's literally asphyxiating.' He frowned, and then smiled whimsically. 'When I need all the fresh air I can get!'

'My dear fellow – what you need first of all is to get away from cities and studios.'

His frown deepened. 'I know; I know all that. Only, you see – well, to begin with, before I turn up my toes I want to do something for mother Kit.'

'Do something?'

'Something to show her that I was – was worth all this fuss.' He paused, and turned his coffee spoon absently between his long twitching fingers.

I shrugged. 'Whatever you do, she'll always think that. Mothers do.'

He murmured after me slowly: 'Mothers – '

'What she wants you to do now is to get well,' I insisted.

'Yes; I know; I'm pledged to get well. But somehow that bargain doesn't satisfy me. If I don't get well I want to leave something behind me that'll make her think: "If he'd lived a little longer he'd have pulled it off".'

'If you left a gallery of masterpieces it wouldn't help her much.'

His face clouded, and he looked at me wistfully. 'What the devil else can I do?'

'Go to Switzerland, and let yourself be bored there for a whole winter. Then you can come back and paint, and enjoy your success instead of having the enjoyment done for you by your heirs.'

'Oh, what a large order – ' he sighed, and drew out his cigarettes.

For a moment we were both silent; then he raised his eyes and looked straight at me. 'Supposing I don't get well, there's another thing . . .' He hesitated a moment. 'Do you happen to know if my mother has made her will?'

I imagine my look must have surprised him, for he hurried on: 'It's only this: if I should drop out – you can never tell – there are Chrissy and Boy, poor, helpless devils. I can't forget what they've been to me . . . done for me . . . though sometimes I daresay I seem ungrateful . . .'

I listened to his embarrassed phrases with an embarrassment at least as great. 'You may be sure your mother won't forget either,' I said.

'No; I suppose not. Of course not. Only sometimes – you can see for yourself that things are a little breezy. . . . They feel that perhaps she doesn't always remember for how many years . . .' He brought the words out as though he were reciting a lesson. 'I can't forget it . . . of course,' he added, painfully.

I glanced at my watch, and stood up. I wanted to spare him the evident effort of going on. 'Mr. and Mrs. Brown's tastes don't always agree with your mother's. That's evident. If you could persuade them to go off somewhere – or to lead more independent lives when they're with her – mightn't that help?'

He cast a despairing glance at me. 'Lord – I wish you'd try! But you see they're anxious – anxious about their future. . . .'

'I'm sure they needn't be,' I answered shortly, more and more impatient to make an end.

His face lit up with a suddenness that hurt me. 'Oh, well . . . it's sure to be all right if you say so. Of course you know.'

'I know your mother,' I said, holding out my hand for good-bye.

• VIII •

SHORTLY after my lunch with Stephen Glenn I was unexpectedly detached from my job in Paris and sent on a special mission to the other side of the world. I was sorry to bid good-bye to Mrs. Glenn, but relieved to be rid of the thankless task of acting as her counselor. Not that she herself was not thankful, poor soul; but the situation abounded in problems, to not one of which could I find a solution; and I was embarrassed by her simple faith in my ability to do so. 'Get rid of the Browns; pension them off,' I could only repeat; but since my talk with Stephen I had little hope of his mother's acting on this suggestion. 'You'll probably all end up together in St. Moritz,' I prophesied; and a few months later a belated Paris *Herald*, overtaking me in my remote corner of the globe, informed me that among the guests of the new Ice Palace Hotel at St. Moritz were Mrs. Glenn of New York, Mr. Stephen Glenn, and Mr. and Mrs. Boydon Brown. From succeeding numbers of the same sheet I learned that Mr. and Mrs. Boydon Brown were among those entertaining on the opening night of the new *Restaurant des Glaciers*, that the Boydon Brown cup for the most original costume at the Annual Fancy Ball of the Skiers' Club had been won by Miss Thora Dacy (costume designed by the well-known artist, Stephen Glenn), and that Mr. Boydon Brown had been one of the stewards of the dinner given to the participants in the ice hockey match between the St. Moritz and Suvretta teams. And on such items I was obliged to nourish my memory of my friends, for no direct news came to me from any of them.

When I bade Mrs. Glenn good-bye I had told her that I had hopes of a post in the State Department at the close of my temporary mission, and she said, a little wistfully; 'How wonderful if we could meet next year in America! As soon as Stephen is strong enough I want him to come back and live with me in his father's house.' This seemed a natural wish; and it struck me that it might be the means of effecting a break with the Browns. But Mrs. Glenn shook her head. 'Chrissy says a winter in New York would amuse them both tremendously.'

I was not so sure that it would amuse Stephen, and therefore did not base much hope on the plan. The one thing Stephen wanted was to get back to Paris and paint: it would presumably be his mother's lot to settle down there when his health permitted.

I heard nothing more until I got back to Washington the following spring; then I had a line from Stephen. The winter in the Engadine had been a deadly bore, but had really done him good, and his mother was just leaving for Paris to look for an apartment. She meant to take one on a long lease, and have the furniture of the New York house sent out – it would be jolly getting it arranged. As for him, the doctors said he was well enough to go on with his painting and, as I knew, it was the one thing he cared for; so I might cast off all anxiety about the family. That was all – and perhaps I should have obeyed if Mrs. Glenn had also written. But no word, no message even, came from her; and as she always wrote when there was good news to give, her silence troubled me.

It was in the course of the same summer, during a visit to Bar Harbor, that one evening, dining with a friend, I found myself next to a slight pale girl with large gray eyes, who suddenly turned them on me reproachfully. 'Then you don't know me? I'm Thora.'

I looked my perplexity, and she added: 'Aren't you Steve Glenn's great friend? He's always talking of you.' My memory struggled with a tangle of oddments, from which I finally extricated the phrase in the *Herald* about Miss Thora Dacy and the fancy-dress ball at St. Moritz. 'You're the young lady who won the Boydon Brown prize in a costume designed by the well-known artist, Mr. Stephen Glenn!'

Her charming face fell. 'If you know me only through that newspaper rubbish. . . . I had an idea the well-known artist might have told you about me.'

'He's not much of a correspondent.'

'No; but I thought – '

'Why won't you tell me yourself instead?'

Dinner was over, and the company had moved out to a wide, starlit verandah looking seaward. I found a corner for two, and installed myself there with my new friend, who was also Stephen's. 'I like him awfully – don't you?' she began at once. I liked her way of saying it; I liked her direct gaze; I found myself thinking: 'But this may turn out to be the solution!' For I felt sure that, if circumstances ever gave her the right to take part in the coming struggle over Stephen, Thora Dacy would be on the side of the angels.

As if she had guessed my thought she continued: 'And I do love Mrs. Glenn too – don't you?'

I assured her that I did, and she added: 'And Steve loves her – I'm sure he does!'

'Well, if he didn't – !' I exclaimed indignantly.

'That's the way I feel; he ought to. Only, you see, Mrs. Brown – the Browns adopted him when he was a baby, didn't they, and brought him up as if he'd been their own child? I suppose they must know him better than any of us do; and Mrs. Brown says he can't help feeling bitter about – I don't know all the circumstances, but his mother did desert him soon after he was born, didn't she? And if it hadn't been for the Browns – '

'The Browns – the Browns! It's a pity they don't leave it to other people to proclaim their merits! And I don't believe Stephen does feel as they'd like you to think. If he does, he ought to be kicked. If – if complicated family reasons obliged Mrs. Glenn to separate herself from him when he was a baby, the way she mourned for him all those years, and her devotion since they've come together again, have atoned a thousand-fold for that old unhappiness; and no one knows it better than Stephen.'

The girl received this without protesting. 'I'm so glad – so glad.' There was a new vibration in her voice; she looked up gravely. 'I've always *wanted* to love Mrs. Glenn the best.'

'Well, you'd better; especially if you love Stephen.'

'Oh, I do love him,' she said simply. 'But of course I understand his feeling as he does about the Browns.'

I hesitated, not knowing how I ought to answer the question I detected under this; but at length I said: 'Stephen, at any rate, must feel that Mrs. Brown has no business to insinuate anything against his mother. He ought to put a stop to that.' She met the suggestion with a sigh, and stood up to join another group. 'Thora Dacy may yet save us!' I thought, as my gaze followed her light figure across the room.

I had half a mind to write of that meeting to Stephen or to his mother; but the weeks passed while I procrastinated, and one day I received a note from Stephen. He wrote (with many messages from Mrs. Glenn) to give me their new address, and to tell me that he was hard at work at his painting, and doing a 'promising portrait of mother Kit.' He signed himself my affectionate Steve, and added underneath: 'So glad you've come across little Thora. She took a most tremendous shine to you. Do please be nice to her; she's a dear child. But don't encourage any illusions about me, please; marrying's not in my program.' 'So that's that,' I thought, and tore the letter up rather impatiently. I wondered if Thora Dacy already knew that her illusions were not to be encouraged.

• IX •

THE months went by, and I heard no more from my friends. Summer came round again, and with it the date of my six weeks' holiday, which I purposed to take that year in Europe. Two years had passed since I had last seen Mrs. Glenn, and during that time I had received only two or three brief notes from her, thanking me for Christmas wishes, or telling me that Stephen was certainly better, though he would take no care of himself. But several months had passed since the date of her last report.

I had meant to spend my vacation in a trip in south-western France, and on the way over I decided to invite Stephen Glenn to join me. I therefore made direct for Paris, and the next morning rang him up at Mrs. Glenn's. Mrs. Brown's voice met me in reply, informing me that Stephen was no longer living with his mother. 'Read the riot act to us all a few months ago – said he wanted to be independent. You know his fads. Dear Catherine was foolishly upset. As I said to her . . . yes, I'll give you his address; but poor Steve's not well just now . . . Oh, go on a trip with you? No; I'm afraid there's no chance of that. The truth is, he told us he didn't want to be bothered – rather warned us off the premises; even poor old Boy; and you know he adores Boy. I haven't seen him myself for several days. But you can try . . . Oh, of course you can try . . . No; I'm afraid you can't see Catherine either – not just at present. She's been ill too – feverish; worrying about her naughty Steve, I suspect. I'm mounting guard for a few days, and not letting her see anybody till her temperature goes down. And would you do me a favor? Don't write – don't let her know you're here. Not for a day or two, I mean. . . . She'd be so distressed at not being able to see you. . . .'

She rang off, and left me to draw my own conclusions.

They were not of the pleasantest. I was perplexed by the apparent sequestration of both my friends, still more so by the disquieting mystery of Mrs. Glenn's remaining with the Brown's while Stephen had left them. Why had she not followed her son? Was it because she had not been allowed to? I conjectured that Mrs. Brown, knowing I was likely to put these questions to the persons concerned, was maneuvering to prevent my seeing them. If she could maneuver, so could I; but for the moment I had to consider what line to take. The fact of her givin me Stephen's address made me suspect that she had taken measures to prevent my seeing him; and if that were so there was not much use in making the attempt. And Mrs. Glenn was in bed, and 'feverish', and not to be told of my arrival. . . .

After a day's pondering I reflected that telegrams sometimes penetrate where letters fail to, and decided to telegraph to Stephen. No reply came, but the following afternoon, as I was leaving my hotel a taxi drove up and Mrs. Glenn descended from it. She was dressed in black, with many hanging scarves and veils, as if she either feared the air or the searching eyes of someone who might be interested in her movements. But for her white hair and heavy stooping lines she might have suggested the furtive figure of a young woman stealing to her lover. But when I looked at her the analogy seemed a profanation.

To women of Catherine Glenn's ripe beauty thinness gives a sudden look of age; and the face she raised among her thrown-back veils was emaciated. Illness and anxiety had scarred her as years and weather scar some beautiful still image on a church front. She took my hand, and I led her into the empty reading-room. 'You've been ill!' I said.

'Not very; just a bad cold.' It was characteristic that while she looked at me with grave beseeching eyes her words were trivial, ordinary. 'Chrissy's so devoted – takes such care of me. She was afraid to have me go out. The weather's so unsettled, isn't it? But really I'm all right; and as it cleared this morning I just ran off for a minute to see you.' The entreaty in her eyes became a prayer. 'Only don't tell her, will you? Dear Steve's been ill too – did you know? And so I just slipped out while Chrissy went to see him. She sees him nearly every day, and brings me the news.' She gave a sigh and added, hardly above a whisper: 'He sent me your address. She doesn't know.'

I listened with a sense of vague oppression. Why this mystery, this watching, these evasions? Was it because Steve was not allowed to write to me that he had smuggled my address to his mother? Mystery clung about us in damp fog-like coils, like the scarves and veils about Mrs. Glenn's thin body. But I knew that I must let my visitor tell her tale in her own way; and, of course, when it was told, most of the mystery subsided, for she was in it, enveloped in it, blinded by it. I gathered, however, that Stephen had been very unhappy. He had met at St. Moritz a girl whom he wanted to marry: Thora Dacy – ah, I'd heard of her, I'd met her? Mrs. Glenn's face lit up. She had thought the child lovely; she had known the family in Washington – excellent people; she had been so happy in the prospect of Stephen's happiness. And then something had happened . . . she didn't know, she had an idea that Chrissy hadn't liked the girl. The reason Stephen gave was that in his state of health he oughtn't to marry; but at the time he'd been perfectly well – the doctors had assured his mother that his lungs were sound, and that there was no such scruples, still less why Chrissy should have encouraged them. For Chrissy had also put it on the ground of health; she had approved his decision. And since then he had been unsettled irritable, difficult – oh, very difficult. Two or three months ago the state of tension in which they had all been living had reached a climax; Mrs. Glenn couldn't say how or why – it was still obscure to her. But she suspected that Stephen had quarreled with the Browns. They had patched it up now, they saw each other; but for a time there had certainly been something wrong. And suddenly Stephen had left the apartment, and moved into a wretched studio in a shabby quarter. The only reason he gave for leaving was that he had too many mothers – that was a joke, of course, Mrs. Glenn explained . . . but her eyes filled as she said it.

Poor mother – and, alas, poor Stephen! All the sympathy I could spare from the mother went to the son. He had behaved harshly, cruelly, no doubt; the young do; but under what provocation! I understood his saying that he had too many mothers; and I suspected that what he had tried for – and failed to achieve – was a break with the Browns. Trust Chrissy to baffle that attempt, I thought bitterly; she had obviously deflected the dispute, and made the consequences fall upon his mother. And at bottom everything was unchanged.

Unchanged – except for that thickening of the fog. At the moment it was almost as impenetrable to me as to Mrs. Glenn. Certain things

I could understand that she could not: for instance, why Stephen had left home. I could guess that the atmosphere had become unbreathable. But if so, it was certainly Mrs. Brown's doing, and what interest had she in sowing discord between Stephen and his mother? With a shock of apprehension my mind reverted to Stephen's enquiry about his mother's will. It had offended me at the time; now it frightened me. If I was right in suspecting that he had tried to break with his adopted parents – over the question of the will, no doubt, or at any rate over their general selfishness and rapacity – then his attempt had failed, since he and the Browns were still on good terms, and the only result of the dispute had been to separate him from his mother. At the thought my indignation burned afresh. 'I mean to see Stephen,' I declared, looking resolutely at Mrs. Glenn.

'But he's not well enough, I'm afraid; he told me to send you his love, and to say that perhaps when you come back – '

'Ah, you've seen him, then?'

She shook her head. 'No; he telegraphed me this morning. He doesn't even write any longer.' Her eyes filled, and she looked away from me.

He too used the telegraph! It gave me more to think about than poor Mrs. Glenn could know. I continued to look at her. 'Don't you want to send him a telegram in return? You could write it here, and give it to me,' I suggested. She hesitated, seemed half to assent, and then stood up abruptly.

'No; I'd better not. Chrissy takes my messages. If I telegraphed she might wonder – she might be hurt – '

'Yes; I see.'

'But I must be off; I've stayed too long.' She cast a nervous glance at her watch. 'When you come back . . .' she repeated.

When we reached the door of the hotel rain was falling, and I drew her back into the vestibule while the porter went to call a taxi. 'Why haven't you your own motor?' I asked.

'Oh, Chrissy wanted the motor. She had to go to see Stevie – and of course she didn't know I should be going out. You won't tell her, will you?' Mrs. Glenn cried back to me as the door of the taxi closed on her.

The taxi drove off, and I was standing on the pavement looking after it when a handsomely appointed private motor glided up to the hotel. The chauffeur sprang down, and I recognized him as the man who had driven Mrs. Glenn when we had been together at Les Calanques. I was therefore not surprised to see Mrs. Brown, golden haired and slim, descending under his unfurled umbrella. She held a note in her hand, and looked at me with a start of surprise. 'What luck! I was going to try to find out when you were likely to be in – and here you are! Concierges are always so secretive that I'd written as well.' She held the envelope up with her brilliant smile. 'Am I butting in? Or may I come and have a talk?'

I led her to the reading room which Mrs. Glenn had so lately left, and suggested a cup of tea which I had forgotten to offer to her predecessor.

She made a gay grimace. 'Tea? Oh, no – thanks. Perhaps we might go round presently to the Nouveau Luxe grill for a cocktail. But it's rather early yet; there's nobody there at this hour. And I want to talk to you about Stevie.'

She settled herself in Mrs. Glenn's corner, and as she sat there, slender and alert in her perfectly-cut dark coat and skirt, with her silver fox slung at the exact fashion plate angle, I felt the irony of these two women succeeding each other in the same seat to talk to me on the same subject. Mrs. Brown groped in her bag for a jade cigarette case, and lifted her smiling eyes to mine. 'Catherine's just been here, hasn't she? I passed her in a taxi at the corner,' she remarked lightly.

'She's been here; yes. I scolded her for not being in her own motor.' I rejoined, with an attempt at the same tone.

Mrs. Brown laughed. 'I knew you would! But I'd taken the motor on purpose to prevent her going out. She has a very bad cold, as I told you; and the doctor has absolutely forbidden – '

'Then why didn't you let me go to see her?'

'Because the doctor forbids her to see visitors. I told you that too. Didn't you notice how hoarse she is?'

I felt my anger rising. 'I noticed how unhappy she is,' I said bluntly.

'Oh, unhappy – why is she unhappy? If I were in her place I should just lie back and enjoy life,' said Mrs. Brown, with a sort of cold impatience.

'She's unhappy about Stephen.'

Mrs. Brown looked at me quickly. 'She came here to tell you so, I suppose? Well – he *has* behaved badly.'

'Why did you let him?'

She laughed again, this time ironically. 'Let him? Ah, you believe in that legend? The legend that I do what I like with Stephen.' She bent her head to light another cigarette. 'He's behaved just as badly to me, my good man – and to Boy. And *we* don't go about complaining!'

'Why should you, when you see him every day?'

At this she bridled, with a flitting smile. 'Can I help it – if it's me he wants?'

'Yes, I believe you can,' I said resolutely.

'Oh, thanks! I suppose I ought to take that as a compliment.'

'Take it as you like. Why don't you make Stephen see his mother?'

'Dear Mr. Norcutt, if I had any influence over Stephen, do you suppose I'd let him quarrel with his bread and butter? To put it on utilitarian grounds, why should I?' She lifted her clear shallow eyes and

looked straight into mine – and I found no answer. There was something impenetrable to me beneath that shallowness.

'But why did Stephen leave his mother?' I persisted.

She shrugged, and looked down at her rings, among which I fancied
I saw a new one, a dark luminous stone in claws of platinum. She
caught my glance. 'You're admiring my brown diamond? A beauty,
isn't it? Dear Catherine gave it to me for Christmas. The angel! Do
you suppose I wouldn't do anything to spare her all this misery? I wish
I could tell you why Stephen left her. Perhaps . . . perhaps because she
is such an angel . . . Young men – you understand? She was always
wrapping him up, lying awake to listen for his latchkey. . . . Steve's
rather a Bohemian; suddenly he struck – that's all I know.'

I saw at once that this contained a shred of truth wrapped round an
impenetrable lie; and I saw also that to tell that lie had not been Mrs.
Brown's main object. She had come for a still deeper reason, and I
could only wait for her to reveal it.

She glanced up reproachfully. 'How hard you are on me – always!
From the very first day – don't I know? And never more than now.
Don't you suppose I can guess what you're thinking? You're accusing
me of trying to prevent your seeing Catherine; and in reality I came
here to ask you to see her – to beg you to – as soon as she's well
enough. If you'd only trusted me, instead of persuading her to slip off
on the sly and come here in this awful weather. . . .'

It was on the tip of my tongue to declare that I was guiltless of such
perfidy; but it occurred to me that my visitor might be trying to find
out how Mrs. Glenn had known I was in Paris, and I decided to say
nothing.

'At any rate, if she's no worse I'm sure she could see you tomorrow.
Why not come and dine? I'll carry Boy off to a restaurant, and you and
she can have a cozy evening together, like old times. You'd like that,
wouldn't you?' Mrs. Brown's face was veiled with a retrospective
emotion: I saw that, less acute than Stephen, she still believed in a
sentimental past between myself and Catherine Glenn. 'She must have
been one of the loveliest creatures that ever lived – wasn't she? Even
now no one can come up to her. You don't know how I wish she liked
me better; that she had more confidence in me. If she had, she'd know
that I love Stephen as much as she does – perhaps more. For so many
years he was mine, all mine! But it's all so difficult – at this moment,
for instance. . . .' She paused, jerked her silver fox back into place, and
gave me a prolonged view of meditative lashes. At last she said: 'Perhaps
you don't know that Steve's final folly has been to refuse his allowance.
He returned the last check to Catherine with a dreadful letter.'

'Dreadful? How?'

'Telling her he was old enough to shift for himself – that he refused
to sell his independence any longer, perfect madness.'

'Atrocious cruelty – '

'Yes; that too. I told him so. But do you realize the result?' The lashes, suddenly lifted, gave me the full appeal of wide, transparent eyes. 'Steve's starving – voluntarily starving himself. Or would be, if Boy and I hadn't scraped together our last pennies. . . .'

'If independence is what he wants, why should he take your pennies when he won't take his mother's?'

'Ah – there's the point. He will.' She looked down again, fretting her rings. 'Ill as he is, how could he live if he didn't take somebody's pennies? If I could sell my brown diamond without Catherine's missing it I'd have done it long ago, and you need never have known of all this. But she's so sensitive – and she notices everything. She literally spies on me. I'm at my wits' end. If you'd only help me!'

'How in the world can I?'

'You're the only person who can. If you'd persuade her, as long as this queer mood of Stephen's lasts, to draw his monthly check in my name, I'd see that he gets it – and that he uses it. He would, you know, if he thought it came from Boy and me.'

I looked at her quickly. 'That's why you want me to see her. To get her to give you her son's allowance?'

Her lips parted as if she were about to return an irritated answer; but she twisted them into a smile. 'If you like to describe it in that way – I can't help your putting an unkind interpretation on whatever I do. I was prepared for that when I came here.' She turned her bright inclement face on me. 'If you think I enjoy humiliating myself! After all, it's not so much for Stephen that I ask it as for his mother. Have you thought of that? If she knew that in his crazy pride he was depriving himself of the most necessary things, wouldn't she do anything on earth to prevent it? She's his *real* mother. . . . I'm nothing. . . .'

'You're everything, if he sees you and listens to you.'

She received this with the air of secret triumph that met every allusion to her power over Stephen. Was she right, I wondered, in saying that she loved him even more than his mother did? 'Everything?' she murmured deprecatingly. 'It's you who are everything, who can help us all. What can I do?'

I pondered a moment, and then said, 'You can let me see Stephen.'

The color rushed up under her powder. 'Much good that would do – if I could! But I'm afraid you'll find his door barricaded.'

'That's a pity,' I said coldly.

'It's very foolish of him,' she assented.

Our conversation had reached a deadlock, and I saw that she was distinctly disappointed – perhaps even more than I was. I suspected that while I could afford to wait for a solution she could not.

'Of course, if Catherine is willing to sit by and see the boy starve' – she began.

'What else can she do? Shall we go over to the Nouveau Luxe bar and study the problem from the cocktail angle?' I suggested.

Mrs. Brown's delicately penciled brows gathered over her transparent eyes. 'You're laughing at me – and at Steve. It's rather heartless of you, you know,' she said, making a movement to rise from the deep armchair in which I had installed her. Her movements, as always, were quick and smooth; she got up and sat down with the ease of youth. But her face startled me – it had suddenly shrunk and withered, so that the glitter of cosmetics hung before it like a veil. A pang of compunction shot through me. I felt that it *was* heartless to make her look like that. I could no longer endure the part I was playing. 'I'll – see what I can do to arrange things,' I stammered. 'If only she's not too servile,' I thought, feeling that my next move hung on the way in which she received my reassurance.

She stood up with a quick smile. 'Ogre!' she just breathed, her lashes dancing. She was laughing at me under her breath – the one thing she could have done just then without offending me. 'Come; we *do* need refreshment, don't we?' She slipped her arm through mine as we crossed the lounge and emerged on the wet pavement.

· X ·

THE cozy evening with which Mrs. Brown had tempted me was not productive of much enlightenment. I found Catherine Glenn tired and pale, but happy at my coming, with a sort of furtive schoolgirl happiness which suggested the same secret apprehension as I had seen in Mrs. Brown's face when she found I would not help her to capture Stephen's allowance. I had already perceived my mistake in letting Mrs. Brown see this, and during our cocktail epilogue at the Nouveau Luxe had tried to restore her confidence; but her distrust had been aroused, and in spite of her recovered good humor I felt that I should not be allowed to see Stephen.

In this respect poor Mrs. Glenn could not help me. She could only repeat the lesson which had evidently been drilled into her. 'Why should I deny what's so evident – and so natural? When Stevie's ill and unhappy it's not to me he turns. During so many years he knew nothing of me, never even suspected my existence; and all the while *they* were there, watching over him, loving him, slaving for him. If he concealed his real feelings now it might be only on account of the – the financial inducements; and I like to think my boy's too proud for that. If you see him, you'll tell him so, won't you? You'll tell him that, unhappy as he's making me, mistaken as he is, I enter into his feelings as – as only his mother can.' She broke down, and hid her face from me.

When she regained her composure she rose and went over to the writing table. From the blotting book she drew an envelope. 'I've drawn this check in your name – it may be easier for you to get Stevie to accept a few bank notes than a check. You must try to persuade him – tell him his behavior is making the Browns just as unhappy as it is me, and that he has no right to be cruel to them, at any rate.' She lifted her head and looked into my eyes heroically.

I went home perplexed, and pondering on my next move; but (not wholly to my surprise) the question was settled for me the following morning by a telephone call from Mrs. Brown. Her voice rang out cheerfully.

'Good news! I've had a talk with Steve's doctor – on the sly, of course. Steve would kill me if he knew! The doctor says he's really better; you can see him today if you'll promise to stay only a few minutes. Of course I must first persuade Steve himself, the silly boy. You can't think what a savage mood he's in. But I'm sure I can bring him round – he's so fond of you. Only before that I want to see you myself – ' ('Of course,' I commented inwardly, feeling that here at last was the gist of the communication.) 'Can I come presently – before you go out? All right; I'll turn up in an hour.'

Within the hour she was at my hotel; but before her arrival I had decided on my course, and she on her side had probably guessed what it would be. Our first phrases, however, were noncommittal. As we exchanged them I saw that Mrs. Brown's self-confidence was weakening, and this incited me to prolong the exchange. Stephen's doctor, she assured me, was most encouraging; one lung only was affected, and that slightly; his recovery now depended on careful nursing, good food, cheerful company – all the things of which, in his foolish obstinacy, he had chosen to deprive himself. She paused, expectant –

'And if Mrs. Glenn handed over his allowance to you, you could ensure his accepting what he's too obstinate to take from his mother?'

Under her carefully prepared complexion the blood rushed to her temples. 'I always knew you were Steve's best friend!' She looked away quickly, as if to hide the triumph in her eyes.

'Well, if I am, he's first got to recognize it by seeing me.'

'Of course – of course!' She corrected her impetuosity. 'I'll do all I can. . . .'

'That's a great deal, as we know,' Under their lowered lashes her eyes followed my movements as I turned my coat back to reach an inner pocket. She pressed her lips tight to control their twitching. 'There, then!' I said.

'Oh, you angel, you! I should never have dared to ask Catherine,' she stammered with a faint laugh as the bank notes passed from my hand to her bag.

'Mrs. Glenn understood – she always understands.'

'She understands when *you* ask,' Mrs. Brown insinuated, flashing her lifted gaze on mine. The sense of what was in the bag had already given her a draught of courage, and she added quickly: 'Of course I needn't warn you not to speak of all this to Steve. If he knew of our talk it would wreck everything.'

'I can see that,' I remarked, and she dropped her lids again, as though I had caught her in a blunder.

'Well, I must go; I'll tell him his best friend's coming. . . . I'll reason with him. . . .' she murmured, trying to disguise her embarrassment in emotion. I saw her to the door, and into Mrs. Glenn's motor, from the interior of which she called back: 'You know you're going to make Catherine as happy as I am.'

Stephen Glenn's new habitation was in a narrow and unsavory street, and the building itself contrasted mournfully with the quarters in which he had last received me. As I climbed the greasy stairs I felt as much perplexed as ever. I could not yet see why Stephen's quarrel with Mrs. Glenn should, even partially, have included the Browns, nor, if it had, why he should be willing to accept from their depleted purse the funds he was too proud to receive from his mother. It gave me a feeling of uneasy excitement to know that behind the door at which I stood the answer to these problems awaited me.

No one answered my knock, so I opened the door and went in. The studio was empty, but from the room beyond Stephen's voice called out irritably: 'Who is it?' and then, in answer to my name: 'Oh, Norcutt – come in.'

Stephen Glenn lay in bed, in a small room with a window opening on a dimly-lit inner courtyard. The room was bare and untidy, the bedclothes were tumbled, and he looked at me with the sick man's instinctive resentfulness at any intrusion on his lonely pain. 'Above all,' the look seemed to say, 'don't try to be kind.'

Seeing that moral pillow smoothing would be resented I sat down beside him without any comment on the dismalness of the scene, or on his own aspect, much as it disquietened me.

'Well, old man – ' I began, wondering how to go on; but he cut short my hesitation. 'I've been wanting to see you for ever so long,' he said.

In my surprise I had nearly replied: 'That's not what I'd been told' – but, resolved to go warily, I rejoined with a sham gaiety. 'Well, here I am!'

Stephen gave me the remote look which the sick turn on those arch aliens, the healthy. 'Only,' he pursued, 'I was afraid if you did come you'd begin and lecture me; and I couldn't stand that – I can't stand anything. I'm *raw!*' he burst out.

'You might have known me better than to think I'd lecture you.'

'Oh, I don't know. Naturally the one person you care about in all this is – mother Kit.'

'Your mother,' I interposed.

He raised his eyebrows with the familiar ironic movement; then they drew together again over his sunken eyes. 'I wanted to wait till I was up to discussing things. I wanted to get this fever out of me.'

'You don't look feverish now.'

'No; they've brought it down. But I'm down with it. I'm very low,' he said, with a sort of chill impartiality, as though speaking of someone whose disabilities did not greatly move him. I replied that the best way for him to pull himself up again was to get out of his present quarters and let himself be nursed and looked after.

'Oh, don't argue!' he interrupted.

'Argue – ?'

'You're going to tell me to go back to – to my mother. To let her fatten me up. Well, it's no use. I won't take another dollar from her – not one.'

I met this in silence, and after a moment perceived that my silence irritated him more than any attempt at argument. I did not want to irritate him, and I began: 'Then why don't you go off again with the Browns? There's nothing you can do that your mother won't understand – '

'And suffer from!' he interjected.

'Oh, as to suffering – she's seasoned.'

He bent his slow feverish stare on me. 'So am I.'

'Well, at any rate, you can spare her by going off at once into good air, and trying your level best to get well. You know as well as I do that nothing else matters to her. She'll be glad to have you go away with the Browns – I'll answer for that.'

He gave a short laugh, so harsh and disenchanted that I suddenly felt he was right: to laugh like that he must be suffering as much as his mother. I laid my hand on his thin wrist. 'Old man – '

He jerked away. 'No, no. Go away with the Browns? I'd rather be dead. I'd rather hang on here till I *am* dead.'

The outburst was so unexpected that I sat in silent perplexity. Mrs. Brown had told the truth, then, when she said he hated them too? Yet he saw them, he accepted their money. . . . The darkness deepened as I peered into it.

Stephen lay with half-closed lids, and I saw that whatever enlightenment he had to give would have to be forced from him. The perception made me take a sudden resolve.

'When one is physically down and out one *is* raw, as you say: one hates everybody. I know you don't really feel like that about the Browns; but if they've got on your nerves, and you want to go off by yourself, you might at least accept the money they're ready to give you – '

He raised himself on his elbow with an ironical stare. 'Money? They borrow money; they don't give it.'

'Ah – ' I thought; but aloud I continued: 'They're prepared to give it now. Mrs. Brown tells me – '

He lifted his hand with a gesture that cut me short; then he leaned back, and drew a painful breath or two. Beads of moisture came out on his forehead. 'If she told you that, it means she's got more out of Kit. Or out of Kit through *you* – is that it?' he brought out roughly.

His clairvoyance frightened me almost as much as his physical distress – and the one seemed, somehow, a function of the other, as though the wearing down of his flesh had made other people's diaphanous to him, and he could see through it to their hearts. 'Stephen – ' I began imploringly.

Again his lifted hand checked me. 'No, wait.' He breathed hard again and shut his eyes. Then he opened them and looked into mine. 'There's only one way out of this.'

'For you to be reasonable.'

'Call it that if you like. I've got to see mother Kit – and without their knowing it.'

My perplexity grew, and my agitation with it. Could it be that the end of the Browns was in sight? I tried to remember that my first business was to avoid communicating my agitation to Stephen. In a tone that I did my best to keep steady I said: 'Nothing could make your mother happier. You're all she lives for.'

'She'll have to find something else soon.'

'No, no. Only let her come, and she'll make you well. Mothers work miracles – '

His inscrutable gaze rested on mine. 'So they say. Only, you see, she's not my mother.'

He spoke so quietly, in such a low detached tone, that at first the words carried no meaning to me. If he had been excited I should have suspected fever, delirium; but voice and eyes were clear. 'Now you understand,' he added.

I sat beside him stupidly, speechless, unable to think. 'I don't understand anything,' I stammered. Such a possibility as his words suggested had never once occurred to me. Yet he wasn't delirious, he wasn't raving – it was I whose brain was reeling as if in fever.

'Well, I'm not the long-lost child. The Browns are not *her* Browns. It's all a lie and an imposture. We faked it up between us, Chrissy and I did – her simplicity made it so cruelly easy for us. Boy didn't have much to do with it; poor old Boy! He just sat back and took his share. . . . *Now* you do see,' he repeated, in the cold explanatory tone in which he might have set forth someone else's shortcomings.

My mind was still a blur while he poured out, in broken sentences, the details of the conspiracy – the sordid tale of a trio of society adventurers come to the end of their resources, and suddenly clutching at this unheard-of chance of rescue, affluence, peace. But gradually, as I listened, the glare of horror with which he was blinding me turned into a strangely clear and penetrating light, forcing its way into obscure crannies, elucidating the incomprehensible, picking out one by one the links that bound together his framents of face. I saw – but what I was my gaze shrank from.

'Well,' I heard him say, between his difficult breaths, 'now do you begin to believe me?'

'I don't know. I can't tell. Why on earth,' I broke out, suddenly relieved at the idea, 'should you want to see your mother if this isn't all a ghastly invention?'

'To tell her what I've just told you – make a clean breast of it. Can't you see?'

'If that's the reason, I see you want to kill her – that's all.'

He grew paler under his paleness. 'Norcutt, I can't go on like this; I've got to tell her. I want to do it at once. I thought I could keep up the lie a little longer – let things go on drifting – but I can't. I held out because I wanted to get well first, and paint her picture – leave her that to be proud of, anyhow! Now that's all over, and there's nothing left but the naked shame. . . .' He opened his eyes and fixed them again on mine. 'I want you to bring her here today – without *their* knowing it. You've got to manage it somehow. It'll be the first decent thing I've done in years.'

'It will be the most unpardonable,' I interrupted angrily. 'The time's past for trying to square your own conscience. What you've got to do now is to go on lying to her – you've got to get well, if only to go on lying to her!'

A thin smile flickered over his face. 'I can't get well.'

'That's as it may be. You can spare her, anyhow.'

'By letting things go on like this?' He lay for a long time silent; then his lips drew up in a queer grimace. 'It'll be horrible enough to be a sort of expiation – '

'It's the only one.'

'It's the worst.'

He sank back wearily. I saw that fatigue had silenced him, and wondered if I ought to steal away. My presence could not but be agitating; yet in his present state it seemed almost as dangerous to leave him as to stay. I saw a flask of brandy on the table, a glass beside it. I poured out some brandy and held it to his lips. He emptied the glass slowly, and as his head fell back I heard him say: 'Before I knew her I thought I could pull it off. . . . But, you see, her sweetness. . . .'

'If she heard you say that it would make up for everything.'

'Even for what I've just told you?'

'Even for that. For God's sake hold your tongue, and just let her come here and nurse you.'

He made no answer, but under his lids I saw a tear or two.

'Let her come – let her come,' I pleaded, taking his dying hand in mine.

• XI •

NATURE does not seem to care for dramatic climaxes. Instead of allowing Stephen to die at once, his secret on his lips, she laid on him the harsher task of living though weary weeks, and keeping back the truth till the end.

As a result of my visit, he consented, the next day, to be carried back in an ambulance to Mrs. Glenn's; and when I saw their meeting it seemed to me that ties of blood were frail compared to what drew those two together. After she had fallen on her knees at his bedside, and drawn his head to her breast, I was almost sure he would not speak; and he did not.

I was able to stay with Mrs. Glenn till Stephen died, then I had to hurry back to my post in Washington. When I took leave of her she told me that she was following on the next steamer with Stephen's body. She wished her son to have a New York funeral, a funeral like his father's, at which all their old friends could be present. 'Not like poor Phil's, you know – ' and I recalled the importance she had attached to the presence of her husband's friends at his funeral. 'It's something to remember afterwards,' she said, with dry eyes. 'And it will be their only way of knowing my Stephen. . . .' It was of course impossible to exclude Mr. and Mrs. Brown from these melancholy rites; and accordingly they sailed with her.

If Stephen had recovered she had meant, as I knew, to reopen her New York house; but now that was not to be thought of. She sold the house, and all it contained, and a few weeks later sailed once more for Paris – again with the Browns.

I had resolved after Stephen's death – when the first shock was over – to do what I could toward relieving her of the Browns' presence. Though I could not tell her the truth about them, I might perhaps help her to effect some transaction which would relieve her of their company. But I soon saw that this was out of the question; and the reason deepened my perplexity. It was simply that the Browns – or at least Mrs. Brown – had become Mrs. Glenn's chief consolation in her sorrow. The two women, so incessantly at odds while Stephen lived were now joined in a common desolation. It seemed like profaning Catherine Glenn's grief to compare Mrs. Brown's to it; yet, in the first weeks after Stephen's death, I had to admit that Mrs. Brown mourned him as genuinely, as inconsolably, as his supposed mother. Indeed, it would be nearer the truth to say that Mrs. Brown's grief was more hopeless and rebellious than the other's. After all, as Mrs. Glenn said, it was much worse for Chrissy. 'She had so little compared to me; and she gave as much, I suppose. Think what I had that she's never known; those precious months of waiting for him, when he was part of me when we were one body and one soul. And then, years afterwards, when I was searching for him, and knowing all the while I should find him; and after that, our perfect life together – our perfect understanding. All that – there's all that left to me! And what did she have? Why, when she shows me his little socks and shoes (she's kept them all so carefully) they're *my* baby's socks and shoes, not hers – and I know she's thinking of it when we cry over them. I see now that I've been unjust to her . . . and cruel . . . For he *did* love me best; and that ought to have made me kinder – '

Yes; I had to recognize that Mrs. Brown's grief was as genuine as her rival's, that she suffered more bleakly and bitterly. Every turn to the strange story had been improbable and incalculable, and this new freak of fate was the most unexpected. But since it brought a softening to my poor friend's affliction, and offered a new pretext for her self-devotion, I could only hold my tongue and be thankful that the Browns were at last serving some humaner purpose.

The next time I returned to Paris the strange trio were still together, and still living in Mrs. Glenn's apartment. Its walls were now hung with Stephen's paintings and sketches – among them many unfinished attempts at a portrait of Mrs. Glenn – and the one mother seemed as eager as the other to tell me that a well-known collector of modern art had been so struck by their quality that there was already some talk of a posthumous exhibition. Mrs. Brown triumphed peculiarly in the affair. It was she who had brought the collector to see the pictures, she who had always known that Stephen had genius; it was with the Browns' meager pennies that he had been able to carry on his studies at Julian's, long before Mrs. Glenn had appeared. 'Catherine doesn't pretend to know much about art. Do you, my dear? But, as I tell her, when you're a picture yourself you don't have to bother about other people's pictures. There – your hat's crooked again! Just let me straighten it, darling – ' I saw Mrs. Glenn wince a little, as she had winced the day at Les Calanques when Mrs. Brown, with an arch side glance at me, had given a more artful twist to her friend's white hair.

It was evident that time, in drying up the source which had nourished the two women's sympathy, had revived their fundamental antagonism. It was equally clear, however, that Mrs. Brown was making every effort to keep on good terms with Mrs. Glenn. That substantial benefits thereby accrued to her I had no doubt; but at least she kept up in Catherine's mind the illusion of the tie between them.

Mrs. Brown had certainly sorrowed for Stephen as profoundly as a woman of her kind could sorrow; more profoundly, indeed, than I had thought possible. Even now, when she spoke of him, her metallic voice broke, her metallic mask softened. On the rare occasions when I found myself alone with her (and I had an idea she saw to it that they were rare), she spoke so tenderly of Stephen, so affectionately of Mrs. Glenn that I could only suppose she knew nothing of my last talk with the poor fellow. If she had, she would almost certainly have tried to ensure my silence; unless, as I sometimes imagined, a supreme art led her to feign unawareness. But, as always when I speculated on Mrs. Brown, I ended up against a blank wall.

The exhibition of Stephen's pictures took place, and caused (I learned from Mrs. Glenn) a little flutter in the inner circle of connoisseurs. Mrs. Glenn deluged me with newspaper rhapsodies which she doubtless never imagined had been bought. But presently, as a result of the show, a new difference arose between the two women. The pictures had been sufficiently remarked for several purchasers to present themselves, and their offers were so handsome that Mrs. Brown thought they should be accepted. After all, Stephen would have regarded the sale of the pictures as the best proof of his success, if they remained hidden away at Mrs. Glenn's, she, who had the custody of his name, was obviously dooming it to obscurity. Nevertheless she persisted in refusing. If selling her darling's pictures was the price of glory, then she must cherish his genius in secret. Could anyone imagine that she would ever part with a single stroke of his brush? She was his mother; no one else had a voice in the matter. I divined that the struggle between herself and Mrs. Brown had been not only sharp but prolonged, and marked by a painful interchange of taunts. 'If it hadn't been for me,' Mrs. Brown argued, 'the pictures would never have existed'; and 'If it hadn't been for me,' the other retorted, 'my Stephen would never have existed.' It ended – as I had foreseen – in the adoptive parents accepting from Mrs. Glenn a sum equivalent to the value at which they estimated the pictures. The quarrel quieted down, and a few months later Mrs. Glenn was remorsefully accusing herself of having been too hard on Chrissy.

So the months passed. With their passage news came to me more rarely; but I gathered from Mrs. Glenn's infrequent letters that she had been ill, and from her almost illegible writing that her poor hands were stiffening with rheumatism. Finally, a year later, a letter announced that the doctors had warned her against spending her winters in the damp climate of Paris, and that the apartment had been disposed of, and its contents (including, of course, Stephen's pictures) transported to a villa at Nice. The Browns had found the villa and managed the translation – with their usual kindness. After that there was a long silence.

It was not until over two years later that I returned to Europe; and as my short holiday was taken in winter and I meant to spend it in Italy, I took steamer directly to Villefranche. I had not announced my visit to Mrs. Glenn, I was not sure till the last moment of being able to get off; but that was not the chief cause of my silence. Though relations between the incongruous trio seemed to have become harmonious, it was not without apprehension that I had seen Mrs. Glenn leave New York with the Browns. She was old, she was tired and stricken; how long would it be before she became a burden to her beneficiaries? This was what I wanted to find out without giving them time to prepare themselves or their companion for my visit. Mrs. Glenn had written that she wished very particularly to see me, and had begged me to let her know if there were a chance of my coming abroad; but though this increased my anxiety it strengthened my resolve to arrive unannounced, and I merely replied that she could count on seeing me as soon as I was able to get away.

Though some months had since gone by I was fairly sure of finding her still at Nice, for in the newspapers I had bought on landing I had lit on several allusions to Mrs. and Mrs. Boydon Brown. Apparently the couple had an active press agent, for an attentive world was daily supplied with a minute description of Mrs. 'Boy' Brown's casino toilets, the value of the golf and pigeon-shooting cups offered by Mr. 'Boy' Brown to various fashionable sporting clubs, and the names of the titled guests whom they entertained at the local 'Lidos' and 'Jardins Fleuris.' I wondered how much the chronicling of these events was costing Mrs. Glenn, but reminded myself that it was part of the price she had to pay for the hours of communion over Stephen's little socks. At any rate it proved that my old friend was still in the neighbourhood; and the next day I set out to find her.

I waited till the afternoon, on the chance of her being alone at the hour when mundane affairs were most likely to engage the Browns; but when my taxi driver had brought me to the address I had given him I found a locked garden gate and a shuttered house. The sudden fear of some new calamity seized me. My first thought was that Mrs. Glenn must have died; yet if her death had occurred before my sailing I could hardly have failed to hear of it, and if it was more recent I must have seen it announced in the papers I had read since landing. Besides, if the Browns had so lately lost their benefactress they would hardly have played such a part in the social chronicles I had been studying. There was no particular reason why a change of address should portend tragedy; and when at length a reluctant portress appeared in answer to my ringing she said, yes, if it was the Americans I was after, I was right: they had moved away a week ago. Moved – and where to? She shrugged and declared she didn't know; but probably not far, she thought, with the old white-haired lady so ill and helpless.

'Ill and helpless – then why did they move?'

She shrugged again. 'When people don't pay their rent, they have to move don't they? When they don't even settle with the butcher and baker before they go, or with the laundress who was fool enough to do their washing – and it's I who speak to you, Monsieur!'

This was worse than I had imagined. I produced a bank note, and in return the victimized concierge admitted that she had secured the fugitive's new address – though they were naturally not anxious to have it known. As I had surmised, they had taken refuge within the kindly bounds of the principality of Monaco; and the taxi carried me to a small shabby hotel in one of the steep streets above the Casino. I could imagine nothing less in harmony with Catherine Glenn or her condition than to be ill and unhappy in such a place. My only consolation was that now perhaps there might be an end to the disastrous adventure. 'After all,' I thought, as I looked up at the cheerless front of the hotel, 'if the catastrophe has come the Browns can't have any reason for hanging on to her.'

A red-faced lady with a false front and false teeth emerged from the back office to receive me.

Madame Glenn – Madame Brown? Oh, yes; they were staying at the hotel – they were both upstairs now, she believed. Perhaps Monsieur was the gentleman that Madame Brown was expecting? She had left word that if he came he was to go up without being announced.

I was inspired to say that I was that gentleman; at which the landlady rejoined that she was sorry the lift was out of order, but that I would find the ladies at number 5 on the third floor. Before she had finished I was halfway up.

A few steps down an unventilated corridor brought me to number 5; but I did not have to knock, for the door was ajar – perhaps in expectation of the other gentleman. I pushed it open, and entered a small plushy sitting room, with faded mimosa in ornate vases, newspapers and cigarette ends scattered on the dirty carpet, and a bronzed-over plaster Bayadère posturing before the mantelpiece mirror. If my first glance took such sharp note of these details it is because they seemed almost as much out of keeping with Catherine Glenn as the table laden with gin and bitters, empty cocktail glasses and disks of sodden lemon.

It was not the first time it had occurred to me that I was partly responsible for Mrs. Glenn's unhappy situation. The growing sense of that responsiblity had been one of my reasons for trying to keep an eye on her, for wanting her to feel that in case of need she could count on me. But on the whole my conscience had not been oppressed. The impulse which had made me exact from Stephen the promise never to undeceive her had necessarily governed my own conduct. I had only to recall Catherine Glenn as I had first known her to feel sure that, after all, her life had been richer and deeper than if she had spent it, childless and purposeless, in the solemn upholstery of her New York house. I had had nothing to do with her starting on her strange quest; but I was certain that in what had followed she had so far found more happiness than sorrow.

But now? As I stood in that wretched tawdry room I wondered if I had not laid too heavy a burden on my conscience in keeping the truth from her. Suddenly I said to myself: 'The time has come – whatever happens I must get her away from these people.' But then I remembered how Stephen's death had drawn the two ill-sorted women together, and wondered if to destroy that tie would not now be the crowning cruelty.

I was still uneasily deliberating when I heard a voice behind the door opposite the one by which I had entered. The room beyond must have been darkened, for I had not noticed before that this door was also partly open. 'Well, have you had your nap?' a woman's voice said irritably. 'Is there something you want before I go out? I told you that the man who's going to arrange for the loan is coming for me. He'll be here in a minute.' The voice was Mrs. Brown's, but so sharpened and altered that at first I had not known it. 'This is how she speaks when she thinks there's no one listening,' I thought.

I caught an indistinct murmur in reply; then the rattle of drawnback curtain rings; then Mrs. Brown continuing: 'Well, you may as well sign the letter now. Here it is – you've only got to write your name. . . . Your glasses? I don't know where your glasses are – you're always dropping your things about. I'm sorry, I can't keep a maid to wait on you – but there's nothing in this letter you need be afraid of. I've told you before that it's only a formality. Boy's told you so too, hasn't he? I don't suppose you mean to suggest that we're trying to do you out of your money, do you? We've got to have enough to keep going. Here, let me hold your hand while you sign. My hand's shaky too . . . it's all this beastly worry. . . . Don't you imagine you're the only person who's had a bad time of it. . . . Why, what's the matter? Why are you pushing me away – ?'

Till now I had stood motionless, unabashed by the fact that I was eavesdropping. I was ready enough to stoop to that if there was no other way of getting at the truth. But at the question: 'Why are you pushing me away?' I knocked hurriedly at the door of the inner room.

There was a silence after my knock. 'There he is! You'll have to sign now,' I heard Mrs. Brown exclaim; and I opened the door and went in. The room was a bedroom; like the other, it was untidy and shabby. I noticed a stack of canvases, framed and unframed, piled up against the wall. In an armchair near the window Mrs. Glenn was seated. She was wrapped in some sort of dark dressing gown, and a lace cap covered her white hair. The face that looked out from it had still the same carven beauty; but its texture had dwindled from marble to worn ivory. Her body too had shrunk, so that, low in her chair, under her loose garments, she seemed to have turned into a little broken doll. Mrs. Brown on the contrary, perhaps by contrast, appeared large and almost towering. At first glance I was more startled by the change in her appearance than in Mrs. Glenn's. The latter had merely followed more quickly than I had hoped she would, the natural decline of the years; whereas Mrs. Brown seemed like another woman. It was not only that she had grown stout and heavy, or that her complexion had coarsened so noticeably under the skillful make-up. In spite of her good clothes and studied coiffure there was something haphazard and untidy in her appearance. Her hat, I noticed, had slipped a little sideways on her smartly waved head, her bright shallow eyes looked blurred and red, and she held herself with a sort of vacillating erectness. Gradually the incredible fact was borne in on me; Mrs. Brown had been drinking.

'Why, where on earth – ?' she broke out, bewildered, as my identity dawned on her. She put up a hand to straighten her hat, and in doing so dragged it over too far on the other side.

'I beg your pardon. I was told to come to number 5, and as there was no one in the sitting room I knocked on this door.'

'Oh, you knocked? I didn't hear you knock,' said Mrs. Brown suspiciously; but I had no ears for her, for my old friend had also recognized me, and was holding out her trembling hands. 'I knew you'd come – I said you'd come!' she cried out to me.

Mrs. Brown laughed. 'Well, you've said he would often enough. But it's taken some time for it to come true.'

'I knew you'd come,' Mrs. Glenn repeated, and I felt her hand pass tremblingly over my hair as I stooped to kiss her.

'Lovers' meeting!' Mrs. Brown tossed at us with an unsteady gaiety; then she leaned against the door, and stood looking on ironically. 'You didn't expect to find us in this palatial abode, did you?'

'No. I went to the villa first.'

Mrs. Glenn's eyes dwelt on me softly. I sat down beside her, and she put her hand in mine. Her withered fingers trembled incessantly.

'Perhaps,' Mrs. Brown went on, 'if you'd come sooner you might have arranged things so that we could have stayed there. I'm powerless – I can't do anything with her. The fact that for years I looked after the child she deserted weighs nothing with her. She doesn't seem to think she owes us anything.'

Mrs. Glenn listened in silence, without looking at her accuser. She kept her large sunken eyes fixed on mine. 'There's no money left,' she said when the other ended.

'No money! No money! That's always the tune nowadays. There

was always plenty of money for her precious – money for all his whims and fancies, for journeys, for motors, for doctors, for – well, what's the use of going on? But not that there's nobody left but Boy and me, who slaved for her darling for years, who spent our last penny on him when his mother'd forgotten his existence – now there's nothing left! Now she can't afford anything; now she won't even pay her own bills; now she'd sooner starve herself to death than let us have what she owes us. . . .'

'My dear – my dear.' Mrs. Glenn murmured, her eyes still on mine.

'Oh, don't "my dear" me,' Mrs. Brown retorted passionately. 'What you mean is: "How can you talk like that before him?" I suppose you think I wish he hadn't come. Well, you never were more mistaken, I'm glad he's here; I'm glad he's found out where you're living, and how you're living. Only this time I mean him to hear our side of the story instead of only yours.'

Mrs. Glenn pressed my hand in her twitching fingers. 'She wants me to sign a paper. I don't understand.'

'You don't understand? Didn't Boy explain it to you? You said you understood then.' Mrs. Brown turned to me with a shrug. 'These whims and capers . . . all I want is money enough to pay the bills. . . . so that we're not turned out of this hole too. . . .'

'There is no money,' Mrs. Glenn softly reiterated.

My heart stood sill. The scene must at all costs be ended, yet I could think of no way of silencing the angry woman. At length I said: 'If you'll leave me for a little while with Mrs. Glenn perhaps she'll be able to tell me – '

'How's she to tell you what she says she doesn't understand herself? If I leave her with you all she'll tell you is lies about us – I found that out long ago.' Mrs. Brown took a few steps in my direction, and then, catching at the window curtain, looked at me with a foolish laugh. 'Not that I'm pining for her society. I have a good deal of it in the long run. But you'll excuse me for saying that, as far as this matter is concerned, it's entirely between Mrs. Glenn and me.'

I tightened my hold on Mrs. Glenn's hand, and sat looking at Mrs. Brown in the hope that a silent exchange of glances might lead farther than the vain bandying of arguments. For a moment she seemed dominated; I began to think she had read in my eyes the warning I had tried to put there. If there was any money left I might be able to get it from Catherine after her own attempts had failed; that was what I was trying to remind her of, and what she understood my looks were saying. Once before I had done the trick; supposing she were to trust me to try again? I saw that she wavered; but her brain was not alert, as it had been on that other occasion. She continued to stare at me through a blur of drink and anger; I could see her thoughts clutching uneasily at my suggestion and then losing their hold on it. 'Oh, we all know you think you're God Almighty!' she broke out with a contemptuous toss.

'I think I could help you if I could have a quiet talk with Mrs. Glenn.'

'Well, you can have your quiet talk.' She looked about her, and pulling up a chair plumped down into it heavily. 'I'd love to hear what you've got to say to each other,' she declared.

Mrs. Glenn's hand began to shake again. She turned her head toward Mrs. Brown. 'My dear, I should like to see my friend alone.'

'I should like! I should like! I daresay you would. It's always been what *you'd* like – but now it's going to be what I choose. And I choose to assist at the conversation between Mrs. Glenn and Mr. Norcutt, instead of letting them quietly say horrors about me behind my back.'

'Oh, Chrissy – ' my old friend murmured; then she turned to me and said, 'You'd better come back another day.'

Mrs. Brown looked at me with a sort of feeble cunning. 'Oh, you needn't send him away, I've told you my friend's coming – he'll be here in a minute. If you'll sign that letter I'll take it to the bank with him, and Mr. Norcutt can stay here and tell you all the news. Now wouldn't that be nice and cozy?' she concluded coaxingly.

Looking into Mrs. Glenn's pale frightened face I was on the point of saying: 'Well, sign it then, whatever it is – anything to get her to go.' But Mrs. Glenn straightened her drooping shoulders and repeated softly: 'I can't sign it.'

A flush rose to Mrs. Brown's forehead. 'You can't? That's final, is it?' She turned to me. 'It's all money she owed us, mind you – money we've advanced to her – in one way or another. Every penny of it. And now she sits there and says she won't pay us!'

Mrs. Glenn, twisting her fingers into mine, gave a barely audible laugh. 'Now he's here I'm safe,' she said.

The crimson of Mrs. Brown's face darkened to purple. Her lower lip trembled and I saw she was struggling for words that her dimmed brain could not supply. 'God Almighty – you think he's God Almighty!' She evidently felt the inadequacy of this, for she stood up suddenly, and coming close to Mrs. Glenn's armchair, stood looking down on her in impotent anger. 'Well, I'll show you – ' She turned to me, moved by another impulse. 'You know well enough you could make her sign if you chose to.'

My eyes and Mrs. Brown's met again. Hers were saying: 'It's your last chance – it's *her* last chance. I warn you – ' and mine replying: 'Nonsense, you can't frighten us, you can't even frighten *her* while I'm here. And if she doesn't want to sign you shan't force her to. I have something up my sleeve that would shut you up in five seconds if you knew.'

She kept her thick stare on mine till I felt as if my silent signal must have penetrated it. But she said nothing, and at last I exclaimed: 'You know well enough the risk you're running – '

Perhaps I had better not have spoken. But that dumb dialogue was getting on my nerves. If she wouldn't see, it was time to make her –

Ah, she saw now – she saw fast enough! My words seemed to have cleared the last fumes from her brain. She gave me back my look with one almost as steady; then she laughed.

'The risk I'm running? Oh, that's it, is it? That's the pull you thought you had over me? Well I'm glad you know – and I'm glad to tell you that I've known all along that you knew. I'm sick and tired of all the humbug – if she won't sign I'm going to tell her everything myself. So now the cards are on the table, and you can take your choice. It's up to you. The risk's on your side now!'

The unaccountable woman – drunkenly incoherent a moment ago, and now hitting the nail on the head with such fiendish precision! I sat silent, meditating her hideous challenge without knowing how to meet it. And then I became aware that a quiver had passed over Mrs. Glenn's face, which had become smaller and more ivory-yellow than before. She leaned towards me as if Mrs. Brown, who stood close above us, could not hear what we were saying.

'What is it she means to tell me? I don't care unless it's something bad about Stevie. And it couldn't be that, could it? How does she know? No one can come between a son and his mother.'

Mrs. Brown gave one of her sudden laughs. 'A son and his mother? I daresay not! Only I'm just about fed up with having you think you're his mother.'

It was the one thing I had not foreseen – that she would possess herself of my threat and turn it against me. The risk was too deadly; and so no doubt she would have felt if she had been in a state to measure it. She was not; and there lay the peril.

Mrs. Glenn sat quite still after the other's outcry, and I hoped it had blown past her like some mere rag of rhetoric. Then I saw that the meaning of the words had reached her, but without carrying conviction. She glanced at me with the flicker of a smile. 'Now she says I'm not his mother – !' It's her last round of ammunition; but don't be afraid – it won't make me sign, the smile seemed to whisper to me.

Mrs. Brown caught the unspoken whisper, and her exasperation rushed to meet it. 'You don't believe me? I knew you wouldn't! Well, ask your friend here; ask Mr. Norcutt; you always believe everything he says. He's known the truth for ever so long – long before Stephen died he knew he wasn't your son.'

I jumped up, as if to put myself between my friends and some bodily harm: but she held fast to my hand with her clinging twitching fingers. 'As if she knew what it is to have a son! All those long months when he's one with you. . . . *Mothers* know,' she said.

'Mothers, yes! I don't say you didn't have a son and desert him. I say that son wasn't Stephen. Don't you suppose I know? Sometimes I've wanted to laugh in your face at the way you went on about him . . . Sometimes I used to have to rush out of the room, just to have my laugh out by myself. . . .'

Mrs. Brown stopped with a gasp, as if the fury of the outburst had shaken her back to soberness, and she saw for the first time what she had done. Mrs. Glenn sat with her head bowed; her hand had grown cold in mine. I looked at Mrs. Brown and said: 'Now won't you leave us? I suppose there's nothing left to say.'

She blinked at me through her heavy lids; I saw she was wavering. But at the same moment Mrs. Glenn's clutch tightened; she drew me down to her, and looked at me out of her deep eyes. 'What does she mean when she says you knew about Stevie?'

I pressed her hand without answering. All my mind was concentrated on the effort of silencing my antagonist and getting her out of the room. Mrs. Brown leaned in the window frame and looked down on us. I could see that she was dismayed at what she had said, and yet exultant; and my business was to work on the dismay before the exultation mastered it. But Mrs. Glenn still held me down; her eyes seemed to be forcing their gaze into me. 'Is it true?' she asked almost inaudibly.

'True?' Mrs. Brown burst out. 'Ask him to swear to you it's not true – see what he looks like then! He was in the conspiracy, you old simpleton.'

Mrs. Glenn's head straightened itself again on her weak neck: her face wore a singular majesty. 'You were my friend – ' she appealed to me.

'I've always been your friend.'

'Then I don't have to believe her.'

Mrs. Brown seemed to have been gathering herself up for a last onslaught. She saw that I was afraid to try to force her from the room, and the discovery gave her a sense of hazy triumph, as if all that was left to her was to defy me. 'Tell her I'm lying – why don't you tell her I'm lying?' she taunted me.

I knelt down by my old friend and put my arm about her. 'Will you come away with me now – at once? I'll take you wherever you want to go. . . . I'll look after you. . . . I'll always look after you.'

Mrs. Glenn's eyes grew wider. She seemed to weigh my words till their sense penetrated her; then she said, in the same low voice: 'It is true, then?'

'Come away with me; come away with me,' I repeated.

I felt her trying to rise; but her feet failed under her and she sank back. 'Yes, take me away from her,' she said.

Mrs. Brown laughed. 'Oh, that's it, is it? "Come away from that

bad woman, and I'll explain everything, and make it all right" . . .
Why don't you adopt *him* instead of Steve? I dare say that's what he's
been after all the time. That's the reason he was so determined we
shouldn't have your money. . . .' She drew back, and pointed to the
door. 'You can go with him – who's to prevent you? I couldn't if I
wanted to. I see now it's for him we've been nursing your precious
millions. . . . Well, go with him, and he'll tell you the whole
story. . . .' A strange secretive smile stole over her face. 'All except
one bit . . . there's one bit he doesn't know; but *you're* going to know
it now.'

She stepped nearer, and I held up my hand; but she hurried on, her
eyes on Mrs. Glenn. 'What he doesn't know is why we fixed the thing
up. Steve wasn't my adopted son any more than he was your real one.
Adopted son, indeed! How old do you suppose I am? He was my lover.
There – do you understand? My lover! That's why we faked up that
ridiculous adoption story, and all the rest of it – because he was desperately ill, and down and out, and we hadn't a penny, the three of us,
and I had to have money for him, and didn't care how I got it, didn't
care for anything on earth but seeing him well again, and happy.' She
stopped and drew a panting breath. 'There – I'd rather have told you
that than have your money. I'd rather you should know what Steve
was to me than think any longer that you owned him. . . .'

I was still kneeling by Mrs. Glenn, my arm about her. Once I felt
her heart give a great shake; then it seemed to stop altogether. Her eyes
were no longer turned to me, but fixed in a wide stare on Mrs. Brown.
A tremor convulsed her face; then, to my amazement, it was smoothed
into an expression of childish serenity, and a faint smile, half playful,
half ironic, stole over it.

She raised her hand and pointed tremulously to the other's
disordered headgear. 'My dear – your hat's crooked,' she said.

For a moment I was bewildered; then I saw that, very gently, she
was at last returning the taunt that Mrs. Brown had so often addressed
to her. The shot fired, she leaned back against me with the satisfied
sigh of a child; and immediately I understood that Mrs. Brown's blow
had gone wide. A pitiful fate had darkened Catherine Glenn's intelligence at the exact moment when to see clearly would have been the
final anguish.

Mrs. Brown understood too. She stood looking at us doubtfully;
then she said in a tone of feeble defiance: 'Well, I had to tell her.'

She turned and went out of the room, and I continued to kneel by
Mrs. Glenn. Her eyes had gradually clouded, and I doubted if she still
knew me; but her lips nursed their soft smile, and I saw that she must
have been waiting for years to launch that little shaft at her enemy.

Charm Incorporated

***

'JIM! I'm afraid . . . I'm dreadfully afraid. . . .'

James Targatt's wife knelt by his armchair, the dark hair flung off her forehead, her dark eyes large with tears as they yearned up at him throught those incredibly long lashes.

'Afraid? Why – what's the matter?' he retorted, annoyed at being disturbed in the slow process of digesting the dinner he had just eaten at Nadeja's last new restaurant – a Ukrainian one this time. For they went to a different restaurant every night, usually, at Nadeja's instigation, hunting out the most exotic that New York at the high tide of its prosperity had to offer. 'That sturgeon stewed in cream – ' he thought wearily. 'Well, what is it?'

'It's Boris, darling. I'm afraid Boris is going to marry a film star. That Halma Hoboe, you know . . . she's the greatest of them all. . . .' By this time the tears were running down Nadeja's cheeks. Targatt averted his mind from the sturgeon long enough to wonder if he would ever begin to understand his wife, much less his wife's family.

'Halma Hoboe? Well, why on earth shouldn't he? Has she got her divorce from the last man all right?'

'Yes, of course.' Nadeja was still weeping. 'But I thought perhaps you'd mind Boris's leaving us. He will have to stay out at Hollywood now, he says. And I shall miss my brother so dreadfully. Hollywood's very far from New York – no? We shall miss Boris, shan't we, James?'

'Yes, yes. Of course. Great boy, Boris! Funny to be related to a movie star. "My sister-in-law, Halma Hoboe." Well, as long as he couldn't succeed on the screen himself – ' said Targatt, suddenly sounding a latent relief, which came to the surface a moment later. '*She'll* have to pay his bills now,' he muttered, too low for his wife to hear. He reached out for a second cigar, let his head sink back comfortably against the chair cushions, and thought to himself: 'Well, perhaps the luck's turning. . . .' For it was the first time, in the eight years of his marriage to Nadeja, that any information imparted to him concerning her family had not immediately led up to his having to draw another check.

271

• II •

JAMES TARGATT had always been on his guard against any form of sentimental weakness; yet now, as he looked back on his life, he began to wonder if one occasion on which he had been false to this principle might not turn out to be his best stroke of business.

He had not had much difficulty in guarding himself against marriage. He had never felt an abstract yearning for fatherhood, or believed that to marry an old-fashioned affectionate girl, who hated society, and wanted to stay home and darn and scrub, would really help an ambitious man in his career. He thought it was probably cheaper in the end to have your darning and scrubbing done for you by professionals, even if they came from one of those extortionate valeting establishments that before the depression, used to charge a dollar a minute for such services. And eventually he found a stranded German widow who came to him on starvation wages, fed him well and inexpensively, and kept the flat looking as fresh and shiny as a racing yacht. So there was no earthly obligation for him to marry; and when he suddenly did so, no question of expediency had entered into the arrangement.

He supposed afterward that what had happened to him was what people called falling in love. He had never allowed for that either, and even now he was not sure if it was the right name for the knock-down blow dealt to him by his first sight of Nadeja. Her name told you her part of the story clearly enough. She came straight out of that struggling mass of indistinguishable human misery that Targatt called 'Wardrift.' One day – he still wondered how, for he was fiercely on his guard against such intrusions – she had forced her way into his office, and tried to sell him (of all things!) a picture painted by her brother Serge. They were all starving, she said; and very likely it was true. But that had not greatly moved him. He had heard the same statement made too often by too many people, and it was too painfully connected in his mind with a dreaded and rapidly increasing form of highway robbery called 'Appeals.' Besides, Targatt's imagination was not particularly active, and as he was always sure of a good meal himself, it never much disturbed him to be told that others were not. So he couldn't to this day have told you how it came about that he bought Serge's picture on the spot, and married Nadeja a few weeks afterward. He had been knocked on the head – sandbagged; a regular hold-up. That was the only way to describe it.

Nadeja made no attempt to darn or scrub for him – which was perhaps just as well, as he liked his comforts. On the contrary, she made friends at once with the German widow, and burdened that industrious woman with the additional care of her own wardrobe, which was negligible before her marriage, but increased rapidly after she became Mrs. Targatt. There was a second servant's room above the flat, and Targatt rather reluctantly proposed that they should get in a girl to help Hilda; but Nadeja said, no, she didn't believe Hilda would care for that; and the room would do so nicely for Paul, her younger brother, the one who was studying to be a violinist.

Targatt hated music, and suffered acutely (for a New Yorker) from persistently recurring noises; but Paul, a nice boy, also with long-lashed eyes, moved into the room next to Hilda's and practised the violin all day and most of the night. The room was directly over that which Targatt now shared with Nadeja – and of which all but the space occupied by his shaving stand had by this time become her exclusive property. But he bore with Paul's noise, and it was Hilda who struck. She said she loved music that gave her *Heimweh*, but this kind only kept her awake; and to Targatt's horror she announced her intention of leaving at the end of the month.

It was the biggest blow he had ever had since he had once – and only once – been on the wrong side of the market. He had no time to hunt for another servant, and was sure Nadeja would not know how to find one. Nadeja, when he broke the news to her, acquiesced in this view of her incapacity. 'But why do we want a servant? I could never see,' she said. 'And Hilda's room would do very nicely for my sister Olga, who is learning to be a singer. She and Paul could practice together – '

'Oh, Lord,' Targatt interjected.

'And we could all go out to restaurants; a different one every night: it's much more fun, isn't it? And there are people who come in and clean – no? Hilda was a robber – I didn't want to tell you, but . . .'

Within a week the young Olga, whose eyelashes were even longer than Paul's, was settled in the second servant's room, and within a month Targatt had installed a grand piano in his own drawing room, (where it took up all the space left by Nadeja's divan), so that Nadeja could accompany Olga when Paul was not available.

• III •

TARGATT had never, till that moment, thought much about Nadeja's family. He understood that his father-in-law had been a Court dignitary of high standing, with immense landed estates and armies of slaves – no, he believed they didn't have slaves, or serfs, or whatever they called them, any longer in those outlandish countries east or south of Russia. Targatt was not strong on geography. He did not own an atlas, and had never yet had time to go to the Public Library and look up his father-in-law's native heath. In fact, he had never had time to read, or to think consecutively on any subject but money-making; he knew only

that old man Kouradjine had been a big swell in some country in which
the Bolsheviks had confiscated everybody's property, and where the
women (and the young men too) apparently all had long eyelashes. But
that was all part of a vanished fairy tale; at present the old man was
only Number So-much on one Near East Relief list, while Paul and
Olga and the rest of them (Targatt wasn't sure even yet how many
there were) figured on similar lists, though on a more modest scale,
since they were supposedly capable of earning their own living. But
were they capable of it, and was there any living for them to earn?
That was what Targatt in the course of time began to ask himself.

Targatt was not a particularly sociable man; but in his bachelor
days, he had fancied inviting a friend to dine now and then, chiefly to
have the shine of his mahogany table marveled at, and Hilda's *Wiener-
schnitzel* praised. This was all over now. His meals were all taken in
restaurants – a different one each time; and they were usually shared
with Paul, Olga, Serge (the painter) and the divorced sister, Katinka,
who had three children and a refugee lover, Dmitri.

At first this state of affairs was very uncomfortable, and even
painful, for Targatt; but since it seemed inevitable he adjusted himself
to it, and buried his private cares in an increased business activity.

His activity was, in fact, tripled by the fact that it was no longer
restricted to his own personal affairs, but came more and more to
include such efforts as organizing an exhibition of Serge's pictures,
finding the funds for Paul's violin tuition, trying to make it worth
somebody's while to engage Olga for a concert tour, pushing Katinka
into a saleswoman's job at a fashionable dressmaker's, and persuading
a friend in a bank to recommend Dmitri as interpreter to foreign clients.
All this was difficult enough, and if Targatt had not been sustained by
Nadeja's dogged optimism his courage might have failed him; but the
crowning problem was how to deal with the youngest brother, Boris,
who was just seventeen, and had the longest eyelashes of all. Boris was
too old to be sent to school, too young to be put into a banker's or
broker's office, and too smilingly irresponsible to hold the job for
twenty-four hours if it had been offered to him. Targatt, for three years
after his marriage, had had only the vaguest ideas of Boris's existence,
for he was not among the first American consignment of the family.
But suddenly he drifted in alone, from Odessa or Athens, and joined
the rest of the party at the restaurant. By this time the Near East Relief
Funds were mostly being wound up, and in spite of all Targatt's efforts
it was impossible to get financial aid for Boris, so for the first months
he just lolled in a pleasant aimless way on Nadeja's divan; and as he
was very particular about the quality of his cigarettes, and consumed a
large supply daily, Targatt for the first time began to regard one of
Nadeja's family with a certain faint hostility.

Boris might have been less of a trial if, by the time he came, Targatt had been able to get the rest of the family on their legs; but, however often he repeated this attempt, they invariably toppled over on him. Serge could not sell his pictures, Paul could not get an engagement in an orchestra, Olga had given up singing for dancing, so that her tuition had to begin all over again; and to think of Dmitri and Katinka, and Katinka's three children, was not conducive to repose at the end of a hard day in Wall Street.

Yet in spite of everything Targatt had never really been able to remain angry for more than a few moments with any member of the Kouradjine group. For some years this did not particularly strike him; he was given neither to self-analysis nor the dissection of others, except where business dealings were involved. He had been taught, almost in the nursery, to discern, and deal with, the motives determining a given course in business; but he knew no more of human nature's other mainsprings than if the nursery were still his habitat. He was vaguely conscious that Nadeja was aware of this, and that it caused her a faint amusement. Once, when they had been dining with one of his business friends, and the latter's wife, an ogling bore, had led the talk to the shopworn question of how far mothers ought to enlighten their little girls on – well you know . . . just *how much* ought they to be taught? That was the delicate point, Mrs. Targatt, wasn't it? – Nadeja, thus cornered, had met the question with a gaze of genuine bewilderment. 'Taught? Do you have to be *taught*? I think it is Nature who will tell them – no? But myself I should first teach dressmaking and cooking,' she said with her shadowy smile. And now, reviewing the Kouradjine case, Targatt suddenly thought. 'But that's it! Nature *does* teach the Kouradjines. It's a gift like a tenor voice. The thing is to know how to make the best use of it – ' and he fell to musing on this newly discovered attribute. It was – what? Charm? Heaven forbid! The very word made his flesh creep with memories of weary picnics and wearier dinners where, with pink food in fluted papers, the discussion of 'What is Charm?' had formed the staple diet. 'I'd run a mile from a woman with charm; and so would most men,' Targatt thought with a retrospective shudder. And he tried, for the first time, to make a conscious inventory of Nadeja's attributes.

She was not beautiful; he was certain of that. He was not good at seeing people, really seeing them, even when they were just before his eyes, much less at visualizing them in absence. When Nadeja was away all he could ever evoke of her was a pleasant blur. But he wasn't such a blind bat as not to know when a woman was beautiful. Beauty, however, was made to look at, not to live with; he had never wanted to marry a beautiful woman. And Nadeja wasn't clever, either; not in talk, that is. (And that, he mused, was certainly one of her qualities.) With regard to the other social gifts, so-called: cards, for instance? Well, he knew she and Katinka were not above fishing out an old pack and telling their fortunes, when they thought he wasn't noticing; but anything as scientific as bridge frightened her, and she had the good sense not to try to learn. So much for society; and as for the home – well, she could hardly be called a good housekeeper, he supposed. But remembering his mother, who had been accounted a paragon in that line, he gave thanks for this deficiency of Nadeja's also. Finally he said to himself: 'I seem to like her for all the things she is *not*.' This was not satisfactory; but he could do no better. 'Well, somehow, she fits into the cracks,' he concluded; and inadequate as this also sounded, he felt it might turn out to be a clue to the Kouradjines. Yes, they certainly fitted in; squeezing you a little, overlapping you a good deal, but never – and there was the point – sticking into you like the proverbial thorn, or crowding you uncomfortably, or for any reason making you wish they weren't there.

This fact, of which he had been dimly conscious from the first, arrested his attention now because he had a sudden glimpse of its business possibilities. Little Boris had only had to borrow a hundred dollars of him for the trip to Hollywood, and behold little Boris was already affianced to the world's leading movie star! In the light of this surprising event Targatt suddenly recalled that Katinka, not long before, had asked him if he wouldn't give Dmitri, who had not been a success at the bank, a letter recommending him for some sort of employment in the office of a widowed millionaire who was the highest light on Targatt's business horizon. Targatt had received the suggestion without enthusiasm. 'Your sister's crazy,' he said to Nadeja. 'How can I recommend that fellow to a man like Bellamy? Has he ever had any business training?'

'Well, we know Mr. Bellamy's looking for a bookkeeper, because he asked you if you knew of one,' said Nadeja.

'Yes; but what are Dmitri's qualifications? Does he know anything whatever about bookkeeping?'

'No; not yet. But he says perhaps he could buy a little book about it.'

'Oh, Lord – ' Targatt groaned.

'Even so, you don't think you could recommend him, darling?'

'No; I couldn't, I'm afraid.'

Nadeja did not insist; she never insisted. 'I've found out a new restaurant, where they make much better blinys. Shall I tell them all to meet us there tonight at half-past eight?' she suggested.

Now, in the light of Boris's news, Targatt began to think this conversation over. Dmitri was an irredeemable fool; but Katinka – what about giving the letter for old Bellamy to Katinka? Targatt didn't see exactly how he could word it; but he had an idea that Nadeja would tell him. Those were the ways in which she was really clever. A few days later he asked: 'Has Dmitri got a job yet?'

She looked at him in surprise. 'No, as you couldn't recommend him he didn't buy the book.'

'Oh, damn the book. . . . See here, Nadeja; supposing I were to give Katinka a letter for old Bellamy?'

He had made the suggestion with some embarrassment, half expecting that he would have to explain. But not to Nadeja. 'Oh, darling, you always think of the right thing,' she answered, kissing him; and as he had foreseen she told him just how to word the letter.

'And I will lend her my silver fox to wear,' she added. Certainly the social education of the Kouradjines had been far more comprehensive than Targatt's.

Katinka went to see Mr. Bellamy, and when she returned she reported favourably on the visit. Nothing was as yet decided about Dmitri, as she had been obliged to confess that he had had no training as an accountant; but Mr. Bellamy had been very kind, and had invited her to come to his house some afternoon to see his pictures.

From this visit also Katinka came back well-pleased, though she seemed not to have accomplished anything further with regard to Dmitri. She had, however, been invited by Mr. Bellamy to dine and go to a play; and a few weeks afterward she said to Targatt and Nadeja: 'I think I will live with Mr. Bellamy. He has an empty flat that I could have, and he would furnish it beautifully.'

Though Targatt prided himself on an unprejudiced mind he winced slightly at this suggestion. It seemed cruel to Dmitri, and decidedly uncomfortable as far as Targatt and Nadeja were concerned.

'But, Katinka, if Bellamy's so gone on you, he ought to marry you,' he said severely.

Katinka nodded her assent. 'Certainly he ought. And I think he will, after I have lived with him a few months.'

This upset every single theory of Targatt's with regard to his own sex. 'But, my poor girl – if you go and live with a man first like . . . like any woman he could have for money, why on earth should he want to marry you afterward?'

Katinka looked at him calmly. Her eyelashes were not as long as Nadeja's, but her eyes were as full of wisdom. 'Habit,' she said simply, and in an instant Targatt's conventional world was in fragments at his feet. Who knew better than he did that if you once had the Kouradjine habit you couldn't be cured of it? He said nothing more, and sat back to watch what happened to Mr. Bellamy.

• IV •

MR. BELLAMY did not offer Dmitri a position as bookkeeper; but soon after his marriage to Katinka he took him into his house as social secretary. Targatt had a first movement of surprise and disapproval, but he saw that Nadeja did not share it. 'That's very nice,' she said. 'I was sure Katinka would not desert Dmitri. And Mr. Bellamy is so generous. He is going to adopt Katinka's three children.'

But it must not be thought that the fortunes of all the Kouradjines ran as smoothly. For a brief moment Targatt had imagined that the infatuated Bellamy was going to assume the charge of the whole tribe; but Wall Street was beginning to be uneasy, and Mr. Bellamy restricted his hospitality to Katinka's children and Dmitri, and, like many of the very rich, manifested no interest in those whose misfortunes did not immediately interfere with his own comfort. Thus vanished even the dream of a shared responsibility, and Targatt saw himself facing a business outlook decidedly less dazzling, and with a still considerable number of Kouradjines to provide for. Olga, in particular, was a cause of some anxiety. She was less adaptable, less suited to fitting into cracks, than the others, and her various experiments in song and dance had all broken down for lack of perseverance. But she was (at least so Nadeja thought) by far the best-looking of the family; and finally Targatt decided to pay for her journey to Hollywood, in the hope that Boris would put her in the way of becoming a screen star. This suggestion, however, was met by a telegram from Boris ominously dated from Reno: 'Don't send Olga am divorcing Halma.'

For the first time since his marriage Targatt felt really discouraged. Were there perhaps too many Kouradjines, and might the Kouradjine habit after all be beginning to wear thin? The family were all greatly perturbed by Boris's news, and when – after the brief interval required to institute and complete divorce proceedings against his film star – Boris left Reno and turned up in New York, his air of unperturbed good humor was felt to be unsuitable to the occasion. Nadeja, always hopeful, interpreted it as meaning that he was going to marry another and even richer star; but Boris said God forbid, and no more Hollywood for him. Katinka and Bellamy did not invite him to come and stay, and the upshot of it was that his bed was made up on the Targatts' drawing-room divan, while he shared the bathroom with Targatt and Nadeja.

Things dragged on in this way for some weeks, till one day Nadeja came privately to her husband. 'He has got three millions,' she whispered with wide eyes. 'Only yesterday was he sure. The check has come. Do you think, darling, she ought to have allowed him more?'

Targatt did not think so; he was inarticulate over Boris's achievement. 'What's he going to do with it?' he gasped.

'Well, I think first he will invest it, and then he will go to the Lido. There is a young girl there, I believe, that he is in love with. I knew Boris would not divorce for nothing. He is going there to meet her.'

Targatt could not disguise an impulse of indignation. Before investing his millions, was Boris not going to do anything for his family? Nadeja said she had thought of that too; but Boris said he had invested the money that morning, and of course there would be no interest coming in till the next quarter. And meanwhile he was so much in love that he had taken his passage for the following day on the 'Berengaria'. Targatt thought that only natural, didn't he?

Targatt swallowed his ire, and said, yes, he supposed it was natural enough. After all, if the boy had found a young girl he could really love and respect, and if he had the money to marry her and settle down, no one could blame him for rushing off to press his suit. And Boris rushed.

But meanwhile the elimination of two Kouradjines had not had the hoped-for effect of reducing the total number of the tribe. On the contrary, that total had risen; for suddenly three new members had appeared. One was an elderly and completely ruined Princess (a distant cousin, Nadeja explained) with whom old Kouradjine had decided to contract a tardy alliance, now that the rest of the family were provided for. 'He could do no less,' Katinka and Nadeja mysteriously agreed.) And the other, and more sensational, newcomers were two beautiful young creatures, known respectively to the tribe as Nick and Mouna, but whose difficulties at the passport office made it seem that there were legal doubts as to their remaining names. These difficulties, through Targatt's efforts, were finally overcome and, snatched from the jaws of Ellis Island, Nick and Mouna joyfully joined the party at another new restaurant, 'The Transcaucasian,' which Nadeja had recently discovered.

Targatt's immensely enlarged experience of human affairs left him in a little doubt as to the parentage of Nick and Mouna, and when Nadeja whispered to him one night (through the tumult of Boris's late bath next door): 'You see, poor Papa felt he could no longer fail to provide for them,' Targatt did not dream of asking why.

But he now had no less than seven Kouradjines more or less dependent on him, and the next night he sat up late and did some figuring and thinking. Even to Nadeja he could not explain in blunt language the result of this vigil; but he said to her the following day: 'What's become of that flat of Bellamy's that Katinka lived in before – '

'Why, he gave the lease to Katinka as a wedding present; but it seems that people are no more as rich as they were, and as it's such a very handsome flat, and the rent is high, the tenants can no longer afford to keep it – '

'Well,' said Targatt with sudden resolution, 'tell your sister if she'll make a twenty-five per cent cut on the rent I'll take over the balance of the lease.'

Nadeja gasped. 'Oh, James, you are an angel! But what do you think you could then do with it?'

Targatt threw back his shoulders. 'Live in it,' he recklessly declared.

• V •

IT was the first time (except when he had married Nadeja) that he had even been reckless; and there was no denying that he enjoyed the sensation. But he had not acted wholly for the sake of enjoyment; he had an ulterior idea. What that idea was he did not choose to communicate to anyone at present. He merely asked Katinka, who, under the tuition of Mr. Bellamy's experienced butler, had developed some rudimentary ideas of housekeeping, to provide Nadeja with proper servants, and try to teach her how to use them; and he then announced to Nadeja that he had made up his mind to do a little entertaining. He and Nadeja had already made a few fashionable acquaintances at the Bellamys', and these they proceeded to invite to the new flat, and to feed with exotic food, and stimulate with abstruse cocktails. At these dinners Targatt's new friends met the younger and lovelier of the Kouradjines: Paul, Olga, Nick and Mouna, and they always went away charmed with the encounter.

Considerable expense was involved by this new way of life; and still more when Nadeja, at Targatt's instigation, invited Olga, Nick and Mouna to come and live with them. Nadeja was overcome with gratitude at this suggestion; but her gratitude, like all her other emotions, was so exquisitely modulated that it fell on Targatt like the gentle dew from heaven, merely fostering in him a new growth of tenderness. But still Targatt did not explain himself. He had his idea, and knowing that Nadeja would not bother him with questions he sat back quietly and waited, though Wall Street was growing more and more unsettled, and there had been no further news of Boris, and Paul and Olga were still without a job.

The Targatts' little dinners, and Nadeja's exclusive cocktail parties, began to be the rage in a set far above the Bellamys'. There were almost always one or two charming young Kouradjines present; but they were now so sought after in smartest Park Avenue and gayest Long Island that Targatt and Nadeja had to make sure of securing their presence beforehand, so there was never any danger of there being too many on the floor at once.

On the contrary, there were occasions when they all simultaneously failed to appear; and on one of these evenings, Targatt, conscious that the party had not 'come off,' was about to vent his irritation against the absent Serge, when Nadeja said gently: 'I'm sorry Serge didn't tell you. But I think he was married today to Mrs. Leeper.'

'Mrs. Leeper? Not the Dazzle Tooth Paste woman he met at the Bellamys', who wanted him to decorate her ballroom?'

'Yes; but I think she did not after all want him to decorate her ballroom. And so she has married him instead.'

A year earlier Targatt would have had no word but an uncomprehending groan. But since then his education had proceeded by leaps and bounds, and now he simply said: 'I see – ' and turned back to his breakfast with a secret smile. He had received Serge's tailor's bill the day before, and had been rehearsing half the night what he was going to say to Serge when they met. But now he merely remarked: 'That woman has a two million dollar income,' and thought to himself that the experiment with the flat was turning out better than he could have imagined. If Serge could be disposed of so easily there was no cause to despair of Paul or Olga. 'Hasn't Mrs. Leeper a nephew?' he asked Nadeja; who, as if she had read his thought, replied regretfully: 'Yes, but I'm afraid he's married.'

'Oh, well – send Boris to talk to him!' Targatt jeered; and Nadeja, who never laughed, smiled a little and replied: 'Boris too will soon be married.' She handed her husband the morning papers, which he had not yet had time to examine, and he read, in glowing headlines, the announcement of the marriage in London of Prince Boris Kouradjine, son of Prince Peter Kouradjine, hereditary sovereign of Daghestan, and Chamberlain at the court of his late Imperial Majesty the Czar Nicholas, to Miss Mamie Guggins of Rapid Rise, Oklahoma. 'Boris has a little exaggerated our father's rank,' Nadeja commented; but Targatt said thoughtfully: 'No one can exaggerate the Guggins' fortune.' And Nadeja gave a quiet sigh.

It must not be supposed that this rise in the fortunes of the Kouradjines was of any direct benefit to Targatt. He had never expected that, or even hoped it. No Kouradjine had ever suggested making any return for the sums expended by Targatt in vainly educating and profitably dressing his irresistible in-laws; nor had Targatt's staggering restaurant bills been reduced by any offer of participation. Only the old Princess (as it was convenient, with so many young ones about, to call her when she was out of hearing) had said tearfully, on her wedding day: 'Believe me, my good James, what you have done for us all will not be forgotten when we return to Daghestan.' And she spoke with such genuine emotion, the tears were so softening to her tired magnificent eyes, that Targatt, at the moment, felt himself repaid.

Other and more substantial returns he did draw from his alliance with the Kouradjines; and it was the prospect of these which had governed his conduct. From the day when it had occurred to him to send Katinka to intercede with Mr. Bellamy, Targatt had never once swerved from his purpose. And slowly but surely he was beginning to reap his reward.

Mr. Bellamy, for instance, had not seen his way to providing for the younger Kouradjines; but he was ready enough to let Targatt in on the ground floor of one of those lucrative deals usually reserved for the already wealthy. Mrs. Leeper, in her turn, gave him the chance to buy a big block of Dazzle Tooth Paste shares on exceptional terms; and as fashion and finance became aware of the younger Kouradjines, and fell under their spell, Targatt's opportunities for making quick turnovers became almost limitless. And now a pleasant glow stole down his spine at the thought that all previous Kouradjine alliances paled before the staggering wealth of Boris's bride. 'Boris really does owe me a good turn,' he mused; but he had no expectation that it would be done with Boris's knowledge. The new Princess Boris was indeed induced to hand over her discarded wardrobe to Olga and Mouna, and Boris presented cigarette cases to his brothers and brother-in-law; but here his prodigalities ended. Targatt, however, was not troubled; for years he had longed to meet the great Mr. Guggins, and here he was, actually related to that gentleman's only child!

Mr. Guggins, when under the influence of domestic happiness or alcohol, was almost as emotional as the Kouradjines. On his return to New York, after the parting from his only child, he was met on the dock by Targatt and Nadeja, who suggested his coming to dine that night at a jolly new restaurant with all the other Kouradjines; and Mrs. Guggins was so much drawn to the old Princess, to whom she confided how difficult it was to get reliable window washers at Rapid Rise, that the next day Targatt, as he would have put it, had the old man in his pocket. Mr. Guggins stayed a week in New York, and when he departed Targatt knew enough about the Guggins industries to make some very useful reinvestments; and Mrs. Guggins carried off Olga as her social secretary.

• VI •

STIMULATED by these successive achievements Targatt's tardily developed imagination was growing like an Indian juggler's tree. He no longer saw any limits to what might be done with the Kouradjines. He had already found a post for the old Prince as New York representative of a leading firm of Paris picture dealers, Paul and Nick were professional dancers at fashionable nightclubs, and for the moment only Mouna, the lovely but difficult, remained on Targatt's mind and his payroll.

It was the first time in his life that Targatt had tasted the fruits of ease, and he found them surprisingly palatable. He was no longer young, it took him more time than of old to get around a golf course, and he occasionally caught himself telling his good stories twice over to the same listener. But life was at once exciting and peaceful, and he had to own that his interests had been immensely enlarged. All that, of course, he owed in the first instance to Nadeja. Poor Nadeja – she was not as young as she had been, either. She was still slender and supple, but there were little lines in the corners of her eyes, and a certain droop of the mouth. Others might not notice these symptoms, Targatt thought; but they had not escaped *him*. For Targett, once so unseeing in the presence of beauty, had now become an adept in appraising human flesh-and-blood, and smiled knowingly when his new friends commended Mouna's young charms, or inclined the balance in favor of the more finished Olga. There was nothing anyone could tell him now about the relative 'values' of the Kouradjines: he had them tabulated as if they were vintage wines, and it was a comfort to him to reflect that Nadeja was, after all, the one whose market value was least considerable. It was sheer luck – a part of his miraculous Kouradjine luck – that his choice had fallen on the one Kouradjine about whom there was never likely to be the least fuss or scandal; and after an exciting day in Wall Street, or a fatiguing struggle to extricate Paul or Mouna from some fresh scrape, he would sink back with satisfaction into his own unruffled domesticity.

There came a day, however, when he began to feel that the contrast between his wife and her sisters was too much to Nadeja's disadvantage. Was it because the others had smarter clothes – or, like Katinka, finer jewels? Poor Nadeja, he reflected, had never had any jewels since her engagement ring; and that was a shabby affair. Was it possible, Targatt conjectured, that as middle age approached she was growing dowdy, and needed the adventitious enhancements of dressmaker and beauty doctor? Half-sheepishly he suggested that she oughtn't to let herself be outdone by Katinka, who was two or three years her senior; and he reinforced the suggestion by a diamond chain from Cartier's and a good-humored hint that she might try Mrs. Bellamy's dressmaker.

Nadeja received the jewel with due raptures, and appeared at their next dinner in a gown which was favorably noticed by everyone present. Katinka said: 'Well, at last poor Nadeja is really *dressed*,' and Mouna sulked visibly, and remarked to her brother-in-law: 'If you want the right people to ask me about you might let me get a few clothes at Nadeja's place.'

All this was as it should be, and Targatt's satisfaction increased as he watched his wife's returning bloom. It seemed funny to him that, even on a sensible woman like Nadeja, clothes and jewels should act as a tonic; but then the Kouradjines *were* funny, and heaven knew Targatt had no reason to begrudge them any of their little fancies – especially now that Olga's engagement to Mrs. Guggins' brother (representative of the Guggins interests in London and Paris) had been officially announced. When the news came, Targatt gave his wife a pair of emerald earrings, and suggested that they should take their summer holiday in Paris.

It was the same winter that New York was thrown into a flutter by the announcement that the famous portrait painter, Axel Svengaart, was coming over to 'do' a chosen half-dozen sitters. Svengaart had

never been to New York before, had always sworn that anybody who
wanted to be painted by him must come to his studio at Oslo; but it
suddenly struck him that the American background might give a fresh
quality to his work, and after painting one lady getting out of her car
in front of her husband's motorworks, and Mrs. Guggins against the
background of a spouting oil well at Rapid Rise, he appeared in New
York to organize a show of these sensational canvases. New York was
ringing with the originality and audacity of this new experiment. After
expecting to be 'done' in the traditional setting of the Gothic library or
the Quattrocento *salon*, it was incredibly exciting to be portrayed literally surrounded by the acknowledged sources of one's wealth; and the
wife of a fabulously rich plumber was nearly persuaded to be done
stepping out of her bath, in a luxury bathroom fitted with the latest
ablutionary appliances.

Fresh from these achievements, Axel Svengaart carried his Viking
head and Parisian monocle from one New York drawing room to
another, gazing, appraising – even, though rarely, praising – but absolutely refusing to take another order, or to postpone by a single day the
date of his sailing. 'I've got it all here,' he said, touching first his brow
and then his pocket; and the dealer who acted as his impresario let it
be understood that even the most exaggerated offers would be rejected.

Targatt had, of course, met the great man. In old days he would
have been uncomfortably awed by the encounter; but now he could
joke easily about the Gugginses, and even ask Svengaart if he had not
been struck by his sister-in-law, who was Mrs. Guggins' social
secretary, and was about to marry Mr. Guggins's Paris representative.

'Ah – the lovely Kouradjine; yes. She made us some delicious
blinys,' Svengaart nodded approvingly; but Targatt saw with surprise
that as a painter he was uninterested in Olga's plastic possibilities.

'Ah, well, I suppose you've had enough of us – I hear you're off
this week.'

The painter dropped his monocle. 'Yes, I've had enough.' It was
after dinner, at the Bellamys', and abruptly he seated himself on the
sofa at Targatt's side. 'I don't like your frozen food,' he pursued.
'There's only one thing that would make me put off my sailing.' He
readjusted his monocle and looked straight at Targatt. 'If you'll give
me the chance to paint Mrs. Targatt – oh, for that I'd wait another
month.'

Targatt stared at him, too surprised to answer. Nadeja – the great
man wanted to paint Nadeja! The idea aroused so many conflicting
considerations that his reply, when it came, was a stammer. 'Why
really . . . this is a surprise . . . a great honor, of course. . . .' A vision
of Svengaart's price for a mere head thrust itself hideously before his
eyes. Svengaart, seeing him as it were encircled by millionaires, probably took him for a very rich man – was perhaps maneuvering to

extract an extra big offer from him. For what other inducement could
there be to paint Nadeja? Targatt turned the question with a joke. 'I
suspect you're confusing me with my brother-in-law Bellamy. He
ought to have persuaded you to paint his wife. But I'm afraid my means
wouldn't allow. . . .'

The other interrupted him with an irritated gesture. 'Please – my
dear sir. I can never be "persuaded" to do a portrait. And in the case
of Mrs. Targatt I had no idea of selling you her picture. If I paint her,
it would be for myself.'

Targatt's stare widened. 'For yourself? You mean – you'd paint the
picture just to keep it?' He gave an embarrassed laugh. 'Nadeja would
be enormously flattered, of course. But, between ourselves, would you
mind telling me why you want to do her?'

Svengaart stood up with a faint laugh. 'Because she's the only really
paintable woman I've seen here. The lines are incomparable for a full-
length. And I can't tell you how I should enjoy the change.'

Targatt continued to stare. Murmurs of appreciation issued from
his parched lips. He remembered now that Svengaart's charge for a
three-quarter-length was fifteen thousand dollars. And he wanted to do
Nadeja full length for nothing! Only – Targatt remined himself – the
brute wanted to keep the picture. So where was the good? It would
only make Nadeja needlessly conspicuous; and to give all those sittings
for nothing . . . well, it looked like sharp practice, somehow. . . .

'Of course, as I say, my wife would be immensely flattered; only
she's very busy – her family, social obligations and so on; I really can't
say. . . .'

Svengaart smiled. 'In the course of a portrait I usually make a good
many studies; some almost as finished as the final picture. If Mrs.
Targatt cared to accept one – '

Targatt flushed to the roots of his thinning hair. A Svengaart study
over the drawing-room mantelpiece! ('Yes – nice thing of Nadeja, isn't
it? You'd know a Svengaart anywhere . . . it was his own idea; he
insisted on doing her. . . .')

Nadeja was just lifting a pile of music from the top of the grand
piano. She was going to accompany Mouna, who had taken to singing.
As she stood with lifted arms, profiled against the faint hues of the
tapestried wall, the painter exclaimed: 'There – there! I have it! Don't
you see now why I want to do her?'

But Targatt, for the moment, could not speak. Secretly he thought
Nadeja looked much as usual – only perhaps a little more tired; she had
complained of a headache that morning. But his courage rose to the
occasion. 'Ah, my wife's famous "lines", eh? Well, well, I can't promise
– you'd better come over and try to persuade her yourself.'

He was so dizzy with it that as he led Svengaart toward the piano
the Bellamys' parquet floor felt like glass under his unsteady feet.

• VII •

TARGATT's rapture was acute but short-lived. Nadeja 'done' by Axel Svengaart – he had measured the extent of it in a flash. He had stood aside and watched her with a deep smile of satisfaction while the light of wonder rose in her eyes; when she turned them on him for approval he had nodded his assent. Of course she must sit to the great man, his glance signaled back. He saw that Svengaart was amused at her having to ask her husband's permission; but this only intensified Targatt's satisfaction. They'd see, damn it, if his wife could be ordered about like a professional model! Perhaps the best moment was when, the next day, she said timidly: 'But, Jim, have you thought about the price?' and he answered, his hands in his pockets, an easy smile on his lips: 'There's no price to think about. He's doing you for the sake of your beautiful "lines". And we're to have a replica, free gratis. Did you know you had beautiful lines, old Nad?'

She looked at him gravely for a moment. 'I hadn't thought about them for a long time,' she said.

Targatt laughed and tapped her on the shoulder. What a child she was! But afterward it struck him that she had not been particularly surprised by the painter's request. Perhaps she had always known she was paintable, as Svengaart called it. Perhaps – and here he felt a little chill run over him – perhaps Svengaart had spoken to her already, had come to an understanding with her before making his request to Targatt. The idea made Targatt surprisingly uncomfortable, and he reflected that it was the first occasion in their married life when he had suspected Nadeja of even the most innocent duplicity. And this, if it were true, could hardly be regarded as wholly innocent. . . .

Targatt shook the thought off impatiently. He was behaving like the fellow in Pagliacci. Really this associating with foreigners might end in turning a plain businessman into an opera singer! It was the day of the first sitting, and as he started for his office he called back gaily to Nadeja: 'Well, so long! And don't let that fellow turn your head.'

He could not get much out of Nadeja about the sittings. It was not that she seemed secretive; but she was never very good at reporting small talk, and things that happened outside of the family circle, even if they happened to herself, always seemed of secondary interest to her. And meanwhile the sittings went on and on. In spite of his free style Svengaart was a slow worker; and he seemed to find Nadeja a difficult subject. Targatt began to brood over the situation: some people thought the fellow handsome, in the lean greyhound style; and he had an easy cosmopolitan way – the European manner. It was what Nadeja was used to; would she suddenly feel that she had missed something during all these years? Targatt turned cold at the thought. It had never before occurred to him what a humdrum figure he was. The contemplation of his face in the shaving glass became so distasteful to him that he averted his eyes, and nearly cut his throat in consequence. Nothing of the greyhound style about him – or the Viking either.

Slowly, as these thoughts revolved in his mind, he began to feel that he, who had had everything from Nadeja, had given her little or nothing in return. What he had done for her people weighed as nothing in this revaluation of their past. The point was: what sort of a life had he given Nadeja? And the answer: no life at all! She had spent her best years looking after other people; he could not remember that she had ever asserted a claim or resented an oversight. And yet she was neither dull nor insipid: she was simply Nadeja – a creature endlessly tolerant, totally unprejudiced, sublimely generous and unselfish.

Well – it would be funny, Targatt thought, with a twist of almost physical pain, if nobody else had been struck by such unusual qualities. If it had taken him over ten years to find them out, others might have been less blind. He had never noticed her 'lines', for instance; yet that painter fellow, the moment he'd clapped eyes on her – !

Targatt sat in his study, twisting about restlessly in his chair. Where *was* Nadeja, he wondered? The winter dusk had fallen, and painters do not work without daylight. The day's sitting must be over – and yet she had not come back. Usually she was always there to greet him on his return from the office. She had taught him to enjoy his afternoon tea, with a tiny caviar sandwich and a slice of lemon, and the samovar was already murmuring by the fire. When she went to see any of her family she always called up to say if she would be late; but the maid said there had been no message from her.

Targatt got up and walked the floor impatiently; then he sat down again, lit a cigarette, and threw it away. Nadeja, he remembered, had not been in the least shocked when Katinka had decided to live with Mr. Bellamy; she had merely wondered if the step were expedient, and had finally agreed with Katinka that it was. Nor had Boris's matrimonial maneuvers seemed to offend her. She was entirely destitute of moral indignation; this painful reality was now borne in on Targatt for the first time. Cruelty shocked her; but otherwise she seemed to think that people should do as they pleased. Yet, all the while, had she ever done what *she* pleased? There was the torturing enigma! She seemed to allow such latitude to others, yet to ask so little for herself.

Well, but didn't the psychologist fellows say that there was an hour in every woman's life – every self-sacrificing woman's – when the claims of her suppressed self suddenly asserted themselves, body and soul, and she forgot everything else, all her duties, ties, responsibilities? Targatt broke off with a bitter laugh. What did 'duties, ties, responsibilities' mean to Nadeja? No more than to any of the other Kouradjines. Their vocabulary had no parallels with his. He felt a sudden overwhelming loneliness, as if all these years he had been married to a changeling, an opalescent creature swimming up out of the sea. . . .

No, she couldn't be at the studio any longer; or if she were, it wasn't to sit for her portrait. Curse the portrait, he thought – why had he ever consented to her sitting to Svengaart? Sheer cupidity; the snobbish ambition to own a Svengaart, the glee of getting one for nothing. The more he proceeded with this self-investigation the less he cared for the figure he cut. But however poor a part he had played so far, he wasn't going to add to it the role of the duped husband. . . .

'Damn it, I'll go round there myself and see,' he muttered, squaring his shoulders, and walking resolutely across the room to the door. But as he reached the entrance hall the faint click of a latchkey greeted him; and sweeter music he had never heard. Nadeja stood in the doorway, pale but smiling. 'Jim – you were not going out again?'

He gave a sheepish laugh. 'Do you know what time it is? I was getting scared.'

'Scared for me?' She smiled again. 'Dear me, yes! It's nearly dinner time, isn't it?'

He followed her into the drawing room and shut the door. He felt like a husband in an old-fashioned problem play; and in a moment he had spoken like one. 'Nad, where've you come from?' he broke out abruptly.

'Why, the studio. It was my last sitting.'

'People don't sit for their portraits in the dark.'

He saw a faint surprise in her eyes as she bent to the samovar. 'No; I was not sitting all the time. Not for the last hour or more, I suppose.'

She spoke as quietly as usual, yet he thought he caught a tremor of resentment in her voice. Against himself – or against the painter? But how he was letting his imagination run away with him! He sat down in his accustomed armchair, took the cup of tea she held out. He was determined to behave like a reasonable being, yet never had reason appeared to him so unrelated to reality. 'Ah, well – I suppose you two had a lot of things to talk about. You rather fancy Svengaart, don't you?'

'Oh, yes; I like him very much. Do you know,' she asked earnestly, 'How much he has made during his visit to America? It was of course in confidence that he told me. Two-hundred thousand dollars. And he was rich before.'

She spoke so solemnly that Targatt burst into a vague laugh. 'Well, what of it? I don't know that it showed much taste to brag to you about the way he skins his sitters. But it shows he didn't make much of a sacrifice in painting you for nothing,' he said irritably.

'No; I said to him he might have done you too.'

'*Me?*' Targatt's laugh redoubled. 'Well, what did he say to that?'

'Oh, he laughed as you are now laughing,' Nadeja rejoined. 'But he says he will never marry – never.'

Targatt put down his cup with a rattle. '*Never marry?* What the devil are you talking about? Who cares whether he marries, anyhow?' he gasped with a dry throat.

'I do,' said Nadeja.

There was a silence. Nadeja was lifting her teacup to her lips, and something in the calm free movement reminded him of Svengaart's outburst when he had seen her lift the pile of music. For the first time in his life Targatt seemed to himself to be looking at her; and he wondered if it would also be the last. He cleared his throat and tried to speak, to say something immense, magnanimous. 'Well, if – '

'No; it's useless. He will hear nothing. I said to him: You will never anywhere find such a *plastik* as Mouna's. . . .'

'*Mouna's?*'

She turned to him with a slight shrug. 'Oh, my poor Jim, are you quite blind? Haven't you seen how we have all been trying to make him want to marry Mouna? It will be almost my first failure, I think,' she concluded with a half-apologetic sigh.

Targatt rested his chin on his hands and looked up at her. She looked tired, certainly, and older; too tired and old for any one still well under forty. And Mouna – why in God's name should she be persecuting this man to marry Mouna? It was indecent, it was shocking, it was unbelievable. . . . Yet not for a moment did he doubt the truth of what she said.

'Mouna?' he could only repeat stupidly.

'Well, you see, darling, we're all a little anxious about Mouna. And I was so glad when Svengaart asked to paint me, because I thought: Now's my opportunity. But no, it was not to be.'

Targatt drew a deep breath. He seemed to be inhaling some life-giving element, and it was with the most superficial severity that he said: 'I don't fancy this idea of your throwing your sister at men's heads.'

'No, it was no use,' Nadeja sighed, with her usual complete unawareness of any moral rebuke in his comment.·

Targatt stood up uneasily. 'He wouldn't have her at any price?'

She shook her head sadly. 'Foolish man!'

Targatt went up to her and took her abruptly by the wrist. 'Look at me, Nadeja – straight. Did he refuse her because he wanted *you?*'

She gave her light lift of the shoulders, and the rare color flitted across her pale cheeks. 'Isn't it always the way of men? What they can't get – '

'Ah; so he's been making love to you all this time, has he?'

'But of course not, James. What he wished was to marry me. That is something quite different, is it not?'

'Yes. I see.'

Targatt had released her wrist and turned away. He walked once or twice up and down the length of the room, no more knowing where he was than a man dropped blindfolded onto a new planet. He knew what he wanted to do and to say; the words he had made up his mind to speak stood out in letters of fire against the choking blackness. 'You must feel yourself free – ' Five words, and so easy to speak! 'Perfectly free – perfectly free,' a voice kept crying within him. It was the least he could do, if he were ever to hold up his head again; but when he opened his mouth to speak not a sound came. At last he halted before Nadeja again, his face working like a frightened child's.

'Nad – what would you like best in the world to do? If you'll tell me I – I want you to do it!' he stammered. And with hands of ice he waited.

Nadeja looked at him with a slowly growing surprise. She had turned very pale again.

'Even if,' he continued, half choking, 'you understand, Nad, even if – '

She continued to look at him in her grave maternal way. 'Is this true, what you are now saying?' she asked very low. Targatt nodded.

A little smile wavered over her lips. 'Well, darling, if only I could have got Mouna safely married, I should have said: Don't you think that now at last we could afford to have a baby?'

All Souls'

QUEER AND INEXPLICABLE as the business was, on the surface it appeared fairly simple – at the time, at least; but with the passing of years, and owing to there not having been a single witness of what happened except Sara Clayburn herself, the stories about it have become so exaggerated, and often so ridiculously inaccurate, that it seems necessary that someone connected with the affair, though not actually present – I repeat that when it happened my cousin was (or thought she was) quite alone in her house – should record the few facts actually known.

In those days I was often at Whitegates (as the place had always been called) – I was there, in fact, not long before, and almost immediately after, the strange happenings of those thirty-six hours. Jim Clayburn and his widow were both my cousins, and because of that, and of my intimacy with them, both families think I am more likely than anybody else to be able to get at the facts, as far as they can be called facts, and as anybody can get at them. So I have written down, as clearly as I could, the gist of the various talks I had with cousin Sara, when she could be got to talk – it wasn't often – about what occurred during that mysterious weekend.

I read the other day in a book by a fashionable essayist that ghosts went out when electric light came in. What nonsense! The writer, though he is fond of dabbling, in a literary way, in the supernatural, hasn't even reached the threshold of his subject. As between turreted castles patrolled by headless victims with clanking chains, and the comfortable suburban house with a refrigerator and central heating where you feel, as soon as you're in it, *that there's something wrong*, give me the latter for sending a chill down the spine! And, by the way, haven't you noticed that it's generally not the high-strung and imaginative who see ghosts, but the calm matter-of-fact people who don't believe in them, and are sure they wouldn't mind if they did see one? Well, that was the case with Sara Clayburn and her house. The house, in spite of its age – it was built, I believe, about 1780 – was open, airy, high-ceilinged, with electricity, central heating and all the modern appliances: and its mistress was – well, very much like her house. And, anyhow, this isn't exactly a ghost story and I've dragged in the analogy only as a way of showing you what kind of woman my cousin was, and how unlikely it would have seemed that what happened at Whitegates should have happened just there – or to her.

When Jim Clayburn died the family all thought that, as the couple had no children, his widow would give up Whitegates and move either to New York or Boston – for being of good Colonial stock, with many relatives and friends, she would have found a place ready for her in either. But Sally Clayburn seldom did what other people expected, and in this case she did exactly the contrary; she stayed at Whitegates.

'What, turn my back on the old house – tear up all the family roots, and go and hang myself up in a bird-cage flat in one of those new skyscrapers in Lexington Avenue, with a bunch of chickweed and a cuttlefish to replace my good Connecticut mutton? No, thank you. Here I belong, and here I stay till my executors hand the place over to Jim's next-of-kin – that stupid fat Presley boy. . . . Well, don't let's talk about him. But I tell you what – I'll keep him out of here as long as I can.' And she did – for being still in the early fifties when her husband died, and a muscular, resolute figure of a woman, she was more than a match for the fat Presley boy, and attended his funeral a few years ago, in correct mourning, with a faint smile under her veil.

Whitegates was a pleasant hospitable-looking house, on a height overlooking the stately windings of the Connecticut River; but it was five or six miles from Norrington, the nearest town, and its situation would certainly have seemed remote and lonely to modern servants. Luckily, however, Sara Clayburn had inherited from her mother-in-law two or three old stand-bys who seemed as much a part of the family tradition as the roof they lived under; and I never heard of her having any trouble in her domestic arrangements.

The house, in Colonial days, had been foursquare, with four spacious rooms on the ground floor, an oak-floored hall dividing them, the usual kitchen extension at the back, and a good attic under the roof. But Jim's grandparents, when interest in the 'Colonial' began to revive, in the early eighties, had added two wings, at right angles to the south front, so that the old 'circle' before the front door became a grassy court, enclosed on three sides, with a big elm in the middle. Thus the house was turned into a roomy dwelling, in which the last three generations of Clayburns had exercised a large hospitality; but the architect had respected the character of the old house, and the enlargement made it more comfortable without lessening its simplicity. There was a lot of land about it, and Jim Clayburn, like his father before him, farmed it, not without profit, and played a considerable and respected part in state politics. The Clayburns were always spoken of as a 'good influence' in the county, and the townspeople were glad when they learned that Sara did not mean to desert the place – 'though it must be lonesome, winters, living all alone up there atop of that hill' – they remarked as the days shortened, and the first snow began to pile up under the quadruple row of elms along the common.

Well, if I've given you a sufficiently clear idea of Whitegates and the Clayburns – who shared with their old house a sort of reassuring orderliness and dignity – I'll efface myself, and tell the tale, not in my cousin's words, for they were too confused and fragmentary, but as I built it up gradually out of her half-avowals and nervous reticences. If the thing happened at all – and I must leave you to judge of that – I think it must have happened in this way. . . .

• I •

THE morning had been bitter, with a driving sleet – though it was only the last day of October – but after lunch a watery sun showed for a while through banked-up woolly clouds, and tempted Sara Clayburn out. She was an energetic walker, and given, at that season, to tramping three or four miles along the valley road, and coming back by way of Shaker's wood. She had made her usual round, and was following the main drive to the house when she overtook a plainly-dressed woman walking in the same direction. If the scene had not been so lonely – the way to Whitegates at the end of an autumn day was not a frequented one – Mrs. Clayburn might not have paid any attention to the woman, for she was in no way noticeable; but when she caught up with the intruder my cousin was surprised to find that she was a stranger – for the mistress of Whitegates prided herself on knowing, at least by sight, most of her country neighbors. It was almost dark, and the woman's face was hardly visible, but Mrs. Clayburn told me she recalled her as middle-aged, plain and rather pale.

Mrs. Clayburn greeted her, and then added: 'You're going to the house?'

'Yes, ma'am,' the woman answered, in a voice that the Connecticut Valley in old days would have called 'foreign,' but that would have been unnoticed by ears used to the modern multiplicity of tongues. 'No, I couldn't say where she came from,' Sara always said. 'What struck me as queer was that I didn't know her.'

She asked the woman, politely, what she wanted, and the woman answered: 'Only to see one of the girls.' The answer was natural enough, and Mrs. Clayburn nodded and turned off from the drive to the lower part of the gardens, so that she saw no more of the visitor then or afterward. And, in fact, a half hour later something happened which put the stranger entirely out of her mind. The brisk and light-footed Mrs. Clayburn, as she approached the house, slipped on a frozen puddle, turned her ankle and lay suddenly helpless.

Price, the butler, and Agnes, the dour old Scottish maid whom Sara had inherited from her mother-in-law, of course knew exactly what to do. In no time they had their mistress stretched out on a lounge, and Dr. Selgrove had been called up from Norrington. When he arrived, he ordered Mrs. Clayburn to bed, did the necessary examining and bandaging, and shook his head over her ankle, which he feared was fractured. He thought, however, that if she would swear not to get up, or even shift the position of her leg, he could spare her the discomfort of putting it in plaster. Mrs. Clayburn agreed, the more promptly as the doctor warned her that any rash movement would prolong her immobility. Her quick imperious nature made the prospect trying, and she was annoyed with herself for having been so clumsy. But the mischief was done, and she immediately thought what an opportunity she would have for going over her accounts and catching up with her correspondence. So she settled down resignedly in her bed.

'And you won't miss much, you know, if you have to stay there a few days. It's beginning to snow, and it looks as if we were in for a good spell of it,' the doctor remarked, glancing through the window as he gathered up his implements. 'Well, we don't often get snow here as early as this; but winter's got to begin sometime,' he concluded philosophically. At the door he stopped to add: 'You don't want me to send up a nurse from Norrington? Not to nurse you, you know; there's nothing much to do till I see you again. But this is a pretty lonely place when the snow begins, and I thought maybe – '

Sara Clayburn laughed. 'Lonely? With my old servants? You forget how many winters I've spent here alone with them. Two of them were with me in my mother-in-law's time.'

'That's so,' Dr. Selgrove agreed. 'You're a good deal luckier than most people, that way. Well, let me see; this is Saturday. We'll have to let the inflammation go down before we can X-ray you. Monday morning, first thing, I'll be here with the X-ray man. If you want me sooner, call me up,' And he was gone.

• II •

THE foot at first, had not been very painful; but toward the small hours Mrs. Clayburn began to suffer. She was a bad patient, like most healthy and active people. Not being used to pain she did not know how to bear it, and the hours of wakefulness and immobility seemed endless. Agnes, before leaving her, had made everything as comfortable as possible. She had put a jug of lemonade within reach, and had even (Mrs. Clayburn thought it odd afterward) insisted on bringing in a tray with sandwiches and a thermos of tea. 'In case you're hungry in the night, madam.'

'Thank you; but I'm never hungry in the night. And I certainly shan't be tonight – only thirsty. I think I'm feverish.'

'Well, there's the lemonade, madam.'

'That will do. Take the other things away, please.' (Sara had always hated the sight of unwanted food 'messing about' in her room.)

'Very well, madam. Only you might – '

'Please take it away,' Mrs. Clayburn repeated irritably.

'Very good, madam.' But as Agnes went out, her mistress heard her set the tray down softly on a table behind the screen which shut off the door.

'Obstinate old goose!' she thought, rather touched by the old woman's insistence.

Sleep, once it had gone, would not return, and the long black hours moved more and more slowly. How late the dawn came in November! 'If only I could move my leg,' she grumbled.

She lay still and strained her ears for the first steps of the servants. Whitegates was an early house, its mistress setting the example; it would surely not be long now before one of the women came. She was tempted to ring for Agnes, but refrained. The woman had been up late, and this was Sunday morning, when the household was always allowed a little extra time. Mrs. Clayburn reflected restlessly: 'I was a fool not to let her leave the tea beside the bed, as she wanted to. I wonder if I could get up and get it?' But she remembered the doctor's warning, and dared not move. Anything rather than risk prolonging her imprisonment. . . .

Ah, there was the stable clock striking. How loud it sounded in the snowy stillness! One-two-three-four-five. . . .

What? Only five? Three hours and a quarter more before she could hope to hear the door handle turned. . . . After a while she dozed off again, uncomfortably.

Another sound aroused her. Again the stable clock. She listened. But the room was still in deep darkness, and only six strokes fell. . . . She thought of reciting something to put her to sleep, but she seldom read poetry, and being naturally a good sleeper, she could not remember any of the usual devices against insomnia. The whole of her leg felt like lead now. The bandages had grown terribly tight – her ankle must have swollen. . . . She lay staring at the dark windows, watching for the first glimmer of dawn. At last she saw a pale filter of daylight through the shutters. One by one the objects between the bed and the window recovered first their outline, then their bulk, and seemed to be stealthily regrouping themselves, after goodness knows what secret displacements during the night. Who that has lived in an old house could possibly believe that the furniture in it stays still all night? Mrs. Clayburn almost fancied she saw one little slender-legged table slipping hastily back into its place.

'It knows Agnes is coming, and it's afraid,' she thought whimsically. Her bad night must have made her imaginative for such nonsense as that about the furniture had never occurred to her before. . . .

At length, after hours more, as it seemed, the stable clock struck eight. Only another quarter of an hour. She watched the hand moving slowly across the face of the little clock beside her bed . . . ten minutes . . . five . . . only five! Agnes was as punctual as destiny . . . in two minutes now she would come. The two minutes passed, and she did not come. Poor Agnes – she had looked pale and tired the night before. She had overslept herself, no doubt – or perhaps she felt ill, and would send the housemaid to replace her. Mrs. Clayburn waited.

She waited half an hour; then she reached up to the bell at the head of the bed. Poor old Agnes – her mistress felt guilty about waking her. But Agnes did not appear – and after a considerable interval Mrs. Clayburn, now with a certain impatience, rang again. She rang once; twice; three times – but still no one came.

Once more she waited; then she said to herself: 'There must be something wrong with the electricity.' Well – she could find out by switching on the bed lamp at her elbow (how admirably the room was equipped with every practical appliance!). She switched it on – but no light came. Electric current cut off; and it was Sunday, and nothing could be done about it till the next morning. Unless it turned out to be just a burnt-out fuse, which Price could remedy. Well, in a moment now some one would surely come to her door.

It was nine o'clock before she admitted to herself that something uncommonly strange must have happened in the house. She began to feel a nervous apprehension; but she was not the woman to encourage it. If only she had had the telephone put in her room, instead of out on the landing! She measured mentally the distance to be traveled, remembered Dr. Selgrove's admonition, and wondered if her broken ankle would carry her there. She dreaded the prospect of being put in plaster, but she had to get to the telphone, whatever happened.

She wrapped herself in her dressing gown, found a walking stick, and, resting heavily on it, dragged herself to the door. In her bedroom the careful Agnes had closed and fastened the shutters, so that it was not much lighter there than at dawn; but outside in the corridor the cold whiteness of the snowy morning seemed almost reassuring. Mysterious things – dreadful things – were associated with darkness; and here was the wholesome prosaic daylight come again to banish them. Mrs. Clayburn looked about her and listened. Silence. A deep nocturnal silence in that day-lit house, in which five people were presumably coming and going about their work. It was certainly strange. . . . She looked out of the window, hoping to see someone crossing the court or coming along the drive. But no one was in sight, and the snow seemed to have the place to itself: a quiet steady snow. It was still falling, with a business-like regularity, muffling the outer world in layers on layers of thick white velvet, and intensifying the silence within. A noiseless world – were people so sure that absence of noise was what they wanted? Let them first try a lonely country house in a November snowstorm!

She dragged herself along the passage to the telephone. When she unhooked the receiver she noticed that her hand trembled.

She rang up the pantry – no answer. She rang again. Silence – more silence! It seemed to be piling itself up like the snow on the roof and in the gutters. Silence. How many people that she knew had any idea what silence was – and how loud it sounded when you really listened to it?

Again she waited: then she rang up 'Central.' No answer. She tried three times. After that she tried the pantry again. . . . The telephone was cut off, then; like the electric current. Who was at work downstairs, isolating her thus from the world? Her heart began to hammer. Luckily there was a chair near the telephone, and she sat down to recover her strength – or was it her courage?

Agnes and the housemaid slept in the nearest wing. She would certainly get as far as that when she had pulled herself together. Had she the courage – ? Yes, of course she had. She had always been uregarded as a plucky woman; and had so regarded herself. But this silence –

It occurred to her that by looking from the window of a neighboring bathroom she could see the kitchen chimney. There ought to be smoke coming from it at that hour; and if there were she thought she would be less afraid to go on. She got as far as the bathroom and looking through the window saw that no smoke came from the chimney. Her sense of loneliness grew more acute. Whatever had happened belowstairs must have happened before the morning's work had begun. The cook had not had time to light the fire, the other servants had not yet begun their round. She sank down on the nearest chair, struggling against her fears. What next would she discover if she carried on her investigations?

The pain in her ankle made progress difficult; but she was aware of it now only as an obstacle to haste. No matter what it cost her in physical suffering, she must find out what was happening belowstairs – or had happened. But first she would go to the maid's room. And if that were empty – well, somehow she would have to get herself downstairs.

She limped along the passage, and on the way steadied herself by resting her hand on a radiator. It was stone-cold. Yet in that well-ordered house in winter the central heating, though damped down at night, was never allowed to go out, and by eight in the morning a mellow warmth pervaded the rooms. The icy chill of the pipes startled her. It was the chauffeur who looked after the heating – so he too was involved in the mystery, whatever it was, as well as the house servants. But this only deepened the problem.

• III •

At Agnes's door Mrs. Clayburn paused and knocked. She expected no answer, and there was none. She opened the door and went in. The room was dark and very cold. She went to the window and flung back the shutters; then she looked slowly around, vaguely apprehensive of what she might see. The room was empty but what frightened her was not so much its emptiness as its air of scrupulous and undisturbed order. There was no sign of anyone having lately dressed in it – or undressed the night before. And the bed had not been slept in.

Mrs. Clayburn leaned against the wall for a moment; then she crossed the floor and opened the cupboard. That was where Agnes kept her dresses; and the dresses were there, neatly hanging in a row. On the shelf above were Agnes's few and unfashionable hats, rearrangements of her mistress's old ones. Mrs. Clayburn, who knew them all, looked at the shelf, and saw that one was missing. And so was also the warm winter coat she had given to Agnes the previous winter.

The woman was out, then; had gone out, no doubt, the night before, since the bed was unslept in, the dressing and washing appliances untouched. Agnes, who never·set foot out of the house after dark, who despised the movies as much as she did the wireless, and could never be persuaded that a little innocent amusement was a necessary element in life, had deserted the house on a snowy winter night, while her mistress lay upstairs, suffering and helpless! Why had she gone, and where had she gone? When she was undressing Mrs. Clayburn the night before, taking her orders, trying to make her more comfortable, was she already planning this mysterious nocturnal escape? Or had something – the mysterious and dreadful Something for the clue of which Mrs. Clayburn was still groping – occurred later in the evening, sending the maid downstairs and out of doors into the bitter night? Perhaps one of the men at the garage – where the chauffeur and gardener lived – had been suddenly taken ill, and someone had run up to the house for Agnes. Yes – that must be the explanation. . . . Yet how much it left unexplained.

Next to Agnes's room was the linen room; beyond that was the housemaid's door. Mrs. Clayburn went to it and knocked. 'Mary!' No one answered, and she went in. The room was in the same immaculate order as her maid's, and here too the bed was unslept in, and there were no signs of dressing or undressing. The two women had no doubt gone out together – gone where?

More and more the cold unanswering silence of the house weighed down on Mrs. Clayburn. She had never thought of it as a big house, but now, in this snowy winter light, it seemed immense, and full of ominous corners around which one dared not look.

Beyond the housemaid's room were the back stairs. It was the nearest way down, and every step that Mrs. Clayburn took was increasingly painful; but she decided to walk slowly back, the whole length of the passage, and go down by the front stairs. She did not know why she did this; but she felt that at the moment she was past reasoning, and had better obey her instinct.

More than once she had explored the ground floor alone in the small hours, in search of unwonted midnight noises; but now it was not the idea of noises that frightened her, but that inexorable and hostile silence, the sense that the house had retained in full daylight its nocturnal mystery, and was watching her as she was watching it; that in entering those empty orderly rooms she might be disturbing some unseen confabulation on which beings of flesh-and-blood had better not intrude.

The broad oak stairs were beautifully polished, and so slippery that she had to cling to the rail and let herself down tread by tread. And as she descended, the silence descended with her – heavier, denser, more absolute. She seemed to feel its steps just behind her, softly keeping time with hers. It had a quality she had never been aware of in any other silence, as though it were not merely an absence of sound, a thin barrier between the ear and the surging murmur of life just beyond, but an impenetrable substance made out of the world-wide cessation of all life and all movement.

Yes, that was what laid a chill on her: the feeling that there was no limit to this silence, no outer margin, nothing beyond it. By this time she had reached the foot of the stairs and was limping across the hall to the drawing room. Whatever she found there, she was sure, would be mute and lifeless; but what would it be? The bodies of her dead servants, mown down by some homicidal maniac? And what if it were her turn next – if he were waiting for her behind the heavy curtains of the room she was about to enter? Well, she must find out – she must face whatever lay in wait. Not impelled by bravery – the last drop of courage had oozed out of her – but because anything, anything was better than to remain shut up in that snowbound house without knowing whether she was alone in it or not, 'I must find that out, I must find that out,' she repeated to herself in a sort of meaningless sing-song.

The cold outer light flooded the drawing room. The shutters had not been closed, nor the curtains drawn. She looked about her. The room was empty, and every chair in its usual place. Her armchair was pushed up by the chimney, and the cold hearth was piled with the ashes of the fire at which she had warmed herself before starting on her ill-fated walk. Even her empty coffee cup stood on a table near the armchair. It was evident that the servants had not been in the room since she had left it the day before after luncheon. And suddenly the conviction entered into her that, as she found the drawing room, so she would find the rest of the house; cold, orderly – and empty. She would find nothing, she would find no one. She no longer felt any dread of ordinary human dangers lurking in those dumb spaces ahead of her. She knew she was utterly alone under her own roof. She sat down to rest her aching ankle, and looked slowly about her.

There were the other rooms to be visited, and she was determined to go through them all – but she knew in advance that they would give no answer to her question. She knew it, seemingly, from the quality of the silence which enveloped her. There was no break, no thinnest crack in it anywhere. It had the cold continuity of the snow which was still falling steadily outside.

She had no idea how long she waited before nerving herself to continue her inspection. She no longer felt the pain in her ankle, but was only conscious that she must not bear her weight on it, and therefore moved very slowly, supporting herself on each piece of furniture in her path. On the ground floor no shutter had been closed, no curtain drawn, and she progressed without difficulty from room to room: the library, her morning room, the dining room. In each of them, every piece of furniture was in its usual place. In the dining room, the table had been laid for her dinner of the previous evening, and the candelabra, with candles unlit, stood reflected in the dark mahogany. She was not the kind of woman to nibble a poached egg on a tray when she was alone, but always came down to the dining room, and had what she called a civilized meal.

The back premises remained to be visited. From the dining room she entered the pantry, and there too everything was in irreproachable order. She opened the door and looked down the back passage with its neat linoleum floor covering. The deep silence accompanied her; she still felt it moving watchfully at her side, as though she were its prisoner and it might throw itself upon her if she attempted to escape. She limped on toward the kitchen. That of course would be empty too, and immaculate. But she must see it.

She leaned a minute in the embrasure of a window in the passage. 'It's like the "Mary Celeste" – a "Mary Celeste" on *terra firma*,' she thought, recalling the unsolved sea mystery of her childhood. 'No one ever knew what happened on board the "Mary Celeste." And perhaps no one will ever know what has happened here. Even I shan't know.'

At the thought her latent fear seemed to take on a new quality. It was like an icy liquid running through every vein, and lying in a pool about her heart. She understood now that she had never before known what fear was, and that most of the people she had met had probably never known either. For this sensation was something quite different. . . .

It absorbed her so completely that she was not aware how long she remained leaning there. But suddenly a new impulse pushed her forward, and she walked on toward the scullery. She went there first because there was a service slide in the wall, through which she might peep into the kitchen without being seen; and some indefinable instinct told her that the kitchen held the clue to the mystery. She still felt strongly that whatever had happened in the house must have its source and center in the kitchen.

In the scullery, as she had expected, everything was clean and tidy. Whatever had happened, no one in the house appeared to have been taken by surprise; there was nowhere any sign of confusion or disorder, 'It looks as if they'd known beforehand, and put everything straight,' she thought. She glanced at the wall facing the door, and saw that the slide was open. And then, as she was approaching it, the silence was broken. A voice was speaking in the kitchen – a man's voice, low but emphatic, and which she had never heard before.

She stood still, cold with fear. But this fear was again a different one. Her previous terrors had been speculative, conjectural, a ghostly emanation of the surrounding silence. This was a plain everyday dread of evildoers. Oh, God, why had she not remembered her husband's revolver, which ever since his death had lain in a drawer in her room?

She turned to retreat across the smooth slippery floor but halfway her stick slipped from her, and crashed down on the tiles. The noise seemed to echo on and on through the emptiness, and she stood still, aghast. Now that she had betrayed her presence, flight was useless. Whoever was beyond the kitchen door would be upon her in a second. . . .

But to her astonishment the voice went on speaking. It was as though neither the speaker nor his listeners had heard her. The invisible stranger spoke so low that she could not make out what he was saying, but the tone was passionately earnest, almost threatening. The next moment she realized that he was speaking in a foreign language, a language unknown to her. Once more her terror was surmounted by the urgent desire to know what was going on, so close to her yet unseen. She crept to the slide, peered cautiously through into the kitchen, and saw that it was as orderly and empty as the other rooms. But in the middle of the carefully scoured table stood a portable wireless, and the voice she heard came out of it. . . .

She must have fainted then, she supposed; at any rate she felt so weak and dizzy that her memory of what next happened remained indistinct. But in the course of time she groped her way back to the pantry, and there found a bottle of spirits – brandy or whisky, she could not remember which. She found a glass, poured herself a stiff drink, and while it was flushing through her veins, managed, she never knew with how many shuddering delays, to drag herself through the deserted ground floor, up the stairs, and down the corridor to her own room. There, apparently, she fell across the threshold, again unconscious. . . .

When she came to, she remembered, her first care had been to lock herself in; then to recover her husband's revolver. It was not loaded, but she found some cartridges, and succeeded in loading it. Then she remembered that Agnes, on leaving her the evening before, had refused to carry away the tray with the tea and sandwiches, and she fell on them with a sudden hunger. She recalled also noticing that a flask of brandy had been put beside the thermos, and being vaguely surprised. Agnes's departure, then, had been deliberately planned, and she had known that her mistress, who never touched spirits, might have need of a stimulant before she returned. Mrs. Clayburn poured some of the brandy into her tea, and swallowed it greedily.

After that (she told me later) she remembered that she had managed to start a fire in her grate, and after warming herself, had got back into her bed, piling on it all the coverings she could find. The afternoon passed in a haze of pain, out of which there emerged now and then a dim shape of fear – the fear that she might lie there alone and untended till she died of cold, and of the terror of her solitude. For she was sure by this time that the house was empty – completely empty, from garret to cellar. She knew it was so, she could not tell why; but again she felt that it must be because of the peculiar quality of the silence – the silence which had dogged her steps wherever she went, and was now folded down on her like a pall. She was sure that the nearness of any other human being, however dumb and secret, would have made a faint crack in the texture of that silence, flawed it as a sheet of glass is flawed by a pebble thrown against it. . . .

• IV •

'Is that easier?' the doctor asked, lifting himself from bending over her ankle. He shook his head disapprovingly. 'Looks to me as if you'd disobeyed orders – eh? Been moving about, haven't you? And I guess Dr. Selgrove told you to keep quiet till he saw you again, didn't he?'

The speaker was a stranger, whom Mrs. Clayburn knew only by name. Her own doctor had been called away that morning to the bedside of an old patient in Baltimore, and had asked this young man, who was beginning to be known at Norrington, to replace him. The newcomer was shy, and somewhat familiar, as the shy often are, and Mrs. Clayburn decided that she did not much like him. But before she could convey this by the tone of her reply (and she was past mistress of the shades of disapproval) she heard Agnes speaking – yes, Agnes, the same, the usual Agnes, standing behind the doctor, neat and stern-looking as ever. 'Mrs. Clayburn must have got up and walked about in the night instead of ringing for me, as she'd ought to,' Agnes intervened severely.

This was too much! In spite of the pain, which was now exquisite, Mrs. Clayburn laughed. 'Ringing for you? How could I, with the electricity cut off?'

'The electricity cut off?' Agnes's surprise was masterly. 'Why, when was it cut off?' She pressed her finger on the bell beside the bed, and the call tinkled through the quiet room. 'I tried that bell before I left you last night, madam, because if there'd been anything wrong with it I'd have come and slept in the dressing room sooner than leave you here alone.'

Mrs. Clayburn lay speechless, staring up at her. 'Last night? But last night I was all alone in the house.'

Agnes's firm features did not alter. She folded her hands resignedly across her trim apron. 'Perhaps the pain's made you a little confused, madam.' She looked at the doctor, who nodded.

'The pain in your foot must have been pretty bad,' he said.

'It was,' Mrs. Clayburn replied. 'But it was nothing to the horror of being left alone in this empty house since the day before yesterday, with the heat and the electricity cut off, and the telephone not working.'

The doctor was looking at her in evident wonder. Agnes's sallow face flushed slightly, but only as if in indignation at an unjust charge. 'But, madam, I made up your fire with my own hands last night – and look, it's smoldering still. I was getting ready to start it again just now, when the doctor came.'

'That's so. She was down on her knees before it,' the doctor corroborated.

Again Mrs. Clayburn laughed. Ingeniously as the tissue of lies was being woven about her, she felt she could still break through it. 'I made up the fire myself yesterday – there was no one else to do it,' she said, addressing the doctor, but keeping her eyes on her maid. 'I got up twice to put on more coal, because the house was like a sepulcher. The central heating must have been out since Saturday afternoon.'

At this incredible statement Agnes's face expressed only a polite distress: but the new doctor was evidently embarrassed at being drawn

into an unintelligible controversy with which he had no time to deal.
He said he had brought the X-ray photographer with him, but that the
ankle was too much swollen to be photographed at present. He asked
Mrs. Clayburn to excuse his haste, as he had all Dr. Selgrove's patients
to visit besides his own, and promised to come back that evening to
decide whether she could be X-rayed then, and whether, as he evidently
feared, the ankle would have to be put in plaster. Then, handing his
prescriptions to Agnes, he departed.

Mrs. Clayburn spent a feverish and suffering day. She did not feel
well enough to carry on the discussion with Agnes; she did not ask to
see the other servants. She grew drowsy, and understood that her mind
was confused with fever. Agnes and the housemaid waited on her as
attentively as usual, and by the time the doctor returned in the evening
her temperature had fallen; but she decided not to speak of what was
on her mind until Dr. Selgrove reappeared. He was to be back the
following evening; and the new doctor preferred to wait for him before
deciding to put the ankle in plaster — though he feared this was now
inevitable.

· V ·

THAT afternoon Mrs. Clayburn had me summoned by telephone, and
I arrived at Whitegates the following day. My cousin, who looked pale
and nervous, merely pointed to her foot, which had been put in plaster,
and thanked me for coming to keep her company. She explained that
Dr. Selgrove had been taken suddenly ill in Baltimore, and would not
be back for several days, but that the young man who replaced him
seemed fairly competent. She made no allusion to the strange incidents
I have set down, but I felt at once that she had received a shock which
her accident, however painful, could not explain.

Finally, one evening, she told me the story of her strange weekend,
as it had presented itself to her unusually clear and accurate mind, and
as I have recorded it above. She did not tell me this till several weeks
after my arrival; but she was still upstairs at the time, and obliged to
divide her days between her bed and a lounge. During those endless
intervening weeks, she told me, she had thought the whole matter
over: and though the events of the mysterious thirty-six hours were
still vivid to her, they had already lost something of their haunting
terror, and she had finally decided not to reopen the question with
Agnes, or to touch on it in speaking to the other servants. Dr. Selgrove's
illness had been not only serious but prolonged. He had not yet
returned, and it was reported that as soon as he was well enough he
would go on a West Indian cruise, and not resume his practice at
Norrington till the spring. Dr. Selgrove, as my cousin was perfectly

aware, was the only person who could prove that thirty-six hours had elapsed between his visit and that of his successor; and the latter, a shy young man, burdened by the heavy additional practice suddenly thrown on his shoulders, told me (when I risked a little private talk with him) that in the haste of Dr. Selgrove's departure the only instructions he had given about Mrs. Clayburn were summed up in the brief memorandum: 'Broken ankle. Have X-rayed.'

Knowing my cousin's authoritative character, I was surprised at her decision not to speak to the servants of what had happened; but on thinking it over I concluded she was right. They were all exactly as they had been before that unexplained episode: efficient, devoted, respectful and respectable. She was dependent on them and felt at home with them, and she evidently preferred to put the whole matter out of her mind, as far as she could. She was absolutely certain that something strange had happened in her house, and I was more than ever convinced that she had received a shock which the accident of a broken ankle was not sufficient to account for; but in the end I agreed that nothing was to be gained by cross-questioning the servants or the new doctor.

I was at Whitegates off and on that winter and during the following summer, and when I went home to New York for good early in October I left my cousin in her old health and spirits. Dr. Selgrove had been ordered to Switzerland for the summer, and this further postponement of his return to his practice seemed to have put the happenings of the strange weekend out of her mind. Her life was going on as peacefully and normally as usual, and I left her without anxiety, and indeed without a thought of the mystery, which was now nearly a year old.

I was living then in a small flat in New York by myself, and I had hardly settled into it when, very late one evening – on the last day of October – I heard my bell ring. As it was my maid's evening out, and I was alone, I went to the door myself, and on the threshold, to my amazement, I saw Sara Clayburn. She was wrapped in a fur cloak, with a hat drawn down over her forehead, and a face so pale and haggard that I saw something dreadful must have happened to her. 'Sara,' I gasped, not knowing what I was saying, 'where in the world have you come from at this hour?'

'From Whitegates. I missed the last train and came by car.' She came in and sat down on the bench near the door. I saw that she could hardly stand, and sat down beside her, putting my arm about her. 'For heaven's sake, tell me what's happened.'

She looked at me without seeming to see me. 'I telephoned to Nixon's and hired a car. It took me five hours and a quarter to get here.' She looked about her. 'Can you take me in for the night? I've left my luggage downstairs.'

'For as many nights as you like. But you look so ill – '

She shook her head. 'No; I'm not ill. I'm only frightened – deathly frightened,' she repeated in a whisper.

Her voice was so strange, and the hands I was pressing between mine were so cold, that I drew her to her feet and led her straight to my little guest room. My flat was in an old-fashioned building, not many stories high, and I was on more human terms with the staff than is possible in one of the modern Babels. I telephoned down to have my cousin's bags brought up, and meanwhile I filled a hot water bottle, warmed the bed, and got her into it as quickly as I could. I had never seen her as unquestioning and submissive, and that alarmed me even more than her pallor. She was not the woman to let herself be undressed and put to bed like a baby; but she submitted without a word, as though aware that she had reached the end of her tether.

'It's good to be here,' she said in a quieter tone, as I tucked her up and smoothed the pillows. 'Don't leave me yet, will you – not just yet.'

'I'm not going to leave you for more than a minute – just to get you a cup of tea,' I reassured her; and she lay still. I left the door open, so that she could hear me stirring about in the little pantry across the passage, and when I brought her the tea she swallowed it gratefully, and a little color came into her face. I sat with her in silence for some time; but at last she began: 'You see it's exactly a year – '

I should have preferred to have her put off till the next morning whatever she had to tell me; but I saw from her burning eyes that she was determined to rid her mind of what was burdening it, and that until she had done so it would be useless to proffer the sleeping draft I had ready.

'A year since what?' I asked stupidly, not yet associating her precipitate arrival with the mysterious occurrences of the previous year at Whitegates.

She looked at me in surprise. 'A year since I met that woman. Don't you remember – the strange woman who was coming up the drive the afternoon when I broke my ankle? I didn't think of it at the time, but it was on All Souls' eve that I met her.'

Yes, I said, I remembered that it was.

'Well – and this is All Souls' eve, isn't it? I'm not as good as you are on Church dates, but I thought it was.'

'Yes. This is All Souls' eve.'

'I thought so. . . . Well, this afternoon I went out for my usual walk. I'd been writing letters, and paying bills, and didn't start till late; not till it was nearly dusk. But it was a lovely clear evening. And as I got near the gate, there was the woman coming in – the same woman . . . going toward the house. . . .'

I pressed my cousin's hand, which was hot and feverish now. 'If it was dusk, could you be perfectly sure it was the same woman?' I asked.

'Oh, perfectly sure, the evening was so clear. I knew her and she knew me; and I could see she was angry at meeting me. I stopped her and asked: "Where are you going?" just as I had asked her last year. And she said, in the same queer half-foreign voice: "Only to see one of the girls", as she had before. Then I felt angry all of a sudden, and I said: "You shan't set foot in my house again. Do you hear me? I order you to leave." And she laughed; yes, she laughed – very low, but distinctly. By that time it had got quite dark, as if a sudden storm was sweeping up over the sky, so that though she was so near me I could hardly see her. We were standing by the clump of hemlocks at the turn of the drive, and as I went up to her, furious at her impertinence, she passed behind the hemlocks, and when I followed her she wasn't there. . . . No; I swear to you she wasn't there. . . . And in the darkness I hurried back to the house, afraid that she would slip by me and get there first. And the queer thing was that as I reached the door the black cloud vanished, and there was the transparent twilight again. In the house everything seemed as usual, and the servants were busy about their work; but I couldn't get it out of my head that the woman, under the shadow of that cloud, had somehow got there before me.' She paused for breath, and began again. 'In the hall I stopped at the telephone and rang up Nixon, and told him to send me a car at once to go to New York, with a man he knew to drive me. And Nixon came with the car himself. . . .'

Her head sank back on the pillow and she looked at me like a frightened child. 'It was good of Nixon,' she said.

'Yes; it was very good of him. But when they saw you leaving – the servants, I mean. . . .'

'Yes. Well, when I got upstairs to my room I rang for Agnes. She came, looking just as cool and quiet as usual. And when I told her I was starting for New York in half an hour – I said it was on account of a sudden business call – well, then her presence of mind failed her for the first time. She forgot to look surprised, she even forgot to make an objection – and you know what an objector Agnes is. And as I watched her I could see a little secret spark of relief in her eyes, though she was so on her guard. And she just said: "Very well, madam," and asked me what I wanted to take with me. Just as if I were in the habit of dashing off to New York after dark on an autumn night to meet a business engagement! No, she made a mistake not to show any surprise – and not even to ask me why I didn't take my own car. And her losing her head in that way frightened me more than anything else. For I saw she was so thankful I was going that she hardly dared speak, for fear she should betray herself, or I should change my mind.'

After that Mrs. Clayburn lay a long while silent, breathing less unrestfully; and at last she closed her eyes, as though she felt more at ease now that she had spoken, and wanted to sleep. As I got up quietly to leave her, she turned her head a little and murmured: 'I shall never go back to Whitegates again.' Then she shut her eyes and I saw that she was falling asleep.

I have set down above, I hope without omitting anything essential, the record of my cousin's strange experience as she told it to me. Of what happened at Whitegates that is all I can personally vouch for. The rest – and of course there is a rest – is pure conjecture; and I give it only as such.

My cousin's maid, Agnes, was from the isle of Skye, and the Hebrides, as everyone knows, are full of the supernatural – whether in the shape of ghostly presences, or the almost ghostlier sense of unseen watchers peopling the long nights of those stormy solitudes. My cousin, at any rate, always regarded Agnes as the – perhaps unconscious, at any rate irresponsible – channel through which communications from the other side of the veil reached the submissive household at White-gates. Though Agnes had been with Mrs. Clayburn for a long time without any peculiar incident revealing this affinity with the unknown forces, the power to communicate with them may all the while have been latent in the woman, only awaiting a kindred touch; and that touch may have been given by the unknown visitor whom my cousin, two years in succession, had met coming up the drive at Whitegates on the eve of All Souls'. Certainly the date bears out my hypothesis; for I suppose that, even in this unimaginative age, a few people still remember that All Souls' eve is the night when the dead can walk – and when, by the same token, other spirits, piteous or malevolent, are also freed from the restrictions which secure the earth to the living on the other days of the year.

If the recurrence of this date is more than a coincidence – and for my part I think it is – then I take it that the strange woman who twice came up the drive at Whitegates on All Souls' eve was either a 'fetch,' or else, more probably, and more alarmingly, a living woman inhabited by a witch. The history of witchcraft, as is well known, abounds in such cases, and such a messenger might well have been delegated by the powers who rule in these matters to summon Agnes and her fellow servants to a midnight 'Coven' in some neighboring solitude. To learn what happens at Covens, and the reason of the irresistible fascination they exercise over the timorous and superstitious, one need only address oneself to the immense body of literature dealing with these mysterious rites. Anyone who has once felt the faintest curiosity to assist at a Coven apparently soon finds the curiosity increase to desire, the desire to an uncontrollable longing, which, when the opportunity presents itself, breaks down all inhibitions; for those who have once taken part in a Coven will move heaven and earth to take part again.

*

Such is my – conjectural – explanation of the strange happenings at Whitegates. My cousin always said she could not believe that incidents which might fit into the desolate landscape of the Hebrides could occur in the cheerful and populous Connecticut Valley; but if she did not believe, she at least feared – such moral paradoxes are not uncommon – and though she insisted that there must be some natural explanation of the mystery, she never returned to investigate it.

'No, no,' she said with a little shiver, whenever I touched on the subject of her going back to Whitegates, 'I don't want ever to risk seeing that woman again. . . .' And she never went back.

List of Sources

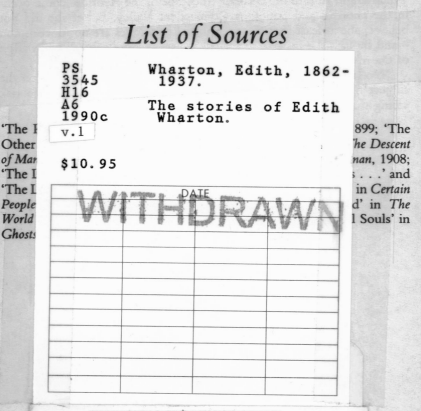
'The F... 899; 'The
Other ... he Descent
of Mar... nan, 1908;
'The L... s ...' and
'The L... in Certain
People ... d' in The
World ... l Souls' in
Ghosts...